RED GEAR 9

Matt Betts

DOG STAR
BOOKS

Red Gear 9 © 2021
by Matt Betts

Published by Dog Star Books
Bowie, MD

First Edition

Cover Image: Bradley Sharp
Book Design: Jennifer Barnes

Printed in the United States of America

ISBN: 9781947879102

Library of Congress Control Number: 2020940466

www.RawDogScreaming.com

Dedication

This book is for all the weirdos, nerds, band geeks, artists, role players, bookworms, gamers, wallflowers, comic book readers, non-conformists, dancers, metal heads, poets, daydreamers, and writers who had a hand in shaping my life.

I wonder what I ever would have done without you.

Acknowledgements

Thanks to:

    Heidi Ruby Miller for editorial skills and encouragement
    The kind staff at Alcatraz Island for maps and advice
    Everyone who asked what the hell was taking me so long to write this book

And the biggest thanks to the wonderful staff at Riverside Hospital, without whom it wouldn't have been possible to finish this book or any other.

Foreword
by Lee Murray

It's 2016 and I'm on the Queen Mary, Long Beach, attending a heady event comprising glittering gowns, award solemnity, and a rousing speech by George R.R. Martin. Then, after the ceremony, when the banquet dishes have been cleared away, I'm introduced to Matt Betts and it turns out to be the highlight of an already stellar evening.

Matt and I share a couple of publishers, so straight away we have some common ground. We start with the usual small talk: writing, books, colleagues we admire, the minutiae of contracts, and squeezing a living out of the stone of writing. A second glass of wine appears, or perhaps it's a third. I nurse my glass as we discuss juggling family when you work from home. We agree wholeheartedly on the blessedness of close-at-hand mothers who are willing to step in and babysit at a moment's notice. We barely notice the round of goodbyes from folk nearby as the guests of honour retire to their cabins. The glasses are cleared away. My husband says goodnight and heads up to bed. By the time the conference staff are putting the chairs up and politely asking stragglers to leave the ballroom two hours later, Matt and I have covered gender politics, social change, and surviving the apocalypse. He's a charming post-dinner companion: informed, funny, and keenly perceptive. I can only imagine what his writing is like. I resolve to add Matt's titles to my reading stack the minute I get home.

I don't regret it for a second. *Indelible Ink. Shadow Beneath the Waves. The Boogeyman's Intern. Godzilla's Better Half.* There's a lot of Matt Betts work to discover, and in myriad formats. As a writer, Matt is a strange beast: a genre-bender and mash-up artist, he refuses to slot neatly into any convenient bookstore category. Instead, he's an all-rounder with a backlist covering urban fantasy, steampunk, bizarro, alternative history, thriller, and even a stomping robotic kaiju sci-fi, all delivered with his unique brand of gritty black humour. In terms of style, he appears to move the goalposts there too, equally adept at breathless action-packed narratives that explode off the page as he is at stories which progress in a steady slow-burn of suspense. He's highly versatile. Did I mention that he also writes rivetingly entertaining speculative poetry? So when I'm approached to write a few words to accompany this, the newest title in his Odd Men Out series, I jump at the chance. A sneak-peek into an alternate history/steampunk adventure? Yes, please. It's the summer holidays in New Zealand, so I grab a coffee, sit on the deck in the sun, and dive right in.

Wow. This new title is a ripping tale, a page-turner which whisks its readers back to the 1890s and the United Nations of America. It's an alternative history account in which Union and Confederacy partisans co-exist in an uneasy truce brought on by their need to face the hordes of undead "chewers" devouring their countrymen. In this context, *Red Gear 9* opens on the prison island of Alcatraz, where Harvey Reeves, a betrayed confederate spy, has been mouldering for close to a decade, but, seeing a rare opportunity, stages a break-out. On the lam and encumbered by his fellow escapees, Reeves wants only to head south to his family, but first he has to make a stop in San Francisco, a city long-since abandoned to the darkness and the chewers. The problem is, things have changed since Reeves' incarceration, and getting home might not be as easy as it first appeared.

For readers who enjoyed the first book, a flurry of your favourite characters from *Odd Men Out* reappear in this adventure, including Office of Military Operations (OMO) operatives Cyrus Joseph Spencer, Trent Lowell, and circus performer Lucinda on the airship Polk, all of whom are getting in the way of Reeves, who is still trying to get home. For those who haven't discovered the first installment, read on anyway, since this story works as a stand-alone. Just know that you're going to want to go back and catch up on what went before.

One of the things that struck me about Matt from that initial conversation on the Queen Mary, quite apart from his passion for writing and his ability to tell a cracking story, was his need to come at a topic from different points of view, to analyse and speculate on why an individual or group might act or react in a particular way. This could explain why he's chosen to write *Red Gear 9* as an ensemble novel, allowing certain key characters to narrate the story in their own words. For this method to be effective, it requires the author to orchestrate a cast of fully-rounded credible characters, each with unique voices and with individual story arcs that drive their actions in consistent and believable ways—*and to tie those story arcs together in a satisfying conclusion.* No mean feat! I don't want to bore readers with the technicalities, but it's an important decision here as it has allowed Matt to offer varied viewpoints on the same events: a retelling of one of the bloodiest periods in American civil history. By electing to write an ensemble novel, Matt suggests there are no pure villains, just ordinary people with conflicting motivations: some desperate to make it home, others keen to make a buck, and still others simply trying to keep the peace. In *Red Gear 9* there's a leader with a secret shame, a nervous recruit trying to impress, and a loyal foot-soldier caught in the crossfire. Decisions taken by any of the characters could influence the course of history. And isn't that the point of speculative fiction? To ask what if, and to test how members of a population might react when confronted with heinous threats, and how those same actions might impact on society? As Glenn McDonald writes in a 2016 article in Future magazine, "…on its most basic level, speculative fiction culls ideas and experiences from the contemporary cultural or technological environment, and extrapolates them towards whatever future event horizon the author has in mind."[1]

Except Red Gear 9 *is set in the past.*

Perhaps Matt's intent is only to regale readers with an entertaining nail-biter of a story. Perhaps *Red Gear 9* is simply the literary vehicle for revisiting a best-loved world, throwing in some steampunk and horror elements, and adding a high-level conspiracy. If that's all its about, then Matt has definitely succeeded. But slot *Red Gear 9* into the rubric of speculative fiction extrapolated from current civil dissatisfaction in the United States, and the book becomes more than just a kick-ass read, it becomes a revelatory work.

I'm heading back to the United States shortly, this time to Grand Rapids, Michigan, where I'm hoping to have another scintillating post-banquet conversation with Matt. I plan to ask him exactly what he was thinking when he embarked on *Red Gear 9*. I also plan to stab him with a fork until he agrees to write another Odd Men Out title.

Lee Murray
Tauranga, New Zealand
January 2019

Lee Murray is an award-winning writer and editor (Australian Shadows, Sir Julius Vogel) whose titles include the Taine McKenna military thrillers (Severed Press), and supernatural crime-noir series The Path of Ra (Raw Dog Screaming Press) which she co-writes with Dan Rabarts. She lives with her family in New Zealand where she writes from an office overlooking a cow paddock. Read more at https://www.leemurray.info/

1.   https://futurism.media/can-science-fiction-predict-the-future

1

It wasn't a storm or a calamity or even the ever-present fog of San Francisco Bay that brought Harvey Reeves his freedom. It was, in fact, a gloriously sunny day and a bright, crisp sky which allowed his escape from incarceration at Alcatraz Island by the Union Army.

Reeves watched out of the barred window of his cell at the soldiers sitting on the pitch at the center of the encampment. Some played cards, others threw around a nut wrapped in yarn; the closest anyone on the island had to a ball at the time. They looked thrilled to be outside in the hint of a breeze after a good rain had kept them soaked for days. The recent rain made the sweet smell of the grass from the common area drift over the whole of the island, which was a welcome change from the dull scent of the salty sea that usually permeated everything. Reeves counted the men— twelve, sixteen, twenty-one. There were only three souls unaccounted for. Somewhere in a prison currently housing forty war captives, three men were on guard.

Reeves walked to his cell door. The iron bars were thick and solid. He'd learned that through the years. No amount of pounding could loosen them, no material he'd acquired could cut them. He'd even tried pissing on a corner section for nearly a month straight before the guards caught him, but it had done nothing to deteriorate or weaken the metal. The smell lingered as a reminder of that failure.

He did his best to peer up and down the corridor at the row of cells that held the other prisoners, scanning for the three remaining guards. There were none. He listened but couldn't hear the familiar crunch of boots on the stone floor.

"Rennie," Reeves said. He talked low, hoping to keep everyone in the prison from hearing.

Across the hall, Jeremiah Rene came to the bars in his cell and peered out. His black hair was wild, and his beard shot in all directions. The longest bit hung down to his bare chest. His eyes were heavy with sleep.

"Rennie? We have an opportunity."

The news woke Rennie somewhat and brought the first cheerful expression that Reeves had seen in years. "Tell me," Rennie said.

"They are out in the yard. Only a trio is unaccounted for. If we can get one, we can get his weapon and key. From there, we work as we've discussed." The two had whispered a plan over the years, evolving it as the fortification was modified and guard numbers had risen and fallen, as battlements were built and dismantled. The basic escape was always the same. Once they had a sufficient number of guards neutralized, they'd open the cell doors and leave other prisoners to delay the remaining guards and then Rennie and Reeves could slip into the bay unnoticed, from there they could swim to the mainland.

There was a small rowboat that the Union soldiers used to patrol the area around the island, but Reeves had decided not to try to take it. The slow craft would be at the mercy of every guard with a gun. Even the worst marksmen could pick off the escapees as they rowed desperately for safety. As swimmers, they could sneak off in the confusion and move with a more discreet profile. After that, the plan was blank. San Francisco had been abandoned long ago and traversing what was left of that city could be treacherous.

Reeves turned and looked out at the men in the field. The sounds of their frolicking and the noise of the ocean would likely conceal any screams for help, and as long as none of the guards inside could hit an alarm, the men outside would be oblivious. "When the next guard comes, make a clumsy grab for him through the bars. He should recoil toward me. I'll dispatch him and take his key."

A methodical scraping sound echoed in the hall. It was a guard named Green who walked with a limp. Reeves counted his luck that the soldier who approached was the weakest of the regiment. It would be easy enough to gain the advantage over him. Reeves stepped back and knelt by his straw bed and blanket near the window. He didn't want to wait by the bars and tip their play to the approaching guard.

Rennie reached out and managed to grab Green by the coat sleeve. He pulled with all the strength his slender fingers could muster, but the guard yanked himself free and stumbled backward toward Reeves. Green grabbed for his sidearm and brought it to bear when Reeves managed to grab the man's collar and yank him hard against the bars. He repeated it again and again to be sure the guard wouldn't get up. Reeves dragged the soldier closer and turned him in order to get at his keys. He unlocked his own cell and picked up the pistol that had fallen into the hall.

He unlocked Rennie's cell and a murmur began to spread among the prisoners. The two men dragged Green's body into Reeves' room and covered it with the tattered blanket. Reeves motioned for them to be quiet as he moved on down the corridor, reassuring each one they'd be free soon too. The chaos of releasing all the prisoners would make the odds better. From a humanitarian aspect, he had a hard time sentencing these men to a fate that he himself could no longer tolerate. He'd been on Alcatraz for nearly a decade and many of the others had been there at least as long.

"I'm going to make my way up the hall and see where the other guards are. I would imagine they're still at the main guard station. Just hold your voices," Reeves said.

The whispers continued.

Reeves knew he could only use the gun in his hand if the situation got desperate. A shot would bring the others from the field before the prisoners were freed and that might end the escape bid before it went any further. When he got to the end of the hallway, he peered around the corner and saw a single soldier sitting behind the guard station more than one hundred feet away. The man was hunched over, reading a book with his rifle against the wall and his warning whistle around his neck. There was no sign of the other guard.

With the knowledge that the other guard could appear at any time, Reeves decided his only option was to charge headlong at the reader, hoping to take him by surprise and tackle him before he could grab his whistle or rifle. Seven years ago, before he was captured, it would've been easier. Reeves was in his top condition then, freshly trained, fearless. Now, after spending that time in a six by eight prison cell, he questioned himself.

The promise of freedom won out. He took a deep breath and rounded the corner, bare feet slapping against the stone floor. The guard looked up from his book far too late to react. Reeves meant to wrap his arms around the man and tackle him to the ground, but he slipped and ended up barreling into him shoulder first. They both toppled in a daze. The guard flailed at the rifle, but only succeeded in knocking it further away. The two grappled on the ground as the guard still made an effort to reach the weapon. Reeves punched him in the side but with little effect. They grabbed each other and held on, rolling over each other and trying to end up on top. The soldier brought his knee up into Reeves' gut, and then pinned him to the ground. Reeves' training came to mind and he remembered his senior officer's admonition to find a weapon or make a weapon. He let go of the guard and slapped around for the book the man had been reading and when he found it, he grasped it tightly, then slammed it into his attacker's head. The guard's grip loosened, and Reeves hit him again. The guard hit back, but Reeves reversed their positions, climbing on top, and when he could, he brought the sharp corners of the book down on the man's throat. There was a crack and Reeves assumed he'd broken the man's windpipe or worse. Blood issued from the man's neck and he gurgled as he grabbed at the wound. Reeves shoved the man's hands away and brought pointed corners down as hard as he could until the guard stopped struggling.

From the direction of the cells, there was shouting and the crack of gunfire. Reeves grabbed the guard's rifle, and discovered a pistol hanging on the wall in a holster. He took them both and ran back toward his cell. As he approached, he saw a wave of prisoners washing over a guard. They clawed at the guard's face and tore at his arms, all while the man tried to shoot them. With a final click of his empty pistol, he fell to the floor and the men set upon him like savages. Some of the escapees turned and blindly ran down the hall, crazed over their freedom. Reeves handed the rifle to a passing prisoner. "Get to the armory and grab a firearm, men."

The guard in Rennie's cell shouted and stuck his pistol out from between the bars and fired blindly down the hall until his pistol clicked empty. Reeves stepped in front of the cell and the man withdrew his arm. Inside, Rennie lay in a pool of blood. Reeves pulled the pistol he'd taken and pointed it at the soldier in Rennie's cell. The guard raised his hands and backed against the far wall. The man was trapped—contained and not a threat at the moment, but if someone freed him the guard could grab a gun or a knife and come up behind the retreating convicts.

Reeves shot him twice. The shots echoed in the cell—two thuds. He allowed himself to stare at Rennie for a second and he wondered what this escape attempt was going to cost in the end. Rennie had been in that tiny room for five of the years Reeves had been on that island. He'd never made the time drag.

The hall had quickly become a mess of running prisoners, rifle reports and a cloud from the smoke of men firing guns in the confined hallway and in the cells. The report of each shot sounded like it was next to Reeves' head, no matter how distant the gunman. The first man with a rifle pointed it out through the bars and opened up on the guards in the field.

The soldiers outside had heard the commotion and were running for the prison. Reeves stood for a moment and watched them fall as the rifle fire cut them down. The only thing that slowed the firing was the rate with which the prisoners could reload the old rifles. The men outside returned fire, but with little effect against the fortified escapees.

By the time he got himself out of the building, there were crowds of men fighting hand to hand. Prisoners had run out the door and leapt at the guards. Reeves kept them all in his sight as best he could, but he was mostly focused on the path to the docks. There, boats moved prisoners, unloaded supplies, and refueled both water and wood for their boilers.

He shoved both prisoner and soldier alike aside, punching a couple who looked to challenge him, but he moved on without engaging. Once he'd passed the largest of the crowd, he allowed himself to run down the trail. At the docks he could see two steam-powered supply boats with smoke already issuing from their stacks. He jumped into one where four prisoners stood on the deck, looking panicked.

"You know how this thing works?" Reeves asked the one nearest the wheel.

"Yes, I do."

"Then move us away from here," Reeves said. The boat moved even as he spoke.

One of the other men raised his rifle and shot at soldiers that were approaching the dock. Several other prisoners jumped onboard the other boat and it pushed away from the island as well.

Neither boat was fast. Not at first. Both sputtered and clanked as the pilots tried to coax some speed out of the engines. Reeves' boat groaned to life a little more quickly than the other. The prisoners grabbed the sides as the boat lurched, then slowed, then lurched again. The other boat fell behind, and though everyone did their best to shoot the guards, there were too many to keep pinned down.

The pilot of Reeves' boat positioned them so that the other vessel was between their craft and the firing soldiers. As Reeves watched, two of the men on the other boat fell overboard, struck by rifle fire. A cloud of splinters flew from their port side and the boat swerved suddenly, seemingly a magnet for the attack from shore.

The men on Reeves' boat hunkered down and stopped firing. They used the hull for cover as much as they could. Reeves lay flat on his back and hoped for the best. Now that his feet were off the soil of Alcatraz, they weren't going to carry him back. He certainly realized that he wouldn't live long if he was captured.

"Head for San Francisco," Reeves shouted.

The men that heard him turned.

"There's nothing there." The pilot was incredulous.

"There's plenty there." Reeves hoped he was right. "There's plenty there."

2

"I would be more than happy to let you open this door," Cyrus Spencer said. He looked at Trent Lowell and gave him an expectant smile. They both stared at the rear entrance to the Lafayette General Store. "I think I might have done the last one. Two, in fact." There were noises coming from inside. Shuffling. Moaning.

There was usually a fancy pistol in Lowell's hand, but today he saw fit to carry a Winchester shotgun. It was a wise idea as far as Cyrus was concerned.

"Oh, I appreciate that. But don't do me any favors. I'm not really keeping track of how many doors we open. There are quite a few of these ahead, I fear." Lowell grabbed the shotgun with both hands and pointed it toward the door. "I'm ready anytime. You go on ahead." He tensed and looked back at Cyrus expectantly. "Go on."

"Jesus, I'll do it." Bethy Nolan shoved her way past them, up the two steps and then gripped the door handle. "You just be ready to run and shoot if we need to." She gave a look that made Cyrus feel useless. He was intimately familiar with the expression.

The plan was simple. The Office of Military Operations was responsible for cleaning up the small towns, making them livable again. Of course, the higher-ups wanted to see the buildings as intact as possible, so as not to make the reconstruction efforts any more strenuous on local resources than need be. If it weren't for that, all the soldiers with the OMO could lounge on an airship while the guns rained down hell; destroying and killing everything on the ground. Instead, to preserve the infrastructure, soldiers were going through the town opening doors, in order to release any horrors that might lurk inside, so they might be dispatched safely and cleanly in the streets. Everyone wanted safety especially, even if it came at the expense of cleanliness. If a chewer bit a body, and didn't eat it on the spot, over the next couple days the body would become fever-ridden and gray. They fell asleep after that, as close to dying as not. Finally, in a matter of hours after drifting off, the infected rose. They were possessed with milky-white eyes and a powerful desire to bite anyone, anything, they could reach. And they walked around snapping their jaws at the air, like something tasty was just out of reach. That was the part that drove Cyrus mad about the chewers from time to time—that snapping sound that occasionally heralded their arrival.

With a steady grip, Bethy turned the handle and pushed inward. "Chewers coming out," she said and backed up quickly. Lowell followed her lead.

Three figures stumbled into the sunlight, mouths opening and closing almost in rhythm with each other. The first one was a woman. *Was.* She was wearing what was left of a green sundress, now in tatters and no longer providing her an ounce of modesty. Her jaw was crushed and opening at an odd angle and she walked with purpose toward Bethy.

Cyrus waited until Bethy was behind him a bit before he decided to move away. None of them fired. Another mandate. While the chewers were being cleaned up and the problem was still very real, the mines in the area weren't being worked yet, and resources were wearing thin to make trivial things like bullets and shotgun shells. The great majority of the available gunpowder was allocated to special troops within the various crews. So, they had to get creative in the face of adversity. Along with their firearms, some of the OMO operatives carried shovels, pickaxes and other makeshift weapons to bludgeon the ghouls to death. Most of the troops were only allocated a handful of bullets to last them a week or more.

The other two chewers wore work clothes and were themselves in various states of decay. One had a hand missing somewhere around the wrist, the other looked like he'd had something slammed against the side of his head – blood had dried around where his ear was sliced away.

The group backed toward the center of the little town, where they were to meet up with the other two groups from the Office of Military Operations who were doing the exact same thing; opening doors, baiting chewers into chasing them and then retreating. Without firing a shot.

Cyrus looked up and saw the number of black birds circling and landing on the roofs of the buildings had grown. He couldn't remember ever being so excited to see the animals.

A man shouted at the other end of the street. Everyone turned to see a newer OMO recruit on the ground, scuttering away from a pair of the monsters near the town's post office on his hands and knees. Cyrus knew him barely well enough to remember his name, Clifton. He was one of a number of people who'd joined the OMO in the last year, eager to help keep the peace. Clifton's teammates ran in and practically dragged the young man safely away from the things that menaced him. Cyrus made a note to keep a closer eye on that one. He was probably fine, but if he couldn't keep his head about him in a situation, Cyrus would find another detail to put him on.

Herding the chewers was relatively easy and the special operatives on Cyrus' squad had it down to a simple process. They gave the chewers a source of food and they made it easy for the grotesque things to follow, yet hard to catch them. Once they were grouped together, the OMO members would run off to safety down the open route that was left opposite the horde. The sharpshooter would take it from there.

Once the dozen officers had gathered and everyone was accounted for, Bethy raised the cavalry sword she'd been carrying for the last few months and waved it to signal they were done. Cyrus marveled at how well she used it, despite her diminutive size and the heft of the weapon. It wasn't an alternative he would have chosen, but she'd dedicated herself to making it work.

Now in the sunlight, the glint of it brought a sigh of relief from deep in his lungs. It meant they were nearly done with this one and they could go home. Hopefully. It was possible their orders could include cleaning out another town on the way back to the outpost.

He waited a beat and there was no shot. Not a report from the marksman's rifle to indicate they'd fired. The chewers were getting closer to the group. Cyrus took a step back and looked up toward the rooftops where the sharpshooters had taken up their positions. One of them was waving and pointing to the near end of the town, in the direction of their escape route. It didn't take Cyrus a second to understand their motions. When they'd scouted this area, they figured there were maybe twenty chewers trapped in the buildings, a few more in the streets, and that number had proven to be pretty accurate, until now. Coming up the trail and blocking their way out were more of the monsters. Many more.

"Oh hell," Lowell said. He'd followed the shooters warning as well. "Gotta be another thirty at least."

It did Cyrus no good to know how many of them there were. Thirty? Fifty? He only knew that they were surrounded, and the situation was quickly getting untenable.

"Where the hell did they come from?" Bethy tensed up and held her weapon at the ready.

"Don't know, don't care. Let's get into that store and see if the shooters can handle this." Lowell moved to the door and slammed it open. He ushered the others in, Bethy and her sword bringing up the rear. The chewers followed.

As the beasts got closer, a sound that had become too familiar echoed through the town. The sharpshooters had opened up with their first volley. Cyrus knew he should stay down in case a stray piece of shrapnel came his way, but he wanted to see the spectacle. Every time he witnessed it, it fascinated him.

Another report, and this time, Cyrus saw it hit. The special ammunition load exploded on impact, shattering a monster's head and showering several of the others nearby with an almost silvery liquid that glimmered in the sunlight. There were more shots, eight in all, each with a similar deadly effect that felled more chewers and spread more of the formula.

The town went silent for a few tense seconds. Cyrus backed from the window and reached for his gun. A half a dozen of the chewers still approached the building.

"I knew this damn stuff wasn't all it was made out to be," Bethy said.

The calm was broken by the single caw of a crow somewhere nearby. It was joined by another, then another until it seemed they were carrying on an angry conversation.

"Just wait." Lowell's arms were folded as he leaned back against a beam. "It'll work. You know the Berley will work." The formula was created by the scientists that worked at Outpost Two-Thirteen, experimenting with notes and samples left behind by a Union doctor after the war.

Cyrus didn't believe Lowell's calm. It was true that in all the tests and all the other towns they'd cleared out, the formula had worked, but Cyrus couldn't help but feel there could always be a first time. He turned to look at the room they were in to see if there was another way out, just in case things went wrong and the dead came pouring through the door.

A sound like waves crashing on coastal rocks erupted outside, somewhere above the store, and Cyrus turned back to the window. He was in time to see the sky turn black and the chewers became obscured by the darkness of crows descending on them and attacking with furious aggression. The birds were so incensed that they flung themselves blindly, slapping against the windows of the building and shoving each other in an effort to get to the monsters that were covered in the slimy concoction the ammunition had unleashed. The crows pecked at the chewers' heads, tearing the eyes from their sockets, digging into open wounds and pulling out sinew and muscle where they could find it. Soon, the birds turned their fury on the chewers that hadn't been doused with the liquid; they leapt and flapped like a tiny black dust cloud blowing through the streets.

One of the recruits shouted in surprise as a chewer with a halo of the birds slammed itself against a store window and pawed at the glass. Its blue-green hand left a trail of puss and blood as it slid down the pane. All the while, the birds tore slimy grey bits of matter from the chewer's head, matted and bloody hair stuck in their beaks, stripping it almost to a skeleton before it fell.

As that monster slid out of sight, the melee in the street became clearer. Crows were everywhere, attacking chewers, knocking them to the ground and feasting on the insides of the dead. Few were standing still, and those that were, stubbornly advanced toward the OMO officers, oblivious to the avian menace that was tearing them apart as they went.

"I miss the old days when we could shoot them in the head and be done with it." Cyrus shuddered as he saw a crow tug at one of the thing's entrails. "It was much less—messy."

"Amen," Lowell said.

The new recruits weren't watching. They'd been on this tour of duty long enough to know that they didn't want to see what was happening, and that Cyrus or someone would let them know if they needed to be alert and ready for a fight. He used to make them watch the melee in the early missions just so they'd get used to it, but he got sick of hearing the retching and smelling the vomit.

"Hey, why in the name of Christ do we even need to be here?" Clifton asked. He was staring steadily at the back wall and asked the question to no one in particular. "I mean, why don't these blackbirds just eat all the chewers on their own while we sat ourselves to home? Nobody told me nothing about this in training."

"I'm sure these crows would love to do that very thing," Lowell said. "They just need a little push. The shit in those rounds does something to get them worked up. That stuff, combined with chewer flesh, gets the ire up in their blood."

"Like Corrigan in a bar on a Saturday night?" Bethy asked. The small group chuckled.

"Something like that. Hell, ask Alek when we get back, or the doctor. They can explain it." Lowell was already checking his gun, having apparently expended his knowledge on the subject.

Cyrus looked out at the carnage in the street, the bones, the guts and the blood-soaked birds carrying off bits and pieces. It was a mess, though it would be picked fairly clean in a day or two. "Well. The buildings are still intact."

"I guess that *is* our objective." Bethy had a stern look that Cyrus interpreted as an effort not to be affected by the scene. "No extra shots fired, either. That's a success. Cashe will be pleased."

They all stood and looked out on the road for a few more moments, lost in the bloody dance of the birds and the chewers.

"There's a back way out of this building, right? I don't want to walk through that mess," Clifton said, huddled with the rest of the recruits.

A crow landed on a window sill, its beak smeared with blood and a thin strip of gray matter hanging from one side. It cawed and pecked at the window, leaving a long streak of crimson on the glass. It bobbed its head a couple of times and managed to swallow the small piece of chewer that had escaped consumption.

Clifton's hand quickly came up to cover his mouth. He gagged a couple of times before he vomited all over the floor and himself.

All of the recruits suddenly went pale, so Cyrus took a step away, unwilling to gamble on their constitutions being stronger than Clifton's.

3

The supply boat *Nathan Prentiss* drifted toward a small dock just south of Russian Hill, near Black Point in San Francisco, powered only by the occasional stroke of the paddle. They took extra time to avoid half-sunken boats and derelicts. The cattails and reeds had grown up unimpeded, obscured the shore from view, and made the approach more difficult. Reeves scanned the city, noting how quiet it was. In days past there'd be fires warming the homes, cooking the food. The smoke would hang over the harbor, mingling with that of the ships giving the area a soothing scent of pine and oak. Reeves saw none of that, and the only smells were of rotting ships and decaying cloth.

If the guard's stories of roving hordes of the living dead were true, he saw no evidence of them. Maybe they'd moved on, or they never existed after all. Nothing moved within his view, save the lightly lapping waves.

"Jesus, Reeves," LaRue said. "This is not a place I want to be right now. We're all free to go. It won't take long for someone to figure out what happened at the prison. They'll start sending out search parties and hunt us down." He gripped a paddle like a talisman.

"When? They won't know something is amiss until the next supply ship is due. That's about two days from now. They'll wait another day just to be sure the boat isn't running late. Then, they'll most likely send another small, slow boat to investigate—that's two more days. Hell, we have close to a week before we need to worry about anything." Odds were good if there were ever problems at Alcatraz, the military would send an airship, and Reeves knew it. The type of prisoners held there, himself included, probably warranted that sort of response. They had a couple of days. Maybe.

"I don't like it," Adams said.

Reeves spread his hands out before them to encompass the whole of the city. "What? There is no one and nothing in this city as far as the eye can see. And whatever the trouble, we will venture in and be gone before anything can cause us a care." He looked around at the dour faces and saw they didn't believe. "Fine. You all stay on the boat. Let me off but wait for me just away from shore. What I have to do will be done by morning."

"What is so all-fire important that you'd find yourself desperate enough to want to go into that haunted city?" Jeffers scratched at his beard. "I can't think of anything but money."

"You got money hidden in the ruins of San Francisco?" Adams asked.

Money would make everything easier, Reeves supposed. But sadly, that wasn't the case. "No. No. I found myself in prison because of money. No, I'm just paying a visit to the office of my old employer to gather some supplies we might need to survive..." Reeves thought a moment about what would motivate the men before them. "...And get home."

"This city has been dead for years. Any food's rotted by now. Bullets and weapons probably in sad shape as well." It was Tremmel this time. They were all taking turns now, pestering him with questions, but Reeves was happy they were focusing on the possibilities, rather than the reasons not to go.

"Supplies, indeed." Adams sniffed. "How do we even know you'll return?"

They drifted close to a dock and Reeves reached out to get a hold on it. "Just wait here in the harbor and I'll be back. I want to get to my family just as much as you all. Ain't no way for me to do it without this boat." He used a paddle to pull the boat closer to the frail ladder that rose to the deck. It creaked when he put his hand on it and a rung fell into the water just from the threat of someone walking on it.

"Whoa." Adams put his boney hand on Reeves' shoulder. "We don't have a whole lot of weapons—you think you're taking one of the fully-loaded ones?"

"You don't expect me to venture into that city alone *and* unarmed, do you?"

Tremmel pushed Adams away. "You ain't going in there alone, that's for certain. I'm going in with you." He hoisted a rifle over his shoulder, staring at Adams as he did. "If the city is empty, no telling what's in there for the taking."

"Hell, I'll go," Reynolds said. He'd been sitting stabbing at the railing with a filleting knife, watching the flurry of woodchips drop the deck. He slid the knife into the rope he was using as a belt and got behind Tremmel. He didn't ask for another weapon or seem to want one.

"Just leave me one of the rifles for a few shots. I don't want no part of this," LaRue said. He'd watched but didn't seem as anxious as the others to find out what Reeves might be venturing into San Francisco for. Patrick looked equally secure in waiting on the boat.

"Probably a wise idea," Reeves said. "Leave a couple with the boat, and we don't want to make the group too big. Five is a nice, easy number to handle." Reeves couldn't help but needle Adams, since he'd started the whole row that got everyone involved.

"I never said I wanted to accompany you on this ridiculous folly. I value my life far more than that," Adams said. "In fact—"

"Christ," Reynolds said. He pushed the others aside and grabbed a rotting rung of the ladder, accidentally pulling it from the dock and knocking it into the water. He met each person's stare defiantly, then grabbed the deck itself and pulled himself onto it. He looked around and gingerly tapped at the planks of wood. Finding them acceptable, he moved on. "Come on," he shouted back to the group. "Stay close to the sides. The middle planks seem a might touchy."

"A little quieter," Reeves said.

Once Reynolds had made it to land, they took turns helping one another up. They were afraid to put more than two people's weight on the structure at any time for fear it would fail just as easily as the pieces of the ladder did.

"Good luck," Reeves said to the two men left on the boat. "I made sure we left you the better rifle. You've got six shots." The men nodded and looked at the gun. "We'll only be gone until first light, but it'll seem a lot longer out here all alone. You're going to be inclined to leave. I would truly appreciate it if you didn't."

"Just don't take longer than you say," LaRue said. "I don't care if the military come looking, or if there's a city full of dead men. I want to get back east. Anything that gets in the way of that…"

"Then we understand each other." Reeves turned and scaled the dock with ease. He watched LaRue and Patrick shove off and paddle as best they could to get out into the harbor farther.

The five men moved through the muddy area just off the docks, easing their way past crates and ropes, ship parts and trunks. "This whole area used to be swamplands," Adams said. "They filled it in and contained it as best they could." Adams walked nearly on tip-toes through the wet mess just off the docks and Reeves took a minute to wonder what the man had done to land himself in prison.

"Quiet," Reeves said. Whether Adams was right or not, the place smelled all the world to Reeves like an open latrine.

They sloughed through the muck at as slow a pace as they dared, though none cared to voice their distaste with the conditions. They looked about for a drier area but found none. If they'd thought about it, Reeves and the rest would have found some boots on the island to steal, to make things like this easier, but as it stood, they walked through the mess in their bare feet, each step making a wet sloshing sound. Adams winced, and looked ready to burst, but said nothing.

There were only two small shacks nearby, and Reeves kept his eyes on them, just in case someone or something came from behind the buildings. Everyone else seemed fixated on what was in front of them. Except Reynolds. It was hard to tell exactly what he cared about. Everyone who had a weapon gripped it tightly—Reynolds' knife was tucked in his waistband and the man seemed happy to feel the earth between his toes. Reeves made the prediction that Reynolds would meet a terrible end sometime soon without better focus on his environment.

They climbed a slight slope out of the muck and up to a road that lead into town and Reeves called everyone close. "We come in here near Baker Street, follow it to Lewis, walk down Lewis for a few blocks until we find Scott Street, turn right and there's houses near the corner. It's a few blocks from Fort Mason at Black Point. We're looking for a row house. Number sixty-three." He kept his voice low and pointed in the direction they needed to go.

"Where is everyone?" Adams asked. "I don't like how quiet it is."

Reeves could tell the silence was affecting the whole group, but to him it was a blessing so far. With nothing but the waves to disturb them, it should be difficult to be surprised. "Just keep it down. We go, we get what we need and leave."

They walked so close to each other, they nearly tripped in a tangle of gangly legs. The streets were little more than paths now; overgrown with weeds and trees that rose up unimpeded by the regular flow of foot traffic. Once they'd managed to get to the first street, the grass was patchy, but regularly above their knees. Anything could be crawling or slithering through it and no one would know.

"I don't like this," Adams said.

"Then go back. And shut up." Reeves was listening to everything around them but couldn't hear over the man's whining.

Adams looked behind them at the long trek through the mud, across the water where the boat had vanished. He held his tongue and walked a little more gingerly.

The streets ended at the water on the left, so the group only needed to worry about what was on their right. At the first street, they found what looked like the remnants of a pair of wagons burned down to their frames, turned on their sides. Rusting and broken weapons were scattered around on the ground. There were barrels, tables and debris stacked on either side of the wagons, looking to Reeves like someone had tried to barricade the street. From the result it looked to him to be unsuccessful.

"Someone lost a fight," Jeffers said.

They pushed on to the next street and found it empty save for the tall grass. The buildings on either side were in sorry shape with shutters askew and glass broken. There were doors hanging on their hinges and roofs with slates missing. These were businesses – dry goods stores, taverns, and offices, all easily accessible to anyone who might happen by.

Tremmel stomped to a stop in the mud. "Surely we can find something in one of these places?" He pointed with his shotgun. "I mean Jesus, there's a mining office right there with the front door hanging wide open. There could be gold, silver, anything in there right now." He looked from man to man to plead his case. "I mean—right?"

Reynolds walked on by the second street and stepped up to a storefront and looked in through a window. "Ain't nothing. Shit scattered everywhere. But ain't no devils or demons inside." He stepped back and stared up at the sign on the building for a minute.

"It's a laundry, you dullard," Adams said. "Not a god damn thing in there worth us stealing, and that's a fact."

Bobbing his head, Reynolds stepped back and looked inside through a different window. "So, it is. So, it is. Anyone need clean sheets?"

"I could use some drawers. These pants I took off that guard are powerful uncomfortable." Tremmel moved toward the building as well.

"Let's keep moving. Just two more streets, I can get what I need, and we can go." Reeves was having a hard time reconciling the tales he heard from the jailors about chewers with the silence now that they were in the city. There were signs of something happened, sure. But it looked as though it had happened a lifetime ago. "If we have time, we can go through the stores on the way out. Besides, any clothes in there have been through the elements, rats, bugs and who knows what else."

"Probably still cleaner than this guard's britches." Tremmel mumbled it low, but the others heard, and they burst out in laughter. Tremmel liked the attention. "All the damn screws in Alcatraz and I take my clothes from the one with dysentery." The laughter grew.

"Shut up." Everyone narrowed their eyes to look at Reeves. "Listen."

Somewhere, the sound of metal on metal found its way through the streets and came to the group of men to break the quiet.

"What? The wind knocked something over." Adams took a step closer to Reeves and Jeffers as he spoke.

Reeves held one finger up to his mouth. The metallic sound came again, paused, then came back a few seconds later. "Not the breeze." He wasn't sure he was right. It could be something rolling in the wind, but he hadn't heard the sound before the men began laughing at Tremmel. They had no real choice: they had to move on and hope to get to the house without incident. To stand still made no sense. They could be surrounded easily, with only the sea as their escape. Turning back was always a possibility for the others, but not for Reeves. Not when they'd made it this far.

With a wave of his hand, Reeves motioned everyone to keep moving. One more street. If the weeds and brush weren't so high and thick, he'd have started running. He could see the street up ahead and it would take nothing to give a burst of speed now. He could see the sign for Scott Avenue in the distance, it was so close, so attainable. But first, they needed to make it past Devisadero Street.

As they cleared the laundry, they entered an area of what Reeves knew to have been decent houses, at least for their time—thin, two-story brick affairs built one immediately next to the other, with barely room to walk between them. These fared a little better than the businesses that were crumbling nearby. They showed signs of wear with broken windows and sun-bleached sides, but they weren't as close to caving in.

The metal sound came to them again and Reeves whirled to see a soldier emerge from the street they'd passed on the other side of the laundry. The man walked as anyone else walked, maybe slower, and Reeves was suddenly seized with the fear that the Union army had quickly discovered the escape at Alcatraz and caught up with them already. The metallic sound came from the man's canteen, rattling against a tin cup on his belt with each step he took. In a matter of a few steps, it became clear that the soldier was not a soldier. Not anymore. He wore a tattered blue uniform, but that was where the similarity ended. This man began to snap at the group, biting at the air between them as if he could swallow the smell of them. He held one arm against his side, while the other swatted and waved just ahead of his mouth. Like the buildings around him, the man was weathered, with great cracks in his face and the color washed out of him.

"Christ. I didn't think they were real," Adams said. "Great Christ I didn't want them to be real."

Reynolds stepped toward it. "Mister? You all right?" He was staring at the soldier, examining it.

"Reynolds. Stop." Tremmel held out his hand to stay the man's movement but didn't move any more himself.

Nothing came out of Reeve's throat as he tried to speak. He didn't want to see the truth. The jailors at the prison had let slip a few words about these things, but it always sounded like another way for those guards to have fun with their detainees. But here one of their jokes appeared to be standing in the street, big as day. Before Reeves was able to collect himself and take charge, Reynolds was on the soldier-thing, the chewer, the guards had called them. He'd leapt with enough force to knock the chewer on the ground, and then Reynolds' knife was out as he stabbed and sliced it enough times that its guts spilled out, filling the air with the horrid stench of a dead man that had been killed again. Reynolds backed off the thing, which was somehow still chomping, and reaching for him, though it had no means to get up.

Adams vomited. He dropped to his knees and heaved in the dirt with a sound like a croaking bullfrog. Reeves kept his composure enough to see more shapes advancing from the area where the soldier had appeared. Three more that he could see. The crunch of weeds drew his attention to Sycamore, just to the immediate left of their original path and there he found even more of them that seemed to come from everywhere at once. They emerged from doorways and alleys, from windows and from God knows where. But they came all the same. If Reeves' group of escapees waited any longer, they'd be cut off and surrounded just as he'd feared. "Somebody grab Adams and drag him along. We need to get to that address."

Tremmel yanked Adams up by his arm and Reynolds snatched up Adams's gun, then wasted no time in turning and shooting the soldier on the ground twice in the face, which finally seemed to stop its chomping motion. Three more shots from the gun felled one of the things that followed the soldier's path.

Reeves ran ahead. He passed the chewers that were emerging onto Lewis, but they were slow and only made motions to grab at him as he passed. It was tough to dodge the weeds and unexpected debris in the street – a wagon wheel here, a bucket or a barrel there – but he managed. He turned at Scott Street to find more of the beasts stumbling ahead, these not quite as sure on their feet as the soldier was, but they plodded on toward him anyway. They seemed to be awakening from a sleep and following whatever senses informed them of movement.

Reeves pulled his gun as he ran and decided which of the ghouls could possibly give him a problem getting to the house that was just a few doors away. One chewer seemed more aggressive and able than the others, so he shot it through the throat, which nearly severed the head clear off, and it fell to the street. "This way," he called to his companions. The gate in front fell off its hinges as he pushed his way toward the house that he'd made home ever so briefly, ever so long ago.

Up the stoop and he turned the knob of the front door. It was locked. All the houses in town with entrances wide open and doors off their frames and this one was shut tight.

4

"It's tough clearing these towns without using additional ammunition," Lucinda said. "Makes it more dangerous for anyone walking into the unknown like that." She'd seen the recruit stumble in the last situation, and there had been similar close shaves in other places. "We need to have some solutions to fall back on if necessary."

"I wish we had something reliable we could give you," Alek said. "We're still actively sorting out the experiments stored in the warehouse." He wiped his hands on his trousers. "Weapons are a high priority, of course. We just only have so many hands to do the work."

"We understand, but we'd surely appreciate if those hands worked a mite faster," Lucinda said. Out in the Nevada desert, a group of OMO men and women—scientists, doctors, builders and tinkerers—were sorting out things they'd received from a Federal scientist named Poley. He'd been hard at work inventing ways for the North to win the war. Not all those ways were ethical, as far as Lucinda was concerned. The mechanical arm she'd been given to replace her crippled one was one of those creations that she still hadn't sorted into a good or evil pile yet. It helped her get along almost like normal, and yet, she couldn't help but hate it more than a little. Lucinda thought of all the men who'd been in the war and lost limbs but didn't have the opportunity to get a new one as she did. *What made her special?*

A number of the Poley inventions had been brought to Santa Rosa, to the OMO tower where Alek set up a workshop for some of the more promising weapons and inventions. The Silver Berley they used on the chewers had been one that Alek's team had improved. While he was no scientist, Alek was a natural with machines, and good with his hands. He was one of a number of Negro soldiers in the OMO, which occasionally caused consternation among the white Confederate recruits. They generally changed their opinions when one of Alek's machines saved their lives in battle. Those that didn't come around, didn't last long onboard the airship *Leonidas Polk* or in the tower.

Lucinda walked the storehouse of odd equipment and machinery with the others. She could identify only the tiniest amount of the things she saw.

Cashe moved deftly through the narrow rows in his wheelchair, turning and dodging loose materials and outright trash. "I think there's bound to be something in here you people can use to clear out towns without wasting resources."

"The crows are becoming a little worrisome," Doctor Hastings said. "I don't trust the formula we're using for the bullets. We all took it on faith when this came to us, because we needed a new way of combating the chewers. But it wasn't tested. Not much."

"We'd have to stop using the ammunition? What other possible choice do we have?" Whatever the doctor's concerns, Lucinda knew the little grey ammunition worked. She'd been there when they first used it and saw the crows stir to action suddenly. It was the most useful way she'd seen to kill the monsters without wasting a bullet or getting right up to them and slicing them with an ax.

"From the reports I'm getting, there have been a few towns the teams cleared out where the birds were a little wilder than you'd expect. Aggressive. Angry. I understand the mixture we're using is doing what we want, but I don't know how it affects the birds. Could those crows take on the properties of what they're eating?"

It was something Lucinda noticed on a previous mission. "They have been showing up in larger groups."

Dex held out a hand to Hastings and Lucinda. "They're just looking for an easy meal and get a little ornery, that's all. Ain't no crows turning into chewers. Let's not be stupid here."

"We're going on the principle that those bullets contain a formula that both accentuates the scent of the chewer's flesh, and creates somewhat of a shimmer. The birds are attracted to the sight and the smell of the exposed matter," Hastings said. "But we didn't test the long-term effect on the birds."

"It makes the chewers powerful tasty to those black birds, saves us the trouble of killing them ourselves," Dex said.

Doctor Hastings nodded. "I'd be happier if we found some alternative, but for now, it's all we have." The doctor moved on. "Maybe we'll find something here?"

Alek, Doctor Hastings, and the team at Outpost Two-Thirteen had all admitted that they didn't know the real use for many of the devices they'd gathered in the room. They'd been developed during the war by a Union doctor named Poley, and he didn't leave instructions for their use. It was a guessing game and the guessing was slow going due to the lethal nature of most of the equipment.

The room smelled like gun polish and worked metal, which made sense to Lucinda, seeing as half of everything in sight was steel and appeared to be made to fire.

"What's this thing?" Dex asked. He nudged a long, heavy rifle lying on the ground with his foot.

Alek wiped his hands with a rag and shrugged. "Not sure what exactly it's called. We've found all of the parts to it, and it's kind of a burden to have to set up on a battlefield." He leaned down and lifted the gun. "Michael? Bring that wagon and load the parts for weapon forty-four. Take everything to the test corridor, if you please." Across the room, a man grabbed a barrow and snaked his way through the maze of junk.

"Any news on the rest of those escaped prisoners, yet?"

"No. After the shootout at the prison, the trail's gone cold. We have to assume they went to ground somewhere, maybe in Santa Rosa. The OMO and sheriff are doing what they can, but no one even knows how many are gone, who they were." A sleek pistol on a shelf caught Lucinda's attention and she went to grab it.

Alek touched her outstretched arm gently. "It's misfired and blown up in every test we've tried. We're calling that one a failure."

"What's it supposed to do?" Lucinda was curious about the small device.

"It's supposed to shoot a small needle into a subject to put them to sleep." Alek moved on toward a door where his companion had disappeared with the barrow. "So, the small explosion in the barrel was a bit of surprise to everyone."

"I can imagine."

Alek shepherded the group to a doorway marked "3" and they found Michael inside, setting up the gun that Dex had asked about. More bits and pieces were strewn about here, all of them fit together to form sections of the weapon. A large oaken barrel, nearly as tall as the man setting everything up seemed to be the centerpiece, a long, flexible tube, like a sausage casing, connected the gun to the barrel. The narrow corridor smelled of oil and smoke, its walls were blackened in spots. Near the large barrel were two smaller ones, clearly marked "Water" in large lettering.

"So, this is a lovely piece of machinery," Alek said. "It'd be perfect for men in the field, but for one thing—" Alek pointed to the apparatus. "It's way too large. No way to move it easily without a train or another vehicle of some type."

"What's it do?" Dex asked. He circled around the large barrel to see inside. "It looks downright dangerous." A gleeful smile exposed his darkened teeth.

The hose went to the rifle from a box near his feet. Alek picked it up and fiddled with a compartment attached to the barrel. "It's particular, that's for sure. If you don't have all the trinkets and dials in place, it doesn't work. You don't have the hose attached to the barrel just so, it won't work. You don't have the hose attached to the stock just so, it won't work." He tightened all the parts as he mentioned them. "But when it does."

"Come on. Show us what it does," Dex said. "Show us." He was obviously getting excited to see what kind of mayhem he could cause with the thing.

"Easy." Lucinda knew how worked up he got about wanton destruction. It was usually helpful, and endearing. But she didn't want to be anywhere near it if it wasn't focused on the right thing.

"Got a match?" Alek asked. Dex dug through his pockets and found one in his coat. Alek took it, scratched it across the table and brought the fire that erupted from it up to the box. "There's nothing in here except a candle." He showed them the tiny flame and slid the lid closed. "Seems like an innocent little thing." He handed the gun to Dex. "Point it that way and put your foot on that box on the floor."

Before Dex could step on the box, everyone yelled at him to point the gun down toward the other end of the corridor. Lucinda ducked and stepped back out the door.

"Great Christ in the morning, man." Alek pushed the gun in the right direction. "Pay attention. And don't shoot this for more than a few seconds at a time. You understand me?"

Dex nodded and grinned. He turned in the direction he was told, pointed the gun where he was told, and placed his foot over the box on the floor. Everyone else moved behind him and flattened themselves against the wall, except Alek who stepped closer to the water barrels.

With a great show, Dex pulled the trigger. And nothing happened for nearly two seconds, and the air seemed to go out of Dex's fun. But then, on the verge of giving up, a long tongue of orange and red flames shot out from the barrel of the weapon. Dex was startled and jerked the gun upward, causing flames to bathe the ceiling.

Lucinda stepped back in the room and moved quickly, kicking Dex's leg out from under him. His foot left the box, and he landed on his rear end with the weapon in his lap. Once his wits were about him, he started laughing. "What do you call this thing again?"

"We're not sure what to call it," Alek said. "I've been referring to it as a fire gun. For obvious reasons."

"Nope." Dex looked down at the rifle in his hands then up to the ceiling, which showed a fresh streak of black from his test. "Inferno something or other." He stood up and swung it around again, causing everyone to duck once more. "*Inferno musket* sounds right."

Lucinda looked at Alek, then at Dex. "You can't have one." Dex looked undeterred.

Alek nodded to Lucinda as she gathered her things to leave. "Got time to adjust that arm?"

She didn't want to, but she might not have a chance again if she headed out. "Yeah. All right." She sighed as she watched the others move toward the mess hall. She'd rather be eating whatever they were heating up in the kitchen.

In a small workroom just off the main storehouse, Cyrus, Alek, and the others had set up a reclining barber's chair next to a tool bench where Lucinda's arm could be tinkered with when needed. The space allowed some privacy, which Lucinda appreciated greatly. In the first few weeks, they either wheeled a cartload of tools into the open infirmary, or they took her down to the hanger and adjusted her like some piece of equipment—a Gatling gun or an airship. One was lacking in privacy, the latter in cleanliness. In either place, she felt stared at and examined. Whenever she flinched or cried out, she was embarrassed.

The men from the *Polk* went to lengths to make sure the new recruits and other soldiers that lived and worked at the tower or Outpost Two-Thirteen kept their prying eyes to themselves. They would stand around near her, forming their own wall whenever she needed attention from the medic or the mechanic, and when that got tiresome, they used blankets tacked to the walls like curtains. Eventually they cleared the former storage area and built solid walls and a door. It was a kindness she appreciated more than she could say.

"Any of it giving you troubles?" Alek took a thin rod covered in cloth and cleaned out the areas at the joints.

"No."

The cloth was filthy and smelled vaguely like lard when he pulled it back out. "Jesus, Lucinda. Maybe don't roll around in the mud so much." His smile was an attempt to soften the process, and he did it every time they had to work on the arm. Usually he told a bad joke or talked about the heat. She'd decided he was sheepish about what he was doing—worried about the pain he could cause.

"Hard to do that when your job is rolling around in the mud."

"You could wear something with long sleeves to cover it," Alek said. He leaned back. "Can you open and close your fist?"

The mechanical hand clenched into a fist and relaxed twice. She still was somewhat repulsed and fascinated by the idea the iron fingers were closing because she told them to do so. "Fashion doesn't really allow for two different size sleeves. One would be normal, and one would have to be huge to cover this monstrosity." She paused, not really wanting to get into the latest styles with Alek. "Besides, it's way too hot out there for long sleeves."

"Ain't that right? Jesus." Alek struggled with a small wrench at one of her elbow bolts.

"The rest of us have to wear full OMO uniforms, sleeves and all." Lowell's voice came from just outside the door. "If I'm going to sweat, why shouldn't you?"

Lucinda wanted to laugh. Lowell was fastidious about his appearance and somehow, she'd never seen him perspire once, even on the hottest day. His uniform was always perfectly creased. "Are you back already?"

"Yep. Cashe wants to speak with us."

"Anything more exciting than feeding the birds?"

"Could be."

Lucinda looked at Alek. "Well, it sounds like adventure calls." She nodded to her arm. "Can I go?"

Alek held up a finger and pulled a small brush coated in some grease from the work bench.

"Oh, come on, not that stuff. That smells like turnips and horse ass," Lucinda said. She started to pull away.

"I'm sorry; this is the best option we have for keeping the arm moving and lubricated. If it dries—"

Sure enough, as Alek got closer the smell hit her nostrils and she cringed. "I know. If it dries, the arm will lock up and I won't be able to play the banjo again."

"Sorry."

"Can I go?" Lucinda asked and stood when Alek nodded.

"Not going with me, you're not," Lowell said. "Not smelling like that."

"Shut it."

Lowell shook his head. "Just walk behind me."

Lucinda pushed him out of the way and moved for the door. She'd thought Cyrus was the only person she'd trust again, but slowly over the course of the last few months, she'd managed to allow the crew of the *Polk*, and the ranks of the OMO to get closer, and even enjoy their company. Bethy was another matter. As that girl had gotten closer to Cyrus, Lucinda felt jealousy, not over Cyrus's affections, but over the time lost. Up until recently, Lucinda and Cyrus and the rest of the crew were locked in a walking tin can called the Turtle for weeks on end. The proximity brought familiarity and now they spent more time apart than together. She missed having him to needle, but sometimes Lowell would do.

They rounded the spiral stairs that led to the upper office and found Cashe in the middle of the room, studying a map at a large table. Dex and Corrigan stood on the other side of the table. The all looked to Lowell and Bethy as they arrived. The room was loud with the hum of the engines of the airships idling, tethered to the tower on the floor above. The fact that both ships were ready to go didn't fill Lucinda with a good feeling.

"Ah, you're both here," Cashe said. He wheeled around in his chair and rolled to another set of papers on the next table. "We need you to leave immediately." He held out a paper for Lucinda and she took it. "We got a telegraph from the prison at Alcatraz Island. The inmates have broken out and they're taking over."

"I didn't know there was a telegraph facility there." Lucinda handed the paper to Lowell.

"It was set up to report any troop movements, mainly in the bay, or ships out to sea," Cashe said. "It was almost never operated. Surprised we got this, honestly."

Corrigan nodded to the two of them. "The airships are ready, and I'll get Alek the information he needs as we prep for departure."

"Wait. You *and* Alek are in the *Polk*? I thought he'd fly the *Polk* and you'd fly the *Valcour Bay*," Lowell said. "Who's flying the *Valcour* if you two are together?"

Cashe and Corrigan glanced at each other.

"Woodward will fly the *Valcour Bay* with Moore assisting," Cashe said.

"Ugh." Lowell looked slightly sick. "Come on."

"We don't have anyone else available and time is short, *The Moon and The Stars* is dropping troops off at Fort Stevens, that means Woodward is all we have at the present. No more bellyaching. Just move out."

Woodward wasn't Lucinda's favorite pilot either, but she had no grudge against the man personally, like Lowell did. On one mission, something had gone poorly. Very poorly. And Lowell had yet to forgive the other man.

Lucinda patted Lowell on the shoulder. "Let's go. We'll ride in the *Polk*." As they all headed up, they were joined by other OMO soldiers coming up the stairs, armed and ready. Lucinda leaned in close to her companion. "So, are we going to be issued actual ammunition for this? They can't expect us to preserve bullets while being shot at, can they?" Lowell shrugged.

Sunlight streamed into the relatively dark building from the huge wide-open doors that held the gangplanks leading to the ships. Lucinda turned toward the *Polk* and put her hands on the railings. She looked down as she left the safety of the building and for a moment there was nothing under the narrow walkway but the ground several stories below. Ahead, one of the many dark shiny crows that called the city home perched on the railing. "On your way." Lucinda waved it off the railing with a swipe of her good arm and it took flight, screaming a string of staccato screeches at her as it moved.

Lucinda continued, but it was back again before she'd taken a half dozen steps. "Shoo," Lucinda said. This time, she swung the metal arm to hurry the bird along. It squawked, spread its wings fully and pecked at the mechanical arm before leaping off the railing and gliding into the air. The crow circled above the walkway as Lucinda paused at the entrance to the airship. When she closed the hatch, the bird came back and landed on the railing, just as it was before.

5

The group ran up behind Reeves as he tried the door again. It was locked solid. "Christ, man," Adams shouted. "They're right behind us." Another shot from Reynolds punctuated the urgency.

They were trapped standing on the porch, and they would die there. That much Reeves knew. He searched. Other houses were open and they could hole up there, but none of them would offer the benefits of the old meeting place. He noticed one of the windows directly above them was cracked, with a pane missing. "Up there." He pointed. "Lift me up there."

Reynolds slung his weapon over his shoulder and bent down and held his hands out. Seeing his plan, Tremmel knelt and did the same. Together they lifted Reeves easily enough for him to grab the window ledge. He pulled himself up, propelled by his legs gaining purchase on the brick wall. The window was locked but he managed to smash his way in. He had his body halfway through the window when gunfire erupted from the porch. Reeves pulled himself in and looked back outside to see the men firing at the approaching mass of monsters. There were two dozen, he guessed. *Minimum.* And more were coming.

Reeves pulled his pistol and fired, downing one of the chewers with a trio of shots.

"Hurry the hell up and open this door," Adams shouted.

With one more shot, Reeves turned and looked around the bedroom he'd climbed into. It was dusty, but otherwise frozen in time. He stepped to the door opposite him and ran into the hall, turning left and running down the stairs he found there. The front door would be through the parlor on his left, he remembered. At the bottom of the stairs, he turned and ran through the room toward the door, only to stop when he realized there was a figure sitting on one of the wide chairs.

Startled, Reeves stopped and stepped back toward the wall. He knew the man, recognized him immediately, even though there was little of his face left. It was his former commanding officer, Zachary Coughlin. Coughlin's sidearm lay on the floor next to the chair, and there was a large hole on the right side of his head. Reeves looked him over before approaching with caution. He was concerned that his old friend was one of them—the chewers—but Coughlin wasn't moving. Reeves thought of his time and training with the man, the few missions they'd managed to work together before Reeves had been captured. Coughlin was covered in dust like the rest of the house and Reeves wanted to brush him off out of respect.

There were more shots outside, accompanied by the shouts of his companions. Reeves picked up Coughlin's pistol and checked it as he moved for the door. The gun was nearly loaded, and Reeves hoped it would work after all the time it had rested on the floor. He lifted the bolt from across the threshold and set it aside. As quickly as he could, he turned the knob and raised his weapon to cover those outside. He was stunned to see his companions fighting hand to hand on the porch.

The area in front of the house was carpeted with the monsters, swarming up to attack the men. Reynolds swung his rifle and knocked his assailant back, then scrambled through the transom, then he turned and fired at the mass of chewers. The rifle report echoed in the close quarters of the house, ringing in Reeves' ears. A bullet found the head of Adams's attacker and Jeffers grabbed him up and they both ran into the house. Tremmel was stuck fast, held by no less than two of the beasts. Reeves aimed at one of them but was pulled backward by Adams.

"Close the god damn door," Adams said.

Before Reeves could protest, Jeffers shoved the door closed and barred it. Reynolds stared ahead, weapon still pointed at the door. Above the din of the chewers outside, Tremmel let out a pathetic scream.

There was a time when Reeves would've made that same decision. It was the right choice, even if it wasn't the humane one. He knew trying to help Tremmel would've made things worse, maybe gotten someone else killed. It was a calculation, with the result being the sum of who lived and who died. Who won and who lost. He was taught that much early on in his training. How important is the mission? How important is it that you survive, so long as the mission gets completed? Here, in this time and place, the mission was getting home and seeing Lydia Jane and the kids. No matter what else had to occur to make that happen, he didn't care.

Adams was still staring at the door, mostly in disbelief, it seemed. The others pulled furniture and other objects in front of the door to further secure it.

"Anyone have matches?" Reynolds was poking around the mantle in the next room. It was hard for Reeves to tell if Reynolds hadn't seen the dead body in the chair or if he'd noticed and just didn't care. "Ah, here's a box," Reynolds said, as a flame erupted in the encroaching darkness, and lit nearby candles.

Reeves grabbed some matches and lit the two lamps he could find with oil still in them. He carried one as he moved to the kitchen. The cupboards were nearly empty—only dishes, cups and silverware remained. He and Reynolds moved on to the pantry and discovered they were empty as well. As Reynolds turned to go, Reeves held up his hand to stop his companion. He grabbed a board that made the framework of the shelves. With a firm grip, he tried to turn it, and broke it off. He looked at Reynolds and sheepishly threw the broken part to the ground. He was sure that triggered something hidden in the kitchen. Reeves thought about it for a moment. *Maybe it was the other end of the shelf, or a different shelf altogether.* As he searched, his hand ran across something under one of the shelves, a metal switch of some kind. He fiddled with it, and with a click, the shelves were free to turn on a hinge, pulling part of the wall away with them. Reeves set the false panel aside and Reynolds came close up to him to see what was behind the façade.

Reeves' heart sank. There were racks and spaces that were meant to hold rifles, a dozen of them, but they stood empty. Not a single gun remained in place. A small tin of musket shot lay at the bottom. Even if they had muskets, they would be devoured trying to reload the relics.

There were shelves where pistols and other firearms should have been, but instead their surfaces held only dust. This was not what Reeves wanted at the moment. With no support, in a deserted town and surrounded by these terrible monsters, he and the others needed weapons.

Further down toward the floor, he spied a cabinet beneath the shelves.

"What?" Adams stumbled close. "We came all this way. It better be worth it."

Reeves waved Reynolds into another room. "Check everything. Surely they left something behind."

"The hell? You don't know what's here? Where's the god damn gold and money?" Jeffers kicked a nearby chair.

"I never said that. *You* said that. You made that up in your own fool head."

The click of a pistol brought Reeves' focus back to Adams. "Then maybe you ought to tell us what this is all about." He stood uneasily, pointing his gun at Reeves from a half dozen paces away. Seeing this, Jeffers pointed his gun as well. "What is this place?"

"It's a base of operations of sorts. It's a safe place where southern operatives met and planned." He looked from man to man to see their reactions.

"Spies?" Adams said.

"Mostly."

"You? A spy?" Jeffers jumped in.

"Not really. I'm just a soldier who got a little more training than the rest." It was true. When he was plucked from the Confederate ranks, he received training in a number of disciplines, whereas most of his compatriots were merely handed a rifle and told to shoot. "I was trained to support spies and generals, operatives and soldiers." Reeves weighed what to reveal to the men. He'd kept it secret for all the years he was in prison, hadn't spoken a word of it since he'd been chosen for the group. "We were more intelligencers, raiders, and whatnot. We observed. We reported. We did what they asked us to do."

"It seems like it was mighty helpful to you," Adams said. "Seeing as you spent so much time in prison and now, you're stuck in a room with people shovin' guns in your face." Adams looked around at the others, confident he was in charge. "Assuming you're telling the truth, your special army training seems kinda lacking."

"And now you're surrounded by chewers, too," Jeffers said. He laughed at Reeves' misfortune until it appeared he realized he shared the same situation.

"You're right. Extra training didn't do a good god damn for me," Reeves said. "In fact," he paused to wave his hands at the room. "The last time I departed from this very abode, I was captured just two days later and went straight to the great island of Alcatraz. Where I met all of you." He smiled his most deprecating smile. "Not exactly a fond memory for me."

They laughed at him, all except for Reynolds, who stood at a window staring silently down at the crowd that was gathering outside. Reeves stole glances around the room. If the previous operatives left in a hurry maybe they didn't take everything. If they grabbed the guns, maybe they left the trinkets. He saw the lantern hanging off a nearby post and remembered it had a dagger hidden in the base. It used to, anyway. The fire poker came apart and became two weapons: a heavy bludgeon and short blade. They kept a single-barrel shotgun hidden in the thick leg of the table. Failing that, any one of the picture frames could be broken into shards of deadly sharp glass. Everything could be turned into a weapon, Reeves was taught that at Camp Moore, but he was never more keenly aware of that than when he was in that room. Were the candlesticks filled with oil, or was that the safe house in Baltimore? Either way, they'd hurt like hell if he smashed Jeffers in the nose with one of them.

"I didn't come back for it, but there is money. Well, there *was* money. I don't know if it's still there." Reeves pointed to the corner in the kitchen. "There's a section of the floorboards that comes up. There used to be a box with some currency hidden underneath."

There was pounding on the outer doors. "Those—those people are going to bust in," Reynolds said. "They's still people, ain't they?"

"Shut up, damn you." Adams stepped toward the area Reeves had indicated and looked.

"They won't bust in. The doors were fortified to withstand much worse." It was true to a point, Reeves thought. Who knew what age and disrepair might have done to those doors?

Adams knelt and leaned close to inspect the floor. His hands ran over the edges of the boards and traced a spot that was just slightly different from the rest of the room. "What do I do?"

"Push down hard and it'll pop up."

The concern on Adams' face was evident, the floor boards could do anything; they could trigger a trap of some sort, they could cause a heavy weight to fall from the ceiling, they could do nothing. His greed quickly won out and he pressed firmly on the wood. With a click, the section did as Reeves had indicated, and it opened about two inches. Adams pulled it up and his face brightened as he saw inside. "There is money. Stacks of it. Union currency, C.S.A. money, coins—" he reached in and pulled out a stack of bills and flipped through them. "Hundreds. Thousands. Enough to get us all home, sure as shit."

Jeffers turned to see for himself and Reeves saw his opportunity. He reached up and pulled the lantern off its peg, and brought it down on the other man's head, shattering the glass. The base, and a considerable amount of glass, clattered to the floor, where no knife fell out. The lantern handle, hood, and some glass shards were all that remained, swinging uselessly in his hand. As Jeffers fell forward, Adams threw down the money and cursed. His gun was next to the hole and he reached for it clumsily.

Reeves pulled the gun from Jeffers' belt and immediately fired one shot that hit Adams square in the shoulder, causing him to grab for the wound as he fell to the floor. Pulling the trigger a second time, Reeves heard the empty click indicating the weapon was out of ammunition.

Jeffers stumbled two steps forward and turned, pulling at his rifle to get it off his back and fire. Reeves turned his attention back to him, bringing the butt of the empty pistol down on Jeffers' trigger hand, with a wet crack of shattering wrist bones, and the man's weapon fell to the ground. Before Jeffers could cry out in pain, Reeves raked the remains of the lantern across his opponent's face. The glass ripped long, dark lines across Jeffers' cheeks and nose. Reeves barely thought about it, his own reactions came so easily. Blood poured from Jeffers' face and it was almost a surprise when Reeves found the sharp instrument the lantern had become was buried in Jeffers' chest. And even as he was falling to the floor, Jeffers seemed unsure of exactly how it had happened.

In the other corner of the room, Adams was moaning and dragging himself back toward the hole and the gun that rested next to it. Quick strides brought Reeves easily to the man's side, and he picked up the pistol just a foot from Adams' grasp. It hadn't been the man's target after all; Adams grabbed a handful of the money out of the hole.

"Never thought I'd get out of the prison," Adams said. His voice strained from the pain. "But I did." He took a deep breath. "Never thought I'd see another dollar again. But look—" He balled the paper in his fist, then let some slide from his hand. "Look at this." The money fell back into the hole, note by note. "Look at it."

"You led a charmed life. Truly," Reeves said. He shot Adams twice in his chest and turned to Jeffers. The man was still breathing, barely, and looked not long for the world. Better to not leave anyone alive and in a position to make things worse, Reeves thought. He made to shoot but realized he should save his bullets for real threats. He stepped up and put his withered boot on Jeffers' neck and then put on as much pressure as he could muster. As he waited for Jeffers to stop breathing, Reeves flipped open the pistol and counted one shot left. One bullet for Reynolds, if he needed. Jeffers' shotgun was lying on the floor nearby, if the pistol failed.

When he heard a final wheeze, and felt the body beneath him go slack, Reeves closed the gun and looked to the remaining man. Reynolds was still leaning against the window when Reeves approached. He hadn't moved from his spot during the fight, and his own weapon was resting on the window sill out of reach. He didn't make to help either side in the conflict.

"They're not going away," Reynolds said. "There's more of them coming." Reynolds pointed up the street and then across the way. "Where are they all coming from? Did the whole city die and now they're coming to drag us off to live in this hell with them?"

"I don't know that." It was hard to grasp the idea that the jailors had been telling the truth and not just spouting a tale to amuse themselves when they talked to prisoners. "But I do know that we need to gather things here and make our escape before morning comes and that boat leaves without us."

"How?"

"I'm working on that. I just need your help. Can you help me?" Reeves wasn't sure he wanted Reynolds' help, travelling and working alone seemed best for Reeves. Things got complicated in a group. One glance around the room at the bodies reinforced that philosophy.

"I'll do whatever you tell me to do. Just don't let me die like Tremmel did out there."

It wasn't clear to Reeves if Reynolds had looked around the room to see their dead partners, or if he was only afraid of dying as the victim of a chewer. "Find a bag or a satchel on one of those tables and fill it with money. I'm going to see what other supplies I can discover." Reynolds went to work immediately, brushing the dust off the table and pulling two messenger bags from one of the other rooms.

Reeves turned his attention to the cabinet below the empty gun racks. He pulled the door open and found it was still stocked with boxes. The first small box revealed some loose change in various denominations and from various countries. He threw it aside and grabbed the largest one. It had maps of the city, shipping schedules, and false identification, and papers for various businesses.

He moved from the kitchen to the lone downstairs bedroom and tossed the identities on the bed. The boxes here proved just as frustrating to Reeves; old clothing, worn shoes, unusable food stuffs. Worst of all: no weapons.

He moved upstairs to the largest room and stepped between the two neatly-made beds there and pulled the drawer from the night stand. It was empty, of course, but he flipped it upside down and removed the dagger that was affixed to the bottom. He dropped the weapon on the bed and the drawer in the corner before moving to the dresser on the west wall. There were still some clothes inside, these in unexpectedly good condition. He threw a couple of shirts, pairs of socks and trousers on the other bed. They smelled musty, but not nearly as bad as what he was already wearing. The second drawer had a false bottom which revealed a Colt Dragoon revolver and a dozen bullets, all in a wooden case. The whole thing went on the bed with the dagger.

He paused, thinking about the less obvious things that were hidden here and all about the house. The bedpost was hollow and contained the barrel of a shotgun, but it was heavy and would only slow them down as they fled, so he left it alone.

"Hey." It was Reynolds downstairs. "There's not just money in here. There's a bunch of papers too. Should I take them?"

"What do they say?"

A quiet pause. "I'm not sure."

The Confederate army certainly didn't teach its soldiers to read. Reeves had learned that particular skill long before the war broke out. He'd even taught some of the prisoners how at Alcatraz, but apparently hadn't gotten around to Reynolds. "Just put it all in, if there's room." He heard shuffling as papers were stuffed carelessly into a bag.

On a shelf, Reeves pulled down a couple of books that turned out to be actual books, rather than hollowed-out hiding places, but reminded himself to check the bookshelf out in the sitting room when he was done. He moved to the closet and pulled out a hatbox. He tossed the expensive head cover aside and pulled out the rest of the hat box's contents. There was a decayed and dirty ball of hair that was originally a blonde wig, and several small jars of make-up. He opened each container, only to find they'd all dried up to the consistency of rock. He tossed them in the far corner with the other useless items. If he needed a disguise, he'd have to start from scratch.

Hanging in the closet were a couple of winter jackets and fine shirts. All useless to him in the warm spring of California. The rest of the clothing was gone.

"That's a nice hat. Lovely wig. Are you planning a festive ball when we get back to the boat?" Reynolds said.

Startled, Reeves dropped the wig and looked to the doorway. "No. Just some useless things." He stood and pointed to the clothes on the bed. "You're free to change if your clothes are as horrid as mine."

"You're worried about how you look and smell now? We could die, we could be stuck here, and you're concerned about your appearance?"

"I'm out of that prison now. I want its stench off of me and I never want it to cling to me again." Reeves took his shirt off and pulled another one from the bed. As he did, he found Reynolds staring at him.

"You must have really angered the guards to have them do that to you." Reynolds pointed tentatively at Reeves' chest. "Good lord."

The shirt covered up the crimson and black scar on Reeves' chest quickly. "So, they know me easier next time." He grabbed pants and a belt and started for the sitting area. "Hard to pretend I'm not the operative they're looking for if my number is burned into my flesh. I'm just thrilled they didn't scorch it into my face." He stopped to look again. "There should be good shoes or boots here somewhere." He looked from room to room in order to get away.

Reynolds followed. "What is that? Some kind of symbol? What's it mean?"

"It's the number nine." Reeves rolled his eyes. "There were twelve of us. I was given the number nine in the program. The Yankees kept track of which ones they had."

"Christ. That must've been painful."

The thought brought back memories he'd buried. The fire where they heated the brand smelled like pine and his own burning flesh reminded him of a rabbit on a spit. "Painful? You don't know. They didn't exactly have a branding iron in the shape of a nine, so rather than branding me once, they took their time. Used a flat line and branded me six separate times, shaping the number as they went—four times to the make the little round part, and twice to make the straight line to go with it." Some boots in the hall closet looked about his size, so Reeves pulled them out and held them up to his foot. "It was hell. Over and over again." He sat down on the floor and pulled on the footwear. "There's a couple pair in there still. Maybe one'll fit you."

The noise outside rose suddenly. Reeves stood and moved toward the bookshelf in the parlor and threw the tomes on the floor, looking for the last hiding place he remembered. It took a minute, but he finally found the box made to look like a stack of books where they kept special weapons and items. He set the container on the table and lifted the lid. Reynolds looked over Reeves' shoulder and inside. It contained three small pepperbox guns, four pocket watches, two coils of thin wire, and a pair of brass knuckles. A number of rounds of ammunition for the small pistols rolled around in the bottom of the box. Reeves sighed. Nothing in the box would help them with the chewers. The guns were too small of a caliber to do any damage from a distance, the watches weren't meant for that kind of thing and a body would have to be real up close with a chewer in order to use the knuckle duster.

Reeves picked up the pistols and cleaned them up as best he could. He made sure there were no obstructions in the barrels, checked the action on the hammer and that the grips were solid. Then loaded each properly and handed one to Reynolds. "This isn't going to bring down one of those bastards unless it's close enough to smell you, and even then, I don't know. Use it as your last hope."

"None of this matters if we can't get out the front door."

Reeves shoved the watches, wire, brass knuckles and small guns into the pockets of a dress jacket and pulled it on. The fabric was soft and felt decadent compared to the prison issue clothes he'd worn for years. It was out of place in the situation he was now facing, but it was comforting, a reminder of what he'd done early in the war— the kind of jobs that had actually gone according to plan. He hated to think the rich black fabric could be soaked in blood by day's end, unless he managed the situation properly.

"We're not going out the front door. Grab the bags and follow me," Reeves said. He picked up Adams' gun and checked it. He knew the other gun was empty and left it. He headed back down the stairs, with Reynolds following cautiously. The sound was louder now, chewers pawing and scratching at the front door. Reeves turned in the other direction and opened the closet door. He reached down and pulled the floor board out of the way. He tossed it and looked down into the blackness below.

6

"You going to make an honest woman out of her?" Lucinda asked. She tossed her rifle on her cot with the rest of the gear she was packing.

"What?" Cyrus asked. He nearly dropped the case he was holding for her.

Each piece of clothing had to be refolded, Lucinda had decided. While she admired Cyrus's ability to pack for a crisis quickly, his method of rolling everything into a ball left much to be desired. "You can't keep carrying on the way you do with that girl and not expect it to lead to something."

"It's only been a few months. Ain't leading to nothing less we want it to."

"Do you? Want it to? And it's almost a year now."

"What're you, my mother all of the sudden?"

"No, but if you look around, you'll realize I've known you longer than anyone," Lucinda snapped a blouse in the air to shake off the dust. "And I know you better than anyone." She watched as Cyrus leaned against the wall and tried to fold his arms. She knew he didn't want to talk about private things with anyone, but occasionally she could wrest something from the dark recesses of his mind.

He shook his head as if realizing she was attempting to trick him somehow. "There are things you don't know."

"I'm sure."

"Don't you need to get aboard the *Polk* and go?"

Lucinda took a minute to stare at him, thinking she could draw him out still. "Maybe we talk when I get back?"

Cyrus shrugged. "Just be careful."

As if on command, the *Polk's* engine suddenly flared out in the courtyard. Lucinda balled up her things and shoved them in her dusty bag, to Cyrus' obvious delight. She stood next to him and hugged him, careful not to hurt him with her unwieldy metal arm. "You, too."

She slung her rifle across her back, shouldered the pack and took the box of precious ammunition and gun cleaning supplies from Cyrus. They nodded, and she was off. Out the door and into the hallway, she half-ran toward the stairs leading to the launch area. The steps were empty, which meant everyone else was already in place or doing their jobs, which meant she was running last to get aboard.

When she got to the top, the noise was louder, the air whipped around inside the common area and spread the stench of burning coal everywhere. She pushed forward to the gangplank to step into the airship. There she found Trent Lowell, standing rail-straight except for one hand which was examining an open pocket watch. He looked up at Lucinda and shook his watch, then looked at it again. As she got closer, he pointed at the watch and shrugged. "I think it's broken."

"I'm not that late," Lucinda said as she pushed past him. Lowell laughed and they both stepped onto the *Polk*. Behind them, two soldiers pulled away the boards and stored them inside. Lowell tugged the portal shut and locked it. He pulled down a tube and yelled into the funnel. "Queen Lucy is aboard. Hatch sealed."

"You're playing with fire, you know." Lucinda liked working with Lowell more than most of the others. At least he enjoyed his work, had some sense of fun, and could carry on a conversation. Occasionally when she was stuck with Dex or one of the others, she struggled to find common ground and it made each patrol or training session incredibly tedious.

Lowell smiled at her. "Well, it's never my intention. Fire is dangerous. I avoid danger when at all possible." He stepped on the stairs and climbed upward. "Seeing as we have hours before we'll be at our destination, I'm going to catch some rack time. Never know what we'll need to be well-rested for when we get there, yeah?" He continued up the spiral steps and disappeared. Not only was Lowell an interesting companion on the job, he liked to take naps and was perhaps the snappiest dresser that Lucinda knew. She was all for naps.

Lucinda went up the stairs, her bag and gun clanking against the rail as she went. On the main floor, she was greeted by the troops, a smattering of men and women lingering in the hall, or on their way to their disembarking stations. There were also enough soldiers that weren't familiar to her, indicating that Cyrus, Bethy and the others had been hard at work training whoever showed up on their doorstep.

A siren sounded throughout the airship, announcing they were pulling away from the tower. Lucinda ducked into the barracks, tossed her kit next to her and clenched the bed frame. The take offs weren't always smooth—a breeze could come in off the Pacific and toss the *Polk* around and she'd learned early on that no one ever saw it coming.

The propellers picked up speed, pushed on by the coal-fired boilers. The thick smell of the fire in the engine room filled her nostrils.

As the ship listed, Dex walked into the room and hefted his own pack onto the bunk above hers. "I'm taking that top bed." His speech was slurred; Lucinda guessed it likely because of a thick wad of tobacco that bulged in his lower lip.

"The hell you are," Lucinda said. She waved to the half a dozen other bunks that were free in the room. "There's plenty down there. It isn't that crowded."

"I like to be close to the door, case I need to relieve myself in the night." He paused, and Lucinda could see him trying to adjust the wad of black in his mouth by moving his jaw and tongue. "I've been having movements at the worst time." Further elaboration was cut off by a clunking from the engines which made them both cock their heads to contemplate.

"Hell was that?" Lucinda said.

Dex sat on the bunk across from her and held the frame. "I don't know. I never heard it before. Ships ain't the area of my expertise, so to speak."

"You have expertise?" Lucinda stopped to listen again, and the racket subsided and disappeared altogether.

"I should've stayed behind. This doesn't feel right."

"What doesn't?"

"Ain't none of it. From the moment I got up today, I said to myself, I said 'Dexter? It all feels wrong.'"

She didn't really think anything was wrong exactly, but Lucinda nodded anyway. She just felt that maybe, just maybe, something wasn't right.

7

"Where does this go?" Reynolds said as he stared down into the darkness under the closet floor.

Reeves grabbed a box of matches from the shelf and lit one. He looked at Reynolds and then the door. "Does it really matter at this point?" He dropped the match down the hole and it extinguished when it hit the ground. He struck another and descended the ladder. He looked side to side for a lantern to light their way. He found a makeshift torch—a thick branch wrapped in rags stuck in the dirt wall—and he lit it with the match. The floor sloshed as he stepped off the ladder, the water on the ground invisible until he was stepping in it. It came to his ankles.

Reynolds was standing at the top, framed in the light streaming into the closet. "Let's go. Close and latch the door behind you. Don't want them falling in with us accidently."

They stopped at the bottom to see the words "Santa Rosa" scrawled in fading white letters on the wall near where they'd descended.

"What's that?" Reynolds asked.

Already walking ahead, Reeves called back to his companion. "I'm guessing it's a hastily left clue for any agents that might be unfortunate enough to find themselves in a tunnel being pursued by the living dead."

The splat of Reynolds' footfalls approached hastily. "Clue for what?"

"Where to go for help." It was not lost on Reeves that the message was in no way coded, or specific, and was left when the city was overrun years ago. So, it was old, untrustworthy and poorly spelled. Would anyone even still be there? Reeves kept moving.

"Anybody could have found that. Couldn't they find your 'help' themselves and captured them?"

"I'm fairly sure whoever wrote this knew that San Francisco was done for. Probably guessed no one would explore down here. Plus, it doesn't say where in Santa Rosa, does it?"

The passage was narrow, with thick beams placed on both sides at intervals that shored up the walls. Reeves moved ahead, trying to keep from stumbling. The torch was warm near his face and bathed him in earthy smoke.

"Why didn't we just come *in* this way?" Reynolds was somewhere behind him, and Reeves wasn't sure how close.

"I had no idea where it came out at this end. I never had to use it. How much time do we have before the boat leaves?"

"I don't know. How in the name of hell do I know?"

Somehow at the time they left, it seemed like it wouldn't be hard to get what he wanted and get back to the boat. Now, after being held at gunpoint and being chased by chewers, time just got away from Reeves.

They moved as fast as they could in the crude tunnel by candlelight. Both ran headlong into a wall after a while as they didn't realize the route took a left turn. Eventually even the light behind them from the hatch of the house disappeared.

Reynolds stopped and stared ahead. "Jesus, Reeves. I can't see a damn thing. How do you know there's nothing ahead?"

He didn't, but that wasn't what he said. "You just have to trust me." He moved past Reynolds and took the lead. Reeves wanted more light as well. He held up his candle to the wall as he went, looking for torches or lanterns that would help light their way and ease their minds. They walked slowly, stumbling and compensating with short steps. Reynolds was breathing heavy and constantly turning his head to look behind them, in front of them and above.

"Calm down. I see a lantern," Reeves said. He opened the shutter to light the lamp with the candle. There was very little oil in it, so he rolled the wick into it as best he could before lighting it. It made a weak flame, but still managed to help.

Ahead, the tunnel ended in a wall, with a ladder dug into the mud there leading up. When Reynolds came beside him, Reeves spoke to him plainly, simply, like he was giving an admonition to a child. "I'm going up first. Understand?"

Reynolds nodded.

"I'll unbolt the door and climb out. We should be fine, but if not, I'll have to shoot and that will draw them to us. Then you're on your own. We'll have to make a mad rush to the boat and if that means leaving you so I can survive, I'll do it. Understand?"

Reynolds nodded again.

"I ain't coming back for you. Got it?"

"Yes. But—"

"I'm going to open this hatch and see what it looks like. If it's still pitch dark, we'll stay here for a few more minutes and rest. If I see the faintest morning light, we run. You fall, I leave you. Understand?"

"I can't—"

"No." Reeves tightened the strap of the bag he was carrying so that it was snug against his chest. He checked the Colt to make sure it was loaded and slid it into his coat pocket. "You fall, I leave you." He put a foot on the first step of the ladder and started climbing. When he was high enough, he reached up and slowly, as quietly as he could, turned the bar that locked the hatch. It groaned and protested, and Reeves braced himself on the wall, struggling with the reddish rusted metal. It gave way with a sandy grinding sound and Reeves turned it until it was no longer an obstacle. He pushed the trap door up just enough to see the room it opened into. It was dark, but with a hint of the dawn to come.

"Let's move out." He pushed the trap door above him open and looked around before climbing out. They were in the laundry building they'd passed on the way in. the door opened under the counter and Reeves found he had a good view of the street outside. More of the chewers were there in the fading dark, moving toward the house, following the crowd. As Reynolds emerged from the hole, Reeves assessed the situation as best he could. There were a good ten chewers visible, and the docks were at least a couple of minutes away, even at a decent run. The large front window made it easy for them to see out, and for the chewers to see in.

Offering a hand, Reeves pulled Reynolds out of the hole. "We're back where we started. If we run, we can dodge these things and get back to the docks. They seem pretty slow."

"I'll follow your lead."

Reeves stood at the door with a hand on the lock. He checked himself again, making sure the gun was safely tucked away, but close enough to get to if he needed it. He planned to run, and shooting would only slow him down. He remembered the things he'd packed in his bag. He fished out the brass knuckles and slid them on his right hand. "Good luck." He nodded to Reynolds, took a breath, opened the door and ran.

8

Reeves was moving as fast as he could, and he could hear Reynolds not far behind. Their steps in the soft earth made mud fly as they ran. They dodged the closest chewers without even so much as a touch and headed through the muck toward the dock. When one of the beasts got in his way, Reeves punched it square in the nose with the brass knuckles, nearly caving the thing's skull in as he did. Black blood and brain matter clung thickly to Reeves' digits as he withdrew his fist and the brass knuckles from the chewer's head. He was disgusted by the sight and spoiled meat stench of the thing's insides.

"Where in hell is the boat?" Reynolds yelled.

It was nowhere to be seen. "Just keep going. They'll be there." The dull light of the morning made the water orange ahead of them.

Both men moved as quickly as they could, but once they hit the muddy section near the dock, it forced them to a horrifyingly slow pace. Reeves pulled his feet out of the muck with as much strength as he could muster, but was merely inching forward at best. Reynolds moved in the same manner, his satchels swinging, feet sloshing loudly with each step as he tried to get out of the mire. Further back, the chewers had turned to pursue, and the things weren't nearly as concerned with the grime and the muck. When they got stuck, they fell to the ground and continued forward, crawling and using their hands and legs to propel them along. They were gaining, even as Reynolds and Reeves hit the halfway point.

"Shoot them," Reeves said.

Reynolds fired at the nearest one, shattering its face in a cloud of red.

"Jesus, help me." Reynolds had stopped. His eyes gleamed in the light. He took time to line up another shot and stopped another chewer.

Reeves kept moving and considered the implications of leaving the man there in order to insure his own escape. Reeves pocketed the knuckles, pulled his gun and shot at two of the beasts. "Let's go." He needed the man for now. And he needed the bag of money if *anyone* was going to get home.

The boat was still not at the dock.

They trudged forward, with more chewers coming at them, excited and drawn toward the noise of the gunfire. They weren't quick, but neither were they deterred by things like mud and bullets. The air was thick with the unpleasant smells of smoke and the filthy, rotting bodies of the chewers coming closer.

Reeves was the first to the dock and ran toward the end as quickly as he could, while keeping himself to the side in hopes of avoiding the broken boards. He stumbled but kept on his feet. Behind him, Reynolds was not quite so careful. His panicked expression told the whole story, he wanted to get away however possible. He ran headlong through the middle of the dock, with each board creaking as he went. He was easily outdistancing the chewers, still mired in the muck.

"Slow down and watch what you're doing," Reeves said, but it was too late. As Reynolds got halfway to Reeves, two planks cracked and gave out, sending Reynolds sprawling. He was able to grab onto what solid wood there was to keep from falling through, but it was cracking even as he clawed to find better support.

The chewers were coming out of the mud and advancing on the dock. "Christ Reeves. Jesus Christ, help me." Another chunk of wood that was supporting him broke away and Reynolds slid down, scrambling for purchase with just one arm.

In the distance, the *Nathan Prentiss* stormed toward the dock previously hidden by half-sunken debris along the shore. Reeves waved to the boat, making sure they saw him, then turned and gingerly made his way toward Reynolds. He shot two chewers as he found his footing, and then put his pistol in his jacket. He held out his hand. "Come on,"

Reynolds was hanging on with one hand on the plank and struggled to get his other up to Reeves. Seeing his dilemma, Reeves reached down and grasped Reynolds' wrist and pulled, but couldn't move him.

"One of the satchels is stuck," Reynolds said.

"Get it loose." Reeves looked up to see a chewer almost within attacking distance. He let go with one hand and reached for the gun in his coat. Reynolds slid back down some. One shot felled the nearest chewer, but the gun clicked empty when he fired for another, so Reeves tossed the gun, grabbed Reynolds with both hands and yanked him as hard as he could onto the dock. "Go," he said. Reeves practically shoved Reynolds ahead of him and kept a hand on his back as the pair ran.

The boat slammed into the dock hard next to them and Reynolds jumped onboard. Some of the chewers fell through the delicate boards and disappeared from sight, but others were making it on sheer luck. He ran as the first few found the same hole that had trapped Reynolds, and he leapt onboard as the boat moved from the dock.

9

The original intent of a base on Alcatraz was to house prisoners in the most terrible place possible, but the site evolved over time to include a post to defend San Francisco Bay and the surrounding area from Confederate attacks by sea and by air. Those weapons were never dismantled once the truce took hold and the chewers made San Francisco uninhabitable. It was those guns, left in place for any future conflicts, that opened up on the *Polk* and its escort ship the *Valcour Bay*.

Explosions burst into black powder a half a mile in front of the OMO force as they arrived. Too far to do real damage, but enough to cause concern on the bridge of the lead ship. "I guess we have an answer as to whether it's just some accident that delayed the boat," Lucinda said.

"It appears we do." Alek nodded and turned to Corrigan, who was already adjusting the *Polk*'s controls in anticipation of the order to come. "Keep your distance, Corrigan," Alek said. He held onto the nearby bar as the navigator put the ship into a tight right turn. He grabbed a tube and shouted more orders into it. "Load up the mini Napoleon and prepare the Gatlings on the port side."

A nearby telescope rolled off the console as the ship maneuvered, and Lucinda snatched it up. She took a moment to focus in on Alcatraz. "I can't tell what the situation is, sir. I see a lot of men in Union uniforms, but I can't tell if they're prisoners wearing the colors to confuse us, or if they're soldiers retaking the fort."

"My guess is the former. But I could be wrong." Alek placed the tube back in its holder, not ready to tell anyone to fire just yet." The good news was that the weaponry on the island had a limited range and the *Polk* was safely out of it. Conversely, the *Polk*'s armaments couldn't hit Alcatraz at the current distance either. It was a stalemate, though it didn't deter the prisoners from firing for the hell of it.

Something below caught Lucinda's eye and she focused on it. "Over there. On the eastern side of the island. There's a handful of what looks like guards entrenched on the beach, firing at prisoners at the wall.

"I see it," Alek said. He'd brought up a smaller spyglass he kept around his neck and looked toward the beach. "We'll call that our rally point."

"*The Valcour Bay* isn't turning fast enough. It could get caught by a lucky shot," Corrigan said. "And they're opening fire on the island."

"Damn Woodward. We told him to keep back. He's got no business flying that ship. He needs more experience." Alek shook his head as he adjusted the wheel.

Lucinda found that no one was fond of Woodward, and it seemed to be more than just the fact that he was the new pilot. "Can we signal them?"

"We can try, but the air's getting pretty thick with smoke already, he may not see our message," Corrigan said.

"Get someone to try, then." One of the men, a recruit named Adam nodded and left, and Alek stared at the scene as the ship shifted to orbit around the island.

Lucinda could see the wheels turning in his mind, working out strategies to end the conflict and keep the *Valcour Bay* safe. They'd left the base in a hurry and hadn't fully loaded the *Polk*'s armaments. That meant it would be useless to climb to higher elevation to drop explosives on the prison; the ship hadn't been loaded up with any, and he didn't want to try to improvise some in the middle of the current volatile situation. "Any ideas?"

"Maybe we should start signaling the men on the island to stop shooting at us? And maybe surrender?" Corrigan called over his shoulder as he gripped the controls a little harder. "That's my vote."

"That's a fine plan. I vote for that, if we're voting," Lucinda said.

Alek laughed. "We're not voting on anything. Besides, I don't know if anyone down there can read our signals. First and foremost, we need to make sure the *Valcour Bay* gets out of harm's way and we can keep them safe."

Corrigan rose from his seat. "Might be too late on that score, sir. I see some smoke trailing the *Valcour Bay* now."

"Lucinda? Would you mind taking a turn at the scope until Adam gets back?"

"Happy to," Lucinda said.

Alek hadn't been commanding ships for long, but he was heartened to see how well the crews had taken to him. Occasionally a southern soldier was slow to respond to a command from a Negro, or openly defied him, but he was replaced quickly by a more willing subject. And sometimes, as in the current situation, the less willing realized following orders might keep them and their cohorts alive a little longer

"I see what he's saying." Lucinda had the scope to her eyes and was adjusting the magnification with her good hand. "They have a dark tendril of smoke escaping from somewhere near the boiler." She turned back to Alek. "If their boiler goes down, they'll be in serious trouble."

The trio watched as the smoke trail got bigger and flames suddenly became obvious.

"You're right. They're dropping quickly. Woodward is guiding the *Valcour Bay* down faster for some reason." Corrigan adjusted their course in order to turn a bit wider and slowed their speed.

It was an odd move to try to crash faster, but Alek quickly saw the strategy the moment the airship hit the water. "It looks like there aren't any of the larger guns that could hit the *Valcour Bay* there. He's close enough that the rock outcroppings prevent the weapons from focusing that low. If they crashed a little in either direction, they're in the open and those Napoleons could just tear them to shreds."

"Won't stay that way for long, I'll wager. Tide'll carry them into the line of fire fairly quickly," Lucinda said.

An echo reverberated through one of the tubes as Dex's hollow voice came up from the cargo deck. "I'm having fun, but some of these new recruits down here are looking a bit queasy. Any chance we can get on the ground and into the possibility of not hurling our biscuits all over this ship?"

Someone put Dex in charge of troops. That idea still made Lucinda's head swim. She grabbed the tube and held it to her mouth. "Gird up the men, Dex. We'll be going in soon.

"He seems a little—I don't know—rowdy to be in charge of other people," Corrigan said.

"He's fine," Lucinda said. "I've been on a few operations with him. He's not rowdy, just enthusiastic." Rowdy seemed like a little more fitting moniker. She raised the tube again. "Fine. Get your rowdy riflemen prepared, we might need them for a rescue. The *Valcour Bay* has gone into the water. Meantime, tell them not to get sick all over the clean ship."

"Rowdy Riflemen?" Corrigan laughed.

"Just you wait. He'll like it. It'll stick."

"If you get around to the other side of the island, their defenses are weakest. You can drop us in the water with a couple of boats and we can row up to the *Valcour Bay* and pull out the crew," Lucinda said. "If things go well, we can approach the island and scout the situation a little closer." She stepped away from the controls and set the telescope on the console as she did.

"I like the rescue part of that plan." Lucinda could hear Alek call to her, but the rest of his response was lost as she moved quickly down the corridor to the spiral staircase that led below. She'd found herself jumping at the chance to join in whatever fight came her way since signing up with the OMO and wasn't sure why. She supposed being cooped up on a Turtle for years made her want to seek a little adventure, but she was quickly discovering there was a line between thrills and actual danger. She tapped the railing with her iron hand as she descended.

As she entered the cargo bay, she found Dex's men were piecing together two large rowboats from a pile of parts in the center of the floor. One was nearly complete, and the other was in sad shape.

"It don't look right, does it?" Dex asked.

There was the general shape of a boat in each of them—a skeleton, really—that gave a sense of what they were trying to do. Otherwise, one of them had far too many holes to suggest that it was supposed to be a water-faring craft. "Are these the only boats we have?"

"It's an aircraft. Why would the *Polk* have a boat onboard?" One of the soldiers tossed a plank of wood onto the pile of parts and folded his arms.

The airship descended, and Lucinda knew their time was short. "Finish this one. It looks closest. Don't try to do them both at the same time. Let's finish the first and launch it with just four or five soldiers when we get close enough to the water. The rest of us will finish up and get in the water when we can." She discovered the parts of the boat were labeled by letters but all mixed in together. She reached into the pile and grabbed a part. "Anyone know where the other 'A' part is?"

"We have another option." Lowell walked up behind them, his approach masked by the noise of the engines and the men. "There's the escape canopies." He pointed to the boxes secured over the doors.

10

Two airships approached from the north, passing almost over the escapees' boat as it moved away from San Francisco. One of the ships was huge, the likes of which Reeves had never seen. Dirigibles were just coming into more common use when he was incarcerated, and most of those weren't even the size of the smaller ship that passed over them now. The big one looked like a small moon and appeared to be heavily apportioned with weapons.

"Shit," LaRue said. He turned and looked accusingly at Reeves. "You said they wouldn't show up looking for their supply boat for almost a week."

The discrepancy wasn't lost on Reeves. He figured the military was either well-disciplined and at peak readiness, or there was so little going on in the outside world that they had nothing else to do with their resources. "The supply ship must've had another deadline to meet and missed it."

"So, what now?" Patrick asked. The men on the boat all stared at Reeves, waiting for an answer. There wasn't much else to do, they'd guided the boat closer to shore and killed the little steam ship's engine as soon as the airship had come in sight. They'd hoped to eliminate the smoke emanating from the engine, as it might give their position away. If they could blend in with the derelict ships near the shore, they might escape detection.

"We look for opportunities," Reeves said. "I certainly don't want to go ashore and get myself back into the situation we just left with those chewers. So, our only hope is to look for a chance to run past them while they're occupied with the prison situation and head out of the bay into the ocean. We'd need to hop onto another ship in the open water and head north if we could, though I guess we go wherever opportunity allows us."

"I sure as hell ain't going into that town," LaRue said. "Not after what you just told us about it."

The ships banked and turned as they headed for the prison. Reeves stared at them, looking for their angles of attack, hoping for an opportunity. "We're not going back into San Francisco, don't worry."

Reynolds was staring at Reeves. "You seem pretty calm about this. We've had freedom for a couple of hours now. Why aren't you panicked about losing it so soon?"

"First, I haven't stepped off that prison island for seven years, and if two hours away from it is all I get, I'm fine with it. Hasn't been a whole good god damn lot of fun, but I'm fine with it." Reeves looked over at Alcatraz and the airships that were approaching it. "Second, this is what I did in the war. I thought, I planned, I schemed. And when something didn't work. I started over."

"And—" LaRue started.

"And if you want to live, you'll listen and do what I say." Reeves looked at the few men on the boat. "That's the end of it. Our ranks are thinner from the men who had their own ideas. Everyone savvy? Everyone?"

It was quiet except for the lapping of the waves against their hull and the nearby rotting vessels that were thumping against each other. The musty smells of the dead city still lingered in his nostrils. "Good. Let's start unloading this ship of anything we don't need. It's not built for speed by any means, but it'll move faster if we toss whatever we don't need." By demonstration, Reeves picked up the empty crate beneath Reynolds' feet and tossed the container into the bay. In a moment, the others joined and started throwing things over, occasionally looking at him for approval if they were undecided if something should stay or go. It was a small vessel, and it didn't take long before it was down to the bare minimum. The cargo hold below was already empty, its contents unloaded at the prison.

Among the last few things in the boat, Reeves found one of Reynolds's satchels. He looked about the boat, then to Reynolds himself. "Where's your other bag?"

The escapee's eyes darted away from contact with Reeves. He spoke a little too quietly. "It came off when I was stuck at the dock, and it fell into the water when you pulled me out."

"What? Which one was it?"

The men were still throwing things over the side. "What's the problem?" Patrick asked.

On his knees, Reeves grabbed the satchel and flipped it open. He reached in, felt the paper there, and his heart sank. He pulled some out to find it was just that: paper. There were sheets of communications and notes, telegraph messages and lists. Crude maps and half-finished letters. There was no money. He closed the bag after stuffing everything back in. He considered tossing it over the side with the rest of the junk but decided there could be something helpful inside—at the very least it could be used to start fires if the boiler went out.

"What the hell is happening?" LaRue moved in closer. "What's wrong?"

Reynolds sheepishly spoke up. "We had another bag that was full of money."

"What?" LaRue looked at the two men. "How much?'

"More than I've seen," Reynolds said. "Would've got us all home."

"Jesus." Patrick looked ill.

"And how much did you keep?" Reeves left the bag and looked up at Reynolds. "Surely if it was more than you've ever seen, you'd see fit to drop some in your pockets, wouldn't you?"

The airships buzzed in the distance as they circled the prison.

"We don't have the time to discuss this now." Reynolds pointed at the ships. "We need to get out of here."

"True. But you did fill your pockets, didn't you?"

"What are you talking about?" Reynolds asked.

Reeves lunged and grabbed Reynolds by the throat, pinning him to the wheelhouse door. "You took some god damned money for yourself, didn't you?" He could feel the man's pulse throbbing through the neck. Reynolds reached for his gun, but Reeves punched him in the gut and the firearm tumbled to the deck.

LaRue and Patrick both moved to intervene but stopped when Reeves looked back at them. "Stay where you are," he said.

"I don't have any money," Reynolds strained.

Still using just one hand, Reeves dragged the man to the side of the boat. Then he took Reynolds by the ankles and lowered him into the water until his head was under. He waited a moment, then another before he pulled him up. "You need time to think about the money?"

"No. I'll—"

Reeves dipped him back into the water anyway. His arms were straining to keep from dropping the man, but luckily Reynolds was slight. As soon as he was able, Reynolds yelled as loud as he could. "My coat. It's in my coat at the front of the boat. Jesus, just pull me back in."

"LaRue? Go check his coat." Reeves kept the man dangling over the water.

They drifted slowly away from San Francisco, pulled by the waves, bobbing while they waited for LaRue. Reeves thought about whether he really needed Reynolds if he wasn't carrying the money anymore.

"Please. It wasn't my fault. The chewers were on us, or I would've climbed down for the bag," Reynolds said.

"It's here." LaRue waved a stack of paper in the air.

"How much?" Reeves asked.

After a quick count, LaRue shrugged. "I don't know... Maybe twenty dollars?"

"All that money, and you only saved twenty?" There had to have been hundreds of dollars in that bag, maybe a thousand and they were down to almost nothing again. He pulled Reynolds on the boat and shoved him toward the aft. Twenty dollars wasn't going to get anyone home.

"If I'd saved more, you would have figured it out. It would've been obvious." Reynolds rubbed his neck.

A rumble erupted from the prison and it was followed by a bright burst of fire near the larger airship. There were more explosions almost immediately, as the island's defenses came to bear. "Jesus. The prisoners are attacking the military with the island's guns." Behind Reeves, Patrick pointed at the bright bursts in the sky, as though the others might have missed the thunderous reports.

Everyone on the boat seemed to forget their own confrontation as they returned to the larger one playing out on the nearby island. The airships took evasive action, turning and diving. The inexperienced men on the island were seemingly having trouble finding their range, as the large ship became what should have been an easy target. Regardless, the fight presented an opportunity. "Let's go. Get us moving."

From the wheelhouse, LaRue squinted at Reeves like he was mad. "The army is here. Where do you think we're going to go?"

Whether through luck or skill, the men on the island managed to strike the smaller ship with something, either Gatling fire, or cannon shot. The craft immediately trailed smoke and began to lose altitude. It banked hard to the starboard and then spiraled toward the water. It hadn't been very high when it was struck and slowed as it descended. From the *Nathan Prentiss*, it looked like the ship was barely damaged.

"Get the boiler stoked up as high as you can again." Reeves saw the opportunity they needed if the airship crashed, it would give them a span of time to run. They'd have to do it in the open, in full view of the other ship, and hope there would be nothing the government vessel could do. It would be too occupied with the island and a rescue. "We need to get moving as soon as we get power and then give it all the engine has." His guess was good, the little ship dipped down and went into the bay.

The others didn't move right away, so LaRue elected himself spokesman. "But we just stopped."

Reeves shoved the man toward the wheelhouse by his prison-issued wool shirt. "And now we go. It might be our only chance. They may have more airships on the way, or a warship. Or something that could run us down. Right now, they're busy." He shoved LaRue hard enough that the scrawny man fell on his ass in the middle of the others. Reeves looked at the men, still unmoving. They had him outnumbered if they wanted to fight, but he figured they wouldn't. Not now. Not with the chance of freedom looming and the quite real possibility of capture circling nearby like a fat, black carrion bird. He pushed Reynolds toward the wheelhouse of the little steamship. There was a small burst of fire from the larger airship and part of the outer wall exploded in a cloud of dust and rock. "Do you see that? I don't think they plan on capturing anyone in this uprising. If they get the chance, they'll kill us. All of us."

The men moved a bit faster, nearly tripping on each other to get the boat moving. Reeves made a note that these men were set in motion by the simplest of motivations. Higher concepts seemed to be lost on them. As they moved forward, he shouted into the wheelhouse. "Stay as close to the shore as you can without having to slow down." He entered the cabin and threw wood and coal into the furnace.

Reeves looked at the equipment and junk covering what seemed like every surface of the boat. "The rest of you start throwing more things overboard. We need to be fast. We need to move so we can take advantage of that situation. They're not going to pay attention to us while someone else is shooting at them."

It seemed to register with the men and they threw more things overboard.

"Nothing essential, save money, food, water, weapons. Everything else goes," Reeves said as he tore loose some wooden steps and let them fly into the water.

11

"These things are supposed to be for emergencies," Lowell said. He pulled the straps around his chest and tugged them. Two soldiers tried to help, but they were just as unfamiliar with the equipment as anyone else.

"This is pretty urgent." The pack on Lucinda's back was as snug as she could make it. "Other ideas?"

The *Polk* was low enough that it could avoid the cannon fire, but as soon as they rose, that would be an impossibility. The big guns couldn't aim low enough, blocked by the contour of the island, a cluster of buildings, and stymied by the inability to make the guns descend beyond being parallel to the ground. But as soon as the *Polk* rose a couple hundred feet, the guns would have a field day. The only hope would be to destroy the cannons or kill their operators.

The choppy water beckoned to Lucinda. She'd been an excellent swimmer not too long ago. Now, it would be difficult, to say the least, with an iron arm. She'd never tried, but that was the impression she got.

With the ship in a holding pattern, Alek had come down to explain the equipment to the both of them as best he could. "Look, we've only tested this a few times. We had a training planned for everyone to try them out."

"Reassuring." Lowell pulled his straps again.

"Completely." The pair looked at each other and rolled their eyes. Above Lucinda, Alek pulled at the boxes that held the other sections of the new apparatuses.

"If the wind is in your favor, you won't even touch the water, you'll land gracefully on the sand," Alek said. "Just hold on to the packs."

"Can we steer which way we're going?" Lowell asked.

"The wind is perfect right now. You need to go." Alek gripped the straps on Lowell's shoulders and pushed him out the open door, using his own body weight to knock him free of the ship.

Lucinda watched in fear and fascination as the ropes attached to Lowell fed farther out of the boxes until larger pieces unfolded and followed him down. After a few seconds the whole apparatus broke free and he was no longer attached to the *Polk* by anything. The larger sections filled with air quickly and immediately slowed Lowell's descent. He fell from the sky hanging from a wide white cover of light canvas.

"You need to go."

"You push me, and I'll take you along with me, got it?" The jump looked like fun; it took her back to the old days in the circus where she flipped carelessly from swing to swing and walked deftly across the high wire. Still, Lucinda needed a moment. This was a different situation. Higher in the sky than ever, more unsure than ever. She took a breath and stepped out into the open air, more out of the fear of leaving Lowell on his own, than out of the need to approach the island and settle the conflict there.

She fell, only for a handful of seconds, but that was enough time to strike fear into her heart that the thing had failed, and she was falling to the sea in a death spiral. There wasn't time to assess her life, or plea for help before a sharp tug of the lines told her the apparatus had unfolded and stopped her from dropping like a cannonball.

She immediately grabbed the straps as she'd been instructed, though it was hard to get the metal fingers of her hand through the loop. With her good hand, she held on until her knuckles started to get cold.

Below, she saw Lowell already landing just behind the line of prison guards on the beach. It was less than graceful as he fell face first in the sand upon touching down. The men on the beach were surprised but stopped him as the wind filled his kites and started to drag him toward the area where the prisoners were under cover and shooting. Luckily, they seemed to be just as shocked to see people falling from the sky, no matter how elegant they were.

The same breeze that pulled Lowell, took hold of Lucinda's apparatus as well and quickly yanked her over the beach and the soldiers, then over the line of convicts that held the higher ground. It seemed to lift her up over an out-building, across a body-strewn field and began to guide her toward the main prison building. Beyond that, she would end up gliding out over the bay, or worse, into it.

The breeze lifted her nearly ten feet above the roof and showed no sign of diminishing. Lucinda tugged at the straps and buckles that held her, gripped by the sudden fear of going over the edge of the building. One buckle came loose, then another. She saw the edge of the prison as she rapidly approached it, driven by some hellish wind that filled the canopies above her again and again.

The harness finally gave her up and she fell to the flat roof and rolled. She stopped herself with her iron arm just short of falling off and over the side into the rocks. Her backpack stayed on, but her harness and the emergency canopies drifted off over the bay, free now that her weight wasn't burdening them.

The contents of the backpack rattled on the stones of the prison, and Lucinda wasted no time in constructing the parts of her sharpshooting rifle. Each piece seemed to fly together in her hands as she half-watched what she was doing and half-scanned the area around her. There was still gunfire, though the *Polk* was silent, waiting for an opportunity.

Once the gun was ready, she reached into the pack for ammunition, and found the box much lighter than she'd expected. Inside, a handful of rounds rolled in the corners. She counted a total of eight. This was a hell of a time for the OMO to enforce the edict to conserve ammunition.

Positioning herself against the prison's smokestack that jutted out of the roof, Lucinda lay on her stomach and scanned for targets. The soldiers on the beach, she could make out Lowell among them through her scope—seemed to be holding fast on their own—so she looked elsewhere. The occasional boom reminded her of the cannons that had brought down the *Valcour Bay*. She swung the sights to the north and found three men at one gun and four more at another. Teams of two operated Gatling guns at various points.

She watched to see which man was pulling the lever that fired the larger cannon. Once he did, and the great gun lunged backward, she took aim and gently squeezed the trigger. The gunner's head jerked, and he fell, slumped over the back of the cannon. His two companions looked around, searching for the shooter before falling to the ground for cover. The men at the other cannon didn't even notice.

She repeated the process, but this time she quickly reloaded and also shot one of the gun's loaders through the neck.

The big guns fell silent.

Behind her, a door swung open and three prisoners ran up a set of stairs, shouting. *Someone noticed that the guns were under attack.*

Lucinda rolled on the ground, dodging the first shots the men fired. She came up with her own rifle and cracked the first one hard on the jaw with the butt of the gun—hard enough that the stock splintered. The next man threw a punch but was hampered by the first prisoner in front of him. With a well-struck kick, Lucinda managed to knock one into the other and the two went sprawling down the stairs. The last man fired a wild shot from his pistol and Lucinda grabbed his wrist to prevent him from pointing the weapon at her for another chance.

"Bitch, let loose of it," the escapee said, as he struggled to aim the gun at her.

She thought about the insult and let it pass, no reason to get angry, make this personal and lose her focus.

The man grunted as he struggled with her until finally, he hauled off with his free hand and punched Lucinda in the jaw. She staggered, the punch didn't have much behind it, but she felt it just the same. Her hand, the iron one, squeezed his wrist just a little more until she heard the cracking of his bones. The soldier screamed, and Lucinda took his pistol and turned back to the stairs just in time to see one of the others climbing up for another turn. She shot him. The other lay at the bottom of the stairs unmoving.

"God. Damn. You broke my arm." The man at her feet bleated.

Lucinda looked at the pitiful thing on the ground holding his wrist and took a breath. She considered killing him. He'd likely hinder her progress if she didn't.

A sudden explosion nearby pulled her focus away, the big guns had begun firing again. This time, it wasn't at the *Polk* or the men on the beach, this time they were firing out into the bay. A small craft was building steam and headed toward the ocean. The men at the guns seemed nearly in a frenzy to stop them.

Pistol in her good hand, Lucinda descended the stairs carefully, making sure no more men were coming to stop her. She ran down the hallway, past open cell doors and a guard station. She cautiously walked into one of the open cells and looked out the window at the fighting going on in the courtyard below. There were only a handful of prisoners still fighting inside. Most of the rest were dead, though a few seemed to be huddling behind cover without participating. Outside, one of the click-together boats was on shore and a large contingent of OMO soldiers were behind cover and helping as best they could.

She ran, nearly knocking Lowell over as he went down the hall. "How the hell did you get up here from the beach?"

"I came around the beach to the rock wall side," Lowell said. "Let's take care of those big guns and we can round the rest up." As they moved to the stairs, they caught a glimpse of the *Polk*, no longer stationary, but rising, unfettered by the guns that were shooting elsewhere.

"Come on." Lucinda led Lowell back to the stairs and up. "Watch out for the con at the top."

"She broke my arm." It was a whimper now, the prisoner laying on the roof rolling around and holding his wrist.

"I'm positive you deserved it, sir."

Lucinda started waving to the *Polk* and jumping around.

"You think they see you?"

"I hope."

"What's the point of this?" Lowell asked, and started waving as well.

"If they see us on this side, they won't have to worry if they're going to hit us, if they want to bomb the ever-loving piss out of those guns."

"Seems like a pretty slim chance of that hap—" Before Lowell could finish, a familiar whistle and whine filled the air. It was the sound of cannonballs sailing earthward from the *Polk*'s forward guns. Both Lucinda and Lowell fell to the rooftop and covered their heads, huddled together as the thuds of the bombardment struck. They were a little closer than Lucinda had expected—one smashed a guard tower not one hundred yards from the building they were in.

She pulled Lowell closer, trying to keep him safe. She was feeling guilty that he'd needlessly risked his life to come farther into the prison than the rest. Until he showed up, she was doing fine on her own. There was a point, she realized, not long ago when she and Cyrus would've been in a situation like this. The difference was that Cyrus would've been protecting her, whether out of some sense of chivalry, affection, or duty. And she let him, to a point. There was little in life that she'd found hard to run from. To have a protector was a godsend, also to a point.

Once the shelling had stopped, she opened her eyes to find Lowell staring back at her. His eyes were narrowed, but it was impossible for her to interpret his emotional state. Was he angry she took the lead? Hurt that he hadn't protected her?

He looked around and up at the *Polk*. "They'll need help with any prisoners that are still willing to fight hand to hand down there." He pointed over to where the cannons had been. There was little left except the support mounts and some twisted iron. "Of course, after that pounding, you'd hope they would think better of it." He stood and brushed himself off while Lucinda looked at the rubble of the weapons emplacements.

"One would hope."

They went down to the field where the battle had come to a head and they found the majority of the convicts were dead. There were small groups gathered in surrender, the few who insisted on shooting were dispatched quickly. The OMO had suffered a few injuries, but no deaths. The guards were not nearly so lucky. Of the garrison that had been assigned to the island, only six were alive, and two of those were in sorry shape.

Once the island was in hand, the *Polk* moved into position to raise the *Valcour Bay*. That ship's crew had been rescued handily by the snap together boats and the airship's own flotation instruments. Both Woodward and Moore were in satisfactory condition, though Woodward had a bloody eye that he didn't seem to want to explain.

12

When the last bit of extra weight plopped into the water, the men turned to Reeves again, looking for direction. He didn't meet their gaze, he was too busy watching the conflict unfolding over at the island. The prisoners there had opened up with the base's cannons and were fruitlessly firing upon the last airborne black government ship. It was obvious, even from Reeves' vantage point that it had moved far out of the cannons' range. Even more unbelievable was that the men on the island weren't using the weapons meant for aircraft yet; the men were firing the cannons which were only useful against water-borne craft.

"They're gonna see our steam," Patrick said.

"Can't be helped. Let 'em see. Just get us moving." He stared at the airship as it came in low and released a rescue craft and then ascended again. Alcatraz's guns weren't meant to shoot in that direction. They were meant to defend the bay from ocean-borne attacks, not threats from inland, not anymore. Reeves remembered well the day they started dismantling the larger defenses on the island. Soldiers came in and, over the course of a few weeks, tore the guns into pieces and loaded them onto cargo ships and they disappeared never to return. The island guards weren't happy, but in the years since the guns vanished, no one attacked the prison from land or sea.

The downed airship and its larger companion were safe for the time being, until the prisoners figured a way around that. Reeves believed they wouldn't have that much time. He was glad he hadn't stayed to make a stand. The sound of gunfire drifted out to their boat from time to time, but it was mostly silent—the sound swallowed up by the sound of the water and the engine. When big explosions came, they were easily heard. The airship unloaded a barrage from their massive cannon, and soon, the lower guardhouse, the docks, and the walls around the beach were either gone or in flames. Reeves felt his chest tighten as he worried that the government might actually mop up the defenses too quickly and send some boat over to pursue his pitiful craft.

The waves lapped at the bow rhythmically as they plowed through the bay at a pace that impressed everyone aboard. The supply ship had a little more power than anyone had originally believed. He looked ahead, to the mouth of the bay, with hope.

The others stayed away from Reeves for a good five minutes, until Reynolds finally approached. "You know as well as I do that there's another fort up ahead, at the Point. What if they're still active?"

"Actually, there are two emplacements; one to the north and one to the south."

After a brief moment, Reynolds attempted to follow up. "That's worse, isn't it?"

"After what we saw in the city? You think they're still manning those guns? Hell, they're dead as King George." Reeves was guessing when he said it, but that seemed like the most logical conclusion after what they'd discovered on the mainland. He didn't want to add that if the guns were manned at either of those forts, they would've likely fired on the boat by now, a warning shot at least, for they were certainly within the range of any major gun at Fort Point.

It was then, as he considered their distance from the mouth of the bay, that he also examined their position relative to Alcatraz. They'd certainly be an attainable target, if the gunners at the prison decided to try.

Reynolds must have seen the sudden panic on Reeves' face. "What? What's wrong?"

"Have them turn us toward the center of the bay, now."

"You said to stay close to shore and—" Reynolds was cut off mid-thought as one of the main cannons on the island rumbled to life. They turned to see where the hissing sound was coming from before a plume of water shot up in the air just a hundred yards to their boat's stern.

"Our former fellow inmates seem to be a little vindictive about us leaving them behind," Reeves said. "Let's start varying our course before they get a bead on us."

Reynolds ran to the wheelhouse as another cannon fired. The ammunition from this one landed farther away. Immediately, Patrick moved their boat in the opposite direction with enough suddenness that Reeves had to brace himself. Soon, another canon and another were belching fire until the four guns were firing only a minute or so apart. Some of the prisoners must have had experience with guns to be able to achieve that speed of reloading. Or else they really hated Reeves and his companions for leaving them. Possibly some of the first and a lot of the second.

The splashes, cannon shot, and occasional explosions of shrapnel got closer, despite the craft's new zig-zag course toward the ocean. It was a straight run. They'd be out of range of the Alcatraz guns in seconds, and out of the bay minutes after that. "Keep it steady. We'll make it." just as the cannons went silent, the huge, dark airship rose over the prison.

While all the guns were focused on the *Nathan Prentiss*, the large airship had moved into a firing position on the other side of the island. Reeves and his crew were the main distraction that allowed the airship to gain the upper hand.

Reeves wasn't sure if that was irony or just bad luck.

The waves lapped at the boat as they made their way north. They were all jittery at first, looking over their shoulders, watching the sky in case the airship appeared on the horizon. But, as the sun sank below the horizon and the sky turned yellow-orange, it became more likely they were alone.

Reeves did a check of their situation. He found they were all low on ammunition. The rifles had six shots between them, the revolvers had two each. The ship's small cabin had a box of food that wouldn't last more than a day or so if they rationed it, but they were all famished as it was. They had the one satchel that Reynolds had brought from the safe house, having lost the other bag at the docks. They would have to make land quickly and find food and shelter as soon as they could.

"Where are we going?" It was growing late, and Patrick was nervous navigating in the darkness. "This boat was supposed to resupply itself at the prison, but it doesn't look like they got a chance to. We're low on wood, water, everything."

"I don't want to break out of prison just to get swept out to sea and die there," LaRue said.

Reynolds snorted at the group. "Can't go back to the prison, now can we? I think you're stuck here."

"I didn't mean I wanted to go back—" LaRue said.

Reeves interrupted, lost in his own assessment of the situation. "None of us want to go back. And none of us are."

"And I'm not going back into San Francisco, that's for true," Reynolds said. "Not fighting any more of them chewers, that's for damn true."

"We'll do what we have to do to make it." Reeves had been thinking about it since he'd arrived on Alcatraz. Though all those years had passed, he felt a strong urgency to his country and to fulfill his promises. He'd stewed about it in his cell. He wanted to finish that mission badly. For all he knew, the rest of his old group had carried out their objectives and everything else had gone to plan. He had his suspicions though, that that was not the case.

He also needed to get back to his family. He wondered what they'd been told about him since he was arrested. Did they think he'd been killed in the raid on the ship? Andrew was all of ten, and Bernard would be fifteen by now—old enough for conscription and a spot on a front line somewhere. He looked around at the men in the boat and knew he wouldn't hesitate to use any means necessary to get back to the family he loved so dearly.

"Maybe we find a place to stop for the night?" Patrick asked. "None of us want to keep moving through unfamiliar territory in the dark like this."

It was smart. It would give them time to take full stock of what they had and gather whatever they could find. "Slow and bring us closer to shore. Look for other boats we can take or cannibalize for wood." It was ironic that they'd tossed everything overboard in the bay, so they could move faster and escape capture, but now they could use all the equipment they'd thrown away in order to keep going and not get captured.

They drifted among the dead ships, the junk, the castoff garbage and ghostly shapes near the shores of the westernmost areas of San Francisco. They caught occasional glimpses of chewers there, stumbling along the coastal ruins. As the night came down, they saw no lights in the city, and hadn't expected any, really. The city was dead.

They tied the boat to the exposed hull of a ship, and cut usable, dry wood from it. They stacked it neatly by the boiler; enough to get them all the way up the coast if they needed. The hold was empty, having unpacked the supplies back at the prison. They looked for ways to solve their drinking water problem, but with only salt water nearby, they were out of luck if they didn't want to head back into the town and scavenge for some. They figured they had enough water to get them up the coast before worrying about it.

They stayed there, moored to the guts of a destroyed ship and slept for a while.

13

The clean-up on Alcatraz Island continued well into the night. There were cells still intact and usable in the block, though the cons had to be housed two to a room. The new recruits and some of the OMO officers used tents out in the field to sleep in, some even managed to use the guardhouse bunks, though it was very drafty in that building what with holes the size of wagon wheels in the walls. Alek got the telegraph reconnected—another victim of the shelling—and sent messages back to the tower and out to Outpost Two-Thirteen.

Corrigan used the *Polk* to lift the *Valcour Bay* from the water and set it at the loading docks for repair. Word was the damage wasn't nearly as terrible as they'd feared—a little shrapnel took out one of the aft rudders and the secondary propeller took a beating. Nothing that would permanently take it out of commission, but it would require the *Valcour Bay* to remain on the island for repairs, because it sure as hell wasn't limping home on its own.

Lucinda and Lowell helped supervise the inspection of the ship, moving from room to room, making sure the interior was going to be salvageable. "Did you see the supply ship that made for the ocean during the fight?" Lucinda watched as Lowell cranked a door open and closed, then marked it with a white chalk 'X' to indicate it worked and had been inspected.

"No. When was this?"

"Not long after I landed on the island, I suppose. When the guns turned away from the *Polk*," Lucinda said.

"I wondered about that. Couldn't tell what they were firing at. That's when I took my chance and ran."

Another door opened and closed. No damage. White X. "It took off from somewhere around San Francisco and made for the ocean fast as it could. I assumed it was one of ours from the way they all fired at it."

"Huh." White X.

"I suppose some of them could have absconded with a supply boat and gotten themselves gone. Nobody's done it before, but it could happen. Why would they still be around though? Why not leg it for somewhere else?"

"Let's inquire to some of the guards and convicts when we're done." He found one portal that had buckled, likely when the *Valcour Bay* hit the water. He marked it with a star.

In the nearby control room voices caught Lucinda's attention. At least one of them sounded angry. She and Lowell both headed for the area at the same time.

"Jesus, Woodward. What's this you've done to the *Valcour*? Alek told you to stay low and follow his lead." It was the navigator of the *Polk*, helping to inspect the instruments. Just because the damage wasn't bad didn't mean Corrigan wouldn't give Woodward shit for it. "Laddie, this is bad. Very bad."

"Everyone already thinks you're a sad excuse for an airman after the way you bungled things at Fort Humbolt a month ago, why you want to go proving them right?" Dex spat a dark glob of tobacco somewhere near the man's feet.

"I did what I thought was right for the situation," Woodward said.

"That's funny; I was in an airship three times the size as yours, and much less maneuverable. I thought the situation called for not crashing into the ocean, and I managed to do it."

Lowell cleared his throat. "None of this is necessary."

"Tell *him*." Woodward walked on and exited at the other side of the room.

Not that Woodward didn't deserve a tongue lashing for his carelessness, but they had work to do. "Come on."

"You don't think he's an idiot?"

"After today, I'm sure he won't be flying too many war ships," Lowell said. "We all saw what happened. We'll all report it. He'll be flying the training ship soon enough."

"They're all lucky to be alive." Corrigan wiped his hands on a cloth from the nearby console and threw it back as he walked away.

"Is this going to be *our* problem?" Lucinda looked as the men retreated.

"I don't know. Are *we* in charge here?" Lowell asked.

It was funny but frightening to Lucinda. In the OMO for less than a year and people looked to her as a leader. "Let's go talk to people about the boat that fled and hopefully, finish this whole mess."

Lowell nodded and led the way out of the grounded ship. The beach outside was lit by makeshift torches, as just about any other light source was a part of the rubble strewn everywhere. Above them, the *Polk* slowly orbited the island, a dark oval in the early evening sky.

"How angry is Alek about this?" Lowell stepped around what remained of a wooden walkway.

"Pissed." Lucinda had spoken with the OMO's engineer as the cleanup had commenced. She boarded the *Polk* to gather some supplies—shovels and picks, mostly—to make the field and beach safer. She'd walked in on Alek throwing things and breaking any object handy. She thought to try to calm him, but she was expected back with the equipment straight away. She also figured it was best to let his anger abate some before stepping in.

The highest-ranking prison guard remaining was a black sergeant named Lorne. They found him standing near the makeshift morgue that had been created in the gardens. The dead prisoners and guards stretched all the way down the path of the sizable area where the men usually tended a vegetable garden to make sure they didn't have to rely on the shipments from up north quite so much.

"Boat?" Lorne asked. "We had two supply ships here at the time, prisoners took both of them. One got sunk by our men—" He looked out into the bay and pointed at a small dark shadow jutting out of the water. "Right there."

"The other one?" Lucinda asked.

"It got strafed pretty fierce by our guns, but it kept going, off toward Frisco."

That was the general idea Lucinda had in her head about the ship she'd seen. "Know who was on it?"

"No clue." Lorne pointed to the dead men around them. "Still have to figure out who all we have here. Our records are piss-poor and we're shorthanded."

"None of them?"

"I know one guy what got on one of those boats, don't know which one though, so he could be dead."

"One guy?" Lucinda asked. "Why this one guy?"

"It is extremely difficult to forget a man with the number nine branded into his chest," Lorne said. "Name was Reeves. I saw him running for the docks when the melee began."

"A number nine?" Lowell asked. "Any idea why?"

"Yeah. He was a spy or something. Least that's what the captain of the guard told me once. Any other questions? I want to get these covered up before it gets any darker, and more of those show up." The man pointed over to a nearby wall where four crows had landed. They stared over toward the bodies, twisting their heads back and forth. Usually their incessant chatter heralded their arrival, but the ocean and the clang of shovels and the hum of airships had covered their noise.

"They seem a might aggressive as of late. Showing up wherever there's something dead now, not just chewers. They follow us," Lowell said. "Sometimes they follow the *Polk*, have you noticed?"

"They're just birds." Lucinda wasn't entirely comfortable with the crows either. They weren't aggressive with people, but they weren't afraid of them either. She'd make a point to talk to the doctor and his crew when they had the chance, just in case. "Leave them alone, and they'll leave you alone."

"I thought that only worked with bees?" Lowell moved away uneasily. "About the escapees—I have to say I think I recognize the description of this Reeves fellow." Lowell strode from the gardens and headed to the telegraph that Alek had recently repaired.

"You know him?"

"Not exactly. I remember Cashe talking about a group of spies that the Southern Army trained that were meant to be elites, men who could do it all. I remember because he talked about what they did to these men when they caught them."

"Branded them?" Lucinda asked.

"That's what I recall."

14

Reeves woke early the next morning, as was his want, and roused everyone else, who were not so used to the hour. They did their early morning business over the side of the boat and then stoked the boiler to get the craft underway.

For an hour or more after they started, the shoreline remained the same: more dead boats, hulls half-sunk, no lights along the land, certainly no light houses. Once they put some distance from their starting point, they noticed a man trudging through the reeds toward their craft, and they tensed, guns in hand. Reeves watched the odd man in a half-ruined bowler shamble down and into the water, like it didn't bother him none, and Reeves realized it wasn't a man at all. "Just another chewer. Put your guns away. Who knows who'd hear the shot?"

No one put their guns away, but they relaxed their stances and watched as the thing advanced with its eyes fixed on them until he suddenly went under water. Pale hands broke the surface and flailed before disappearing. The men stared long after, just waiting for it to reappear and chase them, but it never did.

No other signs of life other than the occasional silhouette of a gull or a pelican perched on a derelict.

"How far up are we going?" LaRue asked. He stood at the door to the wheelhouse, leaning on the frame, still glancing back toward the shore.

It wasn't clear to Reeves himself how long they'd travel north, but he'd know when he saw it. "San Francisco is gone. I figured an important port like that had to be replaced. There has to be a big city where we can find transportation east or get lost in for a spell."

"How do you know that big city wasn't to the south of San Fran?"

"I don't. I'm guessing here. The prison guards didn't give me a whole lot of information about the outside world. Did they give you some?" Reeves was well aware that the odds were fairly equal, and he may well have chosen wrong. As he spoke, he saw a small plume of smoke on the horizon. LaRue was talking again, but Reeves ignored him, transfixed by the small dark cloud on the water. When it started getting bigger, he broke his silence. "I think there's a boat ahead."

Larue stopped talking and squinted in the direction Reeves indicated. "I don't see nothing."

"Go ask the others what they see."

Soon the trio of soldiers were standing at the front of the boat, staring at the smoke. Reeves watched them and took stock of them. If the airships had appeared at the prison so fast, others may be looking for the escapees. They'd all changed out of their prison issue clothes or covered them up with jackets they found on the steamer. Their main concern would be that they were still on a military boat, and they fit the description of desperate fugitives perfectly. They looked desperate, filthy and wildly out of place, except for Reeves himself, who'd taken the time to put on nicer clothing at the safe house in San Francisco. The only thing guiding him was the note scrawled on the wall of the passage—Santa Rosa.

Patrick was the first to come back to the wheelhouse. "What do we do? Should we speed up? Get back closer to shore, maybe?"

"It's the first vessel we've seen. No need to show ourselves by running. Hell, it might be fishermen, for all we know," Reeves said. "Probably best that two of you hide here out of sight if we get close to them. If it is a military craft, they'd be more inclined to search for four people than two." It was a minor ruse, Reeves figured. If the law of the army was looking for prisoners, they wouldn't care how many. They'd likely search any boat they came across.

As LaRue and Reynolds ducked down out of sight at his feet, Reeves took a good look at them. The two of them, huddled there in the relative dark of the cabin floor, looked every inch a fugitive: their hair was wild and unkempt; their beards resembled rat nests. Patrick at least kept his hair close-cut and appeared to have shaved recently. Reeves himself made a point to keep up his hygiene regimen as best he could—shaving and grooming as often as the guards would let him on the Rock.

The other boat, with a lantern gleaming in the low morning light, approached them directly. It was quiet, with only a few splashes to tell of its coming. Reeves got a good look and found it was a small fishing boat with two men leaning back with their feet up, and another gentleman working the rudder as the sea carried them along.

Reeves looked down at the two hidden men. "Stay there."

They'd both grabbed their weapons and held them close, prepared to shoot.

Reeves stepped out onto the thin deck that surrounded the boat and leaned against the doorway as casually as he could. As the supply ship neared the fishermen, Reeves smiled and nodded at the older gentleman guiding the other ship. The man nodded back and drifted on by.

"What's going on?" Reynolds asked.

"Nothing." Reeves stared ahead to the outline of a city in the distance, not daring to look back at the other boat for fear that it would give something away. "Shut up."

"What should I do?" Patrick tapped the wheel repeatedly.

Counting in his head, Reeves gave it ten more seconds before slowly, off-handedly, turning to look at the other boat out of the corner of his eye. Carried by the ocean, it had moved a good distance away in that short period of time. "Nothing," Reeves said just loud enough to be heard. "Just keep going. We'll start stoking up the boiler, so we can get past this city in a hurry, though."

The morning mist mixed itself with smoke off the outpost ahead. Reynolds pointed out a thick fence on the shore that emerged from the water and snaked its way along the coast before it headed inland and disappeared in the distance. It was wide, braced by chunky timbers on both sides.

"Think that's for them chewers?" LaRue bit on something as he talked, a splinter of wood from the looks of it. "Hell, it's sturdy enough, ain't it?"

"That's my guess," Reeves said.

Even at the early hour, the city was alive with activity. In the harbor, boats of all sizes were coming up to steam or already underway, pulling from their slips. More fishing vessels, supply ships, skiffs and steam freighters moved with purpose in the waters before the escapees.

"Look at this mess. Why don't we just go ashore here? All these boats, all this…" Patrick waved his hands at the dance of the ships before him. "…shit. How the hell is anyone going to notice us?"

It only took Reeves a moment to find something in the city that scared him about going ashore. He pointed to a tall structure up the shoreline. "See that tower? Near as I can tell, it's a launch for airships. I can't be sure, but it could certainly be a place to land those ships that showed up at the prison. If it is theirs, that could mean a large group of soldiers is housed in the city."

Patrick wasn't convinced. "I might want to take my chances. What are the odds they'll find me in a city that size?"

"Look friend." Reynolds was soft-spoken, avoiding confrontation. "I want to agree. We could slip in with no problem."

"True enough. And then what? Just jump on an airship or a train? They'll certainly watch those." Reeves kept watching ahead as their boat glided through the mess of craft steering away from the city. "And look around. Do you see any flags? I don't. Who claimed this land? Is it Southern soil? The war may be over, but I don't know whose land this is. That would be important to us getting away, don't you think?"

"If you really believe that airship that came to our little Yankee prison was also a Yankee vessel, it would stand to reason this would be a Union-controlled city, I suppose." LaRue was the only one who spoke in favor of Reeve's reasoning. "Maybe we should just go a mite more, just so we can find a way to make sure we aren't walking into the enemy's den."

Reeves watched the others, eager to get home, afraid of prison. They all mumbled consent with the exception of Reynolds. He screwed his face up in contempt and folded his arms.

"Something to say?" Reeves asked.

With a grunt, Reynolds shook his head. "Nope. Not a word." He refused to meet Reeves' gaze.

15

Lucinda slept while they waited for a reply to their telegraph. Not on purpose, really, she'd just sat down in some prison rubble, leaned against the wall and it all went black.

She woke to Lowell standing over her whispering and holding a metal cup. "Sorry," he said. "We got a reply. We need to talk to Alek and Corrigan. We need to leave."

"What—" Her eyes were blurry, and she rubbed them with her good hand. "What the hell are you talking about?" She stood, brushed herself off, for what good it did, and took the cup of coffee from him.

"Turns out I was right. Cashe said it sounds like one of an elite group of spies that used to do a bit of everything—they carried out assassinations, stirred up malcontents, lied, stole, and whatever else they could do to aid in the Confederate cause," Lowell said. "Called them Red Gears."

"Why?"

"How in God's name do I know?" Lowell took his coffee back. "We can ask him when you catch him. Cashe says he's top priority."

"And why do we need to tell Alek?"

"There's no other ship but the *Polk* available and we sure as shit aren't letting Woodward fly us about up there."

Lucinda nodded. They really weren't sure that this spy was even alive. He could be dead on the first boat that exploded, but they wanted to be safe. Seemed like a waste to go chasing smoke when the prison could really use all the help it could get.

In the distance, a group of men shouted, "*Rowdy Riflemen*" and cheered.

"I told you it would stick like syrup." Lucinda laughed. "Are we taking them with us?"

"Why not? They don't have much experience as a fighting unit. But they might be useful."

"Rowdy Riflemen" echoed again like they were charging up some hill back in the war.

16

Reynolds was knee deep in the water, wading to the shore. He was the first out of the boat, and probably not a moment too soon. He jabbered incessantly when he was on watch, keeping everyone else on edge. In quick succession, the other men followed Reynolds into the water and off toward the shore; Patrick and LaRue had both been stoic soldiers throughout the whole ordeal. Reeves hoped they still had it in them to continue home without murdering Reynolds in his sleep.

Reeves pulled his knapsack tight about his shoulders and jumped into the surf. He'd grown used to the salt air after all the time on the island, but the scent of the reeds growing along the shore nearly brought tears to his eyes. He inhaled deeply to keep their aroma fresh in his nostrils. Reynolds was already jumping about on the shore, kneeling to kiss the sand and howling like a madman. The others climbed onto land and collapsed. It felt like a big step toward freedom.

"I didn't think we'd ever get back here again," LaRue said.

Patrick raised his head from the cold sand. "You reckon we'll make it home?"

"To Savannah?" Reeves asked. "I can't say I know the answer to that one." He looked off into the distance at the bright lights of the city and then searched the cloudy sky. He saw a couple of dimmer lights in the other direction. "First things first, we need to find out where we are exactly and where we can stay while we figure out what's next. We need an empty barn or a cave or something. I'm not picky anymore."

"We can jump aboard a freighter in that city and catch a ride back home, I'll wager. There's trains, airships, boats, whatever." LaRue said.

"Once we settle, I'll scout the city and get a feel for the situation." Reeves dropped his pack to the ground and stared off toward the nearest glowing light on the horizon.

Reynolds was lying face down in the sea grass nearby, but suddenly pushed himself up. "Ain't no situation. We're doing what LaRue said. We're getting on a boat or some shit and going home." The others said nothing but stared at Reeves expectantly.

"We're still soldiers in the army of the Confederacy. And with that—"

Reynolds stood and pointed at Reeves, sand flying from his hand. "No. No. If I'm a soldier, then Robert E. Lee or whoever the hell the president is now, owes me a god damn wheelbarrow full of scrip. I ain't been paid since the day I set foot on the battlefield." He turned to LaRue. "YOU been getting your pay? How 'bout you, Irish? You squirreling your money away in some secret hidey-hole on that rock that none of us knew about?"

"All you're concerned about is getting your coin?" Reeves said. "Our brothers lost their lives fighting for a better world and you want to stop because you're poor?"

"Jesus, Harvey. I think we can be excused for being a bit weary. Look at us. We're lucky to be alive. What do you expect us to do? Our families have to think we're dead," LaRue's voice caught as he spoke. "My God, I just want to get home and see them."

"I do, too. We just need to know what we're walking into and how that's going to effect our safe passage home. I'm not talking about going to war with the North or nothing, but we are fugitives. There's plenty of people around that want us back on that Rock. We need to be ready."

The four men made their way through the tall grass and weeds together, searching for a main trail or road in the near-darkness, and it occurred to Reeves that they looked for all the world like men who had crawled freshly from hell, little different in appearance than the chewers. None of the other men had shaved in weeks, their clothes were torn and filthy, and their skin was dark and spotted from the crusted scabs years of sun exposure had created. Hell, they even walked in the slow, limping manner that the creatures moved in. They'd been afraid of running across those horrid beasts in the darkness, but Reeves wondered if they might be shot themselves, mistaken for the hellish monsters, if they weren't careful.

Still, they shambled on toward what few lights they saw. As they approached, they found a well-worn dirt road and crossed it, trying to stay out of sight should someone approach. The illumination was from a lantern on the porch of a small house with a barn, shed, and an outbuilding.

"I'll approach the door and see what we've found. Maybe the people in here can shed some details on what's happened in our absence," Reeves said. They'd been told in prison that the war was over, but they were short on details. They said nobody had won but spoke nothing of who owned what or where the borders fell. "Maybe they could let us use their barn to rest."

"Just ask them when the next boat, airship, wagon, horse, or strong woman leaves for home. That's all I want to know," Reynolds said.

Reeves moved to secret himself behind a shed. He motioned the others to do the same.

Patrick spoke up. "Why are we being all secretive? Just walk up and knock on the man's door."

"Tell 'em we're lost. If he's a God-fearing man, he'll be obliged to help us out," LaRue said. "Hell, even if he ain't, most likely he'll tell us whatever just to get us off his doorstep."

Reeves could feel his control slipping away. The group was finally back in an arena that he was familiar with; gathering information, stealth, subterfuge, and yet no one was listening. When he and his military unit left port all those years back, it was all "Yes, sir" and "No, sir," but now these men offered only sass talk and foot-dragging. "We just made it back into the outside world. Do you want to go straight to a stockade?"

"Ain't nobody ever been put in jail for asking for directions," Reynolds said.

"Christ. Just let me do this in my own fashion. We can figure out the bigger plan later."

There was a sound then. Metallic and cold from the direction of the home, no doubt the hammer of a shotgun being pulled back. "Who the hell's out there? You come out now or I start shooting. Ain't no joke, ain't no foolin' around. You come out."

The other men looked at Reeves as though this were his chance. Their eyes narrowed, momentarily daring him to talk his way into the man's graces. *So be it*, Reeves thought, and he stepped out of the cover of the shed and into the light from the house, words flooding his mind, lies to tell. On the porch stood a thin man in what appeared to be his night clothes. He was, as imagined, holding a double-barreled shotgun. "I am sorry, sir. I hope I didn't startle you. See, I thought there was a larger thoroughfare that ran—"

"Where's the others? I heard more voices than just yours."

"Well—"

"Get 'em all out here where I can see 'em. Better be all my belongings out there in the toolshed, too." The man waved his gun.

LaRue and Patrick stepped into the glow from the house and held their hands out in a placating manner.

"We just didn't want to give you a fright, that's all," Patrick said. He waved his hands higher and LaRue followed his lead. "Be easy with that gun."

"You don't tell me what to do with this gun. More god damn scavengers from the city?" the man asked. "Getting mighty bold to come out to a man's home like this. Be easy? I'll pull this trigger easy."

Reeves held his hands in front of him to calm the farmer down. "Look, we've just lost our way a bit. We're not here to steal anything or make any trouble." He backed up. "We just need to know how to get to Santa Rosa."

"I asked you where your friend was and I ain't gonna ask again."

Patrick pointed to the others. "This here is all of us."

"He's telling the truth," Reeves said. His reply was cut short by a shot from inside the house. As the farmer fell on his porch, Reynolds emerged through the doorway, pistol in front of him. He shot the fallen man again, and again. Three times he shot the old man.

"Jesus, stop it," Reeves said. "We don't know who's around here or what trouble gunshots will bring."

Reynolds looked at his companions, and then fired one last round into the farmer's body before heading back inside the house.

17

Reeves and LaRue moved the farmer's body, while Patrick climbed onto the roof of the house to see if the shots had drawn anyone's notice. Reynolds had wandered into the house and hadn't emerged. The others were glad for it.

LaRue stared at Reeves as they carried the farmer's body around the house. "Ain't right. This fella didn't have nothing coming to him." He spit a mouthful of tobacco into the bushes as he walked. He'd discovered the tobacco in the farmer's shirt pocket before they picked him up. "Reynolds is not right in the head. Not by a damn sight."

The thought crossed Reeves' mind from the fight in the safe house and hadn't left him. Reynolds appeared vacant at times, and out of control of his faculties at others. "Once we see the situation in town, find out where we stand, we'll decide what we need to do with him."

"Do with him?"

"We'll need to decide whether to part ways with him or put him down. If we can figure a way home, and he jeopardizes that?" Reeves shrugged. "I don't want anyone standing in the way of my freedom, do you?"

LaRue got quiet. Together they moved the man out to the back of the house into the shade of a large Pepperwood tree and covered him in a horse blanket to keep him somewhat hidden until they could dig a proper grave for him.

Once they'd done their assigned tasks, they met up in the common area of the house. Not that anyone would have gotten lost in the small living space. The main room had a number of chairs, a fireplace that looked like it was both for warmth and function, a large dining table and chairs, pots hanging from the ceiling, a basin for washing. There were two rooms with beds, one disused, tidy and dusty, the other a mess from lack of cleaning. The messy one smelled of sweat and dried meat. There was the stench of something that permeated the whole house, a stew that had gone off, or rotting vegetables, Reeves couldn't decide.

Patrick reported on his reconnaissance. "There's no other farms or houses around, but I could see some smoke way off in the distance to the north and the east. Not real close." He shrugged. "I supposed the echo could have reached them, but—"

"That's something, at least," Reeves said.

"Look like he lived here alone, you think?" Patrick asked.

Reeves waved around to the table and kitchen. "I see about one of everything in the sink and on the table. And it looks like the second bedroom hasn't been used, so I suppose it's likely."

Snoring in the other room brought them to find Reynolds lying across a couch with a quilt pulled up to his chin. Reeves stepped to the kitchen and tried to ignore him. He poured a glass of warm water from a nearby pitcher and looked at the men. "We'll sleep in shifts." He drank the full glass in one go. "We need to rest and keep watch. I'll take the first."

"I ain't arguing." Patrick walked toward the back of the house in slow steps as his weariness set in and the excitement of the day wore off. "I'm gonna visit the shitter and then I'm going to take that empty bed." He pointed to the disused room.

LaRue looked almost angry. "I don't want to sleep in a dead man's room. Ain't proper."

"We're staying in his house. What's proper about that?" Reeves said. "Afraid his ghost'll come haunt you in the night for getting into his bed?" Reeves poured another glass. "Think he'll come for me because I'm drinking his water?"

LaRue looked around at Reynolds and the rest of the house, and then spoke quietly. "I don't know. I shot some people during the war, but I ain't slept in their beds after."

Patrick's belch announced he'd returned from the outhouse. "'Night gentlemen." He walked to the dusty room and shut the door without further discussion.

Taking another drink, Reeves stared out the window in the kitchen. "I don't think it's ghosts you need to worry about. We've got a mess of other people looking for us right now." He patted the man on the shoulder. "I'll wake you for the next watch in a few hours. You can have Patrick take the one after."

As soon as LaRue got himself settled, Reeves started a fire in the fireplace, and walked out back. In the encroaching darkness, he looked at the blanket covering the dead farmer under the tree. He thought about saying a few words, but he didn't know anything about the Bible, and had no idea what to say for a murdered stranger, so he grabbed a shovel from the man's shed and dug a hole until he got too tired to continue. He rolled the man in and covered him in earth.

Once he was finished burying the farmer, Reeves pawed through the house until he found a whetstone, some gun oil, some rags and a knife. He sat himself by the fire with a glass of water and took out the pocket watches. He pulled his favorite and took it apart with the tip of the knife. He sighed at the rust that had formed on the gears inside. He spit on the whetstone and dragged each tiny piece across it; first the cogs and the gears, then the thin line of wire that activated the firing mechanism, and the release lever. Finally, he cleaned the little blade inside, sharpened its edges and buffed out the imperfections. After he reassembled the watch, he cleaned the small pepper grinder guns and made sure they were all loaded.

He took a break and walked the perimeter of the farm in the dark, the farmer's shotgun resting in his hands. He paused to listen occasionally, focusing on a night

sound that vexed him. The last seven years of nights and days in the prison consisted
of the noise of waves pounding rocks, the sounds of seabirds squawking as they circled
on the wind. Here, lonely insects chirped half-remembered songs. The ocean was far
enough in the distance that the waves were all but silent. As he rounded the house, he
looked to the south and spotted the bright lights of Santa Rosa down the coast. The
city was shiny, burning like a new sun in the night. It covered so much land that he
thought his eyes were playing a trick. If they were going to find their way home surely,
they'd do it there. And if the ghosts of all the people he'd killed planned to come for
him, that town looked like as good a place as any to receive them.

18

The *Polk* drifted north up the coast from San Francisco, hugging the waterline as it went. They'd left at first light, scanning for signs of anyone on land, and any trace of an escape boat among the skeletons of ships in the water. They saw the occasional chewer stumbling along, but no sign of the prisoners, no sign of the supply ship *Nathan Prentiss*.

"This is insane," Dex said. "We don't know if they even lived this long. These little turds probably sank way back there some, or they got clever and headed out to sea and took on water out there." Dex had been assigned to keep watch at the fore of the ship with Lucinda and Lowell. Lucinda vowed to punch Lowell for allowing it.

"The fact is some prisoners escaped," Lowell said. "Don't know how many, don't know who. We're here to grab them by the collars and drag them back."

"Nobody knows that for sure." Dex sat on a nearby trunk and set his spyglass across his lap. He used his free hand to dig at a wad of tobacco in his mouth. "I mean, how do we know that a boat full of prisoners escaped?"

"I saw them." There was no doubt in Lucinda's mind, nor was there any in her tone. "That's how we know."

"That boat could've been anything. Smugglers, thieves, scavengers, hell, it could've been some friends from on down Mexico way, stealing guns for Santa Anna or some stupid shit like that." Dex pulled a dark dripping ball of chew out of his mouth and tossed it toward a spittoon in the corner. He missed.

"Santa Anna died sometime during the war, of that I'm certain, son," Lowell said. "And besides, I doubt his army is stupid or desperate enough to travel all the way to San Francisco and attack a city full of the undead just to get a few weapons for their army. I think it's safe to say, they'd lose more men than they'd gain in firearms," Lowell said.

"Aw, you lot don't know what you're talking about, Santa Anna is alive and gathering his forces. He survived, you'll see." Dex smiled wide. "His men got him up to the dead nation in the middle of the country. They're gathering with all the escaped slaves and those savages. He'll own The Confederate States soon enough. Then he'll work his way up north for the Yankees."

"Ridiculous rumors," Lowell said. "Nobody survives in the middle of the country, not slaves, not Navajos, not Apaches, none of them, not even the ghost of Santa Anna," Lowell folded his arms, digging in for an argument.

Lucinda started to ask what the men were on about but decided she really didn't want to know. She gave Lowell her most unhappy look, and then turned to the window. Her eyes caught a glimmer in the morning sun, a flash of light that recurred in the distance. She focused in on it with her scope and found it was a reflection from a fishing boat.

"Alek? Any way you can get us down a bit and hold it steady? Maybe these fine gentlemen have something to tell us."

"I can get us down a bit, what do you plan on doing?"

With a flourish, Lucinda smiled and made her way to the door. "Why, I just might revisit my circus glory. Surely our amazing craft has a trapeze on it somewhere." She walked to the hall and descended the stairs with purpose.

19

"What do you mean you're leaving by yourself?" LaRue asked.

The night had passed without incident, everyone except Reynolds took a turn at watch and they awoke in the morning, mostly invigorated, partly sore from all the strain of the previous day, and most of them had one thing on their mind: Going home.

"Look," Reynolds said. "I'm going to the city. I need to assess what's happening there. They're looking for four men escaped from Alcatraz, and here are four strangers come to town soon after. We'd get netted for certain."

"They're not looking for four prisoners," Patrick said. "We lost men in San Francisco on your little side mission. The inmates on the island shot several men on the other boat when we escaped, so they have no idea how many made it off the island. No idea how many survived."

Reynolds was sitting next to the fireplace smoking a small cigar he'd found half-smoked in the kitchen. "I don't want to sit around here waiting to get captured any more than the rest of you. But this man has a kitchen full of booze and cigars. There are worse places to be stuck." He blew a ring of smoke over his head and coughed. "Like prison."

"I'll be gone for a couple of days," Reynolds said. "Come back with news, and if it's safe, I'll have a way to get home all lined up for us." Reeves stood near the kitchen table and secured his satchel. He'd emptied out the papers and loaded it for the trip already, packing some bread, the nice Colt pistol, a handkerchief he'd found in the closet and a few other things. "I'm taking some of the money, so I can buy supplies, and I've left the rest here. I told Patrick where to find it if you need it. If it's all clear, I'll get us passage on a train and we can go home. If I'm not back, leave on the morning of the third day, take the money and go."

"And that's it? You're leaving, we're waiting?" LaRue asked. "Where the hell would we go? The city? Light out across the country on foot?"

"Yes. If I'm not back, you're on your own." Reeves lifted his satchel loaded with some provisions and slung it over his shoulder. He walked out the open front door, into the low light of the morning.

Behind him, murmurs erupted among the others, but he didn't stick around to listen, he was only interested to start up road, such as it was, toward the city. It looked like wagons frequented the trail from their impressions baked into the dirt. Reeves guessed it had been twelve days, maybe fifteen since someone had come through from the boot prints and hoof marks. Of course, he had no idea what the weather had been this far north of the prison. The ground was hard and uneven, making the walk unpleasant and Reeves stumbled occasionally.

He felt bad for making them stay, but only for a passing moment. They'd easily give the group away if they'd come. They weren't trained like Reeves, and clearly didn't have the discipline to maintain their decorum for an extended time in the city. Reeves had done things like this a dozen times; went into a city, got necessary information and got out.

But there was a bigger reason for leaving them all behind. After seven years in prison with dozens of men, a day of being cramped in a boat with his fellow escapees, and a night in a small house, Reeves needed to be alone. He wanted the constant questions and inane plays for power to go away. The chatter rang like a dinner bell. As an agent of the Confederate government, he generally worked alone. He made his way by wits and skill and travelling with the others slowed him down and dulled his senses. They buzzed in his mind like a nest of hornets, but he still felt some sort of allegiance to them as fellow soldiers. Now that he'd helped them flee prison, he couldn't shake the need to get them to safety. He would be glad when he found a way to send them off for their respective homes and he could disappear into smoke like a good spy should.

The road got better as Reeves neared Santa Rosa. It was more well-worn with footprints and signs of carts and animals. There were occasional wooden benches presumably placed for weary travelers to rest. It was almost civilized, which was something relatively new for him. Along the way, Reeves hadn't seen a single soul on his journey. No one moving in either direction and none of the footprints seemed to be more recent than a day or two.

About a mile from the city, fences started on either side of the path. The wood and wire structures looked sturdy, like the type used in places at the prison. Reeves stopped and looked around one side. It stretched all the way to a large building and then seemed to encircle the city itself as far as he could tell. At intervals, there were wooden towers, maybe thirty feet tall, in which Reeves could see at least one sentry. The space between the fences was wide enough for two large wagons to travel abreast.

Reeves took a breath, checked behind him, and started walking toward the building in the distance. The ground here was wet, and a little muddy, which made walking all the more tiresome and difficult. The stench of horse dung hung in the air through most of the trek. As he neared the first tower, he looked up to see a guard with what appeared to be a Sharps & Hankins Carbine cradled in his arms. "Howdy," Reeves said. He tried to sound as friendly as possible. The man nodded. Reeves noted the man wore a Union uniform.

"Do I just keep walking?" Reeves pointed forward.

The man nodded again.

"Thanks." Reeves assumed the man wasn't in the mood to talk, being stranded out in a tower as he was, or that he was trained to be silent for some reason. Or he was just a sign of the new civilization Reeves was about to walk into.

As Reeves neared the next tower, a large black crow came down and noisily landed on the top of the fence, flapping its wings, and cawing into the air. It danced a bit, finding its footing, and then settled, only to turn and twist its dark, shiny head to stare at Reeves with yellow eyes.

"Keep moving," the man in the second tower said.

Reeves hadn't realized that he'd even stopped to marvel at the bird. "What?"

A second man stood up in the tower. "He said to keep moving." This man had his hand on his holster, ready to draw a pistol.

The bird danced on the fence in agitation.

Just as he started moving again, Reeves tripped on something half buried in the muck. He got himself up and discovered a scattering of bones that had been hidden by the mud. He recognized a skull and made out a forearm from the tatters of a sleeve still attached. He stood, brushing off the dirt as best he could.

"Sir?" The second soldier had pulled his pistol and held it at his side.

"I'm going. I'm moving." Reeves started walking. "See?" He stepped carefully as he went. He thought about his own pistol buried in the pack. It would be hard to get to and would be tough to use against these men that were under good cover, high up, and far apart. They'd cut him down, even if they weren't good shots. He passed the tower and found himself nearly to the city. He'd have to pass one more tower, then get to the large gate at the end. That barrier had a wall built over the top with raised guard houses built on either side. Gatling guns protruded from each guard house window.

A few yards from the large gate, Reeves stopped. There wasn't a bell to ring or a lever to pull to open the gate anywhere to be found. As he looked into the guard houses, he found men in each one staring back at him.

"You're a new face," a man in Union uniform strode out onto the wall.

Reeves wondered if the news of the prison escape had made it to the guards out there, and if they knew what they were looking for if it had. "Just headed to the city for supplies."

The Yankee nodded. "You armed?"

"Yessir." Reeves patted his bag. "Never know what you'll run into outside Santa Rosa." He hoped that was acceptable. If the city had some law against firearms, he'd leave the Colt and keep the smaller guns, if he could.

The Yankee nodded again and twisted his mouth up in thought. He waved to someone in the nearest guardhouse and the gate swung open. "You'll want to mind your manners with it. We're pretty free with weapons in Santa Rosa, as long as they don't cause no trouble."

Reeves saw the men still tending the guns on the wall. The city's stance on weapons was perfectly clear. "I understand."

"See that you do."

The gate opened fully, and Reeves slung the bag across his chest and took in the city that unfolded. Before he'd gone into the prison, Santa Rosa was a tiny town, located a good distance to the north. Now it was a bustling city that stretched to the sea on one side and off as far as the eye could see in the other directions. The buildings were two- and three-story affairs, some taller; a far cry from the early days. He supposed many of the people who made it out of San Francisco found their way here and started over. What he could see of the port was filled with cargo ships, which made sense if it had taken over for San Francisco in that respect.

The path ahead was a transition from the gateway to the streets and it was strangled with stalls and shops on either side. The street was alive with the smell of cooking meats, and tanning leather. In order to get to any of them, Reeves would first have to pass by a gauntlet of people leaning against buildings or sitting on boxes. They all stood and straightened themselves as Reeves came closer. They were all positioned just right in that they could bother people coming in through the gate, and people that passed by on the city street ahead.

"Hello there, friend." One man wasted no time in approaching Reeves. He wore a tattered bowler and a threadbare shirt. "Hey friend," he said. "New? What brings you here?"

Another gentleman approached with papers in his hand. "Looking for a little companionship?" He held out a card with an image of a sparsely-dressed woman on it. Reeves took it and flipped it over to find an address and the name Seaside Saloon.

"We got whatever you're looking for."

The man in the bowler shoved the other aside. "The girls at the Montgomery are much more accommodating, if you know what I mean. Here." He reached into his jacket and pulled out a similar card, just with a different girl and a different venue; The Montgomery Red.

Reeves put the cards in his pocket and held up his hands to quiet the men. There were hustlers and barkers in San Francisco all those years ago and in every other big city he'd ever visited, but he'd grown rusty in his ability to brush them off. He was surprised today, to see them after so long. "Thanks, gents." He got moving a good pace. "I'm at a loss for funds today, but I do appreciate your kindness."

The man with the bowler stayed with Reeves while the other fell away. "You get to the Montgomery; you tell them Uncle Larry sent you. They'll treat you right, and that's a promise."

Reeves smiled thank you and started up the street, though he was blocked by one more man who came at him from the other side. This one looked to be a preacher. "My boy, do you know God's word?" He shoved a folded piece of paper into Reeves' palm that showed a pair of praying hands on the cover.

"Friend, I am personally acquainted with God's word. He told it to me himself on the banks of the James River in Richmond where I lay bleeding in the mud. The Lord surely spoke to me that day." Reeves put the paper in his coat and patted it sweetly. "But if I ever stumble, I will call upon you to refresh my memory."

The man in the black coat and collar stared after Reeves for a moment as he left.

Santa Rosa was all new to him and he hadn't formulated a plan of attack just yet. For the moment, he'd decided to move toward the tall tower in the distance with the airships gathered about it. Seemed logical that would be a good place to start looking for information on fleeing east toward home, and in the meantime, he could work on gathering a little information of his own.

On the street, there were booths and barkers, fruit stalls and live chickens, all too expensive by his estimations. He pushed through the crowds that had gathered to line up for the vendors, looking up at the tall buildings crowded together down the block. The structures here, on the outskirts, seemed fresher and more recent, though the construction appeared hastier and cheaper, with ugly thin planks used in their build. The paint tried to cover it, but that too was showing wear, peeling and flaking. Losing the battle with the salt air, Reeves reckoned.

Reeves entered a thick crowd and felt a familiar sensation as he jostled between the people. It took him a moment to realize that his change purse was missing from inside his coat. The crowd kept flowing in both directions as he scanned for anyone who might have nimbly lifted the leather pouch. Two men stood out: a taller, thicker man in a hat; and a smaller man trailing not far behind him. They would have blended in better, but they were a little too quick and purposeful in their movements, almost in perfect step with each other, while everyone else drifted like leaves on a summer breeze. He moved swiftly to catch up with them. They stayed together, in step, as he closed on them. When he came within fifty feet, the men suddenly turned and moved away, each toward opposite alleys to the left and right. He couldn't decide who would have been the actual thief, but he guessed the smaller man. Or wished it was the smaller man, in case things got physical.

Reeves turned to his right and headed for the alley behind the smaller of the two. He pushed through the throng, eyes still on the back of the man's balding head. Near the alley, a trio of people slowed Reeves and as he pushed them aside, he raced into the alley to find it empty. There were a couple of doors—one on each side—but he decided not to pursue the man. The doors would likely be locked, or else there would be more large men waiting to beat Reeves senseless. No, he knew better than to race headlong into a situation he knew nothing about, instead he figured it best to move on. The pouch they'd stolen only contained a few coins, as Reeves had been smart enough to keep the bills and larger change inside his coat. He'd lost a little money, but he'd made contact with the city's criminal element, and that was all that mattered. It was certainly quicker than expected, but there it was. He guessed that one of the men at the entrance to town was some sort of spotter who signaled others when he saw an easy mark. The others then lifted a wallet, stole a necklace, or dragged some poor bastard into an alleyway for a beating, and then he'd wake up with nothing.

That was just smart business, at least as far as Reeves' profession was concerned. You followed a man into the darkness and did what needed to be done. You beat some information out of him, took his money if your operation was in need of funds, or outright killed him if the mission called for it. Hidden alcoves were practically his business office.

Reeves stared out at the massive town of Santa Rosa and considered how many blind alleys there had to be out there. He knew for certain that if the army or any other of his pursuers managed to catch up with him, he wouldn't hesitate to pull them into the darkness and show them his stock in trade.

20

The *Polk* bypassed Santa Rosa, slowing down only to exchange signals with the launch tower. As Alek attended to the flurry of activity to open and close the signal light, he would mumble the responses from the tower, which one of the literate new recruits wrote down for reference later. "No news. No captures. Deputies searching east side... winds from the north at six knots..."

"Tell them about the fishermen," Lucinda said. "How they said they'd seen our beat-up supply boat."

"Getting to that." Alek clicked the light's shutter.

Lucinda walked out to the hall and down the stairs to the observation deck. She pulled one of the wide magnifiers closer to her face and looked through it to see the city and its bustle of inhabitants. People walking everywhere and any of them could turn out to be the escapees they were looking for.

Lowell came to the deck carrying two tin mugs filled with water and handed her one. "Spot our fugitives yet?" He asked as he looked through the magnifier.

"Hmmm. If only it were that easy." Lucinda drank the water in one swig and put the mug on a nearby table. "Any news from the tower?"

"They want us to continue on to the north and then work our way back to the city. They feel certain that the escapees won't try to make it up to the Territories." Lowell stopped to dab at a spot on his shirt, then rubbed it with his thumb. "It's too far for them to aim for with limited supplies and they likely have no idea what they're getting into."

"They land in the wrong place, they could end up surrounded by chewers."

"True," Lowell said. "I think that it's certain they'll know enough to stay away from any areas that are served by a large military presence, and if they understand the OMO, they'll give us a wide berth, that's one thing we can count on."

Lucinda wasn't one to jump to conclusions, but she felt that was an obvious statement on Lowell's part. She watched the city as the *Polk* pulled away, passing the outer fence. From there, the land turned to farmland, relatively flat and broken up only by the occasional farmhouse. "I'd say you're right. Although if this man's some sort of spy or what have you, he might be a little more prone to surprising us than we think."

21

Close to the tower, the buildings were gone; a flat area around it was covered in beautiful flowers in a fenced-in park on both sides of the street. The closest park continued up the hill and away from the buildings. He could see tables among the foliage, just outside of a business, a restaurant, he guessed. A couple of customers sat with tea cups, looking over the park and nearby buildings.

A wooden bench near the park looked inviting to Reeves, so he sat to rest. The walk had been long and tedious. He sighed, realizing that if he stayed long, he might not get up. He reached into his bag and pulled out a handful of bread and ate it as slowly as he could. Even though it was a little stale, it was sustenance. He tore off another small piece and nibbled at it, trying not to choke. His water was gone, and his lips were dry. He figured he had to find something to drink soon at one of the bars.

From the bench, he had an amazing view of the two airships nearly over his head, moored to the tower. Neither of them were the vessels that had come to the prison to try to quell the escape. They were much too small, Reeves was sure he could've recognized the big one from that fight in an instant. The two small ones here were never meant for war it seemed. One was a cargo freighter, the other a small personal craft, which looked to be modified for combat or patrols, a sleeker wheelhouse and guns added.

At the base of that tower, men and women came and went, with a fairly steady flow. Some were dressed like any other person in the town, dungarees and a coat, a dress and hat, but most wore dark uniforms with the letters OMO on them. He wasn't entirely sure who they were, but he'd seen the uniforms before. They'd come to the prison from time to time. And they'd left with prisoners in tow.

Reeves stood and ventured closer to the tower, not looking right at it, but at the stores across the street or the people in the crowds. It didn't escape him, however, that at least one of the buildings across from the tower was vacant—suffering from fire damage that was evident around the windows.

He averted his eyes from the soldiers in the OMO uniforms. As he approached the entrance to the tower, he could see some coming down the stairs and considered trying to pick one of their pockets, but decided it was too risky, and that they probably wouldn't carry anything of value anyway.

Reeves kept walking, passing more people and more stores. He eventually came to a great sign for the Montgomery, the one the barker had mentioned. He considered it for a minute but thought about how much money he had with him. It wasn't nearly enough to cover food, lodging or anything else if he had to stay more than one night. He looked at the crowds around him and felt sure he could steal money if he had to, but it was his first day in Santa Rosa, and he had no idea of what alleys he could use as escape routes, what doors led where, and what faces he could trust. It was best to explore a little, look for his old contacts and stay out of the way before heading back to the farm.

"You look like you need a little fun," a man out in front of The Montgomery said. He wore a ragged vest and a week's worth of stubble. "We have that here. All kinds of it." He stepped down into the street. "You fancy a card game? WE got keno. WE got poker. There's a euchre tournament going on right this very moment, and it won't cost you but a penny to buy in."

Reeves raised his hand and moved away.

"Maybe you like checkers? Dominoes?" The man asked. "What's your game, friend?"

"Not much for games today."

"How about the ladies? You much for the ladies today?" The man pointed up to the windows of the second floor, where, Reeves assumed a gaggle of women were supposed to be staring down, but there were none. Curtains billowed in the breeze, but nothing else was visible. The barker looked flummoxed. "They're up there, I assure you."

"Thanks, but no." Reeves kept on moving, but he was tired. He stepped through the door of a nearby saloon and walked to the bar, welcoming the blend of alcohol and cigar smoke that assailed his nose. He supported his weight on his elbows and waited patiently before asking for a whiskey and water from the bartender. He dropped a few coins to cover the cost, careful not to give away his money's hiding place and stepped back. He drank half the whiskey in one gulp, not wanting to finish it all, wanting to make it last. He followed with half the glass of water. The alcohol was weak, likely diluted, but it tasted fine all the same. It was his first drink in years. A full-strength bottle would put him on his ass in minutes.

He waved to the bartender and finished the rest of the booze.

"Another?" The bartender asked.

Reeves dropped more money on the bar. "No, thanks. I do have a question though."

The bartender took the money and stared at Reeves, waiting.

"You know a fellow named Moose?"

"Moose?" The bartender took his towel and wiped the bar. "Would you be surprised that I know about half a dozen guys that go by that name?"

"I suppose I wouldn't. I'm—"

"My little nephew's name is Moose, in fact. He's about—" The bartender held his hand up to his waist. "He's about yay tall now."

Reeves shook his head. "That's a little young."

"You mean the fur trader from up in the territories, lost his hands to the cold and everyone started calling him Stubbs after that?"

"No, I mean—"

"That guy that mooed every time he got stinking drunk and ran himself head-first into the side of the stables?"

"No." Reeves sighed.

"Then did unspeakable things with the mayor's horse until someone dragged him home?"

"Not—*No*. No. I'm thinking of more like a hired hand, lowlife, would do about anything for money," Reeves said.

The bar was relatively clean, and the bartender tossed the towel over his shoulder. "A criminal? Huh. I have to say, I haven't been here that long. I haven't met every fella named Moose, I suppose."

"There was one guy." A man with stringy gray hair and less teeth than he needed waved from a nearby stool.

"Shut up, Ronald." The bartender waved him off.

"No. That circus guy had a man named Moose helpin' him out once in a while," Ronald said.

It was a start, Reeves supposed. "He was a criminal?"

"Kind of a snitch, really. A ne'er-do-well." Ronald tossed back his drink and smacked his lips. "Big one. Did whatever for money. A jackass, if I remember right."

"I got it. He still around?"

"Don't know."

"What about the circus guy?"

"Dead," the bartender said.

"…As a god damn chewer," Ronald said. "Dead as a god damn chewer."

He'd only been in town for a short time, so Reeves considered it a small victory that he'd already narrowed down the possibilities for one of his old contacts to a horse lover, a five-year-old and a potential circus freak.

As much as he hated to, Reeves realized he needed to move on and find a place to hole up for the night. Night was still a good ways off, but he didn't want to get caught in the town with nowhere to rest. His muscles protested as he stood. As much as he'd tried to keep fighting fit, the walk had strained his body more than expected. He limped out of the bar and looked up and down the street. There was plenty more of the town to explore, but he had the day ahead of him tomorrow for that.

22

Reeves turned and walked back up the main thoroughfare the way he'd come. Something had caught his attention earlier and he wondered if it would work for a resting place. He walked back until he got to the tower and then casually strode past, looking closer at the burnt-out husk of a building that sat ugly and black in the late-day sun across from the launch. A painted sign admonishing people to keep out was tacked to the front door and the windows had long planks covering them on the first and second floors. The third floor was mostly gone, burnt out and planks jutting like a hag's smile.

He walked into an open lot next to the building and stood staring at it thoughtfully as a small group passed him on the street. He found that if you did your best to not look like you were sneaking around, generally people accepted you. Of course, he was a wanted escapee wearing ill-fitting clothing from a dead farmer and standing in a plot of weeds next to a perfectly good street in the middle of town. So, a confident demeanor only carried him so far.

His real concern wasn't the shoppers or the merchants or the townies. He worried about the tower itself. It was full of the people who were searching for him. He looked over at the fire-ravaged building next to him. One thing he remembered from training was that the best place to hide was in the place they least expected you. Who would think to look for a fugitive this close to the jailors?

Once he was confident that he was being ignored, he shuffled quickly to the side and ran behind the building. As he stood there, back against the peeling paint, he found it was probably not his finest effort. As his now dead training officer, Coughlin, would say it was, "done with the grace of an amorous caribou," and he generally wasn't wrong. There were things he did repeatedly to get them right in training. Coughlin said they might save Reeves' life one day, and many of them had. Of course, just as many of those things he practiced ended someone else's life.

He thought of Coughlin. Sitting there in that chair in San Francisco. He'd taken his own life, rather than face, what? The chewers? The Union? The man was rigid and unbendable, a shining example for the Confederacy and every soldier he met. He could see the horrors of those creatures caving a man's mind. But there were ways out; there was the tunnel, and other hidden passages that could have taken Coughlin to other parts of the city. Were those any better? Had things gotten so bad there?

Reeves rubbed his temple and took a deep breath. A few feet down, he found a doorway that was relatively stable, though lacking an actual door. Inside, it was a mess, with boards hanging down from the ceiling, planks missing in the floor, though Reeves made his way by testing each step. The boards below his feet crackled, and Reeves took his steps as carefully as he could. The fire had been worse farther back in the building, so he moved to the front and found the stairs to the second floor. There, the damage was much the same, worse toward the back. The shell of the building closest to the street was darker, shaded by a full set of walls and an intact ceiling. He stayed close to the walls, hoping the area had more support and made his way to the boarded window nearest him.

Reeves looked through the wooden slats and could see the tower and the street below easily. The afternoon crowds were thinning and the parade of uniformed people from the tower had all but stopped. He could still see some of the city beyond the launch tower, but not much. He leaned against the wall gently, making sure it wasn't going to crumble. The city was so much bigger than he'd anticipated. It was impossible to guess if any of his contacts were out there or if they'd fled years ago. What's more, he wondered if he'd told the others back at the farmhouse to give him enough time to scout the place out. Of course, he had the usual thorn that made him wonder if they shouldn't just go on without him, so he could be quit of them.

"Hey. Hey, what're you doing here?" A weak voice came from the dark corner of the room opposite Reeves. "You just get the hell out. Ain't no need for two people in here." The figure of an older man wrapped in a dark blanket emerged.

Reeves raised his hand slowly. "Look, I'm sorry, I didn't know anyone was in here."

The man stepped carefully but surely around on the center of the room. "No. You don't know how things work here, you don't know where to step, you don't know how to hide proper-like. You don't belong here." He shrugged off the blanket, revealing a large Arkansas toothpick in his right hand. The blade was dinged and scratched, but there was no mistaking it.

Reeves moved along the wall, keeping away from both the man and the center of the room, which crackled with each of the man's steps. "I don't want any trouble, let's just say I made a mistake and I'll be on my way." He realized that with his own movements, he'd accidently managed to get the man in between himself and the door. He'd have to hope the man let him leave, or Reeves would have to fight his way out.

One of the powder box pistols weighed heavy in his jacket pocket, and Reeves considered using it to end this fight before it actually got physical, but he wasn't sure if the sound of that small gun would carry to the street and bring anyone to check it or not. Plus, the old pistol was meant to be used at the closest possible range. It might not kill the man.

The vagrant thrust with his knife wildly, though he was still too far away to do any damage. As he started to move back in the other direction, he felt something at his feet—the end of the man's cast-off blanket. Reeves reached down and scooped it up.

"Put that down. That's not yours, that's mine." This time the man checked his footing and stopped as he sized up the situation. "You put that down, now."

Reeves felt the thick material of the old blanket as he turned it over in his hands to get a better grip. He scanned the area for some sort of a better weapon, but there was little to go on. He'd have to stay with the blanket and hope an opportunity presented itself.

"Put it down." The vagrant lunged with surety across the faded floor.

Before the man could find his footing and swipe or thrust with the knife, Reeves tossed the blanket over him and constricted his arm movements, however temporarily. He then landed a solid punch to the gut, followed by a second in the face. Reeves heard something crack from the blow to the face and the man screamed, though it was muffled by the heavy blanket. The knife rattled to the floor as the man tried to raise both hands to his face in pain. Reeves let go of the blanket and grabbed the knife from the floor while the vagrant struggled to get the blanket away from his face.

Reeves watched as the other man tried to get free, listened to him grumble and growl in anger with a rising pitch. In the seconds he stood motionless, he felt the weight of the man's oversized knife in his own hand, and he thought about a line that he needed to cross in order for he and his team to get back home. He scowled at the idea that he'd called the escapees his team in any way.

The blanket was nearly off the vagrant when Reeves stabbed him with the knife. It felt easy and familiar. The thick knife cut deep into the man's neck and Reeves held it there with his left hand as his right covered the man's mouth and shoved him back against the wall.

It only made strategic sense—the man was getting louder and could alert someone, or if he let him go he could walk across the street and alert someone. Neither was a situation Reeves could afford right now. It was different from the farmer that Reynolds killed; they could have tied him up and let him live when they left. Here, there was no sensible alternative.

Reeves took a deep breath and waited for the other man to stop struggling.

23

Cashe looked out the window to the town below. It was quieting down, as it tended to at this point. "Think we need to send Lucinda some help? There's some more trainees available that could do scut work, maybe we can task the *Moon and the Stars* to help."

"We're already down a lot of men helping with the prison," Cyrus said. "And we're short an airship from that as well. I don't know how much we can spare. Besides," Cyrus said. "They said they were fine. We need those green troops here to search for the escapees." Cyrus didn't dwell on it, Lowell and Lucinda could handle whatever. He almost felt sorry for the escapees if she caught them. In their travels together, he'd seen more than one man underestimate Lucy to disastrous results. He scratched at his wild beard and stared out toward the ocean and the few buildings that stood between the water and the tower. The lights were shining in a few structures, but one stood out. "There's a candle or something burning across the way."

"Vagrants sleeping in the burnt-out store again?" Bethy asked.

"Most likely. It's just too unstable in there." Cashe sipped his water. "I'll get a deputy to roust them tomorrow? Bout time the local constable and his deputies did some shit around here."

Bethy nodded. "That place sure needs to come down, before someone gets hurt."

"I guess we'll add that to our list," Cashe said. He wheeled himself back to the nearby table and poured some more water. "The bottom of the list."

Cyrus nodded and started toward the stairs with Bethy. "Don't be too hard on the sheriff. He's a busy man."

"Nickel says he's over at The Seaside Inn with that lady-friend of his, playing euchre and drinking," Bethy said low. "Or getting his hee-haws with the other one behind the old boathouse. Honestly, I don't when the man sleeps, let alone does a lick of work."

Her entire statement struck Cyrus funny and he snorted. "You are certainly attuned to the comings and goings of our local lawmen."

"Since things have been slow around these parts, I've had to amuse myself somehow."

They continued down the steps another flight before a thought hit Cyrus. "You don't ever refer to what we do as 'getting our hee-haws' do you? That's not how I think of it."

"I'm just joshing."

"Well, honestly, how do you see us?" Cyrus cursed Lucy for putting thoughts in his head about love and marriage. "I mean to say; how do you think about what we do? About us being together?"

"What? Do you want to know if I think this is just a brush?"

"It's gone on a little longer than a brush, I'd say." He was joking at first, but the conversation felt too serious suddenly. They hadn't spoken of the future much.

"You mean the whole thing, or just our amorous congress?"

His face grew warm at that. "I certainly feel like we've gone a mite further than just—"

"Giving me the old green gown?" It was clear from the smirk on Bethy's face that she intended to make the discussion as difficult on Cyrus as she could.

"I ain't never thought about getting wed none. Not ever." Cyrus looked around for help from anyone who could step in, but they were all but alone. "And with all this—" Cyrus waved to the tower and indicated the OMO flag waving in the breeze. "I don't know anything anymore." He took Bethy's hand in his own and looked her in the eyes. "You rescued me."

"No, I mean the whole crew did that. That's nothing I did on my own."

"You don't understand. I don't mean when the *Polk* saved us on the Turtle. I mean to say that you saved me from the hole I put myself in and didn't ever want to crawl out of."

24

Reeves awoke to the sun shining through a busted window. He rolled over to shield his face from the light and started to drift off before he realized how late into the day it must've been. The light was high in the sky, and well past morning. He rose, did his morning business in a room missing most of its floor and drank what little was left of his water. With the light as bright as it was, Reeves had no problem rifling through the vagrant's things. He had two piss-poor excuses for cigars in his coat, stale as Reeves passed them under his nose and hesitantly put them in his own pocket. There was little else Reeves decided to keep—the large-bladed knife, a handkerchief, a pair of spectacles—all useful items and easy to carry. He left the half-eaten moldy meat, the pungent clothing, and the dusty jacket the man used as a pillow. The blanket was too bloody to salvage and there was no money, not even coins.

Reeves looked at him, wondering what to do with the man. He couldn't drag him out in the daylight. The docks and the ocean weren't that far away. Reeves was sure if he dumped the squatter in the bay, it wouldn't come back to him, but there was no way to do anything about it in the daytime. He doubted anyone would venture into the dilapidated structure, but just in case, he covered the man with the blanket and rolled him to face the wall.

He made his way toward the back of the structure slowly, stopping as boards creaked beneath him. He had come in the near-darkness to mask his movements, but that would be difficult in the bright light of morning. He stood at the hole of a torn-out window, and seeing the way was clear for the moment, he stepped down and made his way through the overgrown foliage. He moved quickly onto the already crowded street. He darted into the crowd and thought about how easy it was to hide there in the sea of people. He feared the sheer number of people might make it too hard to find others there.

Within minutes, Reeves had stolen a nice jacket off an unattended cart, clean trousers off a line and located a bath house where he cleaned up with a long hot soak in relatively clean water. He paid extra for the use of a razor and some shaving cream to rid himself of the growth and be presentable again. He was feeling less and less like an animal. Less and less like a criminal. The city brought something alive in him that hadn't been there since his incarceration.

As he pulled the razor across his face, he thought what it might be like to stay in Santa Rosa, live as a free man in this place by the sea, with the salt air to greet him each morning. The others back at the farm could get on a train and head east without him. They wouldn't care, wouldn't hesitate. For all he knew, they'd left him already. They might've packed up the instant he was out of sight. He heard a rumble like thunder above him, one of the airships leave its mooring and glide off toward the south.

They'd hunt him here, at least for a while. That was a definite mark against staying. Maybe in time they'd give up and assume he'd gone back East or was dead at sea. But how long would that be?

He needed information on his old contacts if he was going to sort things out and catch up on the Confederacy, the aftermath of the war, and everything else. There didn't seem to be any urgency about the city. He looked around at the beautiful buildings and the sprawling streets. War usually led to suffering. It led to people doing without the luxuries they craved. So far, no one seemed to be wanting for much in Santa Rosa.

He walked the streets of the city, looking for anyone familiar. He stole small things as he went—a loaf of bread here, a bracelet there. It was easy, and the people seemed ill-prepared for a man with light fingers in their midst. He almost wished he could stay and enjoy the easy pickings.

Ahead, the crowds got thinner and nearly disappeared. Those that remained, seemed a little more like rough trade than the shoppers and vendors of the other areas. They watched Reeves out of the corner of their eyes. He wasn't afraid of them, not yet. They all seemed to be individuals that were assessing him and his potential as a target. They were calculating the possible weight of his purse, his ability to fight, the proportion of one to the other.

In his own mind, he weighed whether any of those people would be of use to him. Who had information on the men that betrayed him and sent him to prison? Sent him to prison away from his family.

Reeves stumbled and stopped. His mission today was to gather information and purchase train tickets, but his anger got the better of him.

Or was it curiosity? He wondered where they all had gone after they'd cost him his freedom. If they wanted to disappear, Santa Rosa looked to be several times bigger than San Francisco, so surely, they'd have made their way here at some point. But had they stayed? He had that nagging feeling since he arrived in the city that vengeance was within his grasp if he wanted it. That hatred was hotter than the workhouse on Alcatraz in August. That fire was stoked by the whispers of other prisoners that came and went, some bringing confirmation, by word-of-mouth at least, that he and his team had been done in by some informants.

Reeves had suspected them but had no way of knowing while sitting in a cell. The backstabbers were otherwise reliable and loyal to the Confederacy: a man named Moose, a young woman named Effie, and her brother, Hirim Calloway. The Union gold that Reeves and his men were in the process of stealing disappeared after they were arrested, leading Reeves to believe that Calloway and the others had somehow stashed it and then taken it for themselves. His mind burned at the thought that it was their fault he'd been locked away from his wife and children for so long.

But seven years of prison softened that view. Surely, he still hated all of them, but he found some sort of peace at the thought that he could go home. These thoughts led him out of despair at his situation on that god-forsaken island and gave him something to work toward. Whenever he was tired, hungry, or feeling weak, he turned his focus on how to get out and get himself back East instead of reveling in the idea of hunting for the ones responsible for his misery. His new attitude led him to interact more with the other prisoners. He taught some to read and write when they had free hours and weren't laboring on something or other. Some nights he sang songs at dinner while other prisoners joined in with makeshift instruments like the mouth harp or spoons. He'd managed to lift his own spirits as he helped others do the same. It allowed him to get to know people and their strengths.

And yet, despite all that goodwill and all the thoughts of home, he found himself walking far away from the train station and searching for those lowlifes that had ruined him.

25

On his way to buy the tickets home, Reeves was grabbed roughly and shoved into a nearby alley. He fought to stay on his feet, when a solid punch and another shove sent him reeling into the shadows. This time he spun around and backed himself further into the alley before his assailant could hit or push him again. It wasn't ideal to move into an unknown situation, but Reeves knew the next punch might be worse.

Reeves quickly assessed the area. It was certainly where he'd set up if he wanted to cut a few purses or help a rube part with his treasured belongings. He got quickly upright, scanning the crates and trash that lined one side and the wet laundry that hung low from one window to its counterpart across the way. At the end of the alley, debris was stacked in an obviously deliberate way. The air suggested that more than one person had been using the alley as their personal outhouse. It smelled like horse shit and beer vomit.

In the dim light, he could see movement almost immediately. There was the rustle of paper and wood as a man stood up and brushed the trash off himself at the end of the alley. Another lurker climbed out from the behind the crates and, finally, the big man that had grabbed Reeves took another step closer into the alley from the street where Reeves had entered.

"What're you up to out here, marigold? This isn't your pasture." The smaller man stepped forward and put his hand in his jacket pocket. "You look lost."

The gesture was meant as a threat, Reeves assumed, though he wasn't sure if the man had a gun in the jacket, or a knife, a rock, or just a closed fist. He didn't care. The small man was no problem—it was the big one that could cause real trouble.

"Smells like someone's pasture, that's for sure."

"Let's just be quick about this and no one will get hurt. Give us your goods and money." The little man's eyelids were droopy as if he were tired or bored and he talked in a low, flat tone.

"Since you're covered in dirt and filth, I'd imagine you're not the mastermind of this operation." He nodded to the thin thief at the far end of the alley. "The man behind me is probably the strong arm, but brainless." He turned to the other street tough that had emerged from behind the crates. "The leader wouldn't stoop to hiding behind containers of god knows what, kneeling in the waste someone threw from their window."

The crate hood looked down, noticing the wet spots prominent on the pant knees. This one wasn't nearly as large as the others and Reeves assumed it was a youth. "So, I can't exactly figure out which of you are in charge here. Who should I talk to?"

"Very astute," the man from the other end of the alley said. "You're a smart man." He cocked his head and sneered. "Better be a rich man, too. We been waiting in this alley all morning with nary a passerby. We were getting anxious."

Reeves looked around again at the bricks of the structures and the street. Everything was haphazard and patchwork, like they'd built the town with no plan, much like he'd seen on his way around Santa Rosa earlier. There was no other way out of this confined space that he could see other than a boarded-up door to the building on his left, and the way he came in, which was blocked by the boss.

"Least you're out of the sun. The shade of this alley must be nice." Reeves smiled at them and enjoyed the way the underlings shifted uncomfortably in their places. He moved himself just enough that he could see all three of the attackers at once. He reassessed the one with the wet knees. He'd seen a little of this one's face in the light, and discovered she was a young woman, though he couldn't guess how old.

"Just shut up and give us all your valuables. Your money, your jewelry and whatnot." The boss was not so interested in talking nicely, it seemed. "And do it quickly."

His gang moved on Reeves with practiced steps. The big one produced a sap from his pocket and slapped it into his own palm with a smile.

"Sorry. I have nothing of value really. No money to speak of." He reached into his pocket without taking his eyes off the men. "I guess I just have this." He pulled out the large gold pocket watch that he'd found in San Francisco. It was tedious, but he'd spent the previous night doing what he could to restore it. He wound the watch carefully and nodded to himself as he felt the workings come to life inside it.

"Just give it to us and let's not make this bloody," the short man said. "And by the way, I'm in charge here. I'm leading this..." He looked around at the other two and winced. "I'm the leader."

Reeves held up one finger and then continued to wind the timepiece carefully. The watch wobbled in Reeves' hand as the mechanism inside got up to speed. He watched the leader and the large thug advance, while the girl hung back cautiously.

There was a click and Reeves stopped winding. "This is it. I just want a little information."

The big man said nothing, his mouth hung slack as he stepped forward again.

It took only a second to gauge the distance, level off the watch a little to the left and depress the button. There was a sound like the crack of a walnut as the watch launched the tiny circular blade Reeves had sharpened to perfection, and sent it spinning toward the big man in front of him. However, instead of imbedding itself in the man's thick neck, it spun out of control almost immediately; darting upward as if caught by an intense wind. It sliced through the clothes line above them with ease, kept going and bounced harmlessly off the wall before falling to the ground and rolling around in circles. Everyone in the alley watched it go until it finally fell on its side in the street.

The gang turned back to look at their quarry and advanced just as the clothesline snapped and fell, taking all of the laundry with it and landing on the ground midway between the thug and Reeves with a wet slap.

"Uh…" Reeves looked over at the line and then the men. He didn't feel as confident suddenly about fighting any of them. The blade on the ground shone in what little light there was in the alley. He knew the sea air, the elements and time had worn the timepiece down, but he'd done everything he could to revive it. Obviously, it wasn't enough.

The initial shock wore off and the big man chuckled and slapped the sap in his meaty palm again. "Not sure what your play was there, but sorry." His deep voice made his laugh more like a rumble. What he said was true. The move went sour in a way that Reeves truly hadn't anticipated, but he didn't allow himself a beat to consider it. He bent down and grabbed a wet shirt from the downed clothesline. He gripped it firmly from each sleeve and began twirling it with both hands, wringing water from it as it got tighter and tighter. Once he felt good about the tension, he stopped and looked at his opponent, careful to pay attention to the others as much as he could.

The large thief stopped advancing and looked at his companions. Reeves watched them all shrug. "What're you doing now?" The big man asked. "Are we still fighting?"

"I'd hoped we could talk, but if you still want to fight, I'm ready." The damp shirt was dripping water across Reeve's knuckles and onto the ground. He hated that he was so out of practice, so ill-prepared for a fight, especially one he'd brought on himself by getting distracted. The gun weighed on him from his pack and he ignored it.

As his opponent took his first step forward, Reeves let go of one end of the shirt and snapped the big man in the face with it.

"Ow. Christ." The man reached up and put a huge hand to his eye. "What in the hell?"

"Did you just hit him with a shirt?" The small thief asked.

To Reeves, it sounded like the thieves were genuinely upset by the way Reeves had chosen to fight, though the big man wasn't actually injured. "We can stop," Reeves said as he wound the shirt up again, making it tighter. "I'm not proud of this particular fight so far, either."

"Hell with you, mister." The small man charged at Reeves and the injured thug stumbled forward at the same time, red-faced, eye twitching. They came at him from almost opposite sides, which made things easier for Reeves. He turned and flicked the one in the chest, stopping that one's charge and knocking him backward. Reeves didn't wait for further results and turned to snap the shirt at the big man, hitting him square in the groin. The man fell like an oak, crashing to the ground on his face without trying to save himself. He groaned and put his hands between his legs.

The leader had fallen, too. He was sitting on his butt gasping for air as Reeves approached him. The last of the three attackers was still standing by the crates, hidden under her dark grey hood.

Reeves walked to the big man and stepped behind him. He put a knee in the man's back and wrapped the shirt around his neck. As he shoved the knee against the criminal's spine, he pulled on the shirt, choking him. It took a moment for the man to pull his hands from his crotch, but by that time, Reeves was firmly entrenched and impossible to reach with the man's fat fingers, so he resorted to trying to pull the damp clothing from his neck.

"All I wanted was a couple of answers. I figured some smart men like you could see the wisdom in helping me with that." Reeves could feel himself sweating. He hadn't put himself in a situation like this in too many years and now he was worrying about all the things that could go wrong. He started looking for other ways out of the alley.

The big man gasped like a wounded bull as he tried to suck in air. It was a pitiful sound coming from a man of his size. He continued to swing his hands, trying to break away.

"You sonofabitch." The leader wheezed as he spoke. He reached into his coat and pulled out a Remington two-shot pistol. "You son of… a bitch. You let him go."

"Now we're taking each other seriously, aren't we?" Reeves knew there was no way the man could shoot a gun like that without a good chance of his own crew getting hit. "Look at it like this; I could have picked any throughway to get myself attacked. I could be fighting any of a dozen groups of street toughs right now, but fate has somehow brought me to you. It's chance. It's fate."

"What're you blathering about? Get away from him," the leader said. He suddenly looked around and fixed on the third member of their group. "Shel? Get the hell over here and make yourself useful."

The third person walked toward the fight. "I don't know." It was definitely a young woman's voice. "You and Thompson told me to stay out of the way. You told me I don't get as much money as you two on account of I don't fight nobody like you do."

"Jesus, girl. Just help us."

Shel pulled the hood back to reveal a red-haired girl with what appeared to be a hard-earned sneer across her lips. "And this time I'll get a full share of whatever we steal?" Shel picked up a chunk of the crumbled brick as she advanced. "I think I should get a fair piece of the take every time from now on."

The leader looked at Shel. "What the hell? Does this look like the time to speak about such things?" He carefully got himself to his feet as she approached him. "You'll get what's fair."

"Like always?"

"Like always." He refocused on the fight and the girl landed a blow to the back of his head, sending him sprawling to the ground again. Blood seeped from his hair and he didn't get up. Reeves looked at the small gun the man had dropped. It had landed at Shel's feet.

The large man finally spoke up. "Girl? Have you lost your mind?"

"I think she's finally found her gumption." An older woman entered the alley from the street and was immediately recognizable to Reeves. The red hair was grey-streaked, she walked slightly bent, and her eyes were deep-sunk in her face, but she was impossible to mistake.

"Mama?"

The big man tried to see Reeves. "Mama? What the hell? She's your mother?"

"No. She's my old boss."

"You want to whack me in the face with a wet shirt, or will you just believe me when I say it isn't properly loaded?" Mama asked.

Reeves looked at the gun on the ground. Shel would get to it long before he could, but he wasn't sure if she'd be able to shoot him with it in time, the sudden appearance of one of his old contacts had his head spinning.

"Maybe you want to try to kill us with that pocket watch of yours? That didn't go so well last time you used it, now did it?" Mama leaned herself against the alley wall.

Shel looked down at her feet. "It ain't never loaded. Couldn't afford the rounds for it."

"What the hell are you talking about 'your boss?' She's nothing but a lookout for us. She ain't nobody's boss," the big man said.Shel took off her cloak as she approached Reeves and handed it to Mama as they met. Mama wrapped it up into a tight ball in front of her. "I was," Mama said. "Back in my youth, I was something. And you missed it."

Reeves was enthralled by Mama's face. He hadn't seen her since a few days before he'd been captured. Time hadn't been kind to her in his estimation. Her wrinkles were deeper, her skin more like sandpaper on her hands and face. Her long hair was pulled up, no longer strawberry, more snow-covered.

"Leave him go, Reeves," she said.

Reeves did as he was told, out of habit. He'd done everything she'd said before and it had kept him alive and kept his place in the Confederacy in perspective. He shoved the big man away with his foot and slid himself back, ready for the inevitable lunge from his sparring partner.

"Finally. Come to your senses, did you?" The thug on the ground rolled onto his butt and rubbed his neck.

Mama stood over him and lowered the hand with the balled-up cloak to his face. There was a quiet trio of pops, and a wisp of smoke emerged from the cloth. She let the cloak fall to the ground to reveal the gun that had been wrapped inside it. "*This* gun, we keep *this* gun loaded."

Reeves nodded, still looking at Mama. "So, what do we do about this?" He indicated the bodies.

"What we do is I get my fair share this time." Shel leaned down and stuck her hand in the former leader's jacket pocket and dug around, finding nothing, she patted the inside pockets as well. She finally pulled out a handful of scrip and held it up. "You lying pig," she screamed at him. "This is three times what you said we took in today." She stood up and kicked him hard in the ribs. Her hands deftly pulled the paper apart as she slowly counted what she had.

Reeves got himself to his feet and stared at Shel.

"Check that dung heap's pockets too." She indicated the man Reeves had strangled. "He had a decent roll in his coat. No one ever tries to cheat a big scary bastard." She wagged her chin at the man as she tried to count. "Go on. Check."

The alley had grown quiet again after the confrontation. No one seemed to pass by the entrance out on the street, at least no one close enough to care what had happened there. Reeves leaned down and started going through the man's clothing, looking for anything of value. The money from the farmer's house wasn't enough to get anything Reeves felt would be useful in the city. After a quick search, Reeves found a number of crumpled pieces of paper money and a few coins. It didn't seem to be nearly as much as what Shel had found, but it would help.

"You said you wanted to know something. What was it?" Mama asked.

Shel cursed as she seemed to lose her place and started counting the money again.

"I have to imagine you have all the answers. I'm happy to see you again." Reeves stuffed his share into his shirt and thought about it. He looked at Shel for a moment and Mama seemed to catch his meaning. While the girl certainly didn't look like a threat, he was wary of her.

"She's not a problem. I took her in when no one else wanted to. Her daddy died fighting back East at the Chickahominy River in sixty-two. Her younger brother went missing just few days later in a skirmish near Lexington. She's not particularly fond of the Union for any of that," Mama said. "She hopped on a train and found her way across country just before this whole chewer business happened. I found her, and she's worked for me ever since."

"Doing?"

Mama looked at the girl counting money and cursing at the dead men. "She's got herself a job serving drinks. She makes some money, she hears some things. She helps me."

"I really didn't expect to find you here. I guess I assumed it would be someone else."

"You found the message in the tunnel? I thought that was a dumb place to leave word on where we'd be, but we weren't set up with a house here or anything. We couldn't say exactly where we'd be." She sounded almost apologetic for leaving Reeves alone in the world.

"I found it," Reeves said. "I came here looking for some of our old cohorts."

"I bet you did."

Reeves nodded. "So, you know they crossed me? It's true?" Reeves patted the small amount of money he'd taken and walked down the alley. He bent to pick up the blade that had flown wild from his watch. It was dinged and scratched, but probably still usable if he could fix the firing mechanism to shoot straight again.

"Yeah." Mama pointed to the dead men. "Let's move along before someone who gives a shit comes by and finds us standing over two dead bodies."

"I'm looking for a couple of people. That's it. I'm trying to get home to my family after that." Reeves moved with Mama as she walked to the edge of the alley.

"Go on, ask. Mama knows a lot about what happens round here." Shel carefully folded the sawbucks and slipped them into her coat and she caught up.

"Well, I'm trying to meet up with a fellow named Moose, first of all," Reeves said. "You remember Moose, Mama?"

"Huh. Sure do. Well Moose is dead. Who else are you looking for?" Mama swiped at her coat to get the dust off. Her hand shook as she did.

"Dead?"

"Yes, dead. No longer living. You understand?" Shel sounded upbeat, despite what had just happened in the alley.

Reeves looked at her for a moment. "How do you know?"

"Moose was a fairly well-known figure in my line of work. I had a cousin that pulled a robbery on a mail coach with Moose back before the treaty. They were working with the Confederacy, trying to steal gold for the war effort." Shel gave him smug smile. "THAT's how I know."

Mama raised her hand to silence the girl as they walked. "Mister Reeves knows about the attempted gold heist. Moose and some others were supposed to hand that gold over to Reeves the day he got captured."

"So, he did double cross me?" It made sense, considering Reeves himself was supposed to meet Moose for exactly that reason. The prison talk was right. "Dead how?"

"Depends on who you ask. Either devoured by chewers last year or shot by a lawman. Neither is a good way to go, if you ask me." The crowds were getting thick again as they made their way through the streets and Mama lowered her voice. "I suppose you'll want to know about the rest of the men working with Moose."

That crossed one of his former contacts off his list. Reeves had only to choose from, unfortunately and since that particular caper took place seven years ago; odds were not in his favor. "Yes. What about Kelly Willis and his wife, Brianna, and that other one, Hirim Calloway?"

"Kelly drowned in the Sacramento River—drunk as all hell and couldn't swim in the first place—so his wife lit out for the East on an airship. Ain't nobody heard from her as far as I know." Mama paused as a group of people nearly ran them down as they hurried toward a nearby general store. "And as for Calloway—""Hell, you must be new to our fair city. Or else you're mistaken about that man's name," Shel said. The look of amusement on the girl's face surprised Reeves. It didn't seem to be a name she struggled to place.

"Why's that?"

"Well, it ain't a common thing to hear a body asking for a man like Moose in the same circles as Calloway. Like putting cats and pigs in the same pen."

"How so?"

"Calloway's a rich fellow. Real community pillar. Owns a fancy eatery, gives to those what need it, helps out. Sometimes I work there when he needs an extra hand. Guy like Moose would stick you in the eye with a fork over a crust of bread." She paused and reflected for a moment. *"God rest his soul."*

"So, Calloway is the only one around from the gang that got me sent to prison?"

"Looks that way."

Since he'd left Alcatraz, it felt like every minute mattered more than it had before, and Reeves felt the time passing quickly in the alley. "Thanks for what you did," he said. He approached Mama and nodded, then continued toward the street. "I appreciate it."

Reeves felt himself deflate a little at the news most of the men responsible for his incarceration were gone from his grasp. Seeing his family and getting his revenge fueled him throughout his stretch on Alcatraz, but he didn't know how to put off seeing his family in order to take the last seven years out of Calloway's hide. Knowing their fates seemed to be enough.

"That's all there is? You're just leaving?" Shel quickly stepped in front of him and walked backward awkwardly as Reeves advanced. "Look. I don't know who you are, but not many men would be stupid enough to come out here looking for trouble on purpose. And that watch thing? What was that?"

"I just want to get my men and get home."

"You came all this way to find her and you're leaving immediately?" She stayed a few feet in front of him, stumbling as she walked backward.

"You two seem more in need of help than I do. We'll take what money we have and take a train east. Our families…"

"Let him go." Somewhere behind Reeves, Mama's voice called.

The words moved Shel out of Reeves' way, only to move her toward Mama herself. "No. You said any of your soldiers or spies or whatever came our way, they'd help us." Shel moved quickly to within an inch of Mama's face. "Well, here one is. Here one is. Let's start striking a blow for the South."

Faces in the crowd suddenly looked their way and Mama grabbed the girl's arm with boney fingers and dragged her along quickly. "Shut the hell up, girl. If you shout about the South in a crowd like that, someone is going to have questions. You know that."

In quick strides, Reeves returned to the women. "Christ, Mama. You best put that one on a leash before she gets herself in some kind of trouble. I think you got more than your fair share of the money this time out. Let's just part ways with a smile and forget about this."

Shel shrugged Mama's hand off and moved up to Reeves again. He reached out to shove her aside.

"I don't know what you are, or what you think you are—" Shel looked down, and Reeves noticed she was holding a thin blade to his gut. "But you are most assuredly not the dandy you have been made out to be."

Maybe the prison had dulled his talents, erased his intuition, but he didn't anticipate the girl giving him a problem. He quickly assessed his options for gaining the upper hand.

"Shel." Mama clenched her jaw and moved forward.

"Look. We don't have much of anybody now." Shel indicated Mama with a quick motion. "We could all help each other. I know the girl that works for the Calloways. Bea and I are good friends. She knows everything."

Reeves reached out and grabbed her arm while the blade was away from him. He swung the girl easily and she wound up on her rear with the knife beside her. "I think you're doing fine on your own." He heard her yell one more time as he stepped away into the crowded street.

Mama was silent.

"You can come back to our home. There's more loot there. Those guys back in the alley had plenty; you can take whatever you find in their rooms and sleep there for the night."

Of all the people he thought he would run into from the old regiment, Mama was the last one he'd expected to see. And worse, she was the last person he thought he needed. "Good to see you, Mama. Goodbye Shel."

26

The cross-country railway prices were a little more dear than Reeves had hoped, but he had enough to get himself and the other escapees' tickets, and still buy some food for the trip if they were cautious. They'd have to travel separately, to attempt to keep their identities secret.

Reeves walked through the small railway office and out onto the platform, just to get a feel for the place. The whole area was covered in the stench of smoke from the frequency of trains that came through. There was a ticket taker, a thin woman with a pushed-up nose, there was a baggage handler sitting on a bench, and, at the moment there was a sheriff's deputy standing and talking to the handler. Reeves calmly stepped up to the ticket booth and looked at the woman there. There was no reason to panic, no reason to make any sudden moves that might alert the deputy.

"Any trains leaving for Atlanta or Savannah tomorrow?" he asked.

The woman tilted her head and sighed. She'd been asked this before apparently. "Trains only go to one place from here: Paducah, Kentucky. From there, you can go just about anywhere. That one?" The lady gestured at a resting engine and its cars on the tracks beyond. "That one leaves in less than an hour. Nothing tomorrow. Nothing the next day. Not another for three days."

"Paducah? Seems a mite out of the way," Reeves said.

"There's one open track that crosses the Middle. One." She pointed to a small map behind her that showed a blue line that meandered from Santa Rosa to Paducah. A dozen or more additional blue lines snaked away across the map from there, to all parts of the East. Across the map there were indications of rail lines drawn in black, with big Xs through them in various places and huge gaps after the Xs, apparently indicating a break in the line or other damage.

"If you want to wait about six months, they should have the southern route open to Mississippi."

There was no way they could make it for six months in the west. Not in Santa Rosa, not anywhere. Not together, at least. Someone would most certainly catch up with them. "No thanks. Paducah would be fine." He stared at the map, making out the lines that would take him home. Paducah down to Grand Junction, from there to about Chattanooga, then on to Atlanta, and over to Augusta and then a run home to the boys and Carrie.

The ticket-taker raised her eyebrows and sighed. "Next train leaves in—" The lady looked at the clock above her map. "Forty minutes. So, are you buying a ticket or just staring?"

"What?" Reeves had locked himself onto the idea of leaving. He had enough in his pocket right now to get on the train and leave. He could be gone immediately on the next train pulling out. But if he wanted to take the men with him, he'd have to wait. There was no way to get to the farmhouse, gather them, and get back in time.

"Not yet," Reeves said. Out on the platform, men in the dark OMO uniforms milled about. Men in railway garb loaded wood, coal and luggage. The water tower fed the engine. The soldiers didn't look like they'd be much of a deterrent if he wanted to get on a train. He thought he'd need a disguise of some sort to make sure he wasn't noticed, but Reeves wondered if they had a good description of any of the escapees. It was just over two days since the breakout. It was doubtful anyone had even sorted out the bodies on the island yet, let alone figured out who was missing and what they looked like.

He turned away from the train station, walking back to the main streets and out of the railyard. It was a quiet afternoon in the city, not many people clogging the way as he went. Reeves turned a corner and considered heading back to the first saloon he'd patronized and grabbing a drink. With the money back at the house, and what he had on him from the alley, there was more than enough for all of them to head home on the train, and still have some left over for a drink or two.

"Thought you were leaving?" Shel stepped out of a doorway and quickly fell in step with Reeves. "Train pulls out of town in, what, half hour?"

"Forty minutes. Why are you following me?"

Shel shrugged. "Just keeping an eye out. I have a bet with Emma, or Mama or whatever you want to call her. She said you'd stay. I thought sure you'd be on that train."

Reeves didn't answer.

"She said you'd stay, *and* she said you'd come help us. She's pretty smart and knows you right well."

Reeves looked for another bar along his journey.

"Just come back to our home, mister. Hear what she has to say about what we can do to help the Confederacy," Shel said. "What do you have to lose?"

"What could I lose? Maybe another seven years of my life. I did my duty, I did what I was paid for and then I sat in a prison on a shithole island for seven years. Seven years." Reeves shook his head. "I owe my family those years and more."

"Then just come for a place to spend the night. Save yourself some money and hassle."

"Look, Mama did right by me, I got no issue with her, excepting that I have a small aversion to her, considering the kinds of things she used to have me do to 'help' the confederacy. No thanks. I'll be seeing you, Shel."

"Soon, Mr. Reeves. You'll be seeing me soon."

Reeves took his time heading to his den. He double-backed, made unnecessary turns, and stopped at several carts and stalls, just to make sure Shel wasn't still following. Eventually, he felt safe enough to approach his temporary hideout. He planned to sleep one more time and leave early to collect his fellow escapees and leave.

Reeves climbed up the dirt path he'd followed before, up through the weeds, to a broken window at the rear of the building. It was quiet until he climbed in and heard a faint skittering and scratching. He stepped carefully, trying not to alert anyone of his presence. Slowly, he removed one of the small pepper pot pistols he'd concealed in his coat. He picked the smaller weapon in hopes that if he had to fire, it wouldn't draw attention from outside the building. He crept forward, for more vagrants, more chewers.

Instead, he heard the flap of wings and the arguing caw of multiple birds. He stopped on the broken stairs that led to the spot where he'd slept the previous night; the noise was coming from another room. He turned, careful on the broken floorboards, and followed the noise into a crumbled bedroom. It was familiar to him, as he'd dragged the man he'd killed in here the night before.

In the center of the room, a dozen crows stood on the dead body of the man. They'd torn the thin blanket off in bits and pieces, leaving the brown shards of cloth around him like a child leaves wrapping paper. They'd torn through the man's clothing as well, his white shirt now covered in blood and torn flesh, his pants were long strips of wool with sinew mingled in. The boots were still intact; apparently the birds were unable to tear into those to get to the feet and toes. In some areas of the man's legs and arms, bone was visible through the rent flesh.

Reeves watched the birds hop toward the other side of the room when they were alerted to his presence, each carrying a prize in its beak—one with an eyeball, one with a strip of muscle, another carried a piece of scalp with hair still protruding from it. Their normally shiny, black-purple wings were dulled by a coating of blood in the sunlight that struggled through the broken window. One hopped up on a tarnished bedframe and screeched loudly in Reeve's direction.

None of the birds made to leave, nor did they seem all that concerned by Reeves' arrival. He quickly decided that he should consider sleeping elsewhere for the night.

In the distance, he heard a train whistle blare a number of times. There was no reconsidering now. He was stuck for at least the next three days.

Reeves started up the stairs to gather the few things he'd hidden in the floorboards when he noticed voices approaching outside. The conversation sounded like a group of men nearing the front of the building. Reeves counted voices; and heard only three. He stepped carefully into the room he'd slept the night before and moved to the nearest window and peered down. Three men had indeed stopped and stood looking at the rickety building. One wore an OMO uniform; the others wore badges on their coats.

"Shit. I don't want to walk in there again," one of the deputies said.

The other nodded his head. "Probably just Beaumont in there. Place is going to crash down around his ears one of these times."

"Sheriff and my people want this place cleared to avoid something like that happening," the OMO officer said. "Let's just get it over with."

"After we get him out, can we just dynamite the place? Save some hassle down the road." The second deputy walked out of sight. "I'll see if I can still get around to the back from this side."

The other two moved forward. "The boards over the front door should still be loose. We'll get in that way if we can."

A bird near Reeves scratched the floor as it bounced into the room on its short legs. It stopped and flapped its greasy wings a couple of times and stared at Reeves. He and the animal looked at each other silently until the men at the front door began making a ruckus pulling the board free. The crow cawed and turned in a circle, giving Reeves a look at how large the bird was. It certainly wasn't a normal crow, at least not like the ones he grew up with.

Reeves leaned down and pulled his things out of the floorboard and slid around the room, keeping to the walls.

"God. Damn. It." One of the men at the front door was having an issue.

"I told you to bring a shitting hammer or something, didn't I?"

"Shut up."

"How do you expect to get these things off with nothing except your hands?"

"*Shut up.*"

At the same time, a floorboard creaked close ahead of him. He fumbled for one of the small pistols, but a man stepped through the door before Reeves could pull the gun.

"Look mister, you ain't supposed to be here. It's unsafe. There's signs outside warning about it." It was the deputy that had gone around the back. He didn't have a gun or any other weapon out. When he spoke, the bird opened its wing fully and stepped slowly away. It looked like a widow with a black umbrella marching in a funeral parade.

Reeves tried to say something, but he was at a loss as to how to keep the others from coming up and making things worse.

"Come on. We ain't arresting you or anything, just get out of here and don't come back, and everything will be right with the world."

The deputy wasn't looking at a wanted poster, nor did he seem to be looking for escaped fugitives. He honestly seemed to be clearing the vagrants from an unsafe structure. If he complied quickly, Reeves figured maybe they wouldn't give him a second look.

The birds on the first floor started squawking and flapping in a tizzy below them and the deputy looked back at the noise. "Jesus. That's another good reason to get the hell out of here. These birds aren't too kind. They get nasty sometimes with people."

The distinctive sound of a shotgun cut through the screeches and the caws, seemingly shaking the walls of the piss-poor structure. Both men outside wailed in pain and surprise. The deputy near Reeves turned around and moved for the stairs but was greeted by a cloud of black birds fleeing up toward him. Another blast shook the house and one of the men outside stopped yelling.

The deputy tried to force his way through the birds but only got as far as the first step down before the shotgun fired again, closer this time. The deputy fell backwards, dark feathers whipping around him; a bird carcass landed next to him. Another shot killed the man and felled two more birds. The other large crows flapped around the room with Reeves, throwing themselves against the windows or flying down the hallway instead of the stairs. Reeves dropped to the floor and reached up to pull at the boards covering the windows to give the crows a way to get out. More voices were coming from outside as the commotion brought more people to help the fallen men at the doorstep.

"Your skills need sharpened. That prison made you soft." Shel's voice was just above a whisper, barely audible in the chaos of the birds and the shouts outside. "You could've been killed."

Reeves could feel his heart pound and his hand shake as he realized that he'd already pulled a gun at the first sound of Shel talking. She ascended the stairs with a still-smoking sawed-off shotgun in her hands. "Christ, girl. Do that again and you may not live to see me sharpen those skills." He looked at the dead deputy. "Jesus. You just made the whole thing worse." The shots and the dead deputies would bring more people with guns, especially being so close to the tower that housed the headquarters of the OMO and the sheriff. They needed to leave.

"Be honest with me. Are you really one of those amazing super-spies Emma's been waiting for?" She slid the shotgun into a holster on her back. "Cuz so far you seem like a right dolt."

27

After a twisting and turning route through town, once they were sure there was no one following them, Shel pointed to a tattered building with mostly missing shutters. Reeves followed Shel up the stairs of the building that she and her fellow thieves and ne'er-do-wells apparently called home. She'd led him through the underbrush behind the rotting building, into a back alley for the store next door, and through a butcher shop. They wound around the block, staying off the main thoroughfare until they crossed the street and headed up the hill. He did his best to remember how they got there, but Reeves found himself confused by her path, and was quickly aware of how exactly she'd followed him to his building without being noticed. She knew the city very well, no doubt learned by evading the same authorities that chased them now.

The dilapidated building Shel led him to, was as Reeves expected, horrible. The lower stairs were rickety and near collapse, the first floor smelled of urine and something rotting and he was relieved once they'd passed it by. He could hear movement on that floor and the next, as they continued farther up to the third floor. The idea of people coming getting behind him so easily didn't sit well, but he had no choice if he wanted a look at what treasures and supplies Shel and her compatriots might have. He'd been surprised by her in the alley, and at the building, he'd hate to get another shock from a whole group of cutpurses. That would be more than embarrassing, it could be deadly.

"How big is this group?" Reeves didn't want to touch the railing for fear of what might be infesting it.

"Hmm?"

Not wanting to talk too loud and draw attention, he cleared his throat and tried again. "How many of you are there living here?"

"Oh. Well? Not including Thompson and Breck, on account of you killed them, I guess there's maybe a dozen that always stay here and maybe another four or so that come and go," Shel said.

A total of sixteen. It wasn't much of an army, but the other three back at the farm could make it interesting if Reeves had to put together some sort of operation on short notice.

He paused, feeling that part of him slipping back into the mindset of a killer, or a soldier. He was planning a fight that didn't exist. He repeated to himself that he owed

Mama nothing other than to listen to her in exchange for a night's rest. Then he could get on with the business of going home.

A door barred their way at the top of the stairs, and Shel began to knock a simple code. One knock, a pause, then two rapid knocks. The door rattled as a chain and then a bolt was scraped aside and then the handle moved. The door opened a little and through the crack appeared the fat face of an older balding black man, maybe ten years Reeve's senior.

"Where are the others?" The man asked. "Who is this?"

"Well—" Shel appeared at a loss to explain. And it was obvious to Reeves from her expression that no one had told him what happened in the alley yet.

"I'm Reeves. Harvey Reeves and I'm here to talk to Mama—*Emma*. She asked me to come."

The doorman's eyes narrowed. "Ain't nobody's mama here, mister. Shelby, you know you don't bring nobody back to this place."

"I'm somebody's mama." A light voice came from behind the doorman.

"Shut up, Clara," Shel shouted. "Not talking about you."

Reeves put his hand on the door before it could shut. Whatever circus Mama was running didn't really amuse him. "Emma asked me back here. I just need a place to sleep for the night."

The doorman thought about it and inhaled a rattled breath through his nose. "Where're Breck and Thompson?"

He kicked himself for not practicing a story with Shel first, but he went ahead with a lie in the hopes she'd follow his lead. "They headed for The Montgomery to talk to some man named Uncle Larry. Said something about having a good time."

Shel stiffened but said nothing.

The man's face went flush with anger. "He went to The Montgomery? Probably wasting money we need."

"Look, Wilhelm, just let us in. I need my things…"

"Things?" A man shouted hoarsely from behind Wilhelm this time. "What things does she have? Her blanket and that cold-weather hat? She has no things. Nothing."

"Andre, you know I have a whole bag of my own things," Shel said. "I've got a pillow and…"

Reeves' patience was nowhere nearly as lengthy as it had once been. He grabbed the door and shoved it with his weight, slamming it into Wilhelm's face and knocking him backward. As the door swung open, Reeves followed it, ready to fight any of the others that came to challenge him.

Wilhelm was on his rear end on the floor, rubbing his head and looking terrified. He brought his arms up to block any punches that Reeves might throw, and Reeves saw that Wilhelm was missing his hand below the wrist. The man Reeves guessed was Andre was sitting on a stool in the corner to the right, and he had to be eighty years old if he was a day. In the opposite corner was a woman knitting what was either a blanket for all of them, or a sweater for Wilhelm. There were three other rooms with doors on the opposite wall, but this one appeared to have several blankets arrangeded for sleeping, a stove for cooking, and a box with firewood. Three more men sat around the stove. Each had obvious wounds on their bodies somewhere. One had a deep scar from his forehead to his chin, another was missing several fingers on one hand and had a deep crater in the left side of his head. The last was shirtless, thin—impossibly thin, Reeves wasn't sure how a man could live on so little—and his eyes were a milky white. Not a one of them was younger than Reeves.

"This is the rest of your gang?" Reeves looked at Shel as he moved on to one of the rooms. There, a man with a missing leg sat near the window. "This is the criminal empire that you wanted me to come back to and split the loot with you?" He looked around the second room and found two tattered blankets spread across a heavy wool coat. At opposite ends of the bed were a pillow and a small box. He grabbed the small box and emptied it out in the middle of the first room. "Is this the stash of valuables we're supposed to divvy up?" He kicked at the pile of things with his shoe. "Cheap rings and empty ammunition casings?"

He threw a shawl to the floor and a box rattled on the wood as Reeves moved on to the last room. This one had a small crate with a cloth on it next to a partially splintered table. "Oh, this must be the boss's room, it has *FURNITURE*." Reeves called over his shoulder but didn't turn around. He kicked the makeshift chair and found a heel of bread wrapped in cloth hidden inside. There was a bowler hat hanging on the wall and when he pulled it down, Reeves found several coins in the lining. He dropped them in his pocket and tossed the hat on the table. For a moment it looked like the weight of it might knock the table down as it teetered on its legs. There was a bag beneath the pillow and Reeves snatched it up to take with him to the other room. "Now we're getting somewhere."

In the main room, he opened the sack and released its content in the same spot as the other, though he noticed that the empty shell casings from the first room had disappeared. This time, the contents clattered and rattled loudly as six forks and a butter knife hit the hardwood floor first, followed by a silver necklace, a broken pocket watch, a shiny ring and a small pouch. Three coins fell from the bag after a good shake.

"Breck said he'd sold that ring two weeks ago," Andre said. He looked from Wilhelm to the woman who said knitting silently. "He said he sold it and paid for that bag of rice and the new kettle."

"God damn pathetic." Reeves reached down and picked up the pocket watch from the small pile of things. He could feel everyone in the room holding their breath in fear he'd take the money or the ring, but he left them. He might be able to scrounge some parts from the watch to repair his own.

"Thank you for convincing me to come back to your wretched little hideaway, but I have to say I find it somewhat lacking." He scowled at Shel.

"The others will be back eventually, you'll see."

Reeves turned. "Back? To what? This latrine? And that is coming from a man who spent the last seven years in a fetid, rat-infested prison on an island surrounded by water and fog, which was in turn surrounded by hordes of ungodly ghouls." He exaggerated a sniff of the air. "This place is so foul that I will leave it, bathe in the river, and then burn the clothing I'm wearing. And this is the only shirt and pants I own."

Reeves stepped out of the room and cursed at himself as he shuffled down the stairs. He was tired and cursed himself for not just getting on the train and leaving everyone behind. He pounded the wall in frustration.

The door at the bottom of the stairs opened and Mama entered from the street. She carried a basket with bread and a jug sticking out of the top. "I take it the crew has failed to convince you to help us out."

"That's about right." The stairs creaked as Reeves continued his descent.

"Let Shel and I go with you when you get your men," Mama said. "If I can't convince you, we'll put it to rest. You have my word. Handshake and a goodbye."

Reeves looked at the woman before him— she was by no means frail, but she certainly wasn't the same woman who'd kept pace with the men in the old days. "It's a long walk."

"I'm sure you'll do just fine," Mama told Reeves.

It was another in a long line of mistakes, Reeves was sure of it, but maybe he owed her a listen, and at the very least, it was a step toward gathering his men and getting them home.

28

"There's men all up and down the street looking for them," Bethy said. "Trainees and the other deputies."

"Who was our man with them?" Cyrus asked.

Indicating the body covered by a sheet nearby with a glance, Bethy replied "You remember Graham? Pulled artillery for the North?"

"Tall guy? Scar just about here?" Cyrus indicated his own left cheek.

"That's him. Caught a shotgun blast at pretty close range. Dead right away, but his body caught enough of the blast that the deputy took a lot less," Bethy said. They stopped walking toward the building long enough to talk to the sheriff, who was standing stock still in the middle of the street.

"Anybody have an actual description of who it was?" Cyrus watched as a field medic worked on one of the deputies outside.

"No. Some people say it was one guy. Some say two," Sheriff Andrews said. His face had been a dark color of red since Cyrus joined them. "Some kid said he saw three." He turned away. "We don't know shit about shit."

Cyrus patted the sheriff on the shoulder. "Go with your deputy to the doctor. We'll work on this for you." The sheriff didn't move.

Bethy led Cyrus to the open front door of the derelict building. He looked up at the broken windows above them. Blankets were flapping in the breeze, nailed to the window frame. "Had to put up some blankets to keep more of those crows from coming in. They were eating everything. God damn *everything*."

They walked together inside and up the stairs. At the top, one of the OMO trainees stood leaning in a doorframe with his back to the body of the deputy.

"You okay?"

The trainee quickly shook his head no. "These godforsaken birds. They'll tear a man's eye out if he isn't careful."

"Thanks for keeping them away," Cyrus said. He didn't know the deputy, other than to see him on the street, but the situation still tightened Cyrus' chest. He could easily have been one of the men checking the situation. Worse, it could have been Bethy. He turned to her, but she stopped him before he could even form words.

"The other one is in the room."

"Other *one*? I thought there were three men dead," Cyrus said.

"There were." Bethy entered the next room and pointed to a twisted heap of bone and cloth against the wall.

"Shit."

Bethy nodded. "Ain't no way to tell what killed him, cuz there ain't enough left of him. These shit birds tore him apart."

Cyrus knelt and looked closer. "These things are only supposed to attack chewers. And even then, only the ones that we shoot with that crap the doctor came up with."

"Or dead things."

"Yes, but this looks like Old Beaumont's coat." Cyrus looked closer at the pattern of patches and tears. "If it is, I just saw him—what?—two days ago? Even if he died the same day, these things should've left him alone. They rarely eat recently-deceased carcasses. He couldn't have been a chewer yet, either. "

"They're getting bolder, Cyrus. You've seen them gathering on the rooftops, like they're waiting for something. They used to stay away from town." Bethy turned and walked out of the room, giving the trainee a sympathetic pat on the shoulder as she descended the stairs. "The crew out in Outpost Two-thirteen keep bringing these horrible experiments to life from Doctor Poley's notes, but I think they're best left alone. I mean, they were all meant to help win the war by any means possible, but not a one of them has been a benefit to us now."

The birds had been such a boon to the effort to clear the chewers that it was painful to think of them as anything but helpful. Cyrus wanted to believe their luck had turned for the better, but there was that part of him that was always ready for things to go sour at the snap of a finger.

29

He could navigate well enough, but it had been a long few days and he was bleary-eyed and sore. Reeves became disoriented and feared they'd taken the wrong path to get to the farmhouse somehow. "I could use a warm bed right about now." He put one foot in front of the other and kept going. Shel had taken them all around some buildings to a hole in the fence, so they could avoid being seen at any of the gates to the city.

"A nice warm bed? So, your men are holed up in an actual house? Hell, I assumed wanted men such as yourselves would be hiding in a cave or a tree somewhere," Shel said.

They'd left Santa Rosa in the morning, carrying the bare essentials—a little bread, a little water, whatever money they could scrape up, and weapons. Reeves slept in one of the dead men's rooms, but only after throwing all the pungent, flea-infested blankets out a window. He still wasn't comfortable, but he managed to wrap his own things around him to keep warm.

On their walk, Shel stayed next to Reeves for a long stretch. "You're going east when you're done here?"

"That's the plan," Reeves said.

Shel looked off for a moment and Reeves could see the wheels turning, the possibilities lining up. "I've never been east, never really left Santa Rosa, other than to work that fishing boat for a piece." She squinted at him, the remains of the sunset turning her eyes red. "What would I have to do to come with you?" It wasn't just a question, Reeves knew that. It was a reminder to him that she had a knife and was pretty good with it.

Seeing an opportunity, Reeves raised his voice so Mama, who was trailing behind by a few yards, could hear. "Well, I don't know what Mama has in mind. We've been walking nearly an hour and I haven't heard a word of this thing she needs help with. Hard to say if we'll have room for anyone on a trip east."

"Go to hell. It's hot out here, you dung fly. Damnably hot," Mama said. She was wheezing lightly with each breath. "I'll talk when we take a rest."

In the distance, Reeves could see the pinprick of light that represented the farmhouse where his own little gang had set up shop. He looked around himself and motioned to a nearby length of fence that had been downed. He motioned to it and spoke. "Let's just rest here. We'll be there soon enough, but we all could use a minute, I think." They both sat on chunks of rotting fence posts, which really made it not much better than sitting on the ground, as Shel did. Once they were comfortable, Reeves looked at Mama expectantly while he uncorked his water.

"You broke out of the Rock, huh?" Shel folded her legs up beneath herself. "I hear that ain't easy." She brushed off her clothing. "We heard the god damn Rock was closed up for years. Ever since San Francisco was overrun, I think."

"You probably should keep your voice down. Isn't this area still fair game for chewers?" Reeves looked around, not really interested in the girl's questions. All he wanted to hear was Mama's story, so he could say no, and move on.

"Eh, they're noisy enough out here. Ain't many this close to the city anymore," Mama said. After heavy gulps on her own water, she nodded. "Okay, okay."

She was playing coy with Reeves, drawing out her tale for dramatic effect. Or stalling to make something up. Both were tactics that Reeves had learned in the Red Gear program.

"I want to go home," Mama said.

"So go." Reeves' water bottle was nearly empty, and he swished it around.

"I want to back east and live in Savannah again. Finish out my years there."

"Do it. You don't need me for that."

"Want to live out my life in Savannah as a hero, as a somebody," Mama said. "Right now, in the eyes of Confederate history, I'm a failure. Since that last mission where you were caught and the rest were killed? Since then, my name's been mud. I lost a team of our best men. I'm lower than pig shit."

"You were betrayed, we were all betrayed." No one knew that better than Reeves.

"I can't prove that."

"So, what? You want to go home a hero? How do you propose to go about that?"

"You saw those men there in our little hovel?" Mama shook her water canteen.

"Yes?"

"All broken men. All heroes in their own right. Left and abandoned by the Confederacy. I think about all the things I had to do, all the boys I sent off to kill or die. I think about them boys and I wonder if maybe saving those outcasts back there might somehow balance things for me. Maybe that bit of good will dilute that shit I created."

"You didn't send those men all on your own. You had orders, you had to work from a greater plan. It wasn't all you."

"It feels like it son, and don't you tell me what I feel." Mama sighed. "I never pulled a trigger, but how many children did I kill? A hundred?"

"Mama…"

"A thousand?"

"I still don't understand where I fit in. What do you want from me?" Reeves handed Mama his bottle of water and let her drink it down.

"I want to get them home—"

"Do it. You don't need me."

"You saw them. Shit, half of them can't stand up. *I* can barely stand up." She pointed at Shel with thin digit. "She can't handle all of us."

"I'm leaving with the other escapees. I don't know if travelling with any of us would be a good idea, anyway." Reeves stood and stretched his arms, getting ready to move on, and to let Mama down in the easiest possible terms.

"No. No. See, that's not what you need to do. See, the president of the Confederacy is visiting here in a few days. Edward P. Alexander himself. Right here. All I need is help getting me and those men in front of him and I know he'll find a way for us to get safe passage back with him."

"That's..." Reeves started.

"Don't say no."

"I think that's crazy. There's no way he'll help you get back," Reeves said. "The OMO will take me into custody, and possibly you, if they find out that you directed the spy syndicate. There's no way they'll help. Every murder, every dead soldier, every citizen that got in the way of an operation you directed—they'll blame you just as much as the people you sent. They'll forget the war now that there's peace. You'll be just another murderer, as much as I am."

"We can do it in quiet. There must be a time he's alone. We plead our case, surely he'll appreciate war heroes that want to come home."

"Sure. He can appreciate a war hero, hell maybe he's even heard of you, though if he's a new president, he probably doesn't know you from the next person on the street. But odds are, he'll want to keep the peace and turn you over for a trial." Reeves stuffed his empty canteen back into his pack and dusted everything off.

"I didn't serve my country all this time just to go home and be treated like everyone else. I made decisions that turned the direction of the war. I sent men and women out there to make history. There are statues of *them*. I'm not going home with my tail between my legs hoping no one sees me and praying I turn to dust before they do. I'll put a gun in my mouth right now, thank you."

The sun was getting higher in the sky and Reeves could feel the sweat roll down his neck and forehead. "We'd best get to it. We can get there in another hour or so."

"That's it then?" Mama stood up and batted at her skirt.

"That's it. I don't know what you want, but it sounds like it involves me not going home. And I can't abide that," Reeves said.

"I want you to help me get to the president. I can take it from there. You have a better head for plans and schemes than I do," Mama said. "I need you."

It was as true as anything else Reeves knew. Mama didn't have the faculties for the machinations of the operations of a spy ring. She was good at people though. She could find the perfect person you needed at that precise moment in time. If you had a guy that needed strangling, Mama always knew a man with a rope.

Once upon a time, she did.

They walked in silence for ten minutes or more, until the light from the farmhouse got too close for them to ignore, and Reeves stopped and looked at her. "I want to help you, I do. But going home is mighty big in my heart right now."

"What about revenge? Where does revenge sit in your heart right about now?" Mama asked.

That simple question pulled at a string in Reeves that he'd been trying hard to ignore.

30

The three men stared at the young girl as Reeves talked. He made it clear she was here to help them, and not a thing to be played with. They all but ignored the older woman that stood not a few feet away, drinking gin from a bottle. When Reeves, Shel and Mama walked into house the men were in various states of inebriation, Reynolds was wearing some bright long johns that he'd apparently dug out of the dead man's bureau and singing a song he'd made up as he sat by the fire. LaRue sat in a large wicker rocker and smoked a pipe with an intensity and singularity of purpose that made his eyes bloodshot and red. Their last companion, Patrick, lay sprawled on the kitchen table, clutching an empty brown bottle to his chest. The air stank of pipe smoke, cheap booze and whatever the men had cooked earlier. None of them were anywhere near a weapon and would've been easily shot or captured if the law had arrived. Certainly, a chewer attack wouldn't have gone well. As he watched the men barely react to their arrival, Reeves wondered if he should've just shot them himself. It wasn't a half-bad idea. He'd have less baggage; he'd have fewer mouths to feed, less back-talk. Of course, he'd have few hands to make his work lighter.

"Reeves." Reynolds almost fell over as he announced the arrival of his companion. "We wondered if you were dead. We hoped not. But we wondered."

"Annnd guess what we found?" Patrick raised the bottle from his breast and waved it around, as drops flew from it. "Bastard had a little stash hidden under a board on the back porch. Lots of good stuff to drink."

LaRue continued to smoke and stare at the fire.

"Reeves is back." Reynolds yelled again. "And he brought a lovely young lady with him." He sauntered over to Reeves and Shel, still dancing to the song he'd been singing when they entered. "Come waltz with me, little girl." He held out his hand and waggled it around.

"We've come a long way, we're tired. She doesn't want to dance with you. Not now, not later," Reeves said.

Shel shot a glance Reeves' way that suggested he could butt out, and she stepped forward. "He's right. I don't want to dance. Not with you," she pointed to Reynolds, then Patrick. "or you." She looked over at LaRue, who still hadn't acknowledged her. "And certainly not you. Any of you so much as touch me and I'll slit all of you all's throats."

It was a bold statement coming from a young lady who was currently in a remote shack with four recently escaped criminals who hadn't had the pleasure of a woman's company in years. Reeves supposed that could be attributed to the things he'd said along the way. Or else she was just plain crazy. Either way, he planned on keeping her safe so long as she was useful.

"Hehehe," Patrick laughed from the table where he was still flat on his back. "Tough girl. Like that. Like it when they're all full of piss like that."

Shel pushed Reynolds' still outstretched hand aside, kicked his knee, knocking his leg out from under him, dropping him to the floor and continued to the kitchen. Before Patrick could rise, she had her thin knife out and she planted it in the table next to his ear. As far as Reeves could tell, she didn't appear to have sliced his flesh, but he screamed like a child when the knife thudded into the wood. It was probably mostly due to the alcohol, but when he sobered, he'd question whether that was true.

"I'm not here for your amusement," she said and turned to see if LaRue would get up and push into the fray, but he hadn't moved other than to draw in smoke and blow it back out.

"Believe me. She isn't." Reeves looked at the state of his companions and thought about putting off his discussion until they were in a clearer state of mind, but if Shel could scare them with the booze's help, surely it would work in his favor as well. "I'm sorry my return was so delayed."

"Yeah. We thought you'd gotten lost or captured or killed or worse," Patrick said. He moved himself away from the knife, and from Shel, and got to his feet on the opposite side of the table.

"Or shot." LaRue finally broke his silence. "Gettin' shot's worse, I'd suppose."

It was a brief flash in Reeves' head, but he again considered that he might be better off without these men. Better to take his chances with Shel and her ring of petty thieves than with this crew of drunkards. Wait 'til they're asleep and burn the pathetic shack down around them. With any luck, the OMO or the law would assume all of the escapees were dead once they sifted through the rubble. They'd find the nearby boat, find four bodies, including the farmer that lived here, and call it a day. Reeves could get his revenge unfettered or hop an airship for home and leave it all behind. He reminded himself it was always an option. He could walk away at any time. "We're in good shape here. We have just enough money to get a train home. Now that's the good news, sure as shit, but there's a hitch. The next train in that direction doesn't leave for a few days. So, we need to keep hid for a bit."

"What about them?" LaRue pointed his pipe toward the women. "What the hell are they doing here?"

"We're former colleagues. We discussed a little business on the way here, but it doesn't look like that will pan out."

"Although—" Shel piped up. "We may be accompanying you back to the heart of Dixie. I ain't seen home in too long."

After an airy belch, Patrick shook his head. "I don't know. We don't know you Miss. No offense."

"Reeves here said it might help you stick out a little less as escapees," Shel said.

LaRue exhaled and turned. "You're a belle of the south?"

She wasn't. She'd told Reeves she was born in the Dakotas and had never been further south than Saint Paul before her family moved to the west to get away from the escalating Sioux violence.

"Why yessir, I am." She tried to affect a southern accent that made Reeves wince.

He shook his head no discreetly, hoping to catch her attention.

"Born and raised."

The men all stepped a little closer. Patrick opened his mouth first. "Whereabouts? Anywhere near Milledgeville, Georgia? My uncle helped build the penitentiary there. I still have cousins that work there, last I heard."

Reeves poured a glass of water from a pitcher and watched as Shel worked on making friends with the other men. She touched them on the arms, laughed at their drunken jokes and smiled wide the whole time. It was much like she'd been trained by someone along the line. He turned to see Mama staring at him, sizing him up. He remembered how she did that—seemed to look through people and pick apart their souls.

The men bitched, but Reeves forced them to let Mama and Shel have the only bedrooms. While Mama made herself busy in the kitchen with tea, Reeves escorted Shel into her room and stood in the doorway as she walked around and got herself acclimated to the surroundings. She quietly touched the dead man's belongings—a single framed picture on the nightstand, a vase with a dead flower, a frilly pillow.

"You didn't have to do that. We could've slept out on the floor or the chairs or something. I don't want to get the men to hating me when I just got here," Shel said. "Plus, we need them to like us. If you decide to go along, of course.

"They'll be fine. They won't bother you none."

"A group of men fresh out of prison won't bother me none?" She pulled her thin blade out of the folds of her blouse. "Excuse me if I sleep with this real close by, won't you?"

"I think they're drunk enough that they'll be out like nothing real soon." That was the hope anyway, Reeves would sleep close to the bedroom and he'd have his own weapon handy as he dozed. "If you need to use the privy, let me know. I'll go out with you. Never know if one of those monsters will come stumbling out of the night when you're trying to do your business."

"They're pretty well in hand in this area, but I'll let you know just the same." She tried to act like she was just making conversation, but she jumped to her next question too quickly to be offhand. "You were in the service, Mama said. What kind of training did you receive? Marching and the like?" She smiled, as if the idea of being a soldier was quaint.

"They taught us a lot of things."

"Like what?"

"Like what? They taught us how to shoot straight and not miss. They taught us to blend in, to hide where no one expected us."

"Shoot and hide? That's it? No wonder we were doing so poorly towards the end. You'd think the Confederacy could come up with some better things to teach soldiers."

Reeves was tired and wanted nothing more than to rest. "There was more. We learned to use disguises. They taught us how to explode things with limited resources."

"Huh. You blew things up?" She sat on the bed and bounced a little, then leaned down and sniffed the blanket.

"Hell yes, I did."

She wrinkled her nose at the smell of the bed covers. "Like what?"

"You know we're not courting here, right? I'm not looking for a roll in the sheets. This is a business arrangement."

"I know that. Just making talk. Making talk to understand what we *are*, in fact, doing. Just finding out what we can do together." She forced a small smile.

"I blew up a bridge back east, to keep troops from crossing. A barge. Blew up a barge full of supplies." Reeves thought about that one. There were more than supplies on the barge. The papers back east said there were a dozen soldiers onboard, three doctors and the barge crew. The supplies were mostly medical supplies, blankets, clothing for the upcoming winter.

It didn't seem like Shel was convinced yet. "That's all you blew up?"

"We practiced on the mountains. Obliterated huge outcroppings of limestone during our training." Reeves felt like the girl was enjoying the story but wanted it to be a mite more violent and exciting. "It was pretty—"

"You ever kill anyone?" She interrupted him. She placed the only bag she'd brought with her onto the dresser with a loud thud. "I mean, you know. Really killed anyone?" She busied herself with pulling a couple of items out and made a show of lining them up.

"Ma'am? I think there's probably not much of a line between killing someone and *really* killing them." He shifted and turned to grab the door handle. "We'll talk in the morning. I'll be right outside. Good night."

Reeves listened but didn't hear her return the sentiment. He moved toward the sitting area, where only LaRue was still awake and staring. The fire from the hearth cast a red glow into the man's eyes.

"We going to get home anytime soon?" LaRue sighed heavily and shifted in his chair. "I just want to get home. I didn't really think we were going to have to fight again once we broke out of that prison. I thought we'd just go home." Tears formed in his eyes and his voice wavered. "I don't want to fight no more. Can't we just go home?"

"You're drunk," Reeves said. "I didn't say anything about having to fight."

After a deep sniffle LaRue spoke again. "I want to go back to my farm and grow something. Tobacco, whatever. Shit, I don't care. It's a farm just like this one. I want to get on an airship tomorrow and go home."

"We can't do that. Not yet. We're wanted fugitives from Alcatraz. Our faces are everywhere by now." He kneeled down next to LaRue and patted his leg in assurance.

"But don't worry. We aren't going to fight. In a few days, we can head east. Maybe not by air, something less flashy."

"It'll be good to get home. I want to go home."

Nearby, Reynolds rolled over, grunted and passed wind.

LaRue and Reeves looked over and smiled. "It'll be good to get home," Reeves said. *It will be good when we can all be quit of each other* Reeves thought.

He moved to the kitchen where Mama was staring at the kettle she'd put on the stove, but hadn't lit.

"There's no tea here. Man has water and alcohol, but no tea, no coffee," she stared some more at the stove. "We should've taken some on the way out of town."

"Look, it's late. Why not get some sleep? You'll feel better in the morning and we'll see what we can come up with then."

"You think about what I said?" She took a deep breath and finally turned to see Reeves. "I think we can both do one last good thing for the South before we call it quits. Don't you?"

Reeves nodded. "Let me sleep on it. I don't know what you have planned, but I just want to go home and see my family. I can't imagine how much those boys have grown." The image of his children came to him and Reeves felt his throat catch and he pushed on, so it wasn't obvious. "Probably driving their poor ma crazy, I'd bet."

Mama leaned forward, lips downturned. "When we met in the alley, you said you wanted to get home."

"Yes." Reeves nodded and took a long drink of water. The moment lingered, and Reeves thought of all the things that needed to be done. Train tickets to purchase. How would they get on the train? Altogether, one at a time? Would Mama and Shel come, and would that be a help to have women mixed in to confuse the people looking for escaped *men*?

"Well. Good luck to you. I hope it all goes to plan."

Reeves nodded and stepped out on the porch for air.

A fire crackled out behind the house. In the dark that had settled in, Reeves sat on a stump and stared at the flames for a bit. He glanced occasionally at the freshly dug earth just beyond it and thought of the dead farmer almost as much as he thought of his Lydia Jane and the boys. The smell of the wood was sweet and dark, and he pictured himself throwing a log in the stove back home, Bernard and Andrew gathering around it to warm themselves from the snow outside. The aroma of fresh bread met his nostrils and he imagined turning to see his wife in the kitchen with a stew boiling, bread on the table cooling.

He looked inside and thought about the men and women there. The simple tenant that Zachary Coughlin had taught him in basic training kept coming back to him: *Use anything around you as a weapon if you can.* He wondered if the people in the little farmhouse were using him, or if he was using them. It wasn't a question he liked to ask.

31

In the late morning, most of them gathered at the dinner table and ate what they could scrounge for themselves. There was oatmeal, a few apples, bread and nuts. Reynolds continued to snore away out on the couch while the rest of the men regaled Shel and Mama with the tale of their daring escape from prison, life-and-death struggle with chewers in San Francisco, and their near-death at the hands of the prisoners firing at their boat.

"We left behind a considerable amount of money there. You don't get any of that? You'd have been set." Mama looked at Reeves. "You forget where we hid it?"

LaRue pointed to the couch. "He had two satchels. Saved the one full of the wrong kind of papers."

Shel got up and moved toward the bag near the couch and lifted it, scrounging inside.

"Have you read these papers?" Mama lifted a stack of documents and waved them at Reeves.

"No," Reeves said.

"None of them?" Mama's brow dipped.

"Once I found out it wasn't full of currency, the bag full of paper didn't seem quite so alluring." He tried to make the failure of losing the money into a joke, but it still smarted.

Shel moved to take a page from Mama, curious. Mama jerked them back and held them to her breast. "You sure?"

"We really didn't have time for manifests and assignments and whatnot," Reeves said. "I just want to do what we planned and make my way home. I told these men we'd go home to our families."

Shel was silent for moment, with one hand still slowly falling away from where the papers had been. "What's so important?"

"See, that's just it. The San Francisco operation was our central location. During the war and after, they sent everything to us. They sent plans, orders—"

"I know all of this. I worked out of that office and others." Reeves worried about Mama's sudden turn. He feared she might have an irritable heart or some uncommon excitability.

"We also received correspondence from time to time. From families. It was rare that they let us do it, due to the sensitivity of what we do. These should have been destroyed before we left San Francisco. Out of respect. We left so quickly, but Coughlin swore he'd burn them as soon as he could," Mama said. "But I suppose he didn't think about it." She gathered the papers in an armload and walked with them toward the fireplace.

"Why are you in such an all-fire hurry to destroy those?" LaRue called from the table. He was eating mush and drinking something from a jug.

Before she threw them into the flames, Mama turned. "They're sensitive. They could have information on our assets still in the field. They could have the names of people we don't want exposed to scrutiny. Hell, they could land more soldiers on the firing lines for murder or other crimes. Present company included." She dropped the stack on a chair and grabbed a handful of papers, tossing them into the fire.

"We're not at war, who would care?" LaRue shoveled another spoonful of food into his mouth.

"There could be retribution from the North."

The spoon clanked into the empty bowl. "So, why don't you take them instead of destroying them? If they're so important?"

Mama tossed another stack of papers in. "We're behind enemy lines here, in point of fact. The OMO may have a strong presence, but this area is legally held by the North. If I got caught, it would compromise our efforts past, present and future." She threw the rest of the papers she'd brought and went back, picking up a few sheets that had fallen on the floor and she picked up the satchel and checked for more documents. Once she'd gathered the stragglers, she burnt them as well. She turned immediately and started checking the floor again. "That's all of them, I believe."

"You sure?" LaRue asked. "Want to look some more?"

Reeves stood. He'd had enough of the constant chatter, so much so that his head hurt. "Enough. Jesus LaRue, leave her alone. She's just doing her duty the best way she sees fit." Reeves watched as LaRue shot an angry glance, not at Reeves himself, but at Mama. Reeves walked through the kitchen and out the back door. He stood on the wooden porch and looked out into the empty countryside.

The mound of earth where they'd buried the farmer caught his attention and Reeves walked over. He sat down with his back resting on the nearby tree and stared at the dirt.

Patrick walked out, followed by Shel. "What're we doing?"

Reeves looked up at him. "Throw more into the bags." He stood up and stepped into the doorway. "Shel, we need to pack up what we can, and head for town to buy the tickets." He watched Shel assess the other men as they came out, and she seemed to resign herself to wait.

"So, we're going to wait around again?" LaRue said. "There's tasty hooch here, but it ain't that good."

"No." Reeves pulled the money from his pocket and felt its heft, and then waved it around for all to see. "There's just enough here to get us on a train to the East. Next one comes along in a couple of days, a quick ride on a locomotive and we're home."

"I still want to ride an airship. That would be the life, now wouldn't it?" Reynolds was staring at the money as he spoke. Reeves thought the man might drool.

"Pack up the supplies. Shel, Mama and I will leave soon. LaRue and Patrick will follow in a few hours. Reynolds will wait a day or so and meet me then. Shel will meet LaRue and Patrick at the station with their tickets, I'll meet Reynolds at a restaurant downtown across from the station. We'll board separately, travel in different train cars and—" Reeves lowered his voice. "God willing we'll never see each other again."

"This is assuming you want to go home with us." Reeves eyed Mama and Shel.

"We've got a spell to decide." Mama eyed some silverware in the kitchen drawer, held it up to the light, then shoved it in her coat pocket.

"The rest of you find anything valuable, in case we need to sell it for quick money. Shel, how about you try to pack up food for us?"

"I'll keep looking for valuables, thanks." Shel walked into the nearest bedroom and disappeared.

"I'll do it," LaRue said on the way to the kitchen. "I'm all for food duty right now."

In a matter of minutes, they'd packed, and the first group was out the door.

Reeves left with every intention of heading straight for the station to buy his tickets and get as far away as he could from Santa Rosa and the west coast.

32

Reeves pushed the glass of water away with a polite smile. He scanned the room to see who might inadvertently hear his conversation. Nobody. A couple had left just as he'd come in, but that was it. No one had replaced them. Something was cooking, or maybe it was the smell of something the departing couple had eaten that was lingering in the room. Reeves thought it was maybe ham with eggs. It was a beautiful open-air restaurant, with a wonderful breeze flowing in. But it was empty. Not a soul. The crowds passed by outside the windows, but none came up the steps.

Reeves and the others had snuck into Santa Rosa using Mama and Shel's shortcut through the fence. They walked into town and immediately split up with plans to meet at a hotel near the train station. Reeves figured it would be good for perceptions if they weren't seen together until they got on the train. He'd intended on getting a drink and buying supplies for the trip, food and the like. He accidently, or unconsciously, found himself passing the restaurant that belonged to Hirim Calloway. The man responsible for double crossing Reeves' team. The man who turned Reeves' life end-over-end. At first Reeves walked on by and continued toward the airship tower and the city beyond. Then he slowly shuffled back, stood at the step, and waited. Then he went in.

"It's a shame, isn't it?" Theresa Calloway said.

"Sorry?"

I noticed you looking around. It's not always this empty. You just caught us at a bad time. We're just opening, and no one has quite found us yet," Theresa said. "Plus, it's been so hot. No one wants to come out in this weather."

The temperature had been absolutely glorious by Reeves' mind. "I'm sure it is a fickle business."

It was a moment before she responded. "It can be. It can be." She took a drink of her own water and put the glass back on the table. She pushed the glass around until it was perfectly centered on the coaster. "How do you know my husband again?"

"Old friend. We were in the war together."

"Mister don't lie. He wasn't in no war. None of them." Theresa looked amused at the thought of her man fighting anyone.

"Well, we knew each other at the time of the war," Reeves said, hoping the correction would stick. "So, Hirim is somewhere about?" He looked around the empty restaurant again, just in time to see a young woman in a dark blue dress emerge from the kitchen and approach the table. Reeves took her for a waitress at first, but she moved far too quickly and with far too great a sense of purpose.

"Mrs. Calloway?" The girl's yellow hair was pulled back tight in a high braid and her fingernails were clean. Her lips neither curled up in a smile, nor hung down in a frown. These were the things that Reeves noticed now. He'd been stuck on an island for years with nothing but men, and here, finally alone in a room with two women, he found himself making note of hair, nails and lips.

"Mr. Calloway is in the garden, with the birds," the woman said. To Reeves, she emphasized the word 'birds' a little more than she needed to. "He'd like you to join him."

Theresa sniffed and looked up at the lattice ceiling. "Did you tell him someone was here for him?"

"I did."

Theresa looked around the room for a moment and then stood, flattening her floral print dress as she did. "Well, then. Let me show you the way."

"I can take him for you ma'am. No need to leave the restaurant," the girl said.

"Thank you, Beatrice, no. We can take him together. You and I can discuss tonight's menu on the way back."

Theresa walked toward the patio dining area and Reeves fell in behind her, with Beatrice following a few paces after. He looked around as they stepped outside into the sunny California morning. The Carbondale had an inspiring view of the city of Santa Rosa. The beautiful buildings, the harbor beyond. Two airships floated gracefully over the water, headed in opposite directions. He tried but couldn't make out any distinguishing flags or markings from the distance.

Theresa put her hand on a railing as she went down some stairs, and Reeves realized how new the wood was; the sea air should've torn it up and blasted the colors from it, but it remained pristine. The same was true of the outdoor tables and chairs. They appeared in almost-new condition.

"It's a wonderful business you have here," Reeves said. He wondered how much of the appearance was meticulous upkeep and how much was disuse.

The compliment brought a smile to Theresa's face and she slowed a bit. "Thank you. We've worked hard to get it the way you see it now. There was a… well… a fire and some other unpleasantness in this very area. Buildings were falling down and abandoned. It was quite a mess. No one wanted to touch it."

"No one had the means to clean it up until Mr. and Mrs. Calloway came along," Beatrice said.

"Oh, thank you, Beatrice. That's kind." Theresa opened a gate and they all stepped onto the sidewalk. "We only wanted to see Santa Rosa restored to its former glory. If you look across the street a piece, you'll see some buildings that still stand even though they're unusable. My husband bought the patch across the street and made it a public garden, but there are still those—those eyesores with too much fire damage to fix. I'd think the city could find a way to knock them down and make it more pleasant through here." They walked toward the airship tower as Theresa continued to talk. "Most of this property was owned by a businessman that died a couple of years ago. I'm sure you heard about it. Everybody heard about that."

"I haven't been around much." Reeves was focused on the tower. There were flags hanging from a number of points around it. He saw the familiar flags of the Federals, one that was a slight variation on the flag of the Confederacy that he was familiar with, and a third that he didn't recognize.

"Oh, surely you know the story. It was absolutely a spectacle. Exploding airship? Giant lizard? The chewers roaming the streets? Eating people and whatnot?" Theresa stopped and stared expectantly at Reeves. "Are you having a joke with me?"

Reeves shook his head and smiled. "I wouldn't talk shit to you ma'am, I've been away." They started moving again, passing the airship launch, walking beneath the lightly wafting flags that hung over the entrance. There were bronze nameplates next to the wide doors that brought his attention.

United States of America Western Air Operations Station-First Floor
Sheriff's Office – First Floor
Office of Military Operations-Second Floor
Volunteer Signing-Third Floor
Viewing and Observation for the Public-Fourth Floor

A smaller, less ornate sign was hanging below the others declaring volunteers accepted daily at ten every morning.

Three men in dark uniforms that Reeves didn't recognize walked past his group and proceeded up the steps and into the building. Their uniforms bore the same unrecognizable flag that he'd seen flying from the building.

Beatrice caught him staring. "The Calloways donated to help renovate that tower as well. It was getting to be an eyesore."

"Now Beatrice, let's not bore the man with our charitable works. I'm sure my husband will bore him soon enough." She pointed to some sort of storefront. "He's right in here."

It looked like a ticket taker's booth was built into the structure next to the wide entranceway. "What's this?"

"Another building we took over. Used to be a circus and a zoo and such. Filthy," Theresa said.

"Smelled like boiled cabbage and cow shit." Beatrice turned red immediately as she realized what she'd said.

"Well put," Theresa said. "And watch your tongue."

"Yes ma'am."

"You honestly don't know this place? I guess you have been way out of town. People came from all over. Paid good money to see the freaks and animals and whatnot." Theresa walked carefully up some steps as though they were covered in dung.

They all stepped through the doors, but there was no "inside"; whatever structure had been there had been torn down and walking through the door frame led to huge gardens lined with hedges and tall flowers. The scent of roses hit Reeves' nose for the first time in too many years, the sweet aroma filled his senses and he thought he would swoon. But noise and movement ahead brought him back to the moment. Ahead, in the middle of the gardens, at the center of the winding paths, was a group of cages surrounded by rows of benches. Four men sat loudly laughing with each other and watching one of the enclosures.

"The mister," Beatrice said from behind Reeves.

"And those damn birds." Theresa walked along the central gravel path as it wound through the flowers and short trees. Bees buzzed among the various petals, creating a steady hum in some areas, but Reeves heard it; the loud screech of several birds. It sounded a lot like a murder of crows in a frenzy of some sort, a little like that birds in the burnt-out building, but louder and more intense. But it wasn't like anything he'd heard before.

Reeves discovered the sound came from inside the cage that the men were watching. He could see the black birds fluttering around inside, diving and cawing to each other. As they got a little closer, he could see what they were attacking; there was a single chewer inside, its clothes in tatters, pressing itself against the bars, reaching for the men, all the while being attacked by a half a dozen of the winged menaces. They pecked and flapped, cawing and cackling as they dove and tore at the creature, pulling flesh, ripping the thing's hair away in strips and bits.

The men roared in laughter.

"Hirim?" Theresa called. No one answered her, so she increased her volume. "Dammit, Hirim." All the men turned and looked.

The one in the middle spoke. "Jesus, Theresa, what is it? Can't you see we're working?" He was lanky, and his blonde hair was matted against his head with sweat.

"Anyone can see that." Theresa rolled her eyes. "This man says he's a friend of yours, but he's a might fuzzy on the details."

Hirim glanced at Reeves and then looked back to the cage. "Don't know him. Henry? Can you get rid of him?" The largest man of the group stood and placed his bowler hat on the bench before approaching Reeves.

"It's funny we'd meet at a place like this. A garden? Reminds me of a song we used to sing way back during the war. How'd it go?" Reeves knew damn well how it went. He'd rehearsed it for months leading up to the mission he'd left on that fateful day. On the island, the lyrics rang in his head over and over.

Reeves stood his ground as Henry advanced.

"The fires are flickering low.
Still are the sleepers that lie around,

As the sentinels come and go."

It took an extra second, but Reeves could see the recognition wash over Calloway's face. *"Tenting on the Old Camp Ground."*

"That's it. How does that last part go again?"

Calloway looked carefully at Reeves before starting.

"Many are lying near;
Some are dead, and some are dying,
Many are in tears."

His wife laughed. "I've never heard you sing that song once in your life, Hirim. How do you even know it?"

"Maybe you all should excuse us."

Theresa turned cross quickly. "I thought you said you'd never met this man."

"I haven't."

Mrs. Calloway snorted. "You're an odd bird, Hirim." She stared at him as she and Beatrice retreated back toward the entrance.

After the women had walked away with more than a little reluctance, and all the men but Henry had stepped off into the distance, Calloway began to circle Reeves, eyeing him from toe to top.

"Look at you. A specter from the past. A ghost. Come to do what? Come to ruin me? Come to tell all the good folk of Santa Rosa about my troubled youth?" Calloway said. "Is that it? Are you here to do grievous harm to my reputation?"

Behind Reeves, Henry shifted his position, his boots crunching the stones as he moved.

"I don't know what you mean," Reeves said.

"That song and the response. I don't know where you got it, but I don't enjoy being intimidated."

"I'm not sure what you're driving at. I'm not here for anything other than information."

"Information?"

It had been a long time ago, but the plan was fresh in Reeves' mind. "I was the leader of the team infiltrating the *U.S.S. Eagle Peak.*" The man didn't believe him. Reeves saw it in his eyes. "The ship unloaded us off the coast of California near San Francisco. We were all to make land, meet you and Moose, and load everything onto a coach and get it home to the Confederate capitol to help fund the war."

It took a moment for Calloway's face to soften. "Really? You were supposed to lead that mission?" He leaned back, curious now. "That would make you Harvey Reeves."

"Yes."

"Yes? *Yes?* Well where have you been? That was nearly a decade ago. You never met with us. Word was all hands were lost when the navy boarded that ship."

"Some were killed. Some were captured. I don't know where the rest of them went, but I ended up on Alcatraz Island. I've been held there ever since." Reeves took a deep breath. He saw no need to expound on the details of the years he was gone. No need to mention the men who starved, who drowned trying to escape, those who just gave up. And at this point, no need to mention that three other men had come aground with him and were waiting at a farm outside the city. Not yet. "What's your story?"

"What's my story?" Calloway ran his tongue over his lips. "You don't know who I am?"

"I know your name."

Calloway laughed and looked at Henry, who had moved closer than Reeves realized. "He wants to know my story. You want to know how I spent the last decade or so? When your team got done, I went to ground. I hid out with anyone who would take me in. I assumed that whoever double-crossed you, also gave MY name to someone and they were after me. Some of the Knights of the Golden Circle took me in and kept me safe. Luckily, the chewer outbreak gave everyone something else to think on for a while."

Shel had mentioned that Calloway was somewhat of a philanthropist and businessman. For a man that had buried himself out of fear of arrest, something had eventually gone right. "For all that hardship, it looks like you somehow did well for yourself. The restaurant, the charity work. That's better than the rest of us on that mission came out," Reeves said. "I mean. However, did you land on your feet?"

"I'm not sure what you're implying, but I worked for my money. Started sweeping floors at a feed store. Saved and sacrificed. I worked."

"That must have been a lot of sacrifice."

"You missed out on all the horrible things that happened. You got to avoid all the fighting and dying. You're one of the lucky ones." Hirim nodded and looked closer. "The apparent lone survivor of that secret mission and here you sit, more like a ghost than anything."

"None of the soldiers from that mission ever came to see you?"

"Not a one."

"Never heard from them?"

Calloway shook his head gravely. "Not a one."

Reeves stood up and moved a few steps back the way he'd come. "So, the Confederacy never got their money?"

"No they did not."

"Would it have made a difference to the war?"

"With the chewers making their appearance the way they did? Not really, not so much to the war effort," Hirim said. "But it surely would have put them in a strong bargaining position once the truce was discussed. As it was, they had to concede a good amount of land to the Yankees hereabouts in the West."

"Well. Thank you for your time, sir. I'd best be on my way and see where the wind takes me."

"That's really it? You honestly just wanted to give me an age-old passphrase, and ask a few questions?" Calloway patted his hair, making sure it was in place, and then wiped his hands on his suit.

"No. I hadn't planned to come here at all. I was on my way out of town when I saw your establishment and recalled someone telling me you owned it." Reeves moved down the path a few steps, but something nagged at his mind. "Did anyone ever figure out who exposed our plot? Do you know who warned the Federals we were coming?"

With a sigh, Calloway shrugged his shoulders. "No. I'm afraid not."

"All this time. You were running around with Knights and lowlifes, but you never went looking for information? No one ever whispered an inkling of what might have happened?"

"No."

"Oh. What about your team? Did any of them get caught?"

"They scattered and ran, like I did."

"But they didn't get caught?"

Indignance spread across Calloway's face. "Are you suggesting they were cowards or something for running?"

"No. Just asking questions."

The crows in the cage were picking at the now still chewers eyes and exposed cranium, squawking happily, wings fluttering in contentment.

"I went looking." Reeves watched the birds as he spoke. "Everyone I asked said you were the one that turned on us. Some men in prison swore they'd heard through acquaintances that you sold us out and made off with the gold yourself. You, Moose, and that lady friend of yours."

Calloway's face darkened, and he stood. "You see here, I am sorry as hell at what happened to you, but I won't have a criminal like you accuse me of something like that in my own place of business."

Henry reached into his coat but before he could draw a weapon, Calloway stilled him with an open hand.

"I am not unsympathetic to your plight, but I'm not the cause of your incarceration." Calloway took a deep breath and looked toward the ground. "And believe me, I'm powerful sorry about what happened to your family while you were in that hellish place. But I can't—"

In a snap, Reeves felt his chest tighten and his hands get cold as he reached out for Calloway. "What? What did you say?"

"I said I was sorry that—"

"About my family."

Calloway stammered as Reeves managed to snag him by the lapel. Henry reached in and tried to pull the two apart.

"I thought you knew." Calloway choked.

A pain in his side told Reeves that Henry had changed to punching rather than trying to just pull the two apart. Reeves turned, swung wildly and missed Henry altogether, but the assailant let go. Reeves focused and landed two jabs to Henry's face, then a solid punch to his gut, sending him on his ass.

Reeves turned back to Calloway, who was trying to regain his breath. "What do you mean after what happened to my family? What happened?"

Hands in front of him, Calloway backed off as he spoke. "I thought you knew. I assumed you got word in prison." He coughed before he could continue, hands still waving in front of him. "They died after you went to prison. They all got sick with the lung disease."

Reeves felt dizzy and unsure on his feet. "How? How the hell do you know this?"

Still hoarse, Calloway replied "Mama told me a few weeks after you went to jail."

His legs nearly failing him, Reeves turned and walked toward the gate. Henry struggled to stand and reached out. Without missing a stride, Reeves kicked the man square in the ribs before moving on.

33

Shel was waiting outside the train station, hands crossed in her lap, sitting on a bench. She showed no sign she recognized Reeves, even when he sat down. "Did you kill him?"

He was surprised by the question, and further startled to wonder why he hadn't even considered it. "No. I'm trying to get out of town with as few entanglements as possible, remember?"

"Did you hurt him at all?"

"Again, the law would take a dim view of that, I believe."

Shel continued looking off in the distance, the very picture of a proper lady in the morning sun. "So, we're leaving on the next train? We could do it, just me and you. Those others are going to drag you down, but I'm your good luck charm."

"Any word from the others?"

"Nope. I'm assuming all is going to plan and everyone else is where they're supposed to be."

"And Mama?" Reeves looked around to see if she was anywhere close.

"Still in the hotel where I left her, far as I reckon.

"Did she send you to check on me? She think I'd leave without her?" Reeves fixed his hair and brushed his jacket as he spoke.

"She says you'll come back."

"She seems to know me pretty well."

"You can prove her wrong," Shel said. She nodded toward the ticket taker. "We can leave and never come back. Take me east and show me the land of Dixie and whatnot."

Despite the ache in his stomach that said he should move on and hop on that train, Reeves shook his head. "She knows me pretty well." He could see a vision of his family before him—their small home, their little plot of land. "I'm staying. We're going to get everyone to notice us. We're going to meet the president and make sure our names aren't left under the march of history."

Shel laughed. "What? I thought you were leaving to see your wife and little cubs. That's all you've said since we met. Now you're willing to take a chance on the kindness of the president and the Office of Military Operations?"

The plan changed because everything else changed. When he left Calloway's garden, Reeves wandered, limbs thick, and head cloudy like a thunderstorm. He drifted to the docks and the market, bumping into people and stumbling on the uneven streets. The idea struck him while he leaned against a wall to rest somewhere near the bars and hotels of the fancier district. He had nothing to return to other than a home, and even that might not be there. So maybe Mama had hit on an idea. Maybe people *should* know his name. The Confederates that had sent him into battle, the Office of Military Operations that had left him to rot in the prison long after the war had ended, all of them. And he surely would make sure Mama got her meeting with the president. That would be the most important thing.

He ran through ideas in his head as he walked. He considered the few assets he had on hand, the equipment, the personnel. He didn't have much going for him in Santa Rosa, too many people whose loyalties he was unfamiliar with, too much land to cover, no—if he was going to be successful, the fight would need to take place on his terms.

It was sheer coincidence, he assumed, that he wound up at the train station. It seemed perfectly reasonable that Shel would be there, out of her less desirable clothing and sitting in a neatly pressed green floral dress. It was stolen, he assumed, and about three sizes too large, but it was perfect for her. What very little he knew of her, it was perfect.

"Let's talk to Mama. I have a few ideas on how to get her the attention she wants and how to get her a meeting with the president," Reeves stared up at the rooftop of the train station, at the group of dark birds that had gathered there. Their heads twitched and bobbed in agitation and they snapped their bills like shears. "Those birds are everywhere."

"Sure seems like it," Shel said. "But the OMO seems to be having just a bundle of good luck using them to clear out them chewers." She stood up and they were walking, headed back the way Reeves had come.

"Those old men that Mama wants to save and get home—you know much about them, about their service?"

"I've been there a stretch, I know them well enough. They generally don't talk too much about the war and whatnot." She twisted the pleat of her dress as she walked.

"Any of them work with explosives that you know of?"

Shel thought about it for a moment, but no longer. "I can honestly say that subject has not come up around our breakfast table that I can recall."

"I guess we'll have to bring it up then," Reeves said. They walked in silence back to the little tenement Mama and the soldiers called home.

Mama smiled a shit-eating smile that told Reeves she knew he'd be there. She wore a dark dress and her hair was fixed high like she was going to dinner with King Louie. The place smelled like stew and biscuits. "This is easy. This is nothing," Mama said. "Nothing. I been here waiting for a way out. You're it, son. You're it."

The crackle of the fire interrupted Reeves' thoughts. "Nothing?"

"That man Calloway took your life from you. Took mine from me. Double-crossed us all." Mama picked up a poker and moved the coals around with it. "Killing him is nothing."

That got his attention.

"You know I'm right. I don't know why you didn't do it earlier," Mama said. "He got some of our men shot, took that gold and blamed it on you. Hell, he could'a got you killed too. I'm stuck here—"

"I don't understand that part. How are you stuck here? There's a peace treaty, and it's been years since this gold job went wrong. Nobody cares anymore. You can board a train easy as anyone."

One of the logs flared up in their hearth and Mama moved it around with the poker, causing sparks to careen into the air. "You happy with everything you done during the war? I mean, are you solid in your belief that every task you've performed in the duty to your country is just and true? Will the good Lord welcome you with open arms when your time comes?"

For all the time Reeves had been in the service of the Confederacy, he'd been able to justify his work in the name the greater good of his country. He'd been able to forget most of it, all but a small handful of deeds. Those deeds woke him some nights. Over the course of seven years in prison, he'd even been able to analyze those and blame them on someone else's orders. But that didn't erase that he'd been the one to physically do them. His hands had the blood on them, even if it was someone else that said it was fair to do the deeds. His training made him a spy, a soldier and an assassin, and he was okay with those first two jobs. Murder was what kept him awake.

"Thinking about it?" Mama said. "Well imagine all those things you did and pile on that many again, and then again. I been at this a damn sight longer than you." Mama put the poker back where it belonged and stood. "I didn't get where I am by shaking hands and smiling." She groaned as she stood up straight. "God. My back is knotted and twisted. I need to go to bed."

"What about the others? Those soldiers? Couldn't you take some of the money that you were stealing and send them back one by one or something? They aren't highly sought-after war criminals. Surely no one would give a shit if they headed home."

"I'm going to bed." Mama walked slower than she had earlier.

"Need help?" Reeves rose and reached for her elbow.

"I don't need no help," she said as she swung her arm at him. "Don't touch me." She kept on until she reached her room and paused to lean on the doorframe. "I took care of important missions for the Confederacy. Coordinated attacks, planned secret missions; things that meant life and death. People's lives depended on me and what happened when the war ended? They left me. Just like you. They left me to rot. I hear they got most of their other coordinators out, but not me. In my youth, I could've gotten myself out of here, but if you haven't noticed, I'm not exactly a pony in the pasture anymore."

"And the others?"

"Did they look like spring flowers to you? I could send them all home, sure. They wouldn't even survive the trip." She turned and disappeared into the darkness of her room, then came back a second later. "And if they did, who exactly would take care of them without me?"

"Don't they have families?"

"How the hell would I know?"

"Doesn't the government have hospitals for soldiers?"

"Jesus. They'd be dead in a week." She waved his idea aside. "No, these people need me. I won't abandon them. If you don't want to help, I'll find some other way."

"I will help. That's why I came back. But it has to be done by my design. I'll get you to see the president, hell I'll even get him to welcome you with open arms, AND I'll make sure these men get home just fine, but it has to be my plan." He looked over at Shel, and then to Mama again. "That's the way it has to be."

The old woman waved him aside on her way to her room. "Then I guess I'd best rest."

As her door slammed, George emerged from one of the other rooms. "We may not be whole, but we ain't children. We can still fend for ourselves." He limped into the kitchen and grabbed a bowl. "I don't believe I heard Mama offer you any food. There's a fish soup on the stove. It's not bad." He ladled some for himself and sat at the table with Shel and Reeves. After his first bite, his beard was white with drips of his watery meal.

With one hand, Reeves refused any for himself, but leaned forward, ignoring the mess George was making. "Look, if I'm going to pull this off and get us all home, I need someone with some experience with explosions and munitions to help me out. Any of this crew fit that description?"

"Shel? You mind handing me a biscuit? They're on the table behind you?" George nodded toward the counter as a stream of soup dribbled out of his mouth. "You know, Mama says we couldn't make it without her, but we're fine. Andre made this soup. He's a great cook. Makes stews, soups, he can cook uhh… let's see. Pie. We got a bunch of berries one time and he made a pie out of them."

"What did you do—"

"Abner. Abner used to be in munitions. He used to fire the cannons off a ship. I think he was on the *Tupelo*, maybe. Says that was a loud job. Doesn't hear so good now. Abner." He nodded as Shel handed him his biscuit.

The Tupelo was a smaller attack boat with the Confederate navy. Reeves remembered it had seen frequent action up the east coast near Union waters. "Anybody work on airships?"

A wet laugh erupted from George. "Never get me up in one of those things, that's for god damn sure."

"Yes, but—"

"Saw a guy fall outta one of them." He held a chunk of his biscuit high in the air and dropped it down into this soup. "Right down onto the ground in front of me." He scooped the crumbs up with his spoon and shoveled it into his mouth. "Gruesome. That's what it was."

Reeves stared at George and wondered about the man's fitness to help with the mission ahead. If he had anxiety or nostalgia, he wouldn't be much good to anyone. "Where are the others now?"

George shrugged.

"Probably out in the back," Shel said. "They like to get out in the sun in the afternoons when they can." Shel pointed toward the front door and led him to the stairs.

"Wilhelm used to fly a spy balloon," George said. Ain't no airship, but he flew."

Outside, Reeves stopped to talk with Shel. "Are they all like that? All addled and scattered? Is that why Mama doesn't think they'd live without her?"

"You try being old as Lot with parts of your body blown clean off, you'd be a little off your nut, too," Shel said. She started walking around their building with long, purposeful strides. "They're fine. They have good days and bad, but they're fine."

Reeves stared after, wondering if he'd catch them on the good days, and how reliable they were on their bad days.

34

The engines of the OMO airship roared to life at the tower, and the group looked up to see it.

"I don't want to do this, Reeves," LaRue said. "I just want to go home. Let's just go home." He spoke in a whisper, so the others wouldn't hear. "We gave our service. We did our time. Let's just go."

Reeves had anticipated someone in the group, more than one probably, balking. "Go home to what?"

"My mother. My sister. I want to go home."

"I understand that. I understand that. But how do you want to get there? As a man with his tail between his legs? Or as a hero of the Confederacy?" He waited to see how his would land with LaRue. The man seemed simple enough and love of country had gotten them this far.

Shel looked concerned. She looked up at the airship at the top of the tower.

"I don't know. I just want to go home." He looked over at the open door across the street. There were men trickling in now. They walked up the stairs quickly, packs across their backs, without pause.

"Look. It's time. You need to go." Reeves nodded toward the building. "We're going home. I'm looking for someone to help us with transportation. You've done the hard part. You just need to finish what's begun."

"I—"

"There's no time to go through all of this again." Reeves said. "It'll be over in the next day. *One* day. I'll have our way home squared, and you will have struck a blow for the south. We'll all return to the South to the cheers of our long-lost friends and family."

LaRue looked to Shel and she nodded.

"Promise," Reeves said. "You just have to go." He reached into the man's satchel and unwrapped the lump of coal there. "All you do is drop it in the ship's coal bin. That's all you do."

George had been mostly correct in his assessment of the other people's roles in the Confederacy. Abner had been a gunner on the *Tupelo* and had a hand in other munitions projects. They'd sat down and talked about the easiest explosives they could create together – coal torpedoes. A soldier could take a good-sized lump of coal, hollow it out, fill it with an explosive substance, cap it with more coal and drop it into a furnace, a boiler, an engine, a stove, or just a bin. The enemy eventually needs it for fuel, or heat and after the outer shell burns away, the explosives inside ignite, and cause a hell of a lot of damage. The Red Gears had refined the art of the coal torpedo by changing up what they put inside; they could create excessive black smoke for cover, noxious chemical clouds, or pack the explosives in such a way that they would cause immense explosions.

They gathered what supplies they had on hand and sent Shel out for the rest. They collected ammunition and tore some of it apart for the gunpowder, found bottles and whatever oil she could walk away with. They worked into the night to be ready for the next day. It was an ambitious plan, that relied on everyone from Mama's camp doing their best, and the other escapees doing the rest. Reeves had managed to weave a plan that served his needs, while advancing what Mama wanted. It was hastily imagined and hinged on so many things going right.

"Dirt simple, friend." Shel patted LaRue on the shoulder. "Get in, drop that thing into a bin and then make an excuse and get out of there."

LaRue took a deep breath, then reached into his inside jacket pocket, and leaned close—sliding a folded paper into Reeves' jacket. The man waited and looked into Reeves' eyes. There was more hesitation, and Reeves grew concerned. "Drop the coal in and then go about your training like they tell you. End of the day, you slip away and come home to us."

"And we all go home?"

"We all go home, LaRue," Reeves said. He put his hand on the opposite shoulder from Shel and they both guided LaRue to the door and Reeves pushed it open with his free arm. When LaRue was on the stoop, they pulled the pub door closed and moved away from the entrance. He and Shel moved back to their table and sat down calmly.

"He's not going," Shel said.

It seemed true. LaRue had moved down the three steps and was staring up at the ship overhead. "He'll go."

"What do we do if he doesn't?"

"Shit if I know. I guess we head back to the farm, shoot LaRue in the head somewhere along the way and get Reynolds to take his place." Reeves drank his beer. "Or we start all over with a new plan." There wasn't much room for change in his current plan, but Reeves could improvise.

"But we really will head east, right? You promised you'd take us with you." Shel sounded a little concerned.

In the street, LaRue had begun moving again. One step after another, he moved toward the entrance to the tower. He looked back once; stared straight at them through the window. Reeves hid his face in an attempt to avoid looking in his eyes. Shel mirrored his actions. They both laughed as though they were having a conversation, so as to not draw attention. Both focused on a painting on the opposite wall of a fat soldier in full Northern regalia. After a minute, Reeves glanced at the street out of the corner of his eye, just in time to see LaRue put his hand on the door to the tower and open it.

"He's going in," Reeves said. "He's doing it."

Shel turned and let out a breath. "Sweet Jesus, I thought he'd give us up with his mewing."

There was only a drop of beer left in his glass, but Reeves savored it, let the last of it trickle down into his mouth. He wondered why LaRue was so secretive about whatever was on the note. He decided to wait until he was quit of Shel before he looked at it. Tried to guess what that man would deem important enough to put on paper.

35

Cyrus stood in the lobby and marveled at the way the tower had been converted into a base of operations so completely. It was a beautiful, lavish place of business under its last owner, but now as he watched the latest batch of recruits tromp through the room, he saw how utilitarian it had become. The tapestries were replaced by signs, poorly painted signs directing the public and soldiers where they should go for complaints, quartermaster, sheriff, armory, and more. The only signs left from the former owners were the ornate ones directing people to the shitter and the elevator. It was orderly, at least. A body shouldn't have many questions when they came in.

The last of the recruits ascended the stairs, as directed by the sign with yellow letters, and Lowell turned to follow them. Today they'd get a chance to try out their wings and ride on the new patrol craft, the *Tunnel Hill*. It made it slightly easier to sort out the future airship crews from the soon-to-be foot soldiers, or cooks. He grabbed the rail and put his foot on the first stair when he heard the creak of the door behind him.

Standing with his pack at his side and his hands holding the strap was a new recruit Cyrus hadn't seen at any of the training before "Can I help you, buddy? Are you supposed to be reporting with the other new recruits?" He turned and stepped back, walking briskly to meet the man. "I'm Cyrus. I'm one of the—officers from the Office of Military Operations." He extended his hand in greeting. It felt weird to be presenting himself as a representative of anything.

The other man shook hands and stammered a greeting.

"And you are?"

"I'm—" The man paused, thinking. "I'm Bret—Uh. I'm Bret LaRue."

It was a strange thing to have to think about, Cyrus thought. You know your name, or you don't. "Need some help?"

"I don't think so." LaRue turned around to face the door and grabbed his pack.

Cyrus stepped in front of LaRue and tried to smile his best. "Let's just have a look around, why don't we? The other volunteers are already headed up to the launch, so you're a little behind." With an easy wave, Cyrus indicated the elevator. "What say we take the lift? I'm supposed to make new recruits walk the stairs for discipline, but let's make an exception." He was practically dragging LaRue when he stepped forward and slid the gate aside for the elevator and got on with LaRue in tow. Once they were onboard, Cyrus slammed the gate shut and pushed the lever forward to set the conveyance in motion. It took a moment as the ropes went taut somewhere above them before the box started upward.

There were better things to be doing than leading men by the hand up to something they were supposed to be volunteering for. *Either you were in or you weren't* Cyrus thought. He tapped his fingers against the wall of the elevator and sighed as the thing dragged itself at a snail's pace. He nodded at LaRue and tried to think of something to say.

LaRue hugged his pack in front of him and looked around in panic as they went upward, and Cyrus was wondering if the recruit would even make it through the airship orientation. Probably heave his lunch on the deck before the day was over, but they had orders to make them try, though. Get the men to ride on one patrol, just to see if they had a feel for it. After that they could try another area, like cannon preparation, prison guard, chewer furnace tender, whatever suited them. The men today were mostly applying for the coastal patrol, but some might have higher aspirations after training.

The elevator jerked to a halt with a loud scraping of metal on metal, and LaRue yelped.

"Sorry about that. One of these days, they'll find a way to make this thing a little more pleasant," Cyrus said as he opened the elevator door. "Maybe they'll serve alcohol on the ride up."

LaRue nodded and stepped out onto the floor of the launch.

"I always liked music to calm myself," Lowell said.

"That's—That's a good idea." LaRue looked back at the elevator thought a moment. "They'd never fit a whole band in one of those."

Across the floor there was one wide open bay that led to the *Tunnel Hill*'s gangplank. The other men were lined up there at a table, checking in with Bethy. Next to them, men pushed carts loaded with supplies across the plank onto the airship. Cyrus watched food, water, coal and even a little ammunition roll slowly across the wooden bridge. He doubted the men would be allowed to fire any weapons, what with the shortage of gunpowder and all. What those men were putting on the ship probably represented a good quarter of the OMO's existing supply. In their first few weeks, most new soldiers in the OMO only had one bullet loaded in their guns, unless they brought their own from home.

"I found one of your lost sheep in the doorway downstairs."

The men all turned and parted so Bethy could see. "He does not appear to be wagging his tail behind him," she said. "In fact, he looks downright uncomfortable."

Terrified was the word that came to Cyrus' mind. "He's fine. You got a LaRue on your list?"

There was a clatter at the gangplank, as one of the carts tipped over, spilling logs across the floor. The soldier pushing the cart knelt and began to slowly attempt to reload the cargo on his own.

"Jesus. You men don't just stand there, help him out," Cyrus said. He pushed LaRue along and they both grabbed some wood to toss back in the pile. Cyrus thought it was odd that LaRue didn't want to let go of his bag, but it was hard to say what made the man so skittish.

There were eight men in the line. Between them, Cyrus, Bethy, and the soldiers pushing the carts, they got everything picked up quickly. As they were finishing up, Lowell looked around for anything they'd missed and found LaRue coming back from the nearby carts holding up a log.

"Missed one." He moved faster than Cyrus expected. "One rolled way over here." He kept his pack hanging at his side as he moved toward the cart and placed the last log on the top of the others.

"Didn't think anything went that far," Lowell said. He stared at LaRue for a moment as the carts got moving again.

"What was his name? LaRue? I don't see him." Bethy was already back looking at her list. "Let's get him in line with the others." When no one moved, she looked over at all the new recruits. "Get in line. All of you." Her voice was stern and impatient, large for her short stature, which startled everyone into lining up. All except LaRue.

"There a problem, Mr. LaRue?" Bethy walked over to him briskly and looked up at his face. "You need to be at the end of that line. Why aren't you?"

Cyrus watched as the man stammered and shook his head. Cyrus pulled out his watch and stared at it for a moment. They needed to get everyone on board and headed out to stay on schedule.

36

"He's not coming out," Shel said. She sipped her tea and continued to keep a polite smile on her face.

It was an eventuality they had considered. "He'll be fine. If he's stuck for some reason, he'll get out when he can. He has the rendezvous point. I told him to just blend in and join us after the day's training if he had to."

"Would they arrest him?" Shel asked. "If they caught him in some lie?"

"For what? Carrying a piece of coal?" Reeves stood and straightened his trousers and jacket. He stepped behind Shel and pulled out her chair for her as she stood. She smoothed her dress until it looked nice. They'd both bought the nice clothing at a sundry store up the street and had barely had time to remove the tags before changing in an alley. They looked quite a bit more presentable than when he was wearing the farmer's threadbare work clothing.

"He'll be fine. I'm sure they have recruits change their mind all the time. It's dangerous work." They paid for their refreshments and walked out onto the street. Reeves didn't look over at the tower to check for LaRue again and hoped Shel knew not to do it, either. There were lunch crowds roaming the streets, including men in OMO uniforms. Reeves wanted to avoid anything that would bring attention on them.

"Let's meet the others and get ready for the next phase," Reeves said. He let Shel lead him through the streets, she being more familiar with the area. They took a leisurely pace, no hurry, and quickly left the crowds. The skinny shops that lined the main thoroughfares turned to larger, dimmer store and warehouses, their stoops peopled by muscular men smoking and sitting on their asses.

Above them, one of the OMO airships rattled as it turned from the tower and made for the sea. It was a smaller craft, but still bore the OMO flag. Reeves marveled at how elegantly it floated there, carried by the breeze like a fat goose gliding across a pond. He hoped that LaRue had made it back and would be waiting at the designated meeting place.

When they arrived at the walkway that overlooked the bay, they found Mama, Patrick and Wilhelm, but no LaRue. Wilhelm was throwing chunks of stale bread to the seagulls that toddled along the wooden bridge. Some of them took flight to gain advantage in retrieving what he threw. Mama sat, greying red hair shifting in the ocean breeze, and leaned against the rail, half-dozing in the sun. Patrick stood a few feet away from the others, watching the tourists go by. Reeves couldn't help but think if he were in Patrick's place, he'd be scanning for soldiers, for OMO, for deputies, anyone who could grab him and take him back to prison. If he were Patrick, Reeves would be watching Mama and Wilhelm, wondering if they were going to double cross him. But Patrick was tipping his hat to ladies as they passed, nodding to the men. He was more concerned with feeling freedom again than with keeping it.

Patrick turned at Shel and Reeves' approach. "Where's LaRue?" Patrick asked.

"He's just going around a different route to make sure he isn't being followed." Reeves did his best to sound sure.

"I don't understand what this is about. All I want to do is get into the president's good graces. How is this helping us get ready for his arrival?" Mama still looked half-asleep or pained with a headache. She kept her eyes shut as she talked. "I think we should sit down and talk about this. Plan it together."

Calloway's words came back, and Reeves wondered who he could trust, who he *should* trust. He hadn't talked to Mama about his family, or about the things Calloway had said. "I'll make this work. I don't need to get anyone else involved. You trusted me to make things tick during the war, you can trust me now."

"I trusted you to lead a squad to steal some gold. That was not a good outcome. You didn't make that one tick so well, now did you?" Mama finally opened her eyes and stared at Reeves. The others did as well.

It stung coming from Mama. In training he'd been taught to follow her orders and make her happy. If Mama was happy, you were allowed to be happy. "Obviously, there were difficult circumstances in that one. People were working against me."

"You should anticipate that. It was your job to assume people were against you. The rest of your men knew that too. Always assume that."

It felt like good advice now, and he'd learned that lesson the hard way all those years ago. "I do," Reeves said. "I certainly do. Thank you for the reminder."

Off in the distance, the airship *Tunnel Hill* lazed across the sky, further and further out to sea, turning slowly and drifting. The ship was beautiful, and Reeves wished he was on it.

"So, what about it?" Patrick leaned in closer to Mama, Shel and Reeves. "I want to get home, and that train leaves tomorrow. I'd like to be on it. If that means getting on it without you, Reynolds and LaRue, I'm fine by it. These little missions you want us to do, they don't seem so helpful to our situation."

Crowds began to gather as the day wore on, and Reeves realized their conversation might not be as private as it was moments before. He lowered his voice "We're going to bring attention to the president's visit in the worst way, and once he arrives, we'll be able to point to our handywork and prove our worth to him."

"I don't understand." Patrick looked at the others. "Do you?"

Mama raised a hand to hush Patrick. "Just walk us through what you think the result of these little demonstrations will be, boy."

He'd given each team bits of his plan, just enough to keep them working in darkness of what the other was doing. He knew that he'd need to feed them more to keep it going, but he had no intention of unspooling the whole ball of yarn. "I was in prison for far too long. Once the war ended, the OMO should have helped secure my release, should have gotten us all off that rock, but they didn't. They all left us to rot." *And so did the Confederates*, Reeves wanted to add. "These side jobs get me a sense of revenge and make you look good to the president."

He looked at Mama for a reaction, but the sounds of screams and screeches brought all their attentions to where Wilhelm had been feeding the seagulls. Some crows had muscled in and tried to take the crumbs for their own, and when the gulls resisted, three of the crows attacked one of the grey birds, pecking and clawing at it until all four of them fell to the walkway, cawing bloody death. The crowd walking on the boardwalk parted to get away from the combatants, gasping and screaming at the scene. Reeves stepped closer, watching the dark birds' ferocity. "What in the name of Grant's beard is happening?"

"Oh, the damn doctors or inventors or whatever messed with something they shouldn't have," Mama said. "I hear tell the formula the OMO uses on the chewers came from this stock of experiments left over from the war. Doctor Poley was the fella's name. He was one of our most wanted targets during the war, but we never found him," Mama said. "He was slippery. And just a bastard, if his creations are any indication."

The winged menaces made Reeves uneasy. He'd seen what they did to that dead man in the dilapidated home, and knew they weren't just looking for chewers; they had a taste for something else. Maybe that formula awakened something, maybe it just melted their little minds, Reeves wasn't sure, but he knew from the moment he'd seen them at Calloway's that they could be useful for more than ending the monster menace.

With a sick squawk, the dark birds killed the gull on the deck in a cloud of dark and light feathers. The crowd that had gathered gasped and collectively brought their hands to their mouths in shock. When the three crows looked up at the men and women, they seemed half-crazed, emboldened by the fight and they all cawed at the people and flapped their wings in triumph. The largest bounced forward on bloodied talons and challenged the crowd with a throaty gurgle. Having seen the result of the previous fight, the good men and women ran from the bird, pushing and shoving each other to get away.

The other two turned to look at Wilhelm, but a sound in the distance, made them flinch and take flight. Out over the ocean, a bright burst of fire exploded out of the side of the OMO craft they'd watched leave just moments ago.

37

The airship *Tunnel Hill* fell from the sky with a grace that belied its situation. The decorative blue sails snapped slowly in the wind, giving the effect of forward motion and of intention. Truly, it wasn't until the vessel had dropped a good one hundred feet or more that the smoke began to billow from the port side and leave a wake that made the craft's distress all too clear to anyone watching. Its course into the ocean below became all too clear.

The men and women fleeing the crows stopped and looked up, forgetting the previous danger in favor of the great spectacle over the water. The birds had taken flight anyway, carrying bits of the gull with them, flapping away from the sound of the explosion. As more and more people pointed and murmured, they quickly made their way back around Reeves, crowding up to the railing.

Reeves extricated himself from the people that had gathered to see the spectacle on the boardwalk. They gasped and shouted. They'd come to see the volunteer coastal patrol show off the new toy they'd claimed from some pirates or smugglers or similar ilk. None other than the Office of Military Operations had assisted in refitting the airship and preparing it for a meaningful new existence in the service of the good people of the Western Coast. Those people would have to fend for themselves, Reeves reckoned. And it was only going to get worse.

Reeves didn't bother to watch the craft hit the water. The explosion was large enough and the boat small enough that there was really no way anyone could have made it through the blast. That didn't stop people from trying to help. He could hear boats already racing their engines up to speed to go out to try to save the crew and render assistance. There was a howl in the air that meant the fire brigade was getting involved.

"Let's meet back at the hotel," Reeves shouted to Shel and Mama. "No reason for us all to be seen together here." He left before they could respond. They'd asked for an accounting of the plan and he'd been fortunate enough to have a timely distraction from explaining further.

The smell of smoke from the boats' boilers blanketed the whole of the harbor area and Reeves quickened his pace. He was a salmon swimming upstream against the crowds that were on their way to see the spectacle. At the Mayfair hotel, some three blocks from the waterfront, he ducked into the elaborate entrance and climbed the stairs immediately to the left of the ballroom. Normally, in a fine hotel like this someone would have stopped him and asked if they could help him in some way, the front desk held all the room keys while the guest were out, but the chaos was so absolute that no one glanced at him, no one was even at their given post.

He climbed the stairs two at a time, knowing he had time to spare, but still eager to take his station. As Reeves came to the next floor, he made a left, following an escape route he'd planned earlier, in case anything went wrong, or he was noticed. From the nearby ballroom, a bride and groom emerged in full regalia to see what the commotion was. Reeves turned immediately at the end of the hall and stepped out onto the small smoking balcony. The air was cleaner here, though he feared the stench from the boardwalk would cling to his good suit. With a small breath, he paused and gathered himself. He pulled his waistcoat down into place properly. Straightened his hat. He stepped to the railing and leaned against it leisurely. In the distance he could see the boats approaching the flaming wreck far out to sea.

He took his eyes from that point out on the horizon and focused down to the point on the wooden walkway where he'd been standing just minutes before. The crowd had thickened there. Multiplied. Doubled and tripled. He couldn't see his previous vantage point at all.

Behind him, men in their wedding finery stepped out onto the porch to see what was happening, and they were followed by a stubby little man hauling what Reeves assumed was the camera brought along for the wedding photos. The man set up the tripod and affixed his camera, aimed it in the direction of the disaster. Adjustments were made.

"Sir?" Reeves addressed the photographer. "Sir? Are you going to take some photographs of the wreck?"

The man nodded. He appeared frustrated to have to speak with Reeves. "Yes, of course."

Reeves stepped back and leaned against the wall next to the door. He watched the photographer load the film and then the man began a little dance as he shuffled his feet and adjusted the angle and inclination of his gear. It was doubtful he'd get a good shot of the boats and the burning airship. It was quite far out in the harbor and Reeves could tell the man only had a lens for close-up pictures.

Reeves walked back into the hotel. He strode down the hallway and exited the establishment through a door on the other side. Here, things were calmer. The calamity hadn't quite spread here yet. He stepped into an alley and moved on to the next street. From there, he turned left, and quickly turned left again, bringing him to the cafe. He pushed his way in and calmly walked to the bar. No one glanced at him. He waved to the bartender and ordered a whiskey. As he downed the first that had arrived, he thought about what had just happened. LaRue had come through and the result was more than he'd hoped. The ship went down and at least a few of those onboard were dead, if not all. LaRue may have been onboard.

He waved for another drink and smiled when it was handed to him. He swigged it just as fast as the first. He could feel the warmth of the alcohol spread through his chest as it settled in. He dropped more money on the bar. He could feel the excitement of what they'd done spread through his chest and arms with the whiskey.

Reeves placed his bowler back on his head. A band started warming up in the dining area and when he looked up to see them, he noticed a figure at a table that made his back suddenly tense and ache. He had to be mistaken. He needed to leave and join the others, but he couldn't look away.

38

The Grey Bufflehead was the best restaurant Santa Rosa had to offer. Actually, it was more likely the best restaurant in Santa Rosa that Cyrus and Bethy could possibly afford. Even that was only made possible because of the extra work both of them had done outside of their duties. The Office of Military operations hadn't paid either of them properly in months. Cyrus had sold the tanned hides of animals they'd killed around Outpost Two-thirteen; deer and coyotes and whatnot. He'd worked with business owners to construct fences and build outhouses. Bethy trained men in the volunteer coastal patrol to shoot straight, perform sea rescues and, in some instances, how to swim. They took on odd jobs where their scheduled shifts allowed, seeing each other when they could. Cyrus hoped it would be worth the effort. In the corner of the restaurant, a small band of musicians were destroying one of Cyrus' favorite tunes with their off-key caterwauling.

"I'm not eating the stewed liver," he said.

"You don't have to. There's plenty of other things you can order," Bethy didn't look up at him.

"We eat liver every other day at the Outpost or the tower, where the hell do all these livers come from?"

"Look at all the other things you can eat." Bethy pointed to her own menu. "You can have this chicken with potatoes. That sounds good."

"Hash. Damn, I thought this was a fancy place."

Bethy finally looked at Cyrus. "Are you concerned that someone will force you to eat hash, or worried that you'll like it better than the hash you get back at the fort? Don't get used to it, we can't afford to come here for fancy hash. You'll have to settle for an elk steak or something here." She patted his hand and smiled. "Eat whatever the hell you want."

Cyrus scanned down the menu further. He was hungry, and everything sounded tasty, but he was still guilty about spending so much money after the effort. "I could try the salmon, I suppose."

"Are you sure? Because that might leave you with less to bellyache about." Her eyes glistened in the light when he met her gaze. "Can we not worry for a night? Hell, can we not worry for a couple of hours?"

Nothing would've given Cyrus more pleasure, but it was hard to shrug off the world's burdens when they were sitting in their black OMO uniforms, firearms at their sides. He'd had visions of her in a lovely floral dress and he in a comfortable shirt and vest, attire conducive to a sociable evening. He was surprised to find she didn't own a dress of any kind and hadn't had a desire to do so. Buying one for her would've been an added expense, and something she would've swatted him for. Their uniforms were the nicest clothes they owned, so they made it a military dress evening.

"Lamb? Lamb. I wonder what lamb tastes like? I've never had it," Bethy said. "I don't know."

Cyrus watched her eyes widen and shine as she mentioned each item that intrigued her, and he decided the expense was probably going to be worth it. Since they'd met, he'd not seen her as excited about such a simple thing as food.

The restaurant smelled like heaven; Cyrus smelled meat cooking as soon as he walked in, and the aroma of fish was undeniable. The mess halls he'd been in lately weren't terrible, but their smells were less desirable, even less identifiable.

"You're right. I'll have a buffalo steak. Why not?"

She smiled. "Good."

Cyrus watched as her expression faded and her eyes narrowed. "What's wrong?"

"There's a man over at the bar. He's staring at us."

Cyrus turned and scanned the far side of the restaurant until he found who she was talking about. The man was, indeed, openly gawking at them.

"You know him?"

There was a flicker, somewhere in Cyrus' mind that he couldn't place. He didn't recognize the man at all, but something suggested he should. "No ma'am."

She looked back down at her menu, but moved her other hand down under the table, Cyrus assumed, knowing Bethy, to the firearm resting at her side. "Well, he's coming over."

It was hard for Cyrus to read the man's face as he made his way past the other diners. He wasn't smiling, didn't look angry. His black suit and bowler fit well and appeared brand new, or well-cared for at minimum. There weren't any weapons visible on the man's person, but when Bethy's hand moved out of sight, Cyrus was sure she was preparing for the worst.

"Cyrus?" The man asked. "Cyrus Spencer?" His tone sounded happy, even if he wasn't smiling.

It took a moment for Cyrus to rise, but he decided that would be the best course of action. Good or bad, it would be best to be on his feet. "Yes?"

"My God, I didn't believe it was you. But here you are." The man finally cracked a grin that showed crooked white teeth. He removed his hat and put it under his arm, then smoothed his wavy brown hair with his free hand. He waited a moment. "You don't remember me. Of course not. It's been years." He stepped closer and extended his hand. "Harvey Reeves."

"Harvey Reeves. Good lord above. Harvey Reeves." Cyrus was dumbstruck by the realization of why he'd known the man from a distance. "How long has it been? I had no idea—"

"Whether I was dead or alive? We haven't seen each other since forever. When I went off to war," Reeves said. He turned to Bethy. "I'm sorry miss. Where are my manners? My name is—"

"Harvey Reeves. I heard that." She seemed mildly annoyed.

"Harvey, this is Bethy Nolan," Cyrus released the man's hand and motioned to Bethy as he spoke.

"A pleasure."

Reeves reached out to take her hand, but she drew it back. Her other hand was still at her side. "I'm pleased to make your acquaintance, mister Reeves."

There were so many things running through Cyrus' head that he wasn't sure where to begin in talking to Reeves. The man looked gaunt, his face thin and cheeks sunken. His hands were cracked and worn. Reeves never would have known him for the child he'd grown up with. Cyrus looked around, remembering their surroundings and then pulled out one of the extra chairs at their table. "Please, join us."

"I won't presume to interrupt your meal, but I thank you for the invitation just the same."

"You... You look well."

"Thank you. The war was a bit kinder to me than many of the others." He stared at Bethy as he spoke. "Some scars. Lost a few toes to the cold that first winter. I'd show you, but taking off my boots in an establishment like this would be impolite now wouldn't it?"

"What is it you do now, Harvey?" It was a ham-fisted attempt to change the subject quickly.

Reeves didn't miss a beat. "Bible salesman. I travel the country selling the word of God to all the good in need of salvation."

"Selling the word of God? Don't most pastors *give* the word of the Almighty away to whoever is in need?" Bethy took a drink of the water they'd left in front of her earlier. Slowly her other hand came to rest on the table. But the way it was lightly tapping on the white tablecloth told Cyrus that she was prepared to go for her gun if she needed.

"Didn't say I was a man of the cloth. I'm a salesman. I sell mostly to schools and churches and larger groups." Reeves reached out and touched Cyrus' shoulder then, running his hand over it lightly. "Speaking of larger groups—what is this you're wearing, Cyrus Spencer? It looks for all the world to me to be a uniform from the Office of Military Operations. Could that be true?"

"It is."

"Now how could that be? Did they find you some nice quiet job where you can sit in a cozy quartermaster's office, handing out blankets and tin cups? Have they taught you to fill out muster rolls and pay records in the back room of a barracks somewhere?"

Cyrus swallowed and shook his head. "No. I'm one of the crew of the flagship. I'm with the *Polk*."

Reeves opened his mouth wide and looked from Cyrus to Bethy. "You're a soldier? I real honest-to-God infantryman?" He pulled his hat to his chest and held it with both hands. "Ain't that a kick right in the crabapples? I'm sure your sainted mother would be proud of you."

Out of the corner of his eye, Cyrus noticed another man standing close to him. It was the waiter, and from the exasperation on his face, he'd been waiting patiently for some time. "Will the gentleman be joining you for dinner?"

"I couldn't possibly. Much as it pains me to say, I have an appointment to keep." Reeves put his hat back on and reached to shake Cyrus' hand again.

Cyrus took the man's hand in return. "Right. The bible salesman. It's been so nice to see you, I would feel remiss if I didn't buy a Good Book or two. Surely the men on board could do with some religion in their off hours." He released his grip on Reeves' hand and began fumbling in his own pockets for money.

"That is mighty kind of you, old friend, but unfortunately I don't carry them on my person."

"Not even some sort of sample? That seems like a missed opportunity." Cyrus stopped patting his pockets.

With a chuckle, Reeves began to step away. "Everyone knows what a bible looks like, Cyrus."

"Maybe we can meet again. I'd love to make a contribution to the spread of the Lord's will. How long are you in town?"

Reeves stopped. "Oh Cyrus. I get the feeling we will surely meet again. And believe me, you will have the chance to make your contribution 'Be still before the Lord and wait patiently for him.'"

"'Fret not yourself over the one who prospers in his way,'" Bethy said.

"Come again?" Reeves asked.

"The next part of psalm thirty-seven-seven? 'Fret not yourself over the one who prospers in his way?'" Bethy stood and offered her hand. "It was nice to meet you, Mister Reeves."

Reeves took her hand and kissed it gently. "Ma'am." He turned and weaved a path through the tables and out through the front door.

"You're going to tell me what that was all about, right?" Bethy gave a curious glance.

"Yes."

Bethy raised her eyebrows and folded her hands in front of her.

"Can we at least eat first?"

Bethy shook her head no.

It had been a long time coming. Cyrus had managed to make a new life for himself with few questions about his prior life until now, even made it into the OMO with no inquiries. Now, though. He couldn't avoid it, certainly not with Bethy. "Harvey Reeves went to war in my place."

It was hard to hide the surprise on Bethy's face.

"My family owned a large mine in Bibb County, Alabama. We provided the Confederacy with a good amount of the coal it needed to continue the war effort as long as it lasted. We also had our hands in a number of iron mines in the area as well. For that area we were pretty wealthy, and as far as the government was concerned, we were close to indispensable." Cyrus took a drink of the warm water that was sitting in front of him. The terrible musicians finally took a break and put down their instruments. Their awful racket had made the storytelling that much more difficult.

"Around the time the war started, they came looking for volunteers and soon enough, they came along conscripting men into the effort." Cyrus paused. Without the terrible noise of the band, he noticed intermittent cries coming from somewhere outside, in the distance, hard to pinpoint. He saw that Bethy had noticed, too. "Should we go see what that is?"

She winced. "Finish your story, quickly."

"*Quickly?* My time came around to 'volunteer,' and my family, my mama especially, didn't feel I needed to heed the call of my countrymen. At the time, there was an opportunity for a man to pay for a substitute to join the army in his place. My family being who they were, had the means to pay someone handsomely to go in my stead. I was opposed to the idea, feeling that I ought to do my part."

"And?"

"And the man they paid was Harvey Reeves. I never saw or heard about him again."

Before Cyrus could get a read on Bethy's reaction, a man burst in the door to the restaurant. "There's been an accident. There's an airship down in the ocean."

The first thought that came to Cyrus' mind when he heard an airship was down, was of The *Polk*, he could tell by Bethy's expression, that she feared the same.

39

"What's going on?" Cyrus was winded from running up the stairs to the launch.

"We're not sure," Alek said. "Our watchmen saw an explosion and the *Tunnel Hill* went down into the water. We don't know anything else."

"Get *the Sun and the Moon* cranked up and tell all the boats in the harbor to start moving for the wreck, looking for survivors." Bethy started gathering gear; rope, life rings, all the rescue gear in her reach. "And let Cashe—"

"I've wired Cashe and he said to do all the things you just did. *The Moon* is wrapped up with the Alcatraz situation, and I sent a runner to the docks to get boats moving on the water, and some already went out on their own."

Cyrus nodded and took some gear from Bethy. "Great. Find us a pilot for a boat and we'll go."

"I'm your pilot." Alek turned and pointed to a ship with *Pride of Seal Bend* painted on the hull. "Your ship." He strode with purpose to the gangplank, and Bethy followed, with Cyrus behind. As Alek threw down his equipment, three soldiers ran up the ramp and set down a huge bell. As they retreated, they pulled the ramp back, cranking it in with a rusty handle near the tower door. When the ladder was clear of the craft, one of the men untied a rope from the dock and threw it toward Cyrus. Luckily, he'd dropped the equipment, else the heavy braided rope might have smacked him in the face, but as it was, he caught it and tied it off inside the craft.

Cyrus caught up with Bethy in the wheelhouse just moments later, where she was conferring with Alek. She pointed off to the harbor. It was faint, but Cyrus made out a cloud of smoke almost a mile from shore.

"They've been in the water for about eighteen minutes," Alek said, as he snapped his pocket watch closed and dropped it in his coat. "It looks like the supply ship *McMannis* and the schooner *October Frost* are on station at the wreck, pulling out survivors."

They watched the wreckage rise and fall with the waves as they approached. Smoke still wafted from the aft of the *Tunnel Hill*. Its huge bladder of gas floated along nearby. With the first pass, none of them could see any of the crew in the water.

"Once you find a good place, we'll go in and get to work," Bethy said. After, they tied one of the thick ropes to the bell. "You ever use one of these?"

Cyrus had to admit he hadn't.

"It'll drop into the water near us. It has some air trapped in it, so we can stick our heads in and breathe without having to return to the surface." Bethy waved a ship's ensign over as he came into the deck area. "This man will raise and lower it as needed, but otherwise, we're on our own."

Cyrus nodded. That seemed simple enough to him. But it was always the simple things that got complicated quickly, he thought.

The ship's engines sputtered as it slowed and turned around the *Tunnel Hill*, and eventually came to a near halt, drifting on the wind and the leftover momentum of flight. They were a few hundred yards from the mostly-sunken hull of the *Tunnel Hill* and still saw no survivors in the water. To the east, the *McManus* drifted toward them, lifeboats already dropping down its sides.

After a few deep breaths, Bethy nodded and slid over the side of the boat, dropping thirty into the water feet first. Cyrus watched and inhaled a few times himself. He noticed the ensign was looking at him with a concerned stare. "Are you going to jump? Are you okay?" The ensign asked.

Cyrus looked at the water and saw Bethy surface, so he bit his lip and propelled himself forward, aiming away from her as best he could. The fall was over quickly, and he was soon underwater. The ocean was much colder than he expected, and he immediately started kicking and paddling for the surface.

He took a deep breath when he broke the surface and turned toward Bethy to bitch about the water, but she was gone, already headed toward the wreckage and distant enough that his moaning would be lost in the din of the waves, the hum of the *Pride of Seal Bend*'s engine and the shouts of the men in the lifeboats that were just hitting the water. He turned and swam, glad they'd shed their heavy clothing as the waves were hard enough to manage as it was.

Bethy disappeared beneath the waves as she approached the wreck and Cyrus struggled to catch up. He dove near where she went down, and he found her swimming alongside the ship's hull, looking in windows and portholes. He swam alongside her, doing the same. The inside of the ship appeared to be full of murky water, clouded by things from the ship like lubricants and coal dust. They were looking in on a hall that lead to the crew quarters and eventually stopped at the command center. Cyrus could feel an aching in his lungs and he tapped Bethy that he had to surface. She reluctantly followed, and as they surfaced and caught their breath, Bethy waved to the ensign to let him know they were in good shape.

"See anything?" Cyrus asked.

Bethy shook her head.

"I think we should move to the control room, see if we can find anyone there," Cyrus said. He heard a shout and saw the rowboats from the ships were closing in. Bethy dove, and again Cyrus followed. They swam to the fore of the bobbing airship and peered into the windows there, finding one had been smashed at some point.

Here the water was clear inside, and it made it easy to see the pilot, Woodward, floating, suspended in the water with his arms outstretched near another airman. Neither showed any signs of movement or life, the pilot stared, directly at Cyrus and Bethy as he hung there in the cold water.

Cyrus swam for the bell and poked his head in for a deep breath. Bethy joined him and asked "Where next? There has to be someone alive in there."

He considered it for a moment, but Cyrus wasn't as optimistic. Seeing the men in the wheelhouse had made him feel survivors were less likely. "If they were going through an exercise, they might have been in the main hold. That's the only place that had room for them all, and it would explain why we don't see any other bodies."

Bethy nodded and slipped back below the surface, swimming at a furious pace for the port side. Together they started looking in for more of the crew. At the portal to the main cargo hold, it was again difficult to see in, this time because of the oil, more coal dust and what appeared to be blood. They could make out a giant hole in the back wall where the rest of the hull was separated from the boiler and the engines. It appeared the whole section had exploded and sent shrapnel through the room and anyone who was in it. As Cyrus made the realization, a body floated by, it was one of the volunteers that Cyrus had worked with earlier in the week, though he couldn't recall the man's name. The body was torn and bloody from the explosion.

Soon, Cyrus made out body parts faintly drifting as the water cleared momentarily. An arm sliced off just above the wrist twisted in the corner, and dark forms that looked like oil spills revealed themselves to be more bodies. Cyrus tried to count—to get an idea of how many were there, but the environment made it too tough to keep track of what was what. To make matters worse, the airship had begun to twist and roll with the tide.

As they both turned to go back to the bell, they heard a flat thump on the hull. Cyrus turned to see a man with his face pressed against the glass nearby. He pounded with his fists in the windows and his face twisted in terror, bubbles escaped his mouth as he appeared to try to shout in the water. Cyrus' lungs burned for air, but when Bethy turned back to swim for the ship, Cyrus followed. He figured the man had found a pocket of air that had disappeared when the ship shifted. Cyrus and Bethy got right to the glass and started pounding as the trapped man did. Cyrus grabbed the handle of the bay door and pulled, but it either was stuck tight, or locked from the inside. The man inside saw and swam to the door and tried it from his side. Bethy grabbed an outside rail and tried to use it for leverage to kick a window in.

No one made any headway.

Bethy motioned to a smaller hole that had been blown in the aft section by the boiler and swam toward it. From his angle, Cyrus decided it was too small to squeeze through and kept at the door. The man inside disappeared for a moment and then reappeared with his hands on the window where they'd first discovered him. He wasn't pounding now; he was barely slapping the window.

Cyrus realized the futility of trying to open the door but had no other option. He felt his own strength slipping away and wanted to take a breath so badly, his chest felt like a rock. His grip on the handle loosened. He felt Bethy's hands envelop his arm and pull him away. As they swam for the bell, Cyrus looked back at the man who was no longer moving, no longer spouting bubbles from his mouth. He'd stopped moving altogether.

40

Lucinda was waist-deep in the water next to the supply boat, pulling debris off it and checking the marks on the stern.

"Look here," she said. There were multiple black marks across the wood. "Looks like scoring from an explosion or something."

Lowell, who'd opted to stay out of the water, leaned over the side and looked. "That lines up with what we saw at the scene. The prisoners on the island really tried to pound this one after they sunk the other."

Lucinda nodded. It was the right boat, but there was no sign of the escapees. They could have easily found another boat near here – a fisherman, another supply ship – and headed north on up the coast. Or, they could have doubled backed with it and went ashore at Santa Rosa. They'd be lost amid the plethora of docks in the harbor. The last possibility, maybe they just abandoned the boat and started out on land. That possibility meant that they could have headed for Santa Rosa as well. Or holed up in the countryside, waiting for things to clear.

"Anything in the boat worth looking at?" Lucinda trudged through the water and onto the beach. They'd gotten lucky that the tide had gone out and exposed the boat. The prisoners had actually hidden it pretty well and the *Polk* would have likely drifted over it.

"Nah. It appears they tossed out anything heavy and took the rest with them," Lowell said. He looked to the other crew members walking up the beach and shrugged. "Maybe they'd find something if we took them to search the area?"

"Maybe." Looking at them, she noticed there were a few tiny plumes of smoke visible in the distance. They were pretty far apart and a few miles inland. "This area has been cleared, right?"

"Probably a few stragglers, but it's relatively free of chewers."

"I count three smoke clouds over there, and I can make out two houses in my view right now. Maybe we should visit each of those, make sure they're all right, and ask if they've seen our wayward criminals?"

Lucinda watched Lowell scan the horizon, picking out the houses. "Should we split up?" Lucinda was ready for this whole thing to be done with. "Cover ground faster that way." She thought about Lowell's experience in law and wondered whether he'd agree to it.

Up the beach, one of the younger recruits was running in a circle, poking a crab with a stick while two others clapped and laughed.

"I'm afraid to let these gentlemen out of my sight, lest they get lost and we have to find them, too."

"They aren't that bad," Lucinda said. There were quite a few of the new soldiers who'd had no military experience, no experience with a weapon at all, but they'd mostly taken to the training. Some had been starving and would sign up for at least one meal a day. It was always obvious which ones needed food and a pair of boots and which ones wanted to help their country or their home. They still tried their best usually. "That one with the stick is—" she thought about it "—agile?"

"He can cut a rug, that's a fact," Lowell said. "And the way you talk, you'd think you'd been an officer in the Army of the Potomac from the get-go."

With her metal hand firmly planted on a cleat, Lucinda pulled herself into the boat and looked around. No, she hadn't been in the OMO for long, hadn't been on a side for the war. She'd run free with Cyrus until the *Polk* swooped in and changed everything. Whether that change was for the better, she debated every day. "There's a pile of clothes here, did you check those?"

"Only two shirts and one pair of prison-issue trousers. Doesn't help us. There had to be more than two escapees."

"So, no help at all. We don't know how many made it here, or even which ones."

"I guess we go with your plan. We canvass the farms and see if we find any locals that may have information." He turned and waved his arms at the men up the coastline to get their attention. "Let's round up the men and get going. I want to be back in Santa Rosa by sundown."

"If you're really worried about them, keep in mind they only have a few bullets between them," Lucinda said. "One each, least while they're training."

"I'm worried about them having any ammunition whatsoever." Lowell waved to the dozen men to get them to line up. "I'm worried that kid over there has a stick, honestly."

41

"He was the son of this man and woman that came and helped out at my family's place," Cyrus said. Few years older than me. His dad helped in the stables getting the horses ready and making deliveries. Reeves' mother worked in our shop. She—" Cyrus had to think about it, it had been so long. "She baked things; pies, cakes, bread, whatever." He looked to Bethy next to him and continued to recount his tail to Cashe and the others that had gathered in the ward room of the tower. "Their kid started sweeping the floors and cleaning out stalls for extra money or food. I'd help him sometimes."

"You were friends?" Cashe asked.

"I wouldn't exactly say that. I knew him," Cyrus said. "Knew him enough to be at his wedding. My mother made him a wedding cake and sewed blankets for their children when they came along. We were friendly, I guess. So, years later when the war started, they came around our town and gathered every able-bodied man in the area." Cyrus felt the pang of disingenuousness eat at him. They'd grown up together. They were close.

"Like every town." It was the most Bethy could say in his defense, but Cyrus appreciated it.

"Pretty much."

"And you were one of them?" Cashe had his hands folded in his lap, listening intently.

"The able-bodied? Yessir. Only my parents weren't having it. They told me I wasn't going. They wouldn't let me go do my duty to the Confederacy. Not that I had any designs on fighting and dying, but it had to be done. You don't duck out on responsibility like that, even if you weren't exactly in line with the South's notions." Cyrus took a deep breath and continued, determined to get the telling over with. "Time comes when I'm supposed to report and there's Reeves standing at our front door, saying goodbye to his mother and father. His two kids were still small, and they were wailing about him leaving."

"He wasn't drafted, was he?" Cashe asked.

"No."

"Your parents paid him as a substitute for you, didn't they?" Cashe nodded. "So he'd fight in your place."

"Yes. I didn't know about it until that very moment when I saw them out front of the house."

"I don't understand, wasn't there a way to just pay your way out of service? Why didn't they do that?" Bethy asked.

Cyrus knew Bethy hadn't been around during most of the war, but he appreciated that she knew something about it. "Commutation. It was a possibility for a while, but they did away with it as they became more desperate for troops. By this time, the only option open to my parents was replacement."

"What happened after that?" Cashe asked.

"He left for the war. I left home not long after that and I never saw him or his family again," Cyrus said. "Never saw my family either, for that matter."

Out in the main room, a team of soldiers pulled a wagon off the elevator and set it up in the middle. Doctor Hastings came out of the stairwell and began directing them. "Line them up by the tables and I'll take them one at a time." The men pulled the sheet-covered bodies off the wagon and placed them as they were told.

The sight of them made Cyrus' spine stiffen and wave of cold wash over his skin.

"Come on," Bethy said. "We aren't needed here and we're going to be in the way." She brushed her hand against Cyrus' arm. "We can't help with this part."

It was no comfort, as Cyrus figured they hadn't been much help with the other parts either. Hadn't saved anyone, hadn't pulled anyone out of the water. Cyrus couldn't help but stare at the men they'd brought up from the wreck of the airship *Tunnel Hill*. It was like the war stories he'd been told by veterans, deserters and civilians about the war. Bodies everywhere. The carnage. The mayhem of trying to make sense of it all. The war was over, yet here it was. The hell had come home to him.

"Come on." Bethy tugged at him. "Standing here isn't doing either of us any good."

He allowed himself to be pulled off the center floor, just as the men took the empty wagon back to the elevator. Bethy led him down a small passage to the narrow stairs in back. They climbed up and up until they reached the door above them and pushed it open.

Bethy reached down and offered her hand to pull Cyrus up and he took it. He'd done the same for her many times, and the change wasn't lost on him. They walked out into the open air, standing on top of the tower at the tallest point in the city. They could see the lights, buildings, houses and people of Santa Rosa stretching out as far as they could see in one direction and the Pacific in the other.

"We should probably talk," Bethy said.

"About what?" Cyrus wasn't dense, they had all of everything to talk about, it was just where to start and what to say.

"Start with Reeves."

"I told it all," Cyrus said. He stared out at the dot of a ship out in the ocean.

"You did. But how did you feel? I mean, a man going off to war was highly unlikely to come back. Your family basically sentenced him to death. Were you guilty?"

"He lived. Okay? It wasn't a death sentence if he lived, now was it?" It was a dumb answer, he knew it.

"Really? You just found out he was alive after nearly what? A decade? You had to carry that around with you for that long, the possibilities of what happened." Bethy stepped up onto the thin wooden railing that ran around the edge of the roof and looked him in the eyes. "Don't be an ass. It's me."

He lowered his gaze, but talked to her, nonetheless. "We grew up together. We got in trouble together. Of course, I was guilty. He was like a brother, but when it came down to it, my family didn't see it that way. They saw him as a solution to a problem and nothing else. I assumed he was dead, okay? From day one when they paid him that money, I assumed he was dead and gone."

"I'm sure."

"And yet, when I saw him in that restaurant, I didn't know him. He wasn't him. What that war must have done to him."

42

Reeves sat in the shadows of an alleyway a block from the tower and stared at the front entrance. From his perch on a crate, he could see the men and women come and go from it, he could see the shadows in the windows of each level appear and disappear. Today, there were no airships to marvel at, he assumed the one was still grounded at the prison and hoped the other was still there as well, otherwise it was searching for him and the others.

As the day wore on, the crowds that clogged the main thoroughfare lessened, headed home to their suppers or back out to their farms, to restaurants—It occurred to Reeves that he had no idea what normal people did with their lives out here. This city was immense—a population gathered from hundreds of other towns seeming a safe place from the chewer menace, so likely every type of person with every type of profession settled somewhere within. But what did they do with themselves? Back home, years ago, he would have taken his kids out to the fields to play or down to the stream to swim or fish when he had a free moment.

But here? There were endless rows of buildings. Here there was the constant stench of waste and the sting of smoke in the air.

There had to be schools in the city, somewhere. They must have places to teach their children something more than tanning leather and curing meat. He himself had taught men to read in prison, surely if men learned in prison, children learned here.

Reeves realized that his observations about the town were not tactical in nature. They all revolved around families, and it forced him to confront the notion that his was gone. He felt his eyes grow wet with tears again. He wanted something to lash out at, something to break, someone to hurt, but he clenched his fists until the feeling subsided. That opportunity would come very soon. He composed himself as quickly as he could. Mama would verify or deny the things Calloway said; certainly she would prove the man to be the liar Reeves knew him to be.

He watched as the sun set and the people cleared the streets, leaving on a few stragglers, OMO personnel and other soldiers to run importantly through the streets.

Patrick walked up to the alley and scanned the street to see who was watching, then quickly slipped in and found a seat next to Reeves. His bag clanged and crackled when he moved.

"You get it?" Reeves said.

With a firm pat on the bag, Patrick mumbled "Yep." The bottles inside clanked together as he shifted. "Everything this little crew of yours could find."

There was movement by the third-floor launch doors. Figures were passing by in the waning daylight. "Do you have a spyglass or a pair of binoculars?"

"No. Why the hell would I have that? You didn't say to bring none of that."

Reeves waved him off. "Never mind." He got off the box and leaned against the nearby brick wall, trying to stay hidden, but dying to know who was inside. He hoped it was Cyrus, but was it? His mind might be playing tricks on him. If they were going to kill these men, he hoped Cyrus would be among them. Or maybe it would be better to check that particular goal off his list with his own hands. He pushed his face against the wall, he needed to be more cautious, if he wanted to finish his tasks. But he had to see Cyrus.

"I'm going inside. You watch that clock over there. I'll be out in five minutes. You be ready to throw those things into the entrance when I run out," Reeves stood and patted his coat. Making sure the pepperbox guns were all available quickly. He kept his Colt at his side in the holster, just in case he needed a real gun if things went bad. He reached into Patrick's bag and pulled out two bottles of oil and slipped them under his coat. He held them there with one hand awkwardly. He figured no one was around to question why he had a hand under his coat the way he did.

"What? You didn't say anything about going in," Patrick said. "We were going to toss these and run."

"If I'm not out in five minutes, *you* start throwing them and *you* run."

43

They came up the road, then crossed into the field near the dwelling. Lowell knelt just outside the farmhouse and dug around by the fence. Whatever was there, Lucinda was amazed that Lowell saw it in the fading sunlight.

"Something amiss?" Lucinda asked. It was fast becoming a long day. All of the farms had their owners accounted for and none of them had noticed anything out of the ordinary in the last few days. "I'm pretty near ready to be done with this." She looked over at Clifton and the two other green recruits that she had been stuck with for the search. One leaned against a fencepost, wiped the perspiration from his neck.

"This gentleman had some chewer alarms set up, but—" he lifted up a string and followed it to a kettle and some spoons. Looks like the string was broken, but no one ever reset it." Lowell dropped the string and looked around. "Not that important, I guess." He stood up and brushed his hands on a handkerchief he produced from his back pocket.

"Let's go see if he's about. We've just got one more after this and we can go home and figure out what's next," Lucinda said. She waved on the probationaries and they moved to the house. Lowell went up the step and looked the window. He shook his head and the others stepped onto the porch. Lucinda moved to the door with Lowell on the other side, Clifton stopped by the window, with the other man behind him.

Lucinda took a breath and rapped on the door twice. There was a crash inside and she looked at Lowell for his assessment. He shrugged. There was more commotion inside and the creaking of floorboards told her that someone was walking across the floor. The knob rattled a bit and the door opened a crack.

"Who—What?" Inside, a grubby, unshaven man looked at them, flinching at the remnants of the day's sun that streamed in on him.

"Hello, sir." Lucinda looked him up and down. "We're sorry to be a bother, but we're looking around to make sure the good people around here are all right."

"What?" The man looked puzzled and it was about then that Lucinda caught the stench of alcohol on his breath.

"There's been some trouble in the area," Lowell added. "We're with the government. Just making sure everything is okay with you and yours, Mister Everston."

The man twisted his face up and rubbed his hands across his twisted mess of hair. "Who?"

"Everston? It's on the fence out front. I'm assuming you're Mister Everston?" Lowell looked over at Lucinda.

The man smiled. "Oh, right. Of course. I'm sorry. You caught me waking up from a nap. I'm him. I'm Everston." He appeared awake now. And he looked from Lucinda to Lowell and back very quickly. "What is it I can help you with again?"

"Just checking to make sure you're okay. Is there anyone here with you?" Lucinda tried to look past him into the room.

"Nope. All alone out here. Just me and the—" he waved his arm toward the field beyond the OMO officers, "—the—what do you call it—wheat and what have you."

Lowell looked at the field and the tall stalks growing there. "The corn? That's corn over there."

"That's right." The man cleared his throat and spit somewhere inside the house. "So, I'm fine. Everything's fine here. Dandy. So, if you don't mind, I'll get back to my business." He closed the door politely. They listened but didn't hear the floorboards creak to indicate the man was walking away. Lucinda stared at Lowell, studying his reaction. He rolled his eyes and Lucinda knew neither of them believed the man.

"Can we go?" Clifton asked. "One more house up the road and we can still make dinner at the barracks in town."

It was subtle, but Lucinda could tell Lowell heard it too; the sound of the hammer of a gun being pulled back just on the other side of the door. Hard to say what kind of gun, rifle, pistol, whatever, but 'Mister Everson' had a weapon and he was ready to use it.

"All right." Lucinda tilted her head to let Lowell know they should talk somewhere away from the house. "It is getting late. We need to get along." She said it as carelessly as she could but made sure it was nice and loud enough.

"I could eat," Lowell said.

Two soldiers turned from their positions on the patio, loose and careless. Clifton glanced at the window. "Hey, he's got a shotgun."

The words propelled Lowell into motion. "Get down." And he tackled Clifton to get him out of the line of fire just as the loud explosion of a shotgun tore out the glass.

Lucinda flattened herself against the wall and watched as the window shattered outward, showering Lowell with glass. He managed to shove the recruit out of harm's way, but Lowell went down hard on the ground. Lucinda took a step toward her fallen comrade, but more gunfire stopped her, this time reports from a pistol instead of the shotgun. She looked up at the trainees standing wide-eyed and staring at her, and nodded her head for them to go around the building and look for another way in. As they moved cautiously away, the sound of Clifton quietly sobbing came to her attention. He was still lying on the ground, where he'd been pushed. He was staring at Lowell and flinching at each shot's crackle.

None of the OMO had fired a shot yet.

"Hey," she said. "Hey." She was more forceful this time and Clifton looked up. "Get up and help him. He saved your god damn life."

Clifton looked at her blankly. She wanted to drop to her knees and help Lowell, but the thought stuck in her mind that she was somehow suddenly the most senior member of this particular search party. She had no idea how many people were inside the house, or how heavily armed they were, but if the trainees came in through the back, they might get cut down if she didn't do something.

"What do I do?" Clifton put his pistol on the porch and moved to Lowell.

She was already in motion and didn't want to stop to explain field medicine now. She gripped her own pistol in her good hand and grabbed the doorknob with the other. As she turned it, more shots thudded against the thick wood. When they stopped, she kicked the door with her heel and raced in. She was just in time to see the same man that answered the door throw his pistol aside and pick up the shotgun again.

"Drop that gun," she said, raising her own weapon. She felt a tug on her fake arm just as the room filled with stinging smoke and a reverberating roar. The shotgun blast put her off balance and her shot went wild into the wall.

The man ran into a nearby room and slammed the door before she could recover properly, so she fell behind a table for cover. She tried to open her pistol to check it, but discovered her mechanical arm wasn't quite working properly—the fingers wouldn't grip, the wrist wouldn't move. She examined it—listening for the gunman's movements all the while—but couldn't figure which part was damaged.

The back door opened and two of her men tentatively stepped into her view a few seconds later.

"He's in that room." She indicated the closed door with her good hand when the other didn't react. "Still armed." She ducked back out of their sight and slammed the arm on the hardwood floor.

Come on. She thought and slammed it against the table. Comeoncomeon Come ON.

A second slam to the table seemed to get the thing working again. She flexed it twice, feeling how sluggish it was in responding.

"Listen in there," one of the soldiers shouted. "We have you—" His words were cut off by the blast of the shotgun tearing through the wall.

"Shut up," the man in the room said. "Go the hell away." His words were slurred and louder than before, and he seemed to be nearly screaming. Lucinda wondered if he was just drunk or if firing the shotgun in the small space had affected the man's hearing. She slid back along the table and looked to the area where the blast had opened up a large hole in the wall. She steadied her arm on the table and aimed, holding her breath as she heard the escapee moving around.

"Where are the other escapees?" She yelled, hoping that she'd get a reaction.

"Shut up," he said again. He fumbled, reloading and cursed as something bounced on the ground. Through the hole in the wall made by the shotgun blast,

Lucinda saw the man's head move by as he bent over to retrieve what she figured was a shell for the gun. She waited a second, and when he rose again, she fired the pistol.

The man shouted inarticulately, and Lucinda stood and ran toward the door. "Shit." The man shouted. "Shiiit."

The door gave way easily to Lucinda's metal shoulder and she entered the room to see the escapee holding the side of his head. When he saw her, he slowly raised his shotgun, only to have it batted away. Lucinda moved to grab him, but her arm wouldn't respond again. She slammed it against the door and reached again for the man, catching his shirt in a tight grip with it that wouldn't open if she wanted.

"Where are the other escapees? We found the boat you all got away in. We saw there were at least three of you, so where are the others?" Her shoulder hurt where the metal connected to her.

The man wouldn't answer, only moaned and grabbed at his head. Lucinda could see blood streaming past his hand, skin and hair sticking out between his fingers— the shot had done more than remove his ear, it had taken a good portion of the flesh around it.

"Who are you? What's your name?" She didn't even know if he could hear her.

Behind them, the two soldier trainees that had come in parted for Clifton.

"What are you doing here? You're supposed to be taking care of Lowell," Lucinda said. The look on Clifton's face told her there was nothing he could do.

"What? What's going on?"

"I tried. I held my hands over his wounds, I cleaned out the glass, I did everything I could think of." He raised his hands to show her the blood on them. "I had the others try to signal the *Polk* to come back for us, but there's nothing they can do now."

Lucinda felt her face flush and she moved toward Clifton, thinking she'd strike him. It was his fault, he got Lowell killed, standing at that window with no cover. He'd let Lowell die, bleeding on the porch. But as she moved, her hand was locked on the escapee's shirt. She unlocked it, using her good hand to pry the dull fingers apart, then bashed the man's face with the metal arm. It may not have worked correctly, but it made a good bludgeoning instrument, at least. She struck him again. She may not be able to beat Clifton for Lowell's death, but she certainly could take out her frustrations on his actual killer. She struck him again.

"Uh, shouldn't we keep him alive, so we can ask about the others?" One of the soldiers in the doorway asked, though both were clearly nervous and thinking the same thing.

"Start searching the rest of the house," Lucinda said. She nodded to Clifton. "You too, make sure the *Polk* gets here quickly. And fill them in."

Clifton left with a nod and a quick glance at the escapee. Lucinda grabbed the escapee's face, meaning only to hold him still while she punched him, but the false arm and fingers betrayed her again and the fist closed of its own volition.

The man screamed as Lucinda's fingers got tighter and tighter, digging into his cheek, his ear, his forehead. He wept a high-gurgling sob. Just when Lucinda began to feel good about his suffering, she realized she couldn't stop. The hand wasn't going to stop. His skull crackled.

"Lucinda." The soldiers behind her called in unison and grabbed at her hand, which was now covered in blood from the prisoner's bleeding ear. The men tried to pry her hand away, then the individual fingers. They were unsuccessful. His head crackled again, and a sharp edge protruded from his forehead and his eyes went unfocused. One of the soldiers hit her arm with the butt of the nearby shotgun and it released, but it was too late. The man lay in a pile on the floor at her feet.

Nearby, she could hear the engines of the *Polk* getting louder.

"Lowell," she said.

44

Reeves walked up the steps of the tower as nonchalantly as he could, holding the bottles under one arm and trying to look confident. He took long strides and did his best to push the anger down inside his mind, the bile in his throat.

The first floor was empty. No one stepped out to ask what business he had at the tower, who he was, why he was there so late. Lights burned in the halls, but the side rooms and offices were dark. He found signs next to the doors that indicated a sheriff's office and jail cells, recruiting station. Signs directed visitors to other levels for the airship launch areas, the OMO offices, mess hall, and other destinations.

The bottom floor was empty; some lights shone in the various offices, but not a single person seemed to be about. It was dark in the corridor, with the only other lights coming from near the elevator stairs. Knowing he was short on time, Reeves took to the stairs, quietly, staying out of the light as much as possible. The second floor seemed to be more offices, more darkness. The only voices he heard came from further up on the next floor. He turned to run up the next flight of stairs and ran into a young, black woman in an OMO uniform coming down.

He managed to knock the woman over, scattering the various small brass cannon shells she was carrying. He retained his own balance, but at the cost of dropping his own bottles he'd been holding under his coat. One of them shattered, the other bounced down a step and came to rest intact.

At first, he leaned down to pick up her shells for her, but mid-crouch he remembered what he was there for. He ran through a list of what weapons he had on his person and made a point to consider which would be easiest to get to at the moment. He scooped up the usable bottle and held it behind himself. "I'm sorry, ma'am. I need to speak with Cyrus Spencer. It's important."

The woman bent to pick the shells up herself. "I'm sorry, but I don't know. I haven't seen him in a bit. Things are a mite hectic." He saw her sniff at the air, trying to get a bead on what the smell was coming from the bottle.

"I know that. That's why I need to see him." Reeves stood straightened.

The OMO soldier stood as well, looking Reeves up and down. She still had one shell in her hand, a large one, but the others were scattered around the base of the stairs. "Maybe if you come upstairs with me, we can find him together," she said. "I'm sure he's still in the building."

It was a defeating moment for Reeves. That this mere soldier could see through him. *That's what her look means, right?* Reeves asked himself. *The slightly raised brows?* He'd learned to read facial cues in training somewhat.

The pause went on and he noticed her hand was near her sidearm; a beauty of a .45, hanging on her left side. He knew he couldn't clear any of his weapons fast enough if she decided to pull on him, so he lunged before she tried. He grabbed at her left hand and held it fast, just inches from that pistol's handle. She tugged at him and he grabbed at her gun with his opposite hand, while trying to keep her away from it.

He realized too late that the big brass shell she held in her other hand was free to bludgeon him at will while both of his hands were occupied. The soldier brought it down with a clank on his temple and swung it again, connecting with his neck as he pulled away. The pain in his temple was immediate and fiery.

He reached back and pulled out one of the small pepperbox pistols, aimed, and pulled the trigger twice. Both bullets struck her square in the chest and she stumbled backward but didn't fall. Reeves figured they'd gotten too far apart for the weak handgun to do too much damage. He moved forward to fire the other two shots where they could do more, but even wounded, the woman managed to pull her own gun and fire.

A beauty of a gun like that tends to do damage at close range, and Reeves felt the bullet dig into his side somewhere. He fell backward, more surprised than anything. He fired the gun as he careened and tried to keep his balance, the last two shots erupting in quick snaps. Reeves landed on his ass at the bottom of the stairs, dazed and aching. Above him, the OMO officer lay slumped a few steps up.

His immediate thought was to look up the winding stairs to see who would come to respond to the gunshots, but he didn't see or hear anyone. Reeves looked down at his side, pulling aside the shirt that was quickly becoming blood-stained. He dug at the wound and turned to see a similar wound further back on his torso. The bullet had struck him and gone through the other side. It was good news in that there wasn't a slug inside him, and that it hadn't rattled around in his body, tearing up organs or causing more damage. He tore off a long swatch of his shirt and leaned up to where his bottle had shattered. He dipped the piece of shirt in the spilled oil there until it was soaked and then he set it a few steps up. From his left pocket, he pulled a flint and steel, striking them together four times before a spark caught the oil on the stairs and a flame ensued.

He wrapped the small spent pistol in the shirt scrap and dipped a loose end in the flames, and it lit quickly. He tossed the ball of fire off toward group of chairs draped with blankets on the tower floor below. Reeve watched the fire on the stairs start to spread from the stone steps to the wooden railings and he hoped it would keep going. He stared at the nearby blankets, hoping they'd catch too.

He waited another precious minute, checking his wound again, hoping it would be better. The pain in his head from where he'd been struck throbbed and he did his best to block it out. He thought of Mama, and what he'd promised her, thought of his family and how he'd been robbed of his chance to ever see them again. Calloway's assertion that Mama knew about their passing and didn't tell Reeves about it riled him again.

He stood and took a deep breath, his resolve strengthened, when someone grabbed his elbow. Reeves turned, fist raised, to see Patrick.

"Jesus, are you okay?" He looked Reeves up and down. "You're bleeding."

"What are you doing here?"

"You were coming in here to set the place on fire, but it's been more than five minutes."

Reeves thought about it and wondered if he'd passed out when he fell down the stairs, or if the fight had taken that long. "You should've just set the place on fire."

"You're welcome. I decided to watch out for you, rather than burn you." Patrick shook his head.

"Do you have a gun on you? Did you bring the bottles?"

"Yes to both." Patrick pulled his pistol and showed Reeves.

"Keep it holstered, but when I say so, pull it and shoot everyone you see," Reeves said. He leaned down over the OMO soldier and took her pistol and put it in his pocket as best he could, and they walked up. He held his arm out, keeping Patrick behind him while he surveyed the new floor. In the center of this room there were sheets and blankets covering what Reeves assumed were the bodies of the crew of the downed airship. He started to count the fallen, but decided it was best not to. He didn't really want to know what this cost. Instead, he counted the living.

On the other side of the room, there were two men in long white aprons tending to one of the bodies. There were three other men and two women assisting, still in their OMO uniforms. The elevator creaked, and more men got off, pulling another of the wagons he'd seen earlier. Four men pulled it—none of them Cyrus. Eleven people in the way.

"Stay here," he whispered to Patrick. Reeves moved from the shadows, bottle held discreetly behind him. He stepped further toward where the men with the cart were unloading bodies. The men went about their work in silence.

"Pardon. Any of you men seen Cyrus Spencer anywhere?" He talked low, nearly a whisper.

All the men at the cart stopped and looked around, shook their heads negatively. One turned and shouted. "I have a message for Cyrus. Is he about?"

The doctors shook their heads and went about their business, but one of their assistants stopped and actually took the time to respond. "No, last I saw, he and Bethy were headed—" The woman paused and looked at Reeves to finish, when her face went tense. "Shit. There's a fire." She pointed. "Behind you men. There's a fire on the floor below."

Reeves turned and saw that the flames had grown considerably faster than he'd assumed they would. It was painfully obvious from the way the light danced behind them on the stairs. The light made Patrick's attempt to stay hidden easily detectable.

That got everyone's attention, and they turned to look. A doctor looked at Reeves and Patrick. "Who are you men? What are you doing?"

The doctors likely wouldn't be armed. He looked at the wagon men and saw at least a couple pistols among them. "Light the bottles," he said to Patrick. Reeves pulled the stolen pistol from his pocket and aimed at the nearest man. He pulled the trigger and was rewarded with only a click. He tried again to the same result. Click after click. *Empty.*

Reeves tossed the useless weapon aside and threw his bottle toward where the doctors were working. He hoped it would shatter on their table and set the whole work area on fire due to the two lamps the men were using.

It didn't.

The glass broke near the doctors' feet, sending oil across the floor, part of the wall and onto the doctors themselves, but there was no ignition. While everyone gaped at what had just happened, Reeves took the opportunity to run toward the soldiers unloading the wagon. He fished in his pocket as he ran, digging for the heaviest object he could get his hands on. Finding it, he pulled out the brass knuckles and dressed his right hand with the weapon.

He made short work of the two startled men he approached, felling one with a sharp cracking punch to the jaw, the next man took a jab to the ribs that crunched on impact. He finished the second one with blow beneath his eye that sent the soldier to the floor.

"What in the hell is going on here?" The tall doctor demanded. Everyone around Reeves seemed dumbfounded to see a man attacking a makeshift morgue, none more so than the doctor whose face was screwed up in a terse look of distaste.

As he reached down for the injured soldier's gun, Reeves looked over at Patrick who was still frozen at the stairs. He held a flame just out of reach of the cloth hanging from the bottle. "Light it and throw it, damn it," Reeves said. "Light it and throw it."

Patrick's head shook no.

"Do it."

The other men and women in the huge room took cover, doing what they had to in order to protect themselves. Two moved behind the wagon, others knocked over a table for cover.

Still, Patrick stood.

"Throw it, now." The whole reason Reeves had left Patrick outside was because he feared the man would hesitate when confronted with the possibility of shooting someone. And this room was even worse; there were bodies all over the floor, something that would give a man pause no matter the situation.

One of the assistants leaned out from behind the table and took a shot at Reeves.

45

"Did you hear that?" It was subtle, nearly covered by the sounds of the nearby ocean, the squawking of the few crows that hopped around on the tower roof, but Cyrus was sure the report of a gunshot was mixed in.

Bethy shook her head. "What?"

"I swear—" There was another one, faint from below. Bethy nodded this time and they both gathered their gear and moved for the door. Cyrus lifted it and Bethy scrambled down onto the stairs before he could insist on going first. He followed her, quietly, and then they wound around until they could see the level below them. Near the stairs, one man had a bottle with some cloth hanging from it held over a flame, while near the surgeon's wagon; Reeves crouched for cover with a pistol.

Cyrus drew his pistol, took a moment to aim, and wondered who the biggest threat was at the moment. He stared at Reeves down the sights for a second and watched him throw away the pistol and dig for a something in his pack. Bethy fired before he could make up his mind and the man with the bottle staggered then fell, bringing the makeshift bomb in contact with the flame as he dropped it, lighting the cloth.

Reeves looked up and adjusted his cover by moving behind some crates nearby. "Cyrus?" The man shouted. "I've been looking for you."

They were open on the staircase, so Cyrus urged Bethy forward to find cover. She still managed to get a couple of shots off at Reeves as she went, better than Cyrus at least. Reeves fired back, but from the high sound of it, Cyrus guessed it was a small caliber gun, likely ineffective at that range. Nonetheless, they nearly dove the last few steps and ducked behind a row of water barrels.

"This friend of yours does not act like a bible salesman," Bethy said. She pulled a couple of bullets from her uniform belt and replaced the spent shells in her revolver. "He seems downright hostile."

Cyrus nodded, trying to smile at the girl's levity be he couldn't. He stared across the room at the flame crawling up the wick of the bottle next to the unmoving man who held it. Cyrus barely had time to consider running over to extinguish it when the bottle exploded, sending flames into the air all around it.

The few birds still strutting through the room took wing and screeched. The people flinched and ducked to protect themselves. When everything had settled, there were puddles of flame around the room, some would likely burn out on their own, but others were dangerously close to material, threatening to make things even worse. The stairs were inaccessible, and the man's body was covered in flames as well.

While Cyrus was surveying the flames, Reeves must have seen that his guard was down and ran at him. Cyrus was bowled over by Reeves' charge and they both fell to the ground, rolling toward the flames and the stairs. He managed to land a trio of punches on Reeves, though they had little effect other than stopping their roll. They pushed and pulled each other, trying to find an advantage, trying to punch, or gouge or tear at the other.

"I'm going to kill you, Cyrus," Reeves said. "Then, I'll finish burning down the OMO."

Cyrus missed with a punch meant to answer the threat, and Reeves got on top of him. "They could have negotiated my release from prison once the war was over, but they didn't."

Prison? The word muddied Cyrus's already murky thoughts. "You're mad," Cyrus said. He knew the OMO was a peacekeeping force but had no idea what sort of power they had as far as prisoners and the like. Besides, the small group he belonged to had too much on their plate to even consider helping with that sort of thing. They could barely keep themselves armed with usable weapons. "The OMO isn't responsible for anyone's arrest." He pulled at Reeves' wrists, trying to get the man off of his chest. The heat and smoke of the nearby flames were already making it hard to breathe.

"And once the Confederate president lands, I'll pay him back for each of those years that he left me languishing there as well." Cyrus watched the man's eyes widen as he punched Cyrus once again. "After the president," Reeves said. "Your family. They paid for me to go to war instead of you. They bear some blame, don't you think?"

Reeves' words barely registered as crimson spots began to cloud his vision. Cyrus closed his eyes to get the image of Reeves out of his sight. He only realized that he was tumbling when his forehead connected with something solid.

He opened his eyes to see he'd rolled down several stairs and hit the wall of the stone staircase. Further down, Bethy and Reeves were fighting on the landing below. Much shorter than her opponent, Bethy still managed to land a series of blows to his torso and chest. Reeves stumbled, raising his arms to block the attack as best he could.

The first attempt to stand almost made Cyrus fall down the rest of the stairs: he was weak, still coughing from the smoke. He steadied himself against the rough wall and slowly pushed himself up before he tried to move forward again. The landing where Bethy and Reeves were fighting was in flames, and more seemed to be coming from the rest of that level. He looked up the stairs and only saw fire as well.

46

In the hold of the *Polk*, Lucinda sat on the floor next to Lowell's blanket-covered body and stared at the horizon as the ship made its way home. She'd left one of the bay doors open to smell the sea air and cool the sweltering room. Not so long ago, she and Cyrus and the others had chased the horizon onboard the Turtle, slowly making their way across the country, taking people and goods from east coast to west. It was only a handful of months since they'd lost everyone, they knew except for each other. The whole crew had died because of the chewers and a rebel faction of the Union.

And here she was, sitting with another departed friend. She concentrated hard to remember why she ever decided to give up that nomadic life. The hum of the huge engines that kept the *Polk* aloft and moving hummed and clanked nearby, keeping a steady rhythm for her reverie.

One of the probationary soldiers came tromping into the hold and, before she could bite his head off, he raised his hands in front of him and said, "I'm so sorry, but Alek needs you on the bridge, says it's important." He kept his hands up and turned to run away, not waiting for a response or a rebuke.

She stood and looked down at Lowell. There was no time to process this. There wasn't adequate time to breathe in and out, let alone say the things that needed saying. Alek needed her on the bridge, and she wondered what the OMO was like before she and Cyrus came along. She moved to find out what the matter was, if she didn't force herself to go, she'd remain there until they got to the Tower and reunited with Cyrus.

In the command center, she didn't have to ask Alek what he needed to tell her, she could see it ahead of them in Santa Rosa; Smoke poured out of the upper levels and flames appeared at the windows and bay doors.

"Good god," Lucinda said. "What's happening?" She stepped up behind Alek and put her hand on his shoulder.

"No idea."

"We noticed the smoke a few minutes ago but couldn't believe it would be the tower." Corrigan, sitting in the navigator's spot was staring as well. He handed Lucinda his spyglass without her asking.

"Have you seen anyone in there?" Lucinda asked. She looked at the image through the glass, searching the windows and open doors for figures.

"No," Alek said. "What's worse, is I don't know where we're going to dock. We can't get too close to those flames without possibly igniting the gas in the *Polk*'s balloons."

Lucinda searched the area, trying to get a look at the base of the tower, to see if people got out, or if there was an effort yet to extinguish the flames, but was blocked by other buildings.

"Get me anywhere close," Lucinda pointed to a building across the street from the tower. "Over there is good, I'll climb down. Hell, fly over the top of the tower and I'll drop down."

Alek turned and looked at her. "Calm down. We will get you there. The top floors have smoke, so even if I could, I wouldn't drop you on the roof, you could be trapped."

"Just get me—" Lucinda searched the area with the glass.

"Calm. Down," Alek said. "We'll get there. Just take a moment to think clearly."

It was almost a reflex to be angry that Alek would say she wasn't being rational, but he was right. The thought of losing more friends buzzed in her head.

47

Reeves blocked the onslaught by the girl with his arms and then took two wild swings, which she dodged, but only by backing away. It gave Reeves a moment to dig in his pocket, looking for a gun or the brass knuckles. They weren't there, but he did feel the thin wire of the garrote he'd taken from the safe house in San Francisco. He pulled it out and kept it tucked in his fist.

"Cyrus is your man?" Reeves asked the girl. He nodded up to where Cyrus lay on the stairs. "He never could fight for himself. Ask his parents."

She threw a punch, unresponsive to the question. It grazed his chin ineffectively and he finally managed to hit her, striking her temple and knocking her back. He pressed his advantage and punched again, connecting solidly with her shoulder and turning her to the side slightly with its force. He gripped the ends of the garrote and wrapped it around her neck, moving behind her and pulling as hard as possible. He needed to end this and get away before too many soldiers showed up and overwhelmed him. The flames were surely already drawing citizens, military and law officers to the area, as well as any other OMO that were out of the tower.

He was struck—bowled over, more accurately—by Cyrus. The man stumbled out of the fire and fell into Reeves from what he could ascertain. The three of them dropped to the hard steps and Reeves rolled to get free, tumbling over flames and steps as he went.

When he could stop, Reeves stood up and turned for his opponents again. They were on the stairs, trying to help each other. Cyrus pressed his sleeve against the cut around Bethy's neck.

Reeves was weary and could feel his own blood drip down his side from where he'd been shot earlier. He wanted to finish this, but not at the expense of his own life, certainly not yet. He weighed whether killing Cyrus would satisfy him without finishing the rest that he owed some payback.

The fire answered him; a beam broke loose and dropped from the wall, slamming into another and showering the stairwell between Reeves and Cyrus with flaming ash. Below him, voices were gathering, and heavy footfalls approached on the stairs. He turned and pulled his coat about him and stumbled down the stairs, making a show that he could be an injured citizen.

Behind him, he heard a hoarse shout from Cyrus. "Reeves. Get back here. We're not done."

There was no cause to turn and face the two again, and Reeves moved faster, meeting a group of men on the next landing. He pointed up the stairs and wrung his hands in woe. When they'd left, he started taking the steps two at a time until he hit the bottom. He ran off into the street and was immediately wrapped in a blanket. He turned to thank the stranger and tell them of his narrow escape, when he noticed it was Shel who'd covered him.

"That doesn't look like any sort of plan, Mister Reeves," Shel said. "Is Patrick coming behind you?"

It took a moment to clear his lungs of the smoke and stench that clung to him even in the open air. He let Shel guide him into the crowd, through it and out the other side. "It's a variation on my plan, and that's all that matters. Let's get to Mama and the others so we can be prepared for our meeting with the president."

Shel stopped and looked at the tower burning behind them, the flames dancing in her eyes. "I don't know what you think is going to happen. But people are going to be pretty pissed off. Can't say the president will want to talk to any of us now."

Engines roared in the distance, and Reeves looked to see the *Polk* approaching from the north.

"You go talk to your friend, Beatrice, and I'll go talk to her employer, Calloway. Tell her you're happy to help and you have some friends that could pitch in should the need arise."

Shel nodded. "Nothing's going to happen to her, is it?"

"What?" Reeves' mind was racing on to the next task.

"Bea. She's not in danger, is she? I mean to say, if I tell her what you want, she's not going to get in any trouble, is she?"

It was touching to Reeves. A girl like Shel, living day to day, doing what she had to, and still finding some way to care about someone other than herself. "No. Why?"

"She's a friend, that's all. Don't want to be the cause of any undue bullshit in her future."

"Beatrice'll be fine. I'll meet you at the restaurant's loading docks when you're done."

Shel nodded again, slower this time and then raised her hand to wave. Then, she tore off up the street, moving among the crowds that were streaming out to help or watch the spectacle.

Reeves kept to the alleys and back streets. He was pretty sure no one cared one way or another about one more person running while the flames in the distance grew, ebbing from every window and door.

It was dark in the alley behind the *Carbondale Sage* as Reeves approached. He stayed to the shadows until he got close to the loading dock. There, a few lights burned near the doors, but just enough to help people keep from falling all over themselves. Reeves sat down behind some barrels and took a breath. It hurt to breath deep, and he remembered to check the wound at his side. It was still bleeding, though it had certainly slowed. He took some bits of his torn shirt and applied it to try to stop the bleeding. He leaned his head against a barrel and waited to see if the rest of the plan came to fruition.

48

Cyrus stayed at the tower, helping with the buckets of water and worked the hand cranks for the hoses. He'd run in and pulled a couple of men out of the barracks before others restrained him. Support beams were falling, the top floors were engulfed. He could feel his muscles trying to quit after the strain of the fight, carrying Bethy to a medic, and fighting the fire. Before that, it had been just as rough.

He told his story to a small group of OMO officers, explained how the fire started, who was inside, and what Reeves had said about the president.

Still, he continued for the better part of an hour, and would have gone on until he dropped, had Corrigan not come down and pulled him away. "We need to talk with Cashe," Corrigan said. "It can't wait."

"It has to," Cyrus said. "They need…" Cyrus saw Cashe in his chair sitting in the doorway of a nearby building. Cashe's face was fixed on the burning building, but his expression seemed even more troubled. Cyrus nodded and handed his empty bucket to the nearest man with a free hand. He walked with Corrigan toward their leader, and he realized that a nudge at his side indicated Bethy was walking alongside him.

"You should be…"

She stopped him with a steel glance, unable apparently to say anything yet.

"Thank you both for everything you've done," Cashe said. He looked them up and down. "I'm sorry you've sustained such injuries and I want you both to get medical attention. But I need you to do something else for me and it can't wait."

A nod from Bethy without hesitation, was followed by a "Yes?" from Cyrus.

"We've sent messages via telegraph to Colorado Station to ask that their airship base tell the president to turn around while we deal with this," Cashe said. "The office said they received several other messages about the president's visit and they don't know which ones to believe. They'll put *Airship One* on hold for a few hours once it arrives, but after that they're sending the ship ahead unless they get some confirmation from us. We gave them whatever codes we had, but they want someone to talk in person."

"Isn't that reason enough for them to turn back?" Corrigan asked. "The confusion over the messages?"

"You'd think, but no. They think if they have the president turn back, there could be a trap on the way back, or some such nonsense."

"And they don't want to wait around, for fear it's a trap and they'd be sitting ducks."

Cashe nodded. "So…we need you two to act as liaisons to the president. Or at least, act as my crew while I talk to President Alexander."

"No." It wasn't something Cyrus would even consider at the moment. "You need our help here."

"No," Cashe said. "From what I gather, this man might have a grudge against you in particular. It might be better to remove you from the situation. They also say that they don't have enough supplies to stock the president's airship once it arrives there. They'd have to wait for a supply ship or for us to come resupply them."

"Have Lowell do it," Cyrus said. "He's more diplomatic and has patience for this sort of nonsense. He likes shaking hands and whatnot."

"He's not back yet from…" Corrigan was interrupted by the sight of someone walking toward them from the parted crowd. It was Lucinda. Cyrus barely recognized his friend. She was cut, bruised, bloody and, unless Cyrus was mistaken, she'd been crying recently.

It took a moment for her to look Cyrus in the eye. "You look horrible," Lucinda said, and she hugged Cyrus. A moment later, she pulled Bethy into the embrace as well. "Lowell is dead." She said it loud enough that everyone nearby could hear.

"What?" Bethy whispered, her voice a raspy mess. She pulled back to look at Lucinda's face.

"We caught up with one of the escapees at a farmhouse up north. Looks like they were all staying there at one time. The guy got squirrely, and we ended up in a gunfight." Lucinda looked away from Bethy and Cyrus. "One of the trainees got themselves in trouble and Lowell helped them. Cost him his life."

The group was silent while the town around them became more chaotic by the second. More townspeople came with buckets and blankets. A group had begun to form a line toward the ocean, but it was so far away, that it would take precious time just to find enough people to make it work.

The noise rose behind them and Cyrus turned to look again at the fire efforts.

"I'll go." Lucinda looked haggard as she said it.

Cyrus would have bet everything he owned that she, too would have stayed, to somehow avenge Lowell. He looked at Bethy, and she nodded.

"We'll go, if there's someone onboard the Polk to give medical attention. We could all benefit from a few days to recuperate," Cyrus said. "Then we can come back and settle this." Cyrus felt his spine tighten. He didn't want to do it.

"I've sent Dex over to speak with Calloway," Cashe said. "He was set to throw a welcome dinner for the president and prepare provisions for when he returned to Savannah. He'll have to speed up his timetable for getting things put together, so we can take those supplies to Colorado Station."

Leaving now felt wrong, and as he looked at the flames, he wondered if he left now, whether there would be a town to come back to.

49

Reeves woke up to the sound of voices talking on the loading dock. He rubbed the sleep from his eyes and pulled out a functioning pocket watch. He'd slept for nearly two hours, which was not his intention. It would have been easy for someone to find him splayed out and snoring in the alley, completely unconcealed. Luckily the fire still seemed to be working for him and no one had come down the narrow alley.

On the dock, he saw Calloway and one of his men speaking to a rather disheveled OMO officer. Through what snippets he could hear from his distance away, it sounded like they were talking about throwing supplies together. More of the restaurant staff came out, including Beatrice. She and the cooks and waiters loaded up large crates with bags of grain, containers of lard, and boxes of flour. They brought fresh vegetables and other foodstuffs until two crates had been filled. Calloway talked with Beatrice and the group moved together with a wagon to get more from a storehouse down by the docks. Finally, all that was left was Calloway and his man Harper. Together they nailed crates shut and marked them with coal.

Reeves waited until they'd nearly finished and crept toward them in the shadows. He ducked to use the dock as cover, when heard a voice from behind him.

"That's far enough." He turned to find one of the other men from the garden, Johns, standing with a gun and moving from the shadows himself.

Harper also pulled his gun and aimed at Reeves. He jumped down off the dock and stood on the opposite side of Reeves from Johns.

"You're like a dog that won't leave off a scent even though you know you should, Reeves," Calloway said. "I knew you'd come back. It's just who you are." He pounded the last of the nails to secure the crate lid.

"I'm not here for the reasons you think."

"I'm not stupid. You're only here for one of two reasons, if not both," Calloway said. The lights of the loading dock were outshone by the flames of the tower burning not far behind Calloway and Reeves found himself mesmerized not by the danger at hand, but the inferno that he'd created of the OMO headquarters. Calloway continued, "You're either here to settle the score and kill me, or you're here because you think I have the stolen gold stashed somewhere."

"Those aren't the two reasons I'm here." Reeves didn't look away from the flames. "You can think what you want. I don't want you dead. In fact, if you were dead, my whole apple cart could be upset."

Harper grew impatient. "Can we kill him?"

"This close to the tower? The OMO might hear the shot and come running." Reeves gestured to the looming building.

"So? You're an escaped prisoner. We might get a reward or something," Johns said.

That was true, and if they killed him, Reeves wouldn't be around to tell the authorities what he knew about Calloway. His own threat was hollow.

"Look at him. You've stumped him. He didn't think so far ahead as that," Johns guffawed.

In his haste, and with the time constraints, Reeves had only considered the objectives, not the risks or obstacles. He assumed Calloway and his men would be the least of his worries. "You've gotten the better of me. I really didn't plan this out so much. I only thought about the two things I needed to do. Figured it would be easy." He hoped the men would oblige him with direction on how to accomplish the rest.

"You've mentioned these two things twice now. What pray tell were you going to do?" Calloway asked.

The men were close, but not close enough to reach. If he lunged, they could move away, and with Calloway himself standing on the raised platform of the loading area, he'd be even harder to fight. "The two things I need to do are—break this gentleman's arm," he pointed to Johns. "And break one of this fella's legs." Reeves pointed to Harper. "There is a third thing. But that's none of your concern." He waited for a reaction. If they hadn't shot him yet, odds were good a few more words weren't going to inspire them.

They laughed. The two men nearest him did, at least. Calloway wasn't so inspired. He stared at Reeves with concern. "Just kill him already," Calloway said, and immediately after he shouted in pain and fell to the loading dock, unconscious. Behind him, Shel stood with a length of thick, knotted rope in her hands and her hood pulled up to hide her face. Johns and Harper turned to see what had happened, leaving Reeves free to attack them. He grabbed Johns and kicked him in the side of the knee as hard as he could. With a loud crack, Johns fell to the ground screaming in pain.

Harper turned back to point his gun at Reeves but wasn't fast enough—Reeves punched him in the throat to disable him, then grabbed the man's right hand, pulling him so his arm descended on the edge of the loading dock at an angle, bringing another crackling sound of bone snapping and eliciting more shouts from the second man.

Reeves stopped and took a breath, letting his racing heart slow a little. He marveled for a moment of that time at how easy it was for him. How the reflexes that had caught the attention of the men at the training camps hadn't dulled even after all the time in prison, after the skills lay dormant.

He looked up to see Shel fading back into the shadows and he nodded. When she was gone, he jumped up onto the dock and approached Calloway. Reeves could hear him moaning over the shouts of his men. "You could have come out of this without a scratch," Reeves said. "I'm sure men will ask you how this happened, and if you mention my name, I'll make certain my fellow escapees come back here and burn your establishment to the ground with you and your wife in it. I will not warn you again."

Reeves moved away, running to the shadows that lead toward the garden where he'd first met with Calloway. The third thing he'd mentioned to the men was waiting there in a bucket near the cage where they kept the chewer and the birds.

50

Cyrus went to his quarters on the *Polk* while Lucinda helped Bethy to the infirmary. He pulled a nice clean uniform, which he never wore, from a trunk and straightened it out. Cashe ordered Cyrus to take a full uniform along, so he would look presentable when he met the president. Cyrus put it carefully on the bed and peeled his clothes off. They smelled like smoke and were blackened in spots. The shirt was torn in a number of places and he tossed it into his trash bin. The pants weren't much better, but he hung onto them. In his closet, he pulled out a washcloth and poured some water in the basin. He scrubbed at his face without looking in the mirror. The water in the basin turned black the first time he tried to wring the cloth out. It felt good to have the cold water on his skin until he got to some of the wounds. His cuts and scrapes stung as he dabbed at them and wiped away the blood. He tossed the dirty water out the side window and poured more from the pitcher.

This time he looked at his face as he wiped his brow and neck. He was older suddenly. Seeing Reeves again made his bones ache, and his skin itch. The years hadn't been kind to his memory. He'd made it a point to try to forget the deal that kept him out of the war, but it refused to be forgotten, popping up over the years, pushing him to keep moving. He crossed the country in a giant mechanical transport for years, just trying to stay focused on anything other than the life he'd left behind. And here was Reeves.

He finished, got dressed in his civilian clothes, knowing he'd be helping load up supplies soon enough and headed back down to the wharf. Without the tower, the *Polk* had to move down to the waterfront and load up like a common freight ship by the water. Wagons were already lining up nearby, and a hose was extended to suck water into the holding tank to supply the boiler with fuel.

Down the walkway and off to the side, Lucinda stood out of the way of the chaos and stared off at the burning tower. "You think we may have outlasted our luck here already?" She asked when he got close.

"I was just thinking about that," Cyrus said. "I thought you liked belonging to something?"

"I did."

Jasper approached with a wagon, filled with more crates. He was dressed in his best Confederate uniform, with a few noticeable recent patches in the cloth. Shel rode with him on the bench. They backed the wagon to the loading dock and pulled the lids off. They were all empty except one, which was nailed shut.

"What's that one?" Reeves asked.

"One of Mama's. She says it's stuff she needs to keep these old bastards alive," Shel said, followed immediately by Jasper's grumbling.

Everyone seemed content to stare at the boxes for a minute. They weren't very accommodating.

"Best get to it," Reeves said as he stepped over the side of a crate and got in. He knelt and eventually sat on his ass and leaned back. He had to curl up on his side to feel comfortable, but even that wasn't ideal. Before he allowed the lid to be sealed, he tested the back wall to make sure it could push away from the inside. After that, he nodded to Jasper and Shel and they put the lid on. After a few hammer strikes, they were done.

Several pinpricks of light came through where they'd made holes, so he could breathe, but it wasn't much. He felt around for the supplies he'd grabbed for himself—a loaf of bread, a jug of water, and an empty jug for when he needed to answer nature's call. He made a point of putting one jug on one side and one on another to insure the two of them didn't get mixed up.

In a few minutes he heard voices again and the wagon began moving. It was a noisy, shaky ride as the wagon hit holes and ruts in the street. The thick smell of smoke filtered in as they got downwind of the tower. They came to a halt and received instructions on how they would unload and wait for their turn. There were other voices and he recognized Shel, and Calloway and Beatrice.

The wagon jostled, and he heard the scraping of crates being pulled off. It was maybe a half hour until Reeves came to rest in what he assumed was the cargo hold of the *Polk*. After another hour of loading and movement around him, it got quiet.

Within the next hour everything shifted, and the ship's engines hammered up to speed before taking to the air. The faint pinpricks of light had disappeared in the blackened hold. There was no chance to make it out without surrendering or dying now, Reeves assumed. He thought of his options; let his thoughts drip into a pool in his mind. He had a couple of days to refine his hasty plan, assuming he wasn't discovered by then.

The *Polk* made good time thanks to favorable winds and a determined crew. Lucinda stared out at the scenery from the observation deck, at a loss for what to do to prepare for their meeting with the Confederate president. Hopefully, it would be a quick exchange and they'd all be on their way. While she agreed with Cyrus that they needed to get back and get things in hand in Santa Rosa, she needed time to process the things she'd seen and learned. She sat back and ran though recent events in her mind before she heard light footfalls on the stairs behind her.

"Good morning," Bethy said. Her voice was a level slightly above a whisper. She moved lightly and dropped herself on the chair next to Lucinda.

"Hello. Glad to see you up and around."

With a nod Bethy said, "Yeah. I needed sleep. It helped with a lot of things." She pointed at her throat where a bandage encircled it. "Not this, but the rest of the aches."

"I'm glad. By the time we're headed home I think we'll all be better off." Lucinda felt herself smiling by reflex. The soft voice was unusual for Bethy, and it felt to Lucinda like it suited her better than her usual gruff, say-whatever-comes-to-mind Bethy. "Can I get you anything?"

Bethy shook her head.

A small group of people walked into the observation room, an older woman, younger woman and two older men. "Sorry if we're interrupting you," the older woman said. "We've never been in an airship before and we heard the view was something to see from here."

"I'm sorry. Do I know you?"

The young blonde stepped forward and put her hand out to Lucinda. "I'm so sorry. I'm Shelby, and this is Emma. That man there is Wilhelm. And the slow one." She pointed to the elderly man navigating the few stairs behind them. "That's George. We're with Mister Calloway's restaurant. We were asked to help since they were shorthanded, what with the fire and all."

Lucinda studied the older people and shook the girl's hand. "I see. I apologize, but we have some security concerns with this trip. I'm sure if their liaison vouched for you, you're fine to be on the *Polk*, but you're really supposed to stay confined to the barracks downstairs. We can't have you roaming the ship freely."

George had finally finished the steps and was shuffling for the giant glass window on the far side of the room when Emma's eyes widened. "Oh, my. I'm so sorry. No one told us. We'll leave right quick." She grabbed George's hand and turned him around toward the stairs.

Lucinda guessed the little group wouldn't be a problem as long as she and Bethy stayed with them. They seemed pretty harmless in their advanced years. "It's okay. You can stay for a few minutes. Just a few, though, and then we'll take you back."

The group thanked her profusely and pressed their noses against the window. "Is that black cloud over there a flock of those damn birds, or is it just a black cloud?" George asked.

Bethy rolled her eyes at Lucinda reclined on her chair.

Lucinda patted Bethy on the shoulder. "Tomorrow. This'll all be over tomorrow."

53

In the darkness, Reeves lay curled up, cramped and uncomfortable. People came and went, but none lingered in the hold. While the crate bumped and jostled occasionally, the trip was good for little except planning and reflection. He considered whether anything would work out and whether it mattered if it did. The old Confederate veterans were certainly capable in their day, but Father Time had taken to beating them something fierce, and their abilities today were in question.

The men he'd broken out of prison with were all gone. He'd told them that they'd get home, but had he promised them? Each died in some bloody battle supporting Reeves himself.

Use any object at hand and turn it into a weapon, the trainers told him. *Any object.*

As he lay there, in the near blackness, he struggled to remember a single one of their names. In fact, one had handed him an envelope at some point, and he'd cared so little, that he hadn't been curious about it for more than a minute. Reeves patted his jacket and heard the light crunch of the very same message in his breast pocket.

He felt around until he got it out and held it in front of his face. The light barely let him know there was something there. He quietly rearranged himself, rolling onto his other side, so he could hold the envelope up to one of the pinpricks of light that shone through the crate—one of the things cut to give him air. The light managed to show him the outside—front and back—was blank. He reached in and pulled the paper inside and could see it had writing on it. Large letters on flimsy paper.

It was on the letterhead of The Southern Telegraph Companies. That much was easy to discern. It was in large bold letters at the top. The standard disclaimers followed in tiny typed letters, but the rest was handwritten.

TO: Ida Plessy   Oct. 6 1876

Deeply regret to inform of HRs family taking ill. Children near death from lung sickness. Wife in early stages. Pull HR out of field with all due urgency and send home with haste. Children not expected to last more than a week.

Regards, Father Clifton

Ida Plessy was an alias of Mama's that Reeves had heard her use a number of times. Father Clifton was code for their contacts in the Confederacy. He had to assume that HR referred to Reeves himself. It was the date that concerned him. October sixth, 1876. Reeves' mission that went wrong happened nearly six months later, on April eleventh, 1877. Reeves held the paper closer to the light and reread each word again.

To his estimation, it meant that Mama had known about his family long before they died. It meant that if he'd known, he could have gone home and been with them before the kids had passed. It meant he could've been with his dear Lydia Jane in her dying days. Reeves hadn't known to believe Calloway before, but here was proof, not only that his family was dead, but that Mama had known.

He folded the paper, put it in the envelope and slid it into his pocket again. He spent considerable time breathing, trying to control his emotions. Weeping would most certainly draw attention to the crate and he would be found out. It would prove to be a long ride for a man alone in the blackness with nothing but idle time and his thoughts.

54

When Cyrus finished his shift navigating, he woke Corrigan and Dex and let them know it was time to switch. Dex had just dropped himself on the floor by his station with a blanket and pillow, while Corrigan had merely reclined his chair and pulled his coat around him.

"Already?" Dex asked. "It really doesn't feel like it." When he stood, he pulled his blanket around his shoulders. "Shit it's cold. Must be closing in on Colorado Station."

In a moment, Corrigan had a pencil and was scribbling in the margin of a map. He checked the instruments and air speed. "If everything is right, we should be there in the next three hours or so."

"Dandy. I'll be in the shitter for my morning constitutional," Dex wandered off, blanket and all. He belched in the hall and shouted "Rowdy Riflemen" with quiet enthusiasm.

If he could've picked his crew, this wouldn't have been it, Cyrus thought. Of course, when he was captaining the Turtle, he picked up strays, not knowing their skills or personalities most of the time, and they worked out fine. This time, he was the stray, though.

Some movement around the mountain up ahead drew Cyrus's attention. "What're those things?"

Corrigan squinted in the direction Cyrus indicated. "Those are small airships they call gold ferries. They bring the valuables from the mines into Colorado Station. Dangerous. Only room for a single man and about a ton of precious materials. Pretty basic controls. Not a lot of safety stuff."

"So if it crashes, the pilot dies on a pile of gold?" Cyrus asked. "That's a hell of a way to go."

Corrigan nodded.

"So they aren't likely a threat to the president?"

"Nah," Corrigan said. "We'll keep an eye on them, but they're probably more focused on making their daily quotas than a visit from the president." Corrigan took a drink from his cup and leaned against the console. "Look, I can command this on my own until Dex comes back. After that, we'll need to start navigating the mountains with a little more precision. Since we have the time, why don't you get an hour or so of sleep? You can't look half-dead when you and Lucinda get all gussied up to see the president."

"Dandy." Cyrus walked to his room and picked his uniform up off the bed. He put it on and made sure it all looked good. All the buttons were on it. It was well-cared for. His boots were shiny and he pulled them on. He stood in front of the mirror, trying to make sure it looked good. The Confederate president wasn't someone he wanted to impress, but he didn't want Bethy or Lucy to think less of him. When he was sure he looked proper, he checked his pocket watch; he had more than two hours to go. He sighed and sat in his only chair and thought about what Lucinda said about leaving.

Lucinda gathered him later and they walked together to the control room. "Christ. When're we going to be able to get on with this and go home?" Cyrus asked.

"You look nice." Lucinda fixed his collar. "A little wrinkled, though. Did you sleep in this?"

Cyrus waved her away.

"This is pretty much it. It'll be done soon, and we can go home," Lucinda said. She used her iron arm to point out the *CSA Kernstown* in the distance with its fat holds and bloated airbags. It was the dirigible that served as the Confederate president's personal aircraft and was most commonly known by its adopted military name of *Airship One*. It carried the president's detail of soldiers, press people, and support staff around as the southern leader visited places that he wanted to impress with the CSA's military prowess. The *Kernstown* was built with more lift than any other ship before it. The array of powerful weaponry it was able to carry was astounding; it could support more men and cannon than a land-based fortification the size of Fort Henry. It was larger than any of the craft the Office of Military Operations used in their efforts to keep the peace in this area of the country—including the *Leonidas Polk*, which was a damned impressive craft in and of itself.

As Cyrus stared at the ship, he suddenly felt a tug at his collar. Lucinda was grabbing at his uniform lapel again, trying to make it look right.

"Stop that. It's good enough," he said.

"It is not good enough. We're about to meet the Confederate president, you ought to look presentable." Lucinda picked something off Cyrus' jacket and flicked it off onto the floor. "Must you look like an urchin every minute of every day?"

"This isn't my uniform and that ain't my president."

There was a whirring that drew closer to Cyrus' ear as Lucinda's iron arm gripped his coat tighter and pulled him close to her face. "I don't give a god damn what you think of that man, it's an honor to be chosen to meet the man and his crew. You'll show him some damn respect, too." They lingered, nose to nose for a moment until she pushed him away. "And that uniform is yours now, so you better get used to it."

There were people around and Cyrus felt it was a show for them. It wasn't his nature to be cowed by a woman, least not any other woman, but Cyrus held his tongue. He'd had a hard time adjusting to military life itself, let alone the tug of war that came with working on a crew with somewhat divided loyalties. Half of the *Polk*'s crew were from the north, the other half from the south, just to keep things even and fair when they had to work out some border dispute or water rights. Still, it was the first place Cyrus had felt welcome in some time.

The *Polk* drew closer to the barren field where The CSA *Kernstown* waited. Colorado Station was too small for a craft as enormous as the president's ship or the *Polk*, so they were forced to land at the largest expanse of flat land near the town. The *Polk*'s engines cut off about a mile out and the crew let out some grey maneuvering sails to bring it in the rest of the way.

Cyrus moved down to help with the docking and the planks down in the storeroom. At the bottom of the stairs, he found a row of Confederate soldiers that were already standing at attention in anticipation of the landing. They were all fairly old, and Cyrus wondered if any of them would pass out before they even docked. He furrowed his brow and looked at Lucinda behind him. "They don't expect *us* to stand like that do they?"

"I met a few of them earlier. They volunteered to help. I guess we should stand at attention like the other soldiers. Seems proper."

"Ugh." Cyrus rolled his eyes and straightened his posture somewhat.

"You can really be a miserable bastard sometimes, you know that?" Lucinda stood tall with her hands at her side.

"You've just discovered that?" The smile was tough for Cyrus to hide.

Lucinda knew him better than just about anyone. They had been stuck on a ship for some time together before joining the OMO and then being cooped up together on board various airships, and within the confines of forts. She gave him some sort of direction in the aimless world that tried to pull him in every direction. He'd tried his best to run away with her to Europe, where word was that the chewer plague hadn't spread. Those plans were dashed, and they ended up with the OMO crew instead.

As the airship maneuvered into place, its engines roared to life, to help move it into just the right spot. The door opened, a ramp was lowered, and Lyle Cashe wheeled himself out in his chair. Several other OMO agents stood behind him and walked out when he was clear of the doors.

"What're you standing around like idiots for?" Cashe asked Cyrus.

Lucinda seemed to deliberately avoid Cyrus' gaze.

"And you certainly don't have to stand at attention or salute or any of that horseshit. We're supposed to be neutral to both countries."

Lucinda spoke up. "We just thought it was courteous."

"Pssh. You don't see me standing, do you?"

Cyrus looked down at their wheelchair-bound leader, who hadn't been on his feet in months. He had an odd sense of humor.

"I'll handle talking to the president, you can stand there and look official," Cashe said. "Once the supplies are off-loaded, we can get to going home, yes?"

Cyrus nodded.

When the doors were open, Lucinda helped Cyrus navigate the wheelchair through the rough grass of the field and the occasional rocks. The president's group approached from their ship as well. Once Cyrus and the Confederate guard had exchanged pleasantries, the guard waved everyone else forward. Lucinda signaled the people on board the *Polk* to begin transferring cargo from one ship to the other.

To Cyrus' surprise, the president was cordial with an immediately likeable smile. "So there really is a threat?"

"Unfortunately, sir," Cashe said. "We've suffered some losses and we believe a former Confederate spy is loose after a prison break and he seems bent on payback for his incarceration. But we aren't sure of the details."

In the tall grass nearby, a mass of crows flapped noisily to a landing and strutted in circles. They flapped their wings and twisted their heads to the side, seemingly waiting patiently for something to happen.

"We don't have a full contingent, but my men might be of assistance," President Alexander said. "This is my assistant, Mister Bradley Lake." The president gestured to a small man with a briefcase behind him. "Lake? How many troops do we have here?"

Cashe spoke before Lake could respond. "At this time, I think we should just send you back and attempt a visit later in the season. Just to make sure we have the situation in hand."

Behind Cashe, men were moving carts and crates on wagons. The men on *Airship One* pulled things aboard, stowing them efficiently and easily. He watched as the old men from the *Polk* took a wagon of their own, all pulling and moving nearly as fast as the strapping men fresh from training camps.

"Well, I hate to hear it, but I'll bow to your judgement." He nodded and Cashe nodded back. "Until next time." He extended his hand and Cashe shook it, then the president turned and shook Lucinda's, then stepped toward Cyrus, who had a single second to think what he'd say, and what he'd do. With no time to think of a rejoinder, and with Lucy's eyes boring into his very soul, Cyrus shook the president's hand and nodded.

"That wasn't so hard, was it?" Lucinda said as they watched the president make his way back to his airship.

55

The two ships lifted simultaneously; smoke pouring out of their stacks, engines rumbling back to life.

"Think they've made any headway in catching this Reeves fella back in Santa Rosa?" Dex sat back in one of the comfortable chairs of the observation deck and put his feet up on the metal railing.

Everyone turned to look at Cyrus. He too, was watching the *Kernstown* as it slowly came about to head back the way it came. "I don't know. Hell, I haven't known the guy for almost a decade now. Obviously, things have changed." It was the same question he'd been asking himself the last few days. "But if he's gone through some sort of special training, I'd say he could be a dangerous man if he sets his mind to something."

"Hell, I don't know. I was in the same god damn army as he was and I ain't never heard of no specially trained spies," Dex said. "Sounds like a lot of horseshit to me."

Cyrus felt Bethy lean up against him. He turned, and she smiled up at him. "We'll handle it when we get back. I think the OMO can handle one man, can't we?"

A high-pitched whistle sounded through the com tubes, followed by Lucinda's voice. *"Cyrus? Are you down on the observation deck?"*

Cyrus reached over and pulled a tube from the wall. "Yes, I'm here."

"Can you get a better look at the Kernstown? It looks like it's putting off an awful lot of smoke from up here," Corrigan Lucinda called over the speaker.

Dex and Bethy walked over to scrutinize the other ship while Cyrus reached up and pulled down a pane of glass from the high ceiling. The president's airship came into better view and the others came to look as well. As the ship had turned, the smoke became clearer on the starboard side. It wasn't coming from the stacks after all, it was pouring thick and black from the portals nearest the boiler room.

"Well, shit." Dex was succinct as always.

Cyrus put the tube up to his mouth again. "Can we signal them? Warn them?"

Lucinda's voice came back through the tube. *"We started that already,* but the *Kernstown* seems to have leveled off and is taking measures to land again on their own. Alek and Corrigan are adjusting the *Polk* to head for the ground as well."

"We'll join you in the wheelhouse presently." Cyrus returned the tube and turned to the others. "Dex? Head down to the hold and get everyone ready to assist the president's airship. They could crash into the woods, or the hills; no telling."

"Malfunction?" Bethy asked.

Cyrus didn't offer an answer. He'd just been on the ship himself and everything seemed to be running perfectly normal. He bounded into the control room, where Alek and Corrigan were leading a couple of recruits in bringing the *Polk* back down for a gentle landing.

"One of the new guys spotted the smoke," Corrigan nodded to an older man in the corner, signaling the *Airship One* with a lamp.

"When did it start?" Bethy asked.

"Don't know," the man with the light said. "Hard to tell when it was turned away from us."

The starboard door opened, and Lucinda strode in, holding a pair of field glasses in her good hand. "They seem to be making a controlled descent. What crew members I can see don't appear too panicked. I can't find any smoke in their control room."

"Hopefully they can get it down before it spreads there." Alek pushed the engines to their stop positions and his hand hovered above the controls. Cyrus knew the pilot was waiting for the engines to grind to a halt so he could reverse them and stop the *Polk*'s forward momentum.

"You don't all find this a little coincidental?" Lucinda asked. "We're rushing to get the president away from potential danger and suddenly his ship has a malfunction?"

"We don't know it's a malfunction." Alek slowly reversed the throttle to ease the airship to a halt, all the while letting the vehicle drop toward the ground. "Do we?"

Cyrus looked at the two. "Are you saying that you think Reeves managed to get aboard the *Kernstown* and he's causing this?"

"Wouldn't be out of order to consider the idea," Lucinda said. "If it is, we unknowingly delivered Reeves to the Confederate president."

Bethy questioned the idea. "If that's the case, why would he sabotage the president's ship? Why not hide out until we're gone and sail home undetected until we're out of sight? That should be his ride home, why muck it up?"

It was silent as they stared at the rapidly descending ship less than a mile away from them.

"Maybe he wanted to kill the president and botched it?" Corrigan threw in.

"Whatever the case, that airship is going to land hard, they're using emergency landing procedures over there." Alek pointed to an area close to some trees in the distance. "Probably land about a half mile to the northeast."

"Land us here." Cyrus turned for the portal.

"I can get us closer," Alek said.

"If that ship explodes, it'll take us with it if we're any closer," Cyrus said. He moved down the corridor and descended the stairs, Lucinda and Bethy immediately behind him. The idea of coming back into contact with Reeves so soon didn't sit well with him. He'd hoped to contain the man back in Santa Rosa and deal with him when they returned, but if he was here—if he was on the president's ship—then that confrontation would happen whether Cyrus liked it or not.

The passengers came streaming out of the president's airship even before it touched the ground. A soldier jumped from the main entry and tugged at a ladder, while others opened the cargo door and leapt, tumbling as they hit the ground. Lucinda took a deep breath and peered through the rifle's scope. She adjusted the focus to see the people as they ran toward her and the *Polk*. She was lying on her stomach on the outer deck, steadying the rifle against one of the railing's posts.

"They're coming out now." Cyrus' voice came from the tube to her left.

"No shit," Lucinda said. She looked at the first two soldiers out of the cargo hold. She'd seen them in the initial meeting when they talked to the president. Her focus shifted to the front door, where more men in uniform came out and pooled at the bottom of the ramp with their weapons drawn and scanning the area. There were four in all when the president himself came out.

"The president is on his way down the ramp. Do you see him? Lucy?"

The tube was too far away for her to grab without breaking her visual on *Airship One* and its evacuees. She also hated that she couldn't turn it off and eliminate the distraction.

The president ran hunched over down the stairs, where he quickly disappeared into the small group of soldiers. The group then moved together toward the *Polk*. She scanned the faces of the Confederates, looking for one that didn't belong.

Back at the rear of the craft, two soldiers were helping the rest of the passengers out of the ship. In quick succession, a number of the staff exited the door and ran. The cooks, the servants, the suppliers from Santa Rosa, and more of the president's staff and advisors all moved as fast as they could away from the smoking airship.

One man began to struggle with the soldiers and drew Lucinda's attention. He was trying to take a satchel with him, but the men at the cargo door were pulling it from his grasp. Lucinda imagined they weren't allowing anyone to take anything with them from the ship, just in case someone might have smuggled a weapon aboard. She adjusted her sights and focused in on the man's face, scrutinizing it for the possibility of a disguise. Cyrus had given them a briefing on what Reeves looked like as they traveled to Colorado Station, but a verbal description wasn't much help in the chaos.

Cyrus pushed past the half dozen or so other OMO soldiers standing at the open cargo door. "Keep your eyes open everyone. There's no telling what this spy may be disguised as." He stepped off the ship and landed on the hard ground with a crunch of rocks. "As soon as the president is aboard, move him over to the other side of the cargo bay. We'll take him and his advisor upstairs to the mess hall as soon as possible."

"How the hell are we supposed to watch for this bastard if we've never seen him?" One of the recruits asked.

It was a good question, one that Cyrus had no answer for. He was running on instinct and hope at that point. He heard someone jump off the ship behind him.

"What's going on? What're you staring at?" Bethy asked.

Cyrus pointed to the president, moving toward them, unimpeded. "We'll have him in a few minutes, we can take off and return to Santa Rosa or the outpost in ten minutes or so."

At the smoky cargo hold of the president's ship, the man in the bowler was still arguing with two soldiers. Everyone else seemed to have left them behind. Cyrus raised his rifle to get a closer look. His gun certainly wasn't nearly as fancy, nor was the sight quite as powerful as the one Lucinda used, but at the short distance to *Airship One*, it did the trick. Midway to the *Polk*, a dozen kitchen staff, servants and resupply personnel were running through the high grass as fast as they could manage. Cyrus moved the sight up a bit and focused as best he could on the three men arguing by the other ship. One of the soldiers looked angry with the man, the other soldier appeared anxious to run away from the downed airship. He moved from foot to foot and looked at the other people fleeing. The man in the bowler's face was red as he shouted at the men in Confederate uniforms. After a few seconds, he shouted what Cyrus could only assume was an obscenity, tossed his bag back into the ship and started running toward the *Polk* with the soldiers in close pursuit.

58

Lucinda took a deep breath and focused as she heard the shot. The sound startled her enough that she pulled her eye from the lens of the rifle and checked the barrel to see if it was smoking from a discharge. It wasn't. She hadn't fired. When she returned her gaze to the scope, it took a moment to find the man. The two soldiers who had been attempting to take his bag were now standing over him, looking from the man's body to the *Polk* with stunned expressions. They each grabbed a wrist and dragged the man along.

The exodus from *Airship One* had ended, with the stragglers making their way across the field, copping glances at the downed man as they ran. A woman in a long dress ran along, stealing glances as she went. Nearby, Lucinda recognized one of the ship's burly workers from the reloading effort. He was hampered by the fact that he was practically carrying an elderly woman through the high growth. His filthy coveralls were a stark contrast to her neatly pressed dining staff attire. She looked bewildered as he took her, and she looked back at the president's airship constantly.

The president himself advanced as quickly as he could, encircled by six men who were trying to shield him, and likely blocking his view of everything around him. He stumbled, only to be lifted again by the man nearest his elbow. Lucinda focused in on each of the soldiers' faces, they looked familiar from the meeting with the president, but she scrutinized each of them closely. Maybe Reeves was in disguise and using the panic to confuse the president and his security detail.

Was he working alone? Had Cyrus in fact killed Reeves and ended the threat?

She took in each of the faces still on the field through her scope, but none of them looked the least bit like Reeves. She got off her stomach and up to her knees to grab the nearby tube. "Cyrus? Are you there? Did you fire that shot? Was that him?" She paused and stared out at the emptying field. "Cyrus?"

She dropped the tube and ran toward the door. She sprinted down the stairs, rifle in her mechanical hand, the other lightly sliding along the stair railing. She could feel her feet barely touch the floor, as though she were nearly flying instead of running.

At the first landing, Corrigan leaned out of the hall. "Who's shooting?" The trainee, Clifton stepped into the hall from behind him with the same question on his face.

"Don't know," she said. She could've told him she thought Cyrus, but what would that have accomplished? She continued without comment, noticing that Clifton followed her as she turned down the next stair and onward into the huge hold where everyone was gathering. As she bounded through the open door, she ran headlong into a Confederate soldier and they both tumbled to the ground.

As Clifton bent down to help her up, she scanned the crowd of people from *Airship One* that had amassed on the other side of the cargo bay, before turning back to the soldier that was scrambling to his feet. Her heart had been punching her chest so hard from the shooting and the run down the stairs that she felt lightheaded and feared she might not be able to stay on her feet.

59

Cyrus stayed standing, gun centered on the man's chest as he fell. It was hard to see that far without a better scope or magnifier of some such like, he couldn't see if the man had given up the case or package or whatever the others were trying to wrest from him. He was ready to fire again when one of the Confederate soldiers put a hand on Cyrus' shoulder and shouted for him to stop. An explanation followed, but Cyrus had a ringing in his ears from the report of the gun that blocked his ability to hear them as well as he should, but the meaning was clear—they wanted him to stop. And the horrified looks told him he'd been mistaken about the notion that the man's identity was Reeves.

Time passed him by as he stared at the soldiers dragging the man's body toward the *Polk*. He turned to see his own people questioning him on what to do next, but their words were lost as well. Bethy came through and pointed the Confederate crew toward the bow hold through a thick door. She then reached out for the president and helped Dex hoist him onboard, followed by his contingent. The president was directed toward the rear of the compartment.

"We need to move out," one of the president's men said. He'd shouted it and Cyrus barely heard him.

"Get on board and cover the president." Cyrus stared at the last two soldiers to approach, the ones dragging the man Cyrus shot. He reached out and helped them lift the man onto the deck. They all got on board themselves and examined the wound in the man's shoulder. Cyrus' ears sounded like a bell reverberating, but he was hearing everything slightly better. "How is he?" Cyrus looked at the wound over one soldier's shoulder.

"He's not breathing," the soldier said.

An older woman in a long dress approached and knelt with them. She looked at the wound and held up the man's hand, holding his wrist. She looked at them sadly. "I'm afraid he's gone." Her eyes welled up with tears, as did one of the soldiers who'd carried him.

"Miss, I'm sorry," Cyrus said. "There has to be something we can do. Let's get a physician in here to look at him. Doesn't the president have a personal doctor? Where is he?"

The woman nodded to the man on the floor. "That was him. I was his nurse assistant."

"We had orders that everyone had to leave their things.

"In case there was a saboteur, we had to leave everything for fear it might have a trap of some kind," the teary soldier said. "He wouldn't give up his medical bag."

Across the room, Bethy was trying to shout into a tube, though it was impossible, even without the high pitch sound and her ruined voice, for him to hear. Though by the sudden lift off of the *Polk*, he inferred that she'd told them to get the hell out of there, lest the president's airship explode and take them with it. It seemed that the craft was smoking more now than before.

The trio of Confederates looked up at Cyrus as he stood. He wanted to apologize, but couldn't think straight, couldn't figure what nudged him to pull the trigger. He figured panic. There was fear, too.

He turned to help get the president upstairs.

60

The airship shook and tilted before leveling off and rising. The airship was moving off from wherever it had landed. The engines clanked as they were suddenly made to give full power to lift the massive craft up and off. The ship tilted again, sharply this time, and Reeves heard a number of people shout at the sudden reorientation. The incline was now so great that Reeves felt his crate slide, though only an inch or so.

"We need to get the president to a secure room upstairs, stand aside," Reeves heard a voice from the crowd. "Stand aside." It sounded vaguely like Cyrus, though encased in a box, it was hard to be sure. The very idea spurred Reeves to move. He reached back and pushed the box side slightly, letting his eyes get used to the sudden influx of light, and giving himself a moment to listen for anyone walking nearby.

It was a matter of unfortunate timing, a thing that even the best spy couldn't avoid. Reeves had managed to pull himself from the crate easily, but as he tried to stand, he inadvertently turned and tripped someone coming down a nearby staircase he hadn't seen behind him. They both tumbled, and she fell to the ground. A man behind her rushed over and helped her up. "Are you okay?" The man asked, and once the woman was standing again, the soldier turned and helped Reeves as well.

Getting his bearings, Reeves looked up to notice the woman was Lucinda, one of the OMO soldiers he'd seen and asked Shel about. She was hard to miss with an exposed metal arm at her side. "I'm sorry. I didn't mean to…"

"Why were you on the ground? Are you all right?" Lucinda asked.

Reeves replied "I fell during that last turn, I guess. It knocked me off my feet." He looked around and saw that it was, indeed, Cyrus and several others that were guiding the president in Reeves' direction.

The woman looked at the crowd of soldiers from the president's ship, far across the hold. "Why are you all the way over here?" She looked at the nearby crates, and Reeves knew she would see the side of his crate off, and nothing else inside. He acted, reaching for his gun before she could sound an alarm or grab him. He had it halfway out when he heard a click near his head.

He turned to find the junior officer that had helped them up had already pulled his own gun and it was leveled at Reeves, the barrel just three feet from his face. "Don't move."

Reeves turned to see the young man grit his teeth and narrow his eyes. It was hard to read him, he seemed frightened and resolved at the same time. With everyone staring and time running short, Reeves decided to raise his hands in surrender. He'd take his chances and try to break free once they all tried to grab him. Maybe he could fight his way to the president if they all swarmed him.

As he moved to give up, he saw the young officer's gaze widen and dart wildly from the hands to Reeves' eyes. "I said don't move."

Before Reeves could react, he heard the familiar click. Reeves could feel his body tense, waiting for the impact, the hot burn of a bullet. The boy had pulled the trigger, whether on purpose or by nerves, but nothing had happened. The hammer of the pistol came down the second time with no sudden report of the gun firing. His pistol was empty.

The stab of excitement pushed Reeves to action; his heart raced as he pulled his own pistol and shot the young soldier in the chest twice and then readjusted his focus and shot one of the soldiers near the president in the head. Cyrus was already pulling the president in the opposite direction and another soldier raced forward. They couldn't be more than fifteen paces away, Reeves figured. As the soldier approached, Reeves swung his pistol and caught the man square in the jaw and he fell to the side.

The president was being dragged toward the door leading to the other half of the hold, where the OMO had herded the Confederates fleeing the *Kernstown*. A small group of ten or so civilians and support staff were still trying to shove themselves in, frantic now that there was gunfire.

Reeves assessed the situation as he moved to cover behind some crates to avoid gunfire from Cyrus now that Cyrus had his own gun in hand. As he scanned the hold, the only other people left were Cyrus, president Alexander, one of the president's guards, the woman with the mechanical arm, and a couple of soldiers. He figured those odds were as good as he was going to get.

Mama and Shel emerged from the dwindling group both holding guns low at their sides. As the stragglers entered the other room, Shel shoved the door shut and when a soldier tried to push back through, Shel fired two shots, striking him in the chest. The door fell closed with his body, and she slid the thick wooden plank into place.

Mama was already pointing her gun at the group of OMO soldiers around the president. Reeves kept his gun trained on the president, while Mama and Shel held their guns somewhere in the open space between him.

"Now everyone just be easy," Reeves said. "And we'll all get out of this with minimal injury." He looked at Cyrus out of the corner of his eye, half-thrilled to see him. "Everyone just be easy. You don't think I can shoot the president right now? You all need to drop your guns, before things go real wrong."

They all stared at him, pointing their guns in his direction. "You see what I did to that man back there? I'm as serious as it gets."

"Reeves—" Cyrus began.

Reeves interrupted him by shooting the president's assistant in the shoulder. The few people left shouted in surprise and moved to help the man.

"Stop. Just stop. He'll live. Just stay away." Reeves scanned the few remaining. "You see that I'm not in the mood for frivolity, now don't you? Put your guns down before someone gets hurt for permanently."

They were still reluctant, and Reeves felt his blood rise and he cocked his pistol. He could see his hand was shaking slightly. "I'm not saying it again." They responded, though unhappily, and put their guns down. While they all complied, Reeves paid particular attention to Cyrus, and the narrow looks the man was giving him.

"Son, I don't know what the hell you're thinking," Mama said. "The plan was to get asylum with the president and head home on his ship. You didn't say anything about this. You didn't say anything about killing nobody else." She was breathing heavy, struggling to keep her gun raised. "Certainly not Confederates."

The *Polk* had risen quickly and continued to climb. In the air around them, more of the crows screamed as they flew near the ship.

"It's all in there." Reeves pointed to the lump beneath a tarp near all of the stacked crates and equipment that jutted out into the middle of the hold. "Everything that's owed. Every penny." He looked at the president and felt his hand shake a little. "I wanted to be the one that delivered it to you."

"There's no gold. We *know* that Calloway didn't have any of it." Mama looked as if whatever was under tarp might bite her. "Mister President. I'm sorry. We just wanted to come home. Me and mine, that is. I thought this man could get me there, but it ain't come out like that." She was shrinking before Reeves' eyes. Playing elderly and infirm for sympathy.

Shel was intrigued though. He watched a smile come to her face and she moved closer to the box. "You tellin' the truth?" She was paying less attention to the president and the men, and more to the covered lump Reeves indicated. He ignored her as best he could, so as not to draw his focus from the room full of people that would shoot him at the slightest provocation.

The *Polk* rattled with turbulence and Shel stumbled as she made her way closer and knelt to pull back the tarp. She tugged with one hand while pointing her gun at the OMO personnel clumsily, but the covering wouldn't budge. She kept on almost comically until she became upset enough to put her gun down and lift it with both hands. She pulled the thick tarp free, uncovering a large chest beneath. Reeves watched the others as their brows furrowed or eyes widened at the sight of the container. He kept a steady eye on Reeves, even though the whole room had guns out and pointed at one another.

Shel reached back behind her to grab her gun, but seconds before she could touch it, someone fired a shot. The girl fell backward with her gun and tried to use the chest for cover. Instinctively, Reeves shot back.

As soon as the girl's gun lay flat on the deck, Lucinda began tracking it. She watched as Shel kept it within reach for a moment and slowly moved farther from it, inch by inch. When the girl grabbed the tarp, Lucinda used the moment to remove a pistol tucked into Cyrus' belt behind his back. She did it slowly and used her good hand. *Her real hand.* So she could avoid any clumsiness.

She held it there, steady, quiet, unmoving. She looked at it out of the corner of her eye and debated cocking it. The noise of the engines and the commotion and the open door might mask the sound, but she wasn't sure, so she stared at it and cocked it in her mind; quickly, like water. Not like her other hand, with the muddy movement, and clumsy, crushing grasping.

Shel reached back for her gun and the room seemed to collectively take a breath, and Lucinda pulled the gun and fired. The movement was fluid, but not as she'd hoped. The girl fell backward as her arm produced a spray of blood from the bullet grazing it. Behind Shel, the elderly woman they'd called Mama fell back against a crate clutching her leg.

The girl crawled away, but the old woman stayed put.

Reeves moved the president between himself and everyone else. He could feel his side throbbing with the pain of the wound he'd received earlier, could feel his shirt becoming wet with the blood that seeped from it. He forced himself not to grab at it and give his pain away for fear it would give his enemies some advantage. He kept his gun in the other hand behind the president's head.

"Jesus, Reeves." Cyrus put his hands before him, weaponless. "Just stop. Just stop before this goes any further."

"Goes any further? Like where? Somewhere we can't come back from?" Reeves shook his head. "We passed that point a few years back. We kept on passing it, too. When my men were betrayed, when we went to prison." Reeves couldn't enumerate the places that things went wrong in one breath. It took him a second before he could find the wind to keep going. "When the president decided to let me languish on that island." He shoved the president, but only felt weaker for the effort and the display. "And what about the OMO? Weren't you supposed to be keeping tabs on the North and the South? Checking to make sure neither side was being a shitweasel to the other?"

It wasn't a question he expected an answer to, but he needed to think. He was drowsy, and dazed, backed against a cargo door with nowhere to go but out and down. He needed a distraction or a diversion.

Or a miracle.

"Well, good work gentlemen," Reeves said. "You turned a blind eye while I rotted."

"Jesus, Reeves." Mama was on the floor in an increasing puddle of red.

"You weren't exactly an innocent babe," Bethy said. "You were arrested for your part in the gold heist, but you were convicted of doing much more." Her voice crackled and popped like a campfire.

The little bitch could turn into the distraction he needed. "It was war. It was what I was trained to do."

"Kill?" Bethy said.

"Yes."

"Spy?"

"Yes."

"Steal?"

"Yes. And more. So much more," Reeves said.

"All of which are criminal acts and punishable by imprisonment or death," Bethy said.

"I was paid to kill people. Paid by your man there, Mister Spencer. Cyrus Spencer paid me to kill Union soldiers and murder anyone who opposed the Confederacy." It felt good to be able to point the finger at the man who had started it all. If the Spencer family hadn't paid for Reeves to go in Cyrus' place, none of those things would've happened. Reeves hadn't looked at it that way in prison, but the more he saw the man, looked in Cyrus' eyes, Reeves knew it had to be true. "Because Cyrus was too yellow to pick up a gun back then."

He'd hoped the accusation would have a greater effect, but no one budged—not a single gun barrel wavered. He elbowed the president in the back again, just to feel some reaction.

To his side, he saw Shel using the sudden dialog to fiddle with the chest. She reached up to flip the lid open on the container. "Don't do it, girl. Leave it be." He could see the mischief and the excitement in her eyes. "Leave it."

Shel ignored him and struggled with the latch until it came loose, and in a quick motion, she flipped the lid open. The exhilaration on her face faded as the contents inside sloshed from side to side with the motion of the ship. The lid flipped some of the gray-silver concoction onto Shel's hand and the floor. She stood without consideration of the people around her, trying to wipe her hands. She gave a glance at Mama on the floor, barely moving, before she remembered what had happened and where she was. Shel ran, ducking low to avoid being shot again, though no one seemed to care as they looked at the material on the deck. She ran through the door next to the stairs and vanished. After a moment, Reeves noticed the shadow of the girl with the mechanical arm move from some boxes and chase after Shel.

The ship tilted, and a huge wave of the liquid burst out of the chest with a loud splash on the deck and as the few remaining in the room were distracted, Reeves knocked the latch on the wall aside with his arm and slid the cargo door open. They were not nearly as high as he would have guess, but the president's smoking ship was not far behind them on the ground. From the slight angle of ship's turn, they appeared to be going in a circle above the landing field. He tried not to linger on the beauty of the mountains in the near distance or the clouds just above the ship.

"What does this mean? What is this?" The president spoke over his shoulder at Reeves.

"This is how it ends, I guess." Reeves turned from the scene outside and looked down at the Berley spilling out across the deck. When the ship tilted, more came out and dripped down the side of the chest.

"Come on, enough discussion," Dex said. "Let the president go and we'll put you back in your cell. If you don't—we'll have to—" Dex knelt behind a crate on the far side of the room. "I don't know. We'll—"

"What? What'll you do? Kill me? It's time you all knew something." Reeves figured it wouldn't hurt to bluff. Maybe he could buy himself some time after all.

"None of us are leaving this ship. Doesn't matter if you shoot me or not. Before we revealed ourselves, we paid a visit to the engine room and planted an explosive powerful enough to bring this ship down and kill everyone on board."

"That's a lie," Bethy said. She still had a weapon and stood at Cyrus' side, close enough that they were touching.

"Is it?" Reeves began to rehearse his move in his head. He knew just how he'd pull out the watch to conceal pulling the chain. The noise of the blade spinning inside would be covered by the sounds of the ship's engine.

Quietly, Cyrus spoke up. "You can still stop it."

"I don't know if there's time." Reeves felt light-headed as he reached for the watch with his free hand. He found it and pulled the chain, trying to point the gun at the president with his other hand. He tisked and shook his head. "There's just five more minutes. I don't see how we can disarm that device in time. He kept the watch level and made sure it was aimed at Bethy's neck.

63

Lucinda stopped in the middle of the corridor, nearly running into Corrigan.

"What the hell is happening down there? Were there shots?" Corrigan asked.

"Yes. It's a trick. One of the escaped prisoners is holding the president. We'll explain later, but right now there's a little blonde girl loose out here that helped him do it."

They both looked up and down the metal and wood tunnel and found nothing but closed doors.

"Where did that little yellow-haired witch go?"

"Could've ducked into any one of these rooms?" Corrigan pulled his pistol.

That was the only option Lucinda saw as well. "Move to the right first and check those?"

There were four doors on the right. Before Corrigan responded, there was a slight sound of metal tapping on metal from the left. Both Lucinda and Corrigan turned to seek out the source. At the end of the hall was a door marked EGRESS. It swayed open and closed in the air.

"That door just went to the head of list," Corrigan said.

Lucinda agreed, and they moved to the door. She put her pistol away and motioned for Corrigan to cover her as she pulled open the door. As she did so, they found nothing but open air beyond the hatch. The blue sky was all that greeted them. Lucinda gripped the rail with her metallic arm for support and then leaned out to look from side to side. The seam of the ship's large gondola formed a ledge here that ran the length of the ship on either side. It was thick enough that anyone could walk it easily. Easily being a relative term she supposed. As she scanned, Lucinda found the girl, edging her way back toward the open cargo hold door.

"I see her." She stepped up and put her foot on the outside rail to probe its strength. A rope as thick as Lucinda's arm hung not far over the seam, making balance slightly easier. "I'm going out."

"What?" Corrigan started to reach for her and she shrugged him off.

"I'll be fine. Get a couple of men and head in through that hall and block off the exit. Try to keep your wits about you in here while I'm gone." She put both feet on the rail and hugged the fuselage as she got her balance. She looked back in at Corrigan. "Go. I'll be fine."

The rail that went around the ship was plenty wide and reminded her of the circus days on the high wire. Of course, back then she didn't have a huge metal object to lean on for stability, and she also wasn't hundreds of feet off the ground with no net. With a careful measure of the wind, Lucinda brought herself forward by taking quick baby steps and keeping herself flat.

The girl had a good lead. Lucinda's instincts told her to pull her gun and shoot, to get herself and others out of danger, but she also couldn't bring herself to shoot the woman in the back. "Let's go in and talk about this," Lucinda said. She shouted to be heard at that great distance, and over the ship's machinations.

The girl stood defiantly. "Talk? Honestly, lady, you think we can talk?" She looked around at the situation. "Talking? I need to concentrate, just so I don't fall to my death." The girl had to pause then as she was beset by crows. A half dozen flew at her, pecking, flapping, trying to gain a hold on her somehow. They were far too large to manage to get a grip on the rail, but that didn't stop them from trying.

64

As he yanked the thin cord, Reeves could feel the watch come to life, the gears spinning, the blade getting up to speed. The tiny instrument fit perfectly in his palm and he took a breath, lining up the weapon in his mind. He couldn't wait too long; the blade would lose momentum and his moment would be gone. He looked at Bethy again, sure of his aim. He pressed the button and the blade zipped free and true.

He couldn't tell if it was a quick reaction from Cyrus, or a sudden shift of the airship, but Cyrus stepped in front of blade at the last moment and the sharp metal disc buried itself in his ribs. His hands went to his side and he fell backward, leaning himself on against a crate to stay standing.

Reeves cursed his luck and moved another step back, keeping the edge of the door in his periphery, so as not to fall out. A sudden shift in the *Polk*'s altitude made that a real fear. Boxes shifted near him, and a tangle of ropes dropped from a container above the door and hung near him and the president. As he righted himself, he caught sight of movement outside of the ship, something larger and more substantial than the dark birds flitting about in massive clumps in and around the ship. He turned his head to glance at what it might be, scared that it was another soldier sneaking up on him, but instead saw Shel making her way toward him, walking onto the thin metal railing that stretched above a narrow walkway. Black birds flew about her as she went.

His shoulder burned like a hot iron suddenly. He looked back to see Bethy had fired with enough precision to hit him without injuring the president. In the moment that he'd turned away, she'd struck. She stood with a fiery look about her, and kept the gun focused on him. He flinched in the sudden pain, and the president saw his advantage, bringing his elbow up into Reeves' face and knocking him off balance. Reeves flailed, felt himself falling backward through the open mouth of the airship. He grabbed for whatever he could—the ropes and strings above him tangled in his arms but gave way under his weight. He fell to the deck, his lower body hanging out of the craft, his chest tangled in the mess. He desperately reached out then and managed to grab the president's pant leg as he tried to scramble to safety. The president himself fell to the floor and Reeves could feel them both slowly sliding out the door.

Someone across the hold shouted, "No," but the speaker was unidentifiable. A number of people ran toward them.

"No," Reeves said. "No." He was sure no one heard him, so he shouted. "I'll take him with me. I *will*." He swung his arm wildly, trying to shake off the ropes that had continued to unravel from the ceiling. The president flailed and scraped at the floor to try to stop his backward motion.

"Hold on," Shel shouted from the rail near him.

It was nearly a relief. But he considered what she'd do if she got to him. They'd be back in the same spot they were before, worse even, they'd be captured and left to fate. He'd die if the ship exploded, or he'd be sent back to prison if it didn't.

As Shel neared, one of the birds that was pestering her flew through the open door, flapped in a circle, and landed in the pool of Berley that had spread there. It screamed a strange blast of delight and splashed in the liquid. The sounds drew more of the birds through the door, and soon they'd mostly left Shel alone.

Reeves' shoulder weakened, and he let go of the president. He immediately felt himself fall a foot or so and waved his arms to grab the edge of the cargo hold. He looked behind himself and saw nothing but open air. His fall was only halted by the ropes entangling him.

More crows made their way into the *Polk*'s hold, flapping at the people and dancing in among the crates. In the middle of the room Reeves could see a group of them hopping about Mama's body where it lay in a pool of the shining liquid. They pecked at her clothes and retreated, testing whether she could stop them.

"I'll get you out. Hold on." Shel held on to the rail with one arm and tried to untangle him with the other, but it seemed to get worse. She tugged on the lines hard and they loosened immediately.

Reeves looked up and discovered why it was suddenly so loose; the ropes had pulled a large apparatus free from the ceiling of the supply room and it was all falling out of the door. The box-like objects unfolded and slammed into Shel, knocking her from her perch and they both fell away from the aircraft along with the debris.

65

The president hung on for his life, clawing at the deck, kicking at the side of the craft to stop his own fall. Lucinda stepped up her pace, moving across on the narrow ledge outside the ship, watching his efforts as he hung half-in, half-out of the *Polk*. "Hold on Mister President," she said, just steps away.

He seemed relieved to see her, and the desperation on his face abated, until a large crow landed just inside the doorway. With what seemed like sadistic purpose, it began pecking at the president's fingers and hands, cawing between attempts.

The ship tilted again, and a small stream of Berley splashed across the president's fingers. The sudden turn threw Lucinda back, but she clung to the rope as tightly as she could. When it was safe, Lucinda started forward, but realized her hand was clamped shut on the rope and wouldn't open. She tugged, trying to balance and get herself free, but the hand wouldn't move.

Over at the door, the president looked desperate. He hung on with one hand while clawing for purchase with the other. From inside the bay, Lucinda could see Bethy fighting her way through the mass of wings to get to the president herself. She jumped at the last second and grabbed the president's hand and held fast. Lucinda yanked at the stubborn hand again and pried it loose. She took the last few steps and pulled herself inside the *Polk*'s hold.

Bethy shouted from the doorway. "I'm slipping." Her slight body was quickly moving out the door, pulled by the president's weight and helped along by the slick coating of Berley.

Lucinda grabbed Bethy's coat and pulled with all the strength she could muster. Together, they managed to pull President Alexander back aboard. They moved as fast as they could to get away from the door and the slippery mess that the entrance had become. Once the president was secure in the other room with the shaken up and confused soldiers, Bethy returned to Cyrus and Lucinda joined Dex, who'd begun swinging at crows with a wooden plank.

The birds weren't content to just cause chaos; they dove at anyone that came near, including Dex and Lucinda.

66

Shel was screaming as they fell. The *Polk* above them grew smaller by the second.

Through his own terror, Reeves managed to notice something curious and hopeful; the giant boxes above them began to flutter in the air, whipping back and forth on the lines, and for a moment he thought they were slowing their descent. He looked up and saw the boxes expand at their middle, filling with air. The closest set wasn't filling like the other two sets, skewed by Shel's tangled wires.

He grabbed Shel's head and shouted. "Stop struggling."

Shel's screaming continued.

Reeves took a section of the rope and tied it around his chest as best he could. The motion made his shoulder burn with pain, but he worked through it, because he had no choice.

They'd been tumbling through the open air, but as the boxes filled, they became more stable. The pair was still falling at a rate that horrified Reeves. He grabbed at whatever tangled mess he could see on Shel's body, pulling at string and rope. As it unknotted, Shel caught onto his progress and stopped screaming. Desperately she shouted to him. "Here. This. This." She indicated a particular strand and they worked together to get it righted. In seconds they'd managed, and all of the boxes above them fluttered open correctly and they slowed.

They were still falling too fast for Reeves' liking.

"What do we do?" Shel asked. Her breathing was ragged as her head tilted to see the ground approaching below. "What the hell are we going to do?"

"We're too heavy."

Shel's eyes widened.

"If we can't slow down, we'll be crushed on the ground," Reeves said. He couldn't think of a thing that could help them other than lightening the weight.

Shel's hand disappeared into her jacket and produced her thin blade. With some hesitation, she attempted to stab him. Luckily, she had no leverage and couldn't produce enough force to penetrate Reeves' jacket with it. He grabbed her wrist and held it.

"Jesus, let's work together. Maybe we can save ourselves." It wasn't true, he knew it. And the ground was rushing at them far too quickly.

"Hell with you."

They were falling, and fighting—Shel wriggled her arm free and tried again. Reeves realized they were doubly fighting for their lives; if he survived her attack, he'd still have to survive the fall. He chanced a look below and could clearly see the president's ship in focus below. Shel swung the blade and Reeves felt a new wound open on his cheek. It occurred to him that since they untangled her ropes, that Shel was only attached to him by holding on tight to the ropes around him.

"Stop." Reeves shouted it as best he could to be heard above the rush of air that assaulted their ears.

He didn't know if she couldn't hear, or if she did and chose to continue anyway, but she cocked her arm back and leaned away to get some momentum. As she thrust forward, he brought his arm down on her fist that was clenching his ropes. Her blade still followed through and stabbed him in the side, but she slid down, unable to hold him with just one hand, she dropped the knife and clutched at him with both hands, then lost contact. When he saw she wasn't touching him, Reeves kicked out, sending her a few feet away. She grabbed at his boots but found she couldn't touch him anymore. She shouted what Reeves had to assume were obscenities at him, but he couldn't hear.

The apparatus, now free of Shel's weight, had yanked on his chest as it slowed his fall considerably. He looked away as she raced toward the ground, hoping it wasn't too late for him.

67

The birds swarmed, hundreds around the ship on all sides. Black birds hurled themselves at the deck and slammed into the portals. Lucinda braced herself, and took a half-dozen shots at the birds, taking a couple down. She vacillated between swinging at the birds with her arm, and shooting at them, whichever worked best.

"Hell with this," Dex said. He'd continued to swing the board he'd found but was having less luck than Lucinda. He pushed his way to a group of crates. "This looks about right," Dex said. "Damn right." He dragged one blanket-covered pallet out toward the open bay door.

"Dex?" Lucinda asked.

Dex didn't respond, other than with a widening smile.

"That's not—"

With a flourish, Dex ripped the blanket aside. "Oh, yes, it is." He cackled as he put the pieces of the inferno musket together.

Nearby, Lucinda saw Bethy and Cyrus put their arms out in an effort to calm Dex's excitement. "You know this airship stays aloft because of flammable materials, yes?" Cyrus said.

"Then I'll just have to aim away from them," Dex said. "I mean, that stuff's all four levels up, right?" He dropped the bellows on the ground at his feet and squeezed the fuel bladder.

Lucinda felt suddenly responsible for the man's behavior. "Dex? Maybe this isn't the best time to field-test this particular piece of ordinance."

Dex slapped a pair of goggles over his eyes and pulled thick gloves over his hands. "Aw. It'll be just fine. You'll see." He spit a wad of tobacco out the open door and watched it fall. "Come on let's get down to brass tacks."

The few people left in the room looked at Lucinda, their eyes were wide in terror. But before they could further voice their concerns, Dex slid the last piece into place. "Bunch of crybabies."

"Dex," Lucinda began. "Think this over. If there's a single leak in the ship's bladders, we're—"

The airship shifted, and everyone was rocked by the sudden change in course. Lucinda fell to her hands and knees and slid toward the door. She looked up and noticed Dex headed in the same direction. Scrambling to her feet, she managed to grab him with her metal hand as he was teetering out of the ship. She pulled him back and they both braced themselves as the ship corrected itself and leveled off.

As everyone stood and recovered, more birds came streaming in from a new group. One, shimmering bird came in and immediately panicked as it looked for the exit. It threw itself against a portal, then fell to floor, and screeched demonically. It hopped from crate to crate flapping and clawing, watching the birds that came in previously.

Dex turned toward it and Lucinda pushed the gun so it pointed toward the open door. *That's all we need*, she thought, him shooting into the ship. She turned and fired her pistol, hitting the bird in mid-leap, and knocking it off the crates, and down to the deck, where it flopped around and screeched. She emptied the pistol's spent shells and started loading again.

More birds flew in, flapping in Dex's face as they came. Lucinda followed the crows as they kept flying, almost hovering inside the craft. Corrigan entered the room and a bird landed in his hair, pecking at his ears. Lucinda moved to help him when she was startled by a sudden whoosh, and a wave of heat.

In the doorway, Dex had unleashed the inferno gun. A thick burst of flame leapt from the end of the musket and struck a nearby cloud of birds outside the *Polk*. The fireball seemed to incinerate a good number of them immediately, while others fell out of the fireball and spiraled toward the ground. The flame died down, seeming to disappear back into the gun, and Dex turned to grin at the others. "Heehee. See?"

Lucinda crushed the crow on Corrigan by grabbing it with her metal hand, and it fell off of him with no more than a gurgle. He dropped to the ground and clutched his head. The bird had torn into his scalp.

"Wooo." Dex yelped and let another burst of flame fly at the birds.

Lucinda missed where it hit, but the cargo hold was smelling vaguely of smoke and roasted chicken. She shielded Corrigan from the remaining birds in the hold before pushing him into one of the equipment lockers. She grabbed a heavy shirt off a hook and had him hold it on his wound. "Stay in here. We'll handle this."

Corrigan opened his mouth to protest, but she shut the door before he got very far.

"Dex," Lucinda said. "You need to stop. Stop, so we can close the god damn door up."

More birds got in, this time a couple of them were on fire. One had only a flaming wing, but the other was a ball of fire. They both flew in a panic, thudding into the walls and the ceiling. The least flaming bird made a break toward the open door, instead slamming itself into Dex's back. To his credit, Dex stopped firing the inferno musket before he turned to see what hit him. Unfortunately, the bird had managed to start a fire on Dex's wool uniform jacket—a small flame, to be sure, but it spread quickly. As Lucinda watched the fire spread across the man's back, she feared the fuel for the inferno gun had saturated his clothing, whether the weapon leaked, or the fumes just hung on the man, she wouldn't speculate. She fumbled for a cloth or rag, to beat the flames out, but Dex had become enfolded in the flames and was fruitlessly smacking at his clothing to put the fire out himself.

Lucinda found a blanket covering a crate and whipped it off in a fluid motion and ran toward Dex.

"No," Dex shouted. "Stay away."

"I can help you." Lucinda held out the blanket to smother the flames and wrap Dex in the process.

Dex kept the gun in one hand but held out the other. "Stop." The fire had burned patches of clothing away and Lucinda could see his blackened flesh below. He looked at Lucinda, his eyes wide. "Please get back." He put his free hand on the heavy fuel tank of the gun and pulled it with him out into the open sky. The heavy fuel apparatus came out of his hand, too heavy to for him to hang onto, but it fell out of the airship anyway.

Lucinda ran after him, but before she got to the door, a sizable explosion rocked The *Polk* hard enough that she had to back away. The door she was headed for was briefly a wall of flames burning intensely for a moment, and then the fire was gone. Lucinda stepped up and looked out, seeing nothing but fiery debris falling to earth, and dozens of black birds circling and diving. She turned away, thinking of Dex, his stupid choices and this sacrifice. He was gruff, but kind to her and he'd worked like a dog at every assignment.

Lucinda's grief was interrupted by Corrigan banging on the locker. "What the hell was that?" He pounded on the door. "Anyone?"

Across the room, Cyrus and Bethy swung at the birds that danced and swooped through the air. Lucinda could see they were holding their own, but the small flames had caught on the crates and rigging around them.

Lucinda pulled the bay door shut to stop more of the things from entering, but as she did, she noticed the president's ship still on the ground. In the distance, she could see the thick smoke had stopped and only a normal stream of smoke emanated from the stacks.

At her feet, one of the birds had burned itself out and was twitching on the deck. She stepped on it, to end its suffering.

She ran over to let Corrigan out. He was still clutching the cloth to his head.

"Jumping Jesus, what in the name of Sherman's—"

"Dex is dead, I need to go help Cyrus, and I need you to get up to the bridge with Alek to determine the condition of the ship," Lucinda said, just as the ship lurched and dropped twenty feet in altitude.

Corrigan fell to the floor, unable to keep his balance. "Shit. I'm confident it's in shit condition."

Across the room Lucinda saw Cyrus and Bethy unbar the door that trapped the other soldiers from the president's airship. He waved them out, yelled to them, and then she saw the men and women remove their jackets and overshirts to begin beating the flames to put them out. The bulk of the birds were dead, but the ones that weren't were overwhelmed quickly.

She saw her friends managing without her, so she put out her good hand, and pulled Corrigan up into the smoke at the top of the stairwell. They moved through the hall as fast as they could, stumbling eventually into the wheelhouse. "Alek?" Lucinda shouted. "We need to land, now." She looked up to see the *Polk* was rapidly approaching the mountains and pointed at a downward angle.

"I know." Alek was at the far side of the room, away from the wheel. "I lost all my assistants and I'm doing my best on my own."

"Sorry," Corrigan said.

Lucinda moved to take over the navigator's position, leaving Alek free to handle the other controls. Even Corrigan moved weakly to take a post to help.

"We're losing altitude. We're on fire. And the engines are cutting out," Alek said. "My only thought is to crash us into a snowbank as soon as we can. We can use the snow to help extinguish the flames, and maybe get everyone off this thing."

"What do we do?" Corrigan asked.

"I already cut the engines. I've pointed us toward that bluff over there." Alek pointed to rocky outcropping that was coming at them from the side of the mountain. "I'll need you to start bleeding that gas out of the bladders, so we fall a little faster, and I'll need Lucinda to help me hold this wheel steady."

Lucinda nodded and grabbed a comm tube. *"Everyone brace for impact. Repeat. Brace for a crash."* She let the mouthpiece dangle by the hose and put her mechanical arm on the wheel. "I'm not letting go until you tell me."

68

At Lucinda's announcement, soldiers began lashing themselves to support beams, bracing against the bulkheads and shouting in terror. Some moved to the parachutes, only to find they'd been destroyed by fire, and were still smoldering.

"I don't know how we ended up here," Cyrus said. He clutched Bethy in one arm and a long stretch of rope coiled to the wall in his other arm as cargo, and people, slid past them. "I thought we were on the easy mission."

"No one really expects to be attacked by flaming crows, to be honest."

The *Polk* ran headlong into the side of the mountain, scraping the hull against rock and bouncing off, slowing as it went, but still steaming hard ahead. The sound turned from the screech of metal on rock to the thud of the hull bottoming against the snowbank. Cyrus held tight as the bow of the airship came to a sudden stop and the stern continued unabated, causing the back of the *Polk* to rise, shifting everything in the hold toward the front wall. Cyrus turned away as one of the Confederates was crushed between two unsecured boxes. The air was dense with the cries of men and women, the howl of twisting beams and crackle of wood.

69

The sound of the parachute's canopies wasn't what woke Reeves from his stupor; it was the high screech of a crow. Reeves scrambled to his feet, swinging his fists to make sure they weren't descending on him to tear out his eyes or pluck out his tongue. He immediately fell back down on his ass, dropped there by the searing pain in his leg. He guessed it was a remnant of his fall, and if that was the worst of it, he would happily suffer it.

He fell backward in the thick weeds, confident he could fend off the crows for a time if he needed to. As he rested, crunching steps in the thick brush brought his attention. It was Beatrice, followed by Wilhelm and George. Andre was somewhere behind, halfway between them and the president's airship. The rest, Jasper, Abner and Clara stood at the top of the ramp of the ship. Smoke drifted idly from the stacks and sunshine glistened off the glass of the command room.

"I told you all to leave," Reeves said.

"You also said you likely weren't coming back." Wilhelm leaned down and started looking at Reeves' various wounds.

"Best get up," George said. "People are coming from the town. They look like lawmen from here. Or maybe just angry folk, can't tell," George said. He held out his hand to help Reeves up.

With a wave, Reeves said, "I can't. Leg's broken."

"Here," Wilhelm and George did their best and slowly raised Reeves to standing.

It was then that Reeves realized Beatrice was staring at him. "Where's Shelby?" She asked. "How'd you make it and she didn't?"

Reeves looked up. "I fell from an airship. Way up there. And I lived." He saw the anger and hurt in her eyes and hoped that she wasn't armed. He'd hate to be shot and killed after what he'd been through.

"The deal was," Beatrice said. "If I helped you get jobs on the loading detail, and I helped you get your boxes on the airships just so, she and I could go with you and take off wherever we pleased." Beatrice held her hands clasped in front of her, her knuckles turning white for gripping too hard, or the cold.

So far, the elderly Confederates had surprised him with their abilities. He hoped they could actually work an airship well enough to make it airborne and fly it home. Behind him, he heard Beatrice following.

Reeves looked at the massive ship and wondered what he could do with it, what contribution he could make to whoever he chose. Or, with a full crew, he thought the kind of revenge he could extract from whomsoever he pointed his finger.

70

The soldiers grabbed whatever instruments they could and shoveled snow onto the flames in various spots on the *Polk*. In the shadow of a nearby outcropping, Cyrus helped Lucinda carry Cashe to a safe spot, before she sat him down to rest. Cyrus' side was bloody from the disc that Reeves had hit him with, as well as all the other injuries. Alek had gone into the *Polk* three times, pulling people out and looking for Corrigan. They were miles from Colorado Station, and high up above some terrible terrain.

Cyrus kneeled down where Bethy lay beneath the rock canopy next to Cashe, her leg injured and bleeding from numerous cuts, but she was still conscious and still itching to get up and help, or fight, or whatever.

At that point, Cyrus wasn't sure what exactly anyone could do. He held Bethy's hand and patted it absently, but his eyes locked with Lucinda's. The idea of belonging to something, anything was painful. They'd lost the crew of the Turtle not long ago, and now the men and women of the *Polk* were gone or holding death at bay.

A hum and rattle echoed through the mountains. Everyone stopped and stilled their shovels, halted their rescue efforts to scan the skies to find its source. To the west, a small airship rose to view. It was one of the compact ferries the mining companies used to haul gold from the mines back to Colorado Station, likely drawn by the thick plume of grey smoke that billowed from the side of the mountain.

A few of the crew members cheered at the sight, but Cyrus remained silent. The tiny ship, with empty holds, could carry maybe a dozen survivors. Meanwhile the rest would have to stay alive on the mountain waiting for their turn. A rescue operation would last into the next day, easily, even if all of the gold ferries were put into use. For some of the injured, that would be too long.

"We can't let this stand." Alek trudged back to where Cashe rested. He pointed to the flaming remains of the *Polk* and waved his hands around to take in the scene of their friends sprawled out on the snow and rocks. "We need to get after that son of a bitch and make him feel our wrath."

It was a sentiment that Cyrus knew well, but was in no position to act on. He did his best to keep his gaze low so as not to meet Alek's stare. Cyrus was already mulling options to get Bethy, Lucy, and himself out east at the first opportunity—North or South, it didn't matter. Revenge would get in the way of the survival of the ones he loved, and Cyrus feared that looking Alek in the eye would only tip his intentions.

"We will." Cyrus took a moment to realize the words had come from right next to him, spoken by Bethy. "We're with the government, right? Can we commandeer whatever we need? Take any airship? We'll chase him down and he'll pay."

Her words made Cyrus shiver more than the cold did.

About the Author

Ohio native Matt Betts is a pop culture junkie—sometimes to levels that are considered unhealthy by the Surgeon General. He grew up on a steady diet of giant monsters, comic books, and horror novels, all of which creep into his own work. Matt's speculative poetry and short fiction have appeared in a number of anthologies and journals.

Red Gear 9 is a sequel to his first novel, the steampunk/zombie/alternate history adventure *Odd Men Out*. His other books include *White Anvil: Sasquatch Onslaught*, *Indelible Ink*, and *The Boogeyman's Intern*. Matt's novel *Carson of Venus: The Edge of All Worlds* and the prequel comics *Carson of Venus: The Eye of Amtor* are continuations of a series created by science fiction legend Edgar Rice Burroughs.

www.ingramcontent.com/pod-product-compliance
Lightning Source LLC
Chambersburg PA
CBHW030113260626
47156CB00008B/2645